ON

VICIOUS

WORLDS

Praise for

THESE BURNING STARS

ON VICIOUS WORLDS

BOOK TWO OF THE KINDOM TRILOGY

BETHANY JACOBS

orbit

orbit-books.co.uk

ORBIT

First published in Great Britain in 2024 by Orbit

1 3 5 7 9 10 8 6 4 2

Copyright © 2024 by Bethany Jacobs

Charts by Tim Paul

Excerpt from *The Mercy of Gods* by James S. A. Corey
Copyright © 2024 by James S. A. Corey

The moral right of the author has been asserted.

A CIP catalogue record for this book
is available from the British Library.

ISBN 978-0-356-52008-7

Printed and bound in Great Britain by Clays Ltd, Elcograf, S.p.A.

Papers used by Orbit are from well-managed forests
and other responsible sources.

Orbit
An imprint of
Little, Brown Book Group
Carmelite House
50 Victoria Embankment
London EC4Y 0DZ

An Hachette UK Company
www.hachette.co.uk

orbit-books.co.uk

For Julianne, the dear friend

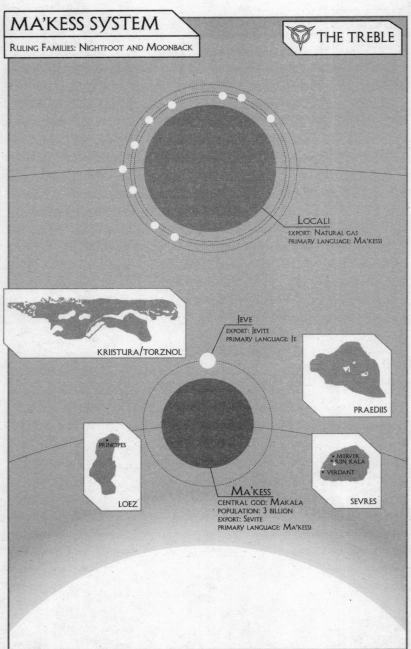

MA'KESS SYSTEM

RULING FAMILIES: NIGHTFOOT AND MOONBACK

THE TREBLE

LOCALI
EXPORT: NATURAL GAS
PRIMARY LANGUAGE: MA'KESSI

KRIISTURA/TORZNOL

JEVE
EXPORT: JEVITE
PRIMARY LANGUAGE: JE

PRAEDIIS

PRINCIPES

LOEZ

MA'KESS
CENTRAL GOD: MAKALA
POPULATION: 3 BILLION
EXPORT: SEVITE
PRIMARY LANGUAGE: MA'KESSI

• MIIRVEK
• RIIN KALA
• VERDANT

SEVRES

CHART BY TIM PAUL

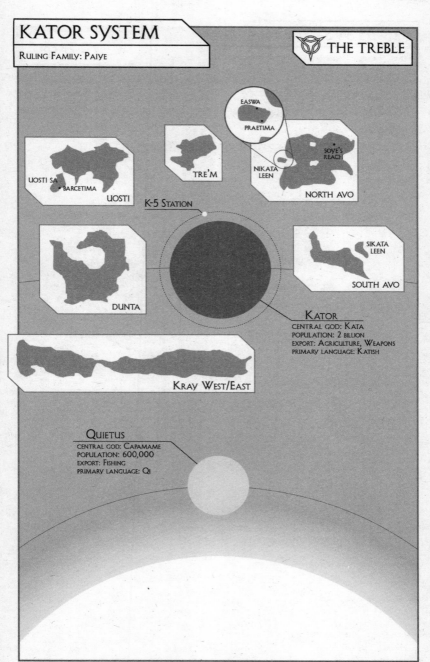

KATOR SYSTEM

RULING FAMILY: PAIYE

THE TREBLE

EASWA

PRAETIMA

SOYE'S REACH

NIKATA LEEN

NORTH AVO

UOSTI SA

BARCETIMA

UOSTI

TRE'M

K-5 STATION

SIKATA LEEN

SOUTH AVO

DUNTA

KATOR
CENTRAL GOD: KATA
POPULATION: 2 BILLION
EXPORT: AGRICULTURE, WEAPONS
PRIMARY LANGUAGE: KATISH

KRAY WEST/EAST

QUIETUS
CENTRAL GOD: CAPAMAME
POPULATION: 600,000
EXPORT: FISHING
PRIMARY LANGUAGE: QI

CHART BY TIM PAUL

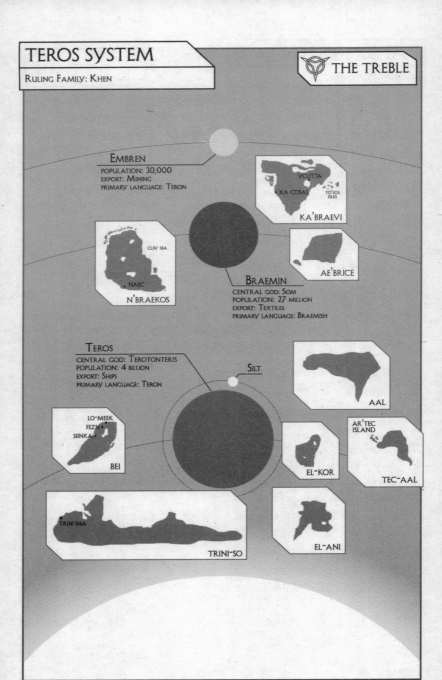

TEROS SYSTEM

RULING FAMILY: KHEN

THE TREBLE

EMBREN
POPULATION: 30,000
EXPORT: MINING
PRIMARY LANGUAGE: TERON

KA'BRAEVI
YCUTTA
XA COSAS
TO'SOS ISLES

AE'BRICE

N'BRAEKOS
CLEV SEA
NAJIC

BRAEMIN
CENTRAL GOD: SOM
POPULATION: 27 MILLION
EXPORT: TEXTILES
PRIMARY LANGUAGE: BRAEMISH

TEROS
CENTRAL GOD: TEROTONTERIS
POPULATION: 4 BILLION
EXPORT: SHIPS
PRIMARY LANGUAGE: TERON

SILT

AAL

BEI
LO-MEEK
FEZN
SIINKAI

EL-KOR

AR'TEC ISLAND

TEC-AAL

TRINI-SO
TRIN-MA

EL-ANI

CHART BY TIM PAUL

CAST OF CHARACTERS

The Hands of the Kindom

Chono, a cleric
Seti Moonback, the First Cloak
Ilius Redquill, a secretary, and the Minor Advocate
Ostiver Ravening, the First Secretary
Lalik Songrider, a secretary, and the Major Advocate
Aver Paiye, the First Cleric

The Ironway Family

Jun Ironway, a caster
Liis Konye, a former cloaksaan, and Jun's lover
Bene Ironway, Jun's cousin
Luja Ironway, Jun's cousin
Tej Redcore, Jun's cousin

The Capamame Colonists

Masar Hawks, a collector
Effegen ten Crost, the Star of the Wheel
Fonu sen Fhaan, the River of the Wheel
Gaeda ben Kist, the Stone of the Wheel
Hyre ten Grie, the Gale of the Wheel
Tomesk ten Ruvo, the Tree of the Wheel
Dom ben Dane, a collector
Aris the Beauty, a colonist

The Nightfoot Family

Alisiana Nightfoot, the Nightfoot matriarch, murdered
Riiniana Nightfoot, Alisiana's great-granddaughter
Torek Nightfoot, Riiniana's guardian

Also

Yantikye the Honor, a revolutionary
Graisa the Honor, a revolutionary, and Yantikye's daughter
Drae sen Briit, a Jeveni, killed in the Jeveni Genocide

and Six

CHAPTER ONE

1648

YEAR OF THE GAME

Barcetima
Uosti Sa Continent
The Planet Kator

It was a warm night in the Katish summer, full of dancing and music and laughter, and they used all of this as cover when they slipped into the bar and took a table by the windows. They sat facing the rest of the room and turned a memory coin in their fingers. They didn't signal for a waiter. They had a perfect view of the road, which wended south and up—toward an estate on the hill that belonged to Ashir Doanye. From their place in the bar, they could see the estate, the grand house, its windows like yellow eyes. They flipped the coin once, but since its tail and head were the same, there was nothing to infer.

They imagined a head and tail onto the coin. If the coin landed on heads, they would give the coin to her. If it landed on tails, they would kill her.

They flipped it again. Impossible to know.

Someone jostled past them, bumping their chair. Easy as breathing, to turn toward the bump, to slip their hand into the woman's coat and lift the coin purse off her belt. When she was gone, they held the purse under the table, digging through the contents. It was mostly Katish currency, plastic plae, but down at the bottom they found a Ma'kessn ingot. Pleased, they sat with the memory coin in one hand and the ingot in the other. One side of the ingot showed the face of the goddess Makala, fecund and lovely. On the opposite side of the ingot was an image of the temple Riin Cosas, the holiest site on Ma'kess. Heads and tails.

They flipped the ingot. Makala appeared. *Hmm.*

It was a noisy night, crowded. But they had picked their location wisely. The bar was attached to a very nice hotel, whose best rooms were reserved for a Kindom delegation that, even now, celebrated in the home of Ashir Doanye. A lucrative weapons contract had been signed, to the benefit of Kindom and warmongers alike. Rolling the memory coin between their fingers, they watched the road. They would be able to see the delegation come down from the estate. They would see her arrive, and slip from their table, and go to her on the street, and offer her the memory coin. Unless the ingot fell on tails. Then they'd kill her.

Flip. Heads. *Hmm.*

The trick was, she would be expecting it. Because she was always expecting it, always anticipating an assassination attempt. This was one of the things they had learned in the past few years of studying her life—that she never *didn't* expect someone to try to kill her, and that it was this expectation that kept her alive. If they appeared out of nowhere, even just to give her the coin, she would expect a kill. So they had to be fast, so fast, faster than her. She was twenty-seven, practically old, surely not as fast as them.

Of course, if they tried to kill her and failed, she would definitely kill them. She might torture them first and figure out who they were, but what good was a failed assassin to her?

Or they might succeed in offering the coin, and still, she'd kill them. She had warned them, once, that it could go that way. Just the insult of startling her was worth a death sentence.

They flipped the ingot, and Makala's face shone once more. They thought of the opposite side of the coin, the temple Riin Cosas. Symbol of the Righteous Hand, of the holy Clerisy. They had never wanted to be a cleric when they studied at the kinschool. Always they wanted to be a cloaksaan, even when Four tried to change their mind. The Cloaksaan, quiet and unnoticed. Brutal. That was the road for them. And it might all work out, if they gave her the memory coin and she accepted them into her cadre of novitiates.

It was all "maybes" now, and they felt somewhat clinical about the possibility of their own death. Not because they were indifferent, but because they had come up against death a dozen times. What was their alternative, now that this crucial moment had arrived? To walk away? After everything?

Yes, said Four in their thoughts, for Four was a pragmatist, and protective. *Walk away.*

Just then a new group came into the bar, taking the table nearest theirs with raucous laughter and congratulatory braying, saying a lot of things, like how well it went, and what a payday, and who should they fleece next? It wouldn't have registered, except that one of them, a tall man with broad shoulders, said arrogantly, "That teacher was *gagging* to meet Doanye. It was a cinch, closing the deal."

That name, Doanye, caught their attention. The man with the estate on the hill. Esek's host, even now. The group ordered drinks, and the drinks came. But no one mentioned Doanye again, so Six lost interest and watched the road through the window. It was already near midnight. Surely the party wouldn't go on much longer. Inside their jacket were two weapons: a pistol strapped under one arm, and a knife in an interior sheath. The knife had a long, curved blade, perfect for gutting fish.

The memory coin was another form of weapon. A crystallized moment in time. Or a half hour, to be precise. Revel Moonback, leader of the Moonback family and rival to the Nightfoots, was a cautious man, but someone betrayed him. Someone recorded him. Six didn't even have to pay much, all things considered, and now they had a recording of him with his mistress, who also happened to be his niece.

It was sordid. And just the sort of secret that Esek Nightfoot would salivate over. If they chose to offer it to her. If they didn't kill her instead. And she didn't kill them.

"When do we get payment, Goan?" asked one of the saan at the table next to them.

The tall one laughed. "I already got the pay I care about. But the rest of it will be in this weekend. You mark my words; these people need us more than we need them. There's going to be lots more contracts that come out of this."

One of them, the smallest, said, "What do you mean you already got paid?"

A beat of silence, and the other four at the table were laughing, slapping their ignorant comrade on the back. Surly, he demanded, "Did you take another cut?"

"Just a finder's fee," said Goan, smug. "You know how it is with the kinschools."

The word buzzed in Six's ear, and though they had only been giving the group half their attention, now the saan had it all. But none of them noticed the teenager flipping the ingot.

Goan went on, "Those masters have more than money on offer, and it's all about connections in this business. You know the right people, you get the best rewards."

Everyone at the table seemed to hold their breath, waiting for the punch line, and Six, too, was waiting for it, wondering—

"A student," Goan crooned.

It took a beat for his small friend's eyes to widen in realization. "No!"

Goan nodded. "They wanted it to have an invitation to the party as well, so I asked to taste the merchandise. Sweetest thing, too. Fifteen, sixteen? Big gray eyes—like moons. Not much of a face, but those kin-school students are built like little gods."

Six's skin prickled with recognition.

"But it's illegal!" the small one said.

They all laughed again. Goan was a big man; his hands were big. He squeezed his friend's shoulder so hard Six imagined bruises spreading like ink in water.

"It's illegal if the Kindom finds out. And the Kindom doesn't find out because it doesn't want to. The students belong to the schools. They can use them for whatever they want, business, pleasure, you name it. What, you think any Hand starts out a virgin? Or haven't you ever seen the way clerics flirt? Bunch of dogs in heat. And if they're sell-ing, I tell you what—I'm buying. That little student made my week. I could have gone for hours."

The waiter came back with a new round of drinks, and the saan at the table raised their glasses and toasted, and cheered Goan on as if he was a hero. Six looked up the road, toward the Doanye estate, and real-ized that Four was at the party with Esek. Four, who they hadn't seen in nearly five years, but who they knew had gone out on a recruiting mission with one of the kinschool masters. They thought of Four's rare gray eyes and strong body, which the man Goan had enjoyed so much. Four, dangerous in its own peculiar way, had never been a sexual per-former. Four was quiet, reserved. Four would not have shared Goan's enjoyment.

They gripped the memory coin. They flipped the ingot. Makala.

The night was getting later. The people in the bar were getting drunker. The revelry of the summer night was starting to affect Six, like a hot wind whipping up their emotions. If they didn't control themself, they would lose their way. Esek Nightfoot was coming down the road soon, a red-plumed bird of prey in her cleric's coat, and she knew nothing of Four, or of Goan, or of Six waiting for her in this bar.

Their only advantage was surprise. If the coin landed on heads one more time, they would give it to her. If it landed on tails, they would kill her.

They flipped the ingot. This time, the temple Riin Cosas winked up at them.

Goan stood, bragging, "I need to piss," and went off.

Six pocketed the ingot and the memory coin. They rose like a shadow and followed him.

The restrooms were empty, and as Goan went to the urinal and started to piss, Six stood behind him, watching. It took Goan longer to notice than it should have, but when he did, he threw a startled look over his shoulder. "What are you looking at, you little freak?"

"I heard you like them young," said Six.

Goan barked, a sound half laughter, half scoff. "Fuck you. Get out of here."

He was zipping up his pants. Six said, "I need money."

Goan stopped still. Turned slowly. Looked Six over with slow, perusing eyes. What did he see? Six wondered. A tall teenager, lean, and dark-skinned as Kata—not fair like Four. Not built solid, the way Four was built. Small dark eyes instead of gray. Attractive in a conventional and generally unnoticed way. And gendermarked. Unlike Four.

"Really?" said Goan with interest. "You know, prostitution is illegal in Barcetima."

"It is illegal if they find out," Six replied.

A snort. "You're a little spy, aren't you?"

"Fifty plae," Six said.

"Thirty."

"Forty."

Another laugh. "All right. Lock that door and come here."

"Not here," said Six, stepping back from the aggressive height of the man, who looked displeased. "Somewhere more private. The alley."

They left the restroom together, walking back toward a rear exit and into an alley that separated the hotel bar from the housing blocks behind it. Six looked left and right, and saw no one, and already Goan was grabbing at them, pawing at their clothes. Six used the confidence of sixteen years learning to survive and pushed Goan back against the alley wall, distracting him with hands on his belt. They opened it together, and Six reached in for his sex, grasping him firmly and beginning to stroke. Goan groaned, head leaning back against the wall as he panted, and after a short while something hot and wet spilled over Six's hands, and they stepped back.

Goan's head had dropped down. He looked at Six with a wide, startled expression. Six held the knife in one hand, the curved blade gleaming red. Goan gripped a hand to his entrails, already spilling out of the wide slash Six had cut through him. Goan made a gurgling sound, near enough a scream that Six stepped forward and slashed out again—this time cutting through his throat. The carotid artery became a geyser, spraying hot blood over Six's face. Six stepped back again, and watched grimly as the man clutched at his belly and his throat.

It was a messy death, a smelly death, but it went quickly, the two wounds overwhelming all Goan's strength in moments. He slumped against the wall, and his legs went out. He fell sideways onto the ground, jerking and gagging on his own blood before at last he went still.

Six wiped a hand down their bloody face. There was very little light in the alley, but still too much. They found the nearest lamp and determined to crush the bulb and leave Goan in a blanketing darkness.

"What's this, little killer?" said a voice in the shadows. "You're not even going to rob the corpse?"

Six drew their gun in an instant, pointing into the dark.

"Do not move," they warned.

In the darkness, a figure stood still. Six felt a kind of horror, as if what stood in the alley would lumber forward and be a doppelgänger of themself.

"Come into the light. But do it slowly."

The figure obeyed, hands held out at their sides, until at last they had stepped into the shallow lamplight. A man. Shorter than Six and built of compact muscle, he looked as if he must be thirty or a little older than that. He stood and looked at Six, and his eyes were narrow and dark and caught the light with a shimmer. Six recognized him at once for a Quietan. He had deep brown skin, rough from sun and surf, and wore his hair in pristinely matted locs, which fell past his shoulders. He wore an oilskin vest over a shirt, and canvas trousers, and a double belt of small knives forming an X across his chest. He was smiling.

"That was brutally done. Are you a cloaksaan?"

Pride and bitterness surged in them, but they squashed it, remembering Four's talent for calm. They pointed the gun at the man. They would have to kill him.

"What are you doing in this alley?" Six asked.

"It's a public alley, nah? Can't a man smoke in peace?"

Now Six could smell the pipe smoke on him, a salty tobacco that Quietans favored. Six had spent some time on Quietus four years ago, before indenturing with a Katish weapons merchant. Six liked Quietus, and Quietans, and maybe this was why they had not pulled the trigger. Also, the gun's report might bring people running. Six would have to get close to the man and cut his throat. Leave both bodies in the alley. Make their way through the shadows to their room in the shanty town. They thought of Esek at the party on the hill. It would have to wait. It would all have to wait, either murder or gift, because this thing had happened.

Six holstered the gun and the knife, wanting to appear harmless. As harmless as they could with blood all over them, of course. They inched forward. The man watched them, thoughtful. "If you're not going to rob the corpse, do you mind if I do it?"

Startled, Six said, "Yes."

A lifted eyebrow. "Really? Why?"

Six hesitated, mouth opening and closing, some ridiculous Godtext edict about respect for the dead washing up on their memory—they dismissed it just as quickly.

"I did not kill him so he could be robbed."

It was a foolish reason. The man laughed. "Then why kill him?"

He had the typical accent of a Quietan, clipped and musical, and it only sounded more musical for the faint mockery of the question. Six kept quiet this time, though they were thinking of their kinschool days, and Four in the cot next to theirs, and Four stealing them food from the kitchen, and Four with bloody teeth scaring off some older students.

The man gave a small nod of understanding, and Six didn't like that. What could he possibly understand? Six took another step toward him, pretending to step away from the pool of blood. The door that went back into the bar was on their left. They could hear noise behind it—somewhere in there Goan's friends were drinking and fantasizing about Four.

"Was he alone?" the man asked.

It was like he had heard Six's thoughts. Six said, "He came here with friends."

"Then his friends will look for him. And you're covered in blood. If you go up this alley and turn right, you'll come to a fountain. Wash in the fountain, and run. Otherwise, they're going to find you."

Six slid closer. "They will not find me."

Or else they would. Let them.

The man sucked his teeth. "That arrogance won't take you far."

In a flash the knife was in their hand—the man was a foot away. Six lashed out, wanting to make it fast. Something jarred against their wrist. It was the leather bracer on the man's forearm. Six stepped right, swiped in the other direction. Another block, and this time the man's free hand came up and cuffed them so hard on the ear that their skull clanged. Startled, furious, they dove at him, a barrage of strikes and thrusts that pushed the man back into the shadows of the alley but didn't overwhelm him. He brandished no weapon but his arms and his hands, and they were like clubs, blocking every strike and cuffing Six again, on the opposite ear.

"Stop that," the man snapped.

Six pulled a second knife from their ankle cuff and went at the man with both hands, and this time when an arm came up, they dove under it toward his belly, saw him barely dodge, and suddenly the man had them by both wrists. They stared at each other.

"Will you *stop*?" he said.

They kneed him. It was a good blow, between his legs, but the man twisted somehow and got the brunt of it in his thigh. He gripped them tighter, so tight. Six choked in pain. They felt the bones in their wrists move, felt the compression like a vise, and panic went through them. They couldn't get past him, couldn't get free of him—

A hard jerk. The man was stronger than them and spun them around like a toy. Shoved them up against the wall. Their head cracked against stone, their back jarred badly. The knives had fallen from their choked wrists, and they were trapped. They snarled and spit like an animal, thinking of Four alone in the dark, forced to do terrible things—

"Damn you, calm down!" hissed the man. "I'm not going to hurt you."

They felt something wet on the back of their head where it had cracked against the wall. They felt a little dizzy, and the man had crossed their arms against their chest and was pinning them like that. His belts of knives were so close. Six wrenched and fought—and had their head knocked against the wall again. Their vision went starry.

"You stop it right now," said the man, as if from far away. "There was no need for any of this, you little fool."

Six felt nauseated, woozy. In humiliation they realized how quickly Esek would have killed them, if they'd gone to her tonight. They were nowhere near ready for her.

The man pulled them away from the wall and threw them down onto the alley floor, right next to Goan's fetal body. Six saw that the Quietan was holding their gun. The two knives were on the ground, by the man's feet. Out of reach. Six lay in the blood and dust and stared up at him. He was pointing the gun at them but also swiping a hand down the front of his clothes.

"Damn you, you got blood on me."

"Shoot me, then."

The man blurted a laugh. "Why are young people in such a hurry to die?"

Six flooded with heat, furious to be laughed at.

"I will not be taken by the Cloaksaan!"

He laughed again, gesturing at Goan in his smelly, motionless heap. "You think a cloak is going to get involved over this fuck? He's a merchant with his dick hanging out of his pants. I doubt the guardsaan will even care that much. You're in more danger from his friends, and I'm not about to tell strangers I ran into some weird little assassin."

That descriptor rankled, but Six was more focused on getting their gun back. As if he sensed it, the man snorted and tucked the gun in his belt. "I'm keeping this. You're a good fighter, by the way, so don't take it too hard. You just lack experience." He kicked the knives across the ground, close enough to grab. Six was so insulted they just sat there. With a vanity that seemed out of place, he took out a handkerchief and wiped at the blood that had gotten on him. "You better not try to stick me again," he warned. "Damn. Try to help someone, and this is what you get. Fucking kids."

Six watched him, suspicious, and thinking the whole thing was not quite right. Guardedly, they asked, "Why help me?"

At once the Quietan met their eyes with a wide smile, as if he'd been hoping they would ask, and said all bright and cheerful, "Well, to be honest with you—I'm a bit of a talent scout. And I saw how you used that knife. Damned impressive, kid. Damned impressive."

Six did not react. This was not the first time they'd met "talent scouts." Most were looking for child prostitutes. One had wanted Six for their actual skills, and she was dead now. They would find a way to kill this man, too, if they had to.

"I do want to know," he went on, still cheerfully, like this was a chat happening in the bar instead of the alley, "why did you kill him, if not to rob him?"

Six thought of Four. "He was a rapist."

The man stopped dabbing at himself. He looked at Six seriously, in a way that said he believed them. Six had said it as a warning rather than a justification—as a way to insist that if the man *was* looking for child prostitutes, this was the wrong tactic.

"Well, then. I suppose that's fair play. But you didn't come to Barcetima to kill this fucker, did you?" Six just looked at him. The man shrugged. "I can spot the difference between a local and the just-passing-through type. So, I ask myself, what does a weird little assassin pass through Barcetima for? Why do they sit in the bar and watch Ashir Doanye's house? Why do they do it on the night he's got Kindom visiting him?"

A thousand icy needles swept the crown of Six's skull as they realized that this strange Quietan had been watching them since before the murder in the alley. Following them, maybe? Were their intentions toward Esek visible on their face? Did the man work for Esek?

"Word of advice on that front," he continued. "It's not an easy thing, going up against Kindom all alone. They'd have you spitted and roasting before you had a chance to name the Sixth God."

Six stood up slowly, swiping the knives. They could get another gun. For now, the blood was drying on their clothes. The shanty town room was ten blocks away, and no one would glance at blood there, but they thought maybe they should get out of town altogether. There were farms four miles outside the city center. A barn would make a good hideout for the night.

"Do not follow me," they ordered, and took a step back.

He looked amused. "The name's Yantikye, in case you're interested. Yantikye the Honor."

"I am not interested," said Six, backing up farther.

Yantikye the Honor tsked. "Come now, little killer. Everyone needs allies sometimes."

Spinning around, they leapt and broke the lamp bulb that illuminated the alley. Thrown under a black blanket, they ran away from the body and the Quietan man, but they heard his voice calling after them like a premonition. "Don't forget my name! You may need it!"

Bruised and with blood on their skull, they didn't look back.

It was months before they learned that Four became Chono that night.

For this reason, it is to the benefit of the Jeveni people and the Treble entire that no separatist community shall exceed one hundred Jeveni citizens, and the Kindom retains the right to disband these communities at will. It is better by far that the Jeveni should assimilate, and adopt the practices of their new planets and cities, for their isolation from civilization has been a blight upon them, and ultimately made them vulnerable to the genocider Lucos Alanye. Thus the Kindom intends that they never suffer such a fate again, and may the Godfire ensure it, by curtailing their pride.

excerpt, the Anti-Patriation Act, Article 3.
Dated 1596, Year of the Brand.

CHAPTER TWO

1664

YEAR OF THE CRUX

Farren Eyce
The Planet Capamame

The body lies at a strange angle, both arms underneath his torso. Half of him lies on the landing, the other half sprawled over the last few steps of this flight of the massive stone staircase that forms the core of Farren Eyce. His neck is broken, one leg snapped at the knee. In this position, his face is hidden, but there's no mistaking Uskel's red hair, matted with blood.

Through Masar flashes an image of Nikkelo, lifted off his feet by the force of a gunshot, a scarlet corona spreading around his head where he fell...

"We should move him," says Fonu sen Fhaan, the River of the Wheel, and Nikkelo's replacement.

No one says anything. Masar's prosthetic eye tics, a quick glitch in his vision; he rubs the corner until it resolves. He looks over at Dom, another collector, whose normally dark complexion has grayed out with shock. Nevertheless he comes at Masar's gesture, and together the three of them crouch and gently lift Uskel's body, carrying him down the last steps and laying him on his back. Masar's stomach churns at the crushed ruin of his face, and Dom makes a soft, strangled noise. From nearby come more sounds of gasps and murmurs. Masar glances up. The crowd has gotten bigger since he arrived five minutes ago. It's not even dawn, but word has already spread. A couple of the junior collectors, Qlios and Siel, stand between him and the crowd, an informal barricade.

Masar asks Dom, "When was the last time you spoke to him?"

Dom stares at Uskel, then looks up at Masar with rapidly blinking, damp eyes. "Two nights ago. We had drinks. Everything…seemed fine."

Masar nods, and suddenly a woman in the crowd approaches. She's carrying a blanket, and though Siel looks uncertain, Qlios stands aside for her. She holds the blanket out to Masar, her eyes fixed on Uskel's body.

"Moon arise," she breathes.

Masar takes the blanket. "Don't look, Auntie."

Her eyes snap up to his. He knows her from a little noodle shop she runs in the Market District. She says, "I saw a death like this in the factories. A woman fell from some scaffolding."

What should he say to that? He and Dom take the blanket as Fonu watches, and they spread it out over Uskel, covering him and most of the blood. Masar turns back to the woman, who looks wan and haunted.

"May the barren flourish," she whispers, and turns away.

For the first time he takes a good look at the crowd, sees the mix of expressions, fear and uncertainty. They're all murmuring to one another, many staring at Masar or Fonu, rather than Uskel. Tension hangs over the crowd like the quiet eye of a storm.

Fonu mutters, "We should disperse these people. It does no good for them to see this."

Masar gives the River a sidelong glance. Not for the first time, he considers how different Fonu is from Nikkelo, whose warmth bred loyalty and confidence in everyone he spoke to.

Dom, looking sick, demands, "Disperse them how, my River?"

His voice holds none of the reverence usually found in that honorific.

Fonu makes an impatient sound, their skinny frame tightening as they sense the rebuke in Dom's question. "Who knows what rumors and exaggerations will spread through the colony?"

Masar pauses, glancing toward the swelling ranks of colonists. Uskel is the third collector to die in the past six months.

"It might be a bit late for that," he says.

Fresh chatter starts up in the crowd as people stand, and Jun Ironway appears. She must have taken the elevator down from her apartment on Level 7. She looks rumpled and cross, and he can tell at once that she's already casting, her eyes distant.

The lights in the courtyard suddenly flicker. Everyone looks up, uneasy at this latest example of a problem that's been plaguing Farren Eyce for months. Jun's limbs tighten. The flickering stops, and she stands beside the body.

"Can you move the blanket?" she asks, voice rough either from sleep or from her caster fugue. Masar lifts the blanket, standing between Uskel and the crowd to block their view. Dom helps. There are voices behind them, but Masar focuses on Jun. She observes the body, clearly assessing with her ocular, feeding information into a vault of evidence. She raises her eyes toward the staircase rising above them. They're on the fourth level of Farren Eyce, and eventually Jun says, "Based on the damage, I calculate he fell from Level 8."

A beat of silence.

"Fell," Masar repeats.

The stone railings of the staircase are as high as Uskel's waist.

Jun amends, "Someone . . . made him fall."

Fonu makes a low, aggressive sound. "Keep your voice down. We don't need hysteria."

Something changes in Jun's eyes, a flicker from distance to presence, as she turns to look at Fonu for the first time. Her eyebrows hike up in that fucking smartass way that keeps getting her in trouble with the Wheel.

"Or else he jumped. But three collector suicides in six months? I doubt they hate your leadership *that* much, Sa."

Fonu's narrow face twists. Masar warns in a rumble, "Jun..."

She rubs her eyes, clears her throat. "A few cameras caught his fall, but none of them show how it happened. He was in a dead spot."

This is the same as it was with the other two collectors. Leios was found hanging in a gymnasium locker room with no cameras. Roq appeared to have shot themself with a nail gun in a construction zone that hadn't yet been connected to the Farren Eyce casting net. And now, this fall in the early hours, no one and nothing to see it happen.

As if hearing his thoughts, someone in the crowd calls out, "What is this? If you can't protect your own from murderers, how can you protect us?!"

Voices rise in agreement. Masar glances at Fonu, expecting them to address the speakers, but the River holds challenging eye contact with Jun. Masar leaves them, walking toward the crowd. To his unease, a few people step back, as if they're afraid of him.

"I know how frightening this is," he says. "But we're doing everything we can to figure out what's happening. Believe me, I want to understand it as much as you. These people who've died—they were my friends. I worked with them for years."

Saying it for the first time makes his throat tighten. Most of the remaining collectors in Farren Eyce only finished their training in the last two years. The veterans Masar came up with, who lived and bled for the cause of the Wheel, are a dying breed. It's just him and Dom left.

Someone says, "We need better methods for preventing suicide."

Someone argues, "This isn't suicide, you fool."

"No one knows anything," says a third. "The Wheel doesn't know *anything*."

More rumbling in the crowd, more anxiety and crackling anger. Before Capamame, when it was Masar's job to seek out the lost descendants of the Jeveni, he had a gift for making people trust him, like him, talk to him. He has used that gift these past eight months, trying to soothe the uncertainty and fear of the Farren Eyce colonists with his natural charisma. But what was once a performance in service of the mission now feels like a costume that no longer fits.

He speaks over the crowd, "You're right. We don't know yet what happened. If it was suicide or something else. But until we're sure, it's better not to make guesses. You should all go home, get a little more sleep. The Gale will send out a newscast once we know more."

Someone scoffs. Masar zeroes in on a man in farmer's coveralls. "And how are you gonna 'know more'? You gonna ask *her*." He flings a contemptuous gesture at Jun, who has stopped her staring contest with Fonu to stand aside and do—whatever it is she does when she casts. "She's a stranger!"

Masar flicks an eye to the farmer's greenish Jeveni tattoo. He's Draeviin—one of the crew of *Drae's Hope*, the ship that left the Treble decades ago on a mission to build a new world where Jeveni could prosper in freedom from the Kindom. *Drae's Hope* crossed forty light-years of the Black to reach the ice planet they called Capamame, birthing new generations of crew along the way, like this farmer—the ones who began the work of building Farren Eyce. Before Masar and seventy-six thousand other refugees jumped to the Capamame System eight months ago, most Draeviin had never seen a non-Jeveni. The Je word that the farmer used, *stranger*, means "outsider," "distrusted," "not one of us." It's a word that matches the suspicion and contempt in the farmer's eyes. Masar feels helpless.

Suddenly Dom appears, his shock and horror taking a back seat as he speaks sternly to the farmer. "That's enough. You're talking about Jun Ironway." He looks around at the rest of the crowd. "You all know what we owe her."

While the farmer looks dissatisfied, most of the rest of them nod somber agreement. Even the angriest, most reluctant citizen of Farren Eyce knows what they owe Jun Ironway.

Somebody says, "Masar is right. We should all go home."

It takes a few seconds, but gradually, with much muttering and whispers, the people begin to disperse. A few stragglers hang back, including the nightshift casters who found Uskel. Jun goes to them, taking them aside and speaking quietly, gathering information that she pings to Masar's neural link. Their reports are harrowing. They had come off shift in the casting labs and were taking the stairs up to their apartment level when the body fell past them. One describes hearing the crack as it hit the stairs. They contacted the River's office as soon as they reached the body, dead on impact. Masar pings her.

Did they hear Uskel scream?

After a few seconds, she pings back.

They don't think so.

Surely if he had been thrown over the railing, he would have screamed?

Morgue workers arrive. They put Uskel onto a float stretcher, still covered by the blanket. Later, maintenance will come down to clean the blood, perhaps even paint over the stain, but people will know.

Fonu sen Fhaan, standing beside Masar again as they watch Uskel carried away, says lowly, "That farmer is right, you know. If this was murder, it's most likely a stranger did it."

Masar shoots them a look. Fonu was the chief engineer of *Drae's Hope* when it reached Capamame. Their election to the Wheel after Nikkelo died was more a gesture of gratitude to the Draeviin than it was an endorsement of Fonu's particular qualifications. If the generation ship's captain and first mate had not died during the construction of the colony, Fonu would never have risen so high.

"There's no evidence it was a non-Jeveni," Masar says.

"No Jeveni would kill a collector," Fonu retorts, pale eyes certain. "Our people revere collectors."

A year ago, Masar would have agreed. Those Jeveni who knew about the collector mission to find lost Jeveni descendants had always held people like Masar in the highest esteem. But many of his perceptions of his own people have changed in the past year. The vast majority of Jeveni in the Treble *didn't* know about the collectors—or about the Wheel, the secret ruling body of their people. It was always the Wheel's plan to invite every known Jeveni to jump to Capamame, to give them the choice. But eight months ago, as the Jeveni gathered for Remembrance Day, Kindom warbirds attacked them. Masar had known what would happen. Death for many. Imprisonment for the rest. The Wheel ordered every Jeveni ship to jump to Capamame, where the vast majority found themselves thrown into a life they hadn't chosen. Many have acclimated to the new world, but huge segments of the population resent it.

What reverence do those segments have for the collectors?

Fonu sen Fhaan and the rest of the Draeviin have little sympathy for those who haven't embraced Farren Eyce. But they also reserve all their contempt for the small population of non-Jeveni who came over in the jump.

Masar tries to think how to challenge Fonu, but he doesn't get a chance. "I want you to go to Effegen and report on this," the River says.

Masar pauses. "You...don't want to do it yourself?"

"I'm going to the morgue to oversee the medical examiner's work. It's possible they'll find a connection between this death and the others. But if someone doesn't go to the Star, she's going to come down here and start pacing the scene herself."

"Effegen likes to be visible," Masar says.

"Yes. But visibility might not be safe right now."

They walk away without saying anything else. Masar notices Qlios and Siel stand aside for them, sending wary looks after their back as they head to the bank of elevators that most people use to travel between the ten levels of Farren Eyce. Even the young collectors, who have little memory of Nikkelo, seem uncomfortable with Fonu's leadership.

Shaking off the thought, Masar looks around for Jun. She's gone. Wandered back to her lab, no doubt, without so much as a word. He rolls his eyes. Ever since Liis left on an expedition to explore the larger planet several weeks ago, Jun's social ineptitude has skyrocketed.

He'll find her later. He throws one last glance at the bloodstains, then looks up the height of the stairs from which Uskel fell. Or was thrown. Effegen is on Level 8. Masar decides to walk.

The other members of the Wheel are waiting for him in the council room. Masar, who had hoped to speak to Effegen alone in her office, feels stiff and inarticulate as he relays everything that he knows. Before Nikkelo died, Masar never had to stand before the Wheel alone. Nikkelo's easy charm and confidence lent confidence to Masar, gave him a solid wall to lean against. Now, Gaeda ben Kist, the Stone and religious leader of the colony, demands, "Where is Fonu?" and he feels small in the face of her disapproval.

"They went with Uskel to the morgue."

Gaeda narrows her eyes and sniffs. "May the barren flourish."

Hyre ten Grie, the Gale, repeats her blessing, and looks at Masar sorrowfully. Masar's skin itches. His eye feels tired and sore.

Tomesk ten Ruvo, the Tree, says, "You're sure no one else saw it happen?"

"I can't be sure of that, yet. The River will launch an aggressive investigation."

"I'll send out a colony-wide communiqué, asking people to come forward," says Hyre. "And I'll have the newscasters put out an obituary right away."

Tomesk throws them a skeptical look. "We should hold off on saying anything until we know more." A quick look at Effegen. "Don't you agree, my Star?"

Gaeda ben Kist snaps the end of her cane against the floor. Eldest of them all, acerbic and proud, she has a gift for bullying the others. "We've already got half the colony distrusting everything we do. Let's not feed the rumor mill by keeping secrets."

Effegen says, "Tomesk, let's let Hyre handle the messaging. It's their office, after all."

Tomesk glowers, which is his typical expression. For a moment no one speaks, the air brittle. A Wheel should never be a placid organization. Its members should argue and challenge one another. But this past year has strained the equanimity among the Spokes. Masar feels certain that if Nikkelo were alive, it wouldn't be this way. Probably wishful thinking.

"I should go, then," Hyre says, lifting their big, voluptuous body from a chair and bowing to the others before leaving the council room.

"I'm going to perform services," Gaeda agrees. "Come along with me, Tomesk. You could use some prayer." Tomesk snorts, and Gaeda gives Masar a piercing look. "You be careful, young man. I don't want to find your body next."

Her words leave a staticky crackle in the air.

When they've all gone and he's alone with Effegen, they watch each other across the length of the round council table. She's wearing her official green robes, the silver embroidery like veins, and her folded hands display several jevite rings. Jevite studs limn the helix of her right ear.

"Have you or Fonu considered that maybe you should take the day off?"

The question startles him. Not for the first time, he feels unnerved by Effegen's steady gaze. She has a calm affect, eyes wise beyond her years. When he first met her, she was sixteen, newly risen to her position as the Star, and even then she had this steady seriousness about her—though she smiled more. He admired her instantly, even if her keen insights and poise made him feel like a big, lumbering oaf. But the leader of the Wheel, and of the Jeveni, has historically wielded a certain gravitas.

"I'm sorry," he says. "I'm not sure what you mean."

She tilts her head. "Masar, this is the third close friend of yours to die in six months."

It's unsettling that she knows this. Though of course she has dossiers on him and every other Jeveni who ever served the Wheel, and that would certainly include which saan he worked with under Nikkelo. Her expression is patient. She has this habit of digging into parts of him that he's not inclined to advertise.

"I appreciate your concern, my Star, but I'm fine. Yes, we were friends, but—"

"More than friends. Collectors are family to one another."

She flicks her fingers through the air, and a cast appears. "I'm looking at a report here from Nikkelo, of eleven senior Jeveni collectors who worked missions together. The cream of our crop, you might say. Far more experienced than most of the collectors here in Farren Eyce. Of those eleven, six died before the jump. Now three more have died here. Am I correct?"

The mathematics make his teeth hurt. He nods shortly, wondering what the point is. Effegen flicks the cast away, clasping her hands.

"Four of them died on a single mission in 1660," she says, giving him a long, careful look. "Do you mind telling me about it?"

Masar hesitates, but discipline and years of soldierly obedience click into place. "Nikkelo received intelligence from within the Kindom. An anonymous Hand had evidence that the Wheel was still operating. They were seeking information about you. According to Nikkelo's sources, someone had offered to sell your name. We knew it was bullshit—excuse me—nonsense."

"Bullshit is fine," she says dryly.

"Anyone who would know your names was thoroughly vetted and trustworthy, which meant the seller was lying. But Nikkelo wanted us to track down the Kindom buyer. He sent seven of us altogether, because we didn't know how much heat we'd be up against. The meetup was in an open-air market in Ycutta, on Braemin. When we had eyes on the rendezvous point, there was just one person there, in an armored uniform. We couldn't get any cast readings on them. They waited for over two hours, and no one arrived, so we decided to fall back. But guardsaan came at one of our positions, and Leios...She shot at them. There was a firefight. I got hit early, and Uskel carried me out. Leios managed to escape, too, but...no one else survived."

Masar's voice goes a little soft at the end, remembering. From the time he was recruited at barely seventeen, he had trained ceaselessly for the task of infiltrating whatever places or systems necessary to track down his targets. This was the appeal for him as a teenager. Espionage. Combat training. And all in the service of his people. Make his grandmother proud. Honor the memory of his dead fathers. It had all seemed so heroic, back at the beginning.

Effegen says quietly, "That must have been terrible for you."

A ringing starts in his ears, like the shrieking whistle of the alarm when shots broke out in the commercial galleria. He is overwhelmed by the scent memory of air-conditioning, smoke grenades, blood—and the sickly sugary smell of a taffy shop nearby.

"Masar."

Effegen's voice is like the snap of a rubber band, jerking him back into the room with her, his new eye half a beat behind the old as it refocuses on her somber face.

"I apologize for asking you to relive painful memories. I ask because Nikkelo said in his report that the firefight was particularly hard on Leios, Uskel, and Roq."

Masar frowns. "Roq wasn't even there."

"Yes, neither was Dom. Both of them contacted Nikkelo afterward, angry that he hadn't included them. Roq was especially upset, because their lover died. Ademi, wasn't it?"

Masar resettles his weight. Roq and Ademi had tried to keep the romance quiet, but everyone knew. They could never seem to stop smiling, when they were together.

"Yes."

"This event...It hurt you all badly. It left wounds in you. I suppose what I'm asking is...were those wounds deep enough to explain three collector suicides?"

Masar grimaces. "Until today I . . . thought it might be suicide. Leios took that firefight the hardest; she blamed herself for firing on the guards. And then the battle on *The Risen Wave* set her back even worse. Our first few months in Farren Eyce she was . . . pretty quiet. Jumpy. Roq was closer to Leios than anyone, so when she died, it made a kind of . . . sick sense that Roq would follow her. Especially because they'd never stopped grieving Ademi. But Uskel . . ." A spike of anxiety makes him want to run. Uskel's face, caved in. Nikkelo's body, sprawled and broken in the landing bay. "Uskel's been so happy since we got here. He threw himself into helping wherever he could. Always lit up the room."

Effegen smiles sadly. "Sometimes the happy ones hide a secret darkness."

"I know all about that. But Uskel always passed the psych check-ins with flying colors. I'm sorry, my Star, but I just . . . I don't think it was suicide, for him."

"An accident, perhaps?"

"The railings are tall and made from solid stone."

"Then we are back to murder."

". . . Yes."

"And if we're back to murder for Uskel, then the fact that two other collectors have died means they might have been murdered, too."

"But why kill us?" Masar asks. "We're not fighters anymore. The army has been disbanded. All we do is help solve problems when they arise. No one has cause to hate us."

"Could it be connected to any of the other troubles in Farren Eyce?"

She is referring to a half dozen unexplained incidents over the past eight months: six coops of fowl that took ill and died from suspected poisoning; an electrical failure in the hospital; rashes of vandalism that might be kids but seem somehow more sinister. Five weeks ago, a fire in the Market District showed signs of arson. All of this on top of the power fluctuations, which Jun insists are due to an overburdened electrical grid, but which always seem to set her on edge, as if she suspects something worse. Still . . .

"Murdering collectors seems like a lot worse than those troubles," Masar says. He, like many, hopes these events don't mean anything. What he hopes and what he fears, however...

"And what about the Kindom agent who wanted to buy my name?" Effegen asks.

Masar frowns, surprised. "What about them?"

"Nikkelo never identified them. It seems to me that this was the first sign that the Kindom was aware of our existence and was trying to sabotage us."

Masar considers.

Effegen continues, "We have every reason to believe the Kindom had spies among us before we jumped. Masar, there are tens of thousands of people in this colony. Isn't it possible that one or many of them were those spies? That they work for the Kindom, even now?"

"To what purpose? Jun controls communication out of Farren Eyce. There's no way for our people to contact the Treble. And it's not as if they can jump to them, or the Kindom can jump to us."

Indeed, this is the only reason why Farren Eyce is possible. Without the Capamame gate key, Kindom agents can't reach them. And with only a select few in Farren Eyce privy to that key (the Wheel, and Jun herself), their protection from the Kindom is secure.

"Even if there are spies," Masar continues, "they have no way to receive instructions from Kindom operatives."

Effegen's lip curls in a slow, amused smile. "I admit it surprises me to think that I might be more paranoid than a collector."

"My Star, whoever was behind the Ycutta mission was after the Wheel. There haven't been any assassination attempts against you or any of the others."

"*Yet*," Effegen says ruefully.

"We'll protect you," Masar says.

"Who, exactly? I have every confidence in your diligence, but our senior collectors are almost all dead. The ones we have left are novices. Eda is just eighteen!"

Masar exhales restlessly. Could she be right? Could it be a long game, to take out all the Wheel's strongest protectors and leave them at the mercy of the untried?

Effegen says, "Let us imagine that these deaths have nothing to do with the mission on Ycutta. Many people in Farren Eyce are angry that they ended up here, and the collectors were instrumental in making that happen. Which would certainly make them targets."

"The people who are angry have only the Kindom to blame for forcing us to run."

"That may be *factual*, but it hardly feels *true* to those who don't want to be here. And the Kindom did what it did because it believed that the Wheel was fomenting an uprising."

"We never did," Masar presses.

"But some of our actions appeared to do it. Another reason for people to be angry at us. In any case, our dream was to give the Jeveni a choice of whether or not they wanted a life on Capamame. Now, the vast majority of them are stuck here through no fault of their own, because a ruling body they didn't know about was acting on their behalf—without their permission."

Masar bristles. "You sound like you think Farren Eyce is a mistake."

"Not at all," she hums. "But on the one side, we have the beauty and freedom of a colony beyond Kindom reach; on the other side, we have the injustice of tearing tens of thousands of people away from the only life they ever knew."

"You haven't forced anyone to stay here," he reminds her.

Effegen gives him a droll look. He shifts restlessly. It's true that in the days after the jump, the Wheel agreed to send back anyone who wished it. But most understood that the Kindom was prepared to annihilate their fleet. They recognized that it was not safe for them to return. Only about five thousand of them took the risk. They were promptly arrested and thrown into a sevite labor camp.

No one has tried to go back since.

Effegen stands up. Masar rises as well and watches a bit warily as she comes to stand before him. The first time he met her, Effegen looked up at him and said with a mischievous smile that they hardly seemed to be the same species. Masar is tall and muscular, broad through the shoulders and narrow through his hips, a soldier at heart. Even since cutting off his unkempt tangle of Braemish kill braids, he has retained his tattoos and his scars. Effegen, on the other hand, is more than a head shorter than him, with a plump build and a sweet, beautiful face. She has no scars—at least in physical terms.

Yes, they could be a different species. But as she gazes up at him with eyes like moss-threaded gold, he sees the ghosts haunting her. They are of a kind with the ghosts that haunt him.

Effegen reaches into a pocket of her dress, withdrawing a small book. It's little more than a pamphlet, yet he recognizes it for a publication of the speeches of Drae sen Briit. He half expects Effegen to start quoting him the maxims of their colony's symbolic founder, but instead she withdraws a piece of folded laminate from inside the pages. She holds it out to him. Confused, he unfolds it, instantly recognizing Nikkelo's distinct scrawl:

My Star,

I must keep this brief, though I know how you love detail. You're grieving the deaths of the collectors; you're angry that they died hiding your name. I'm grieving, too. But this is their mission, and always has been: to protect our people. That includes you. We are your sword and shield, and we will do what needs to be done.

That said, I'm placing Roq, Uskel, and Leios on leave, until they've had time to recover. Then we'll resume the hunt for whichever Hand wants to buy our names.

I'm also reassigning Masar. He seems the steadiest of them all, but I need that steadiness elsewhere. He's a leader among the collectors, respected and admired, and we'll need leaders on Capamame. I want him on a less dangerous mission.

He'll be angry about the reassignment, so I'm sending him to you first. Tell him about Sool ben Leight. If he knows he's tracking down a family that the Nightfoots themselves may have killed, it'll inspire him. To say nothing of the special gravity that he will give to your request. He is quite devoted to you. As am I.

Your River

Masar reads the letter twice. He remembers distinctly when Nikkelo ordered him to visit Effegen, so this letter must have come just before. On the one hand, the cadence of Nikkelo's written words is like hearing his voice, and it burns through Masar, pure love and grief. On the other hand, Nikkelo speaking of Masar's devotion to Effegen embarrasses him. But the most potent emotion of all is anger, realizing *why* Nikkelo took him off the hunt for the Kindom Hand. It wasn't because finding the descendants of Sool ben Leight was more important. It was because Nikkelo calculated that *Masar* was more important.

"Ironic, isn't it?" Effegen says. Masar raises a questioning eyebrow. "The Sool ben Leight mission was supposed to be safe—yet you ended up right in the Kindom's crosshairs, and responsible for bringing in Jun Ironway. Turned out to be quite the most dangerous mission Nikkelo could have given you."

"Maybe if it had been someone else, Nikkelo would still be alive," Masar says without thinking.

Her look chastises him. "You know that's not true. And Nikkelo wanted you there. He viewed you as his inheritor."

Masar balks. "*Fonu* is his inheritor."

"And I would never undermine my River," she replies. "But Fonu is new to this role, and inexperienced with a population this size—not to mention politics this fraught. The Draeviin were always of one purpose. Fonu needs your expertise, and I need you to commit all your skill and energy to this. I'm convinced that whoever is killing the collectors has bigger aims than murder. I need you to be my sword and shield, Masar. I need you to find who is responsible. Whatever it takes."

The grimness of the directive worries Masar. Effegen more than anyone believes in the pacifist vision of Farren Eyce. The Jeveni warriors who fought on *The Risen Wave* are now retired into community-focused work. Masar's beloved shotgun is locked away in the armory. There are no guardsaan, no weapons, no jails, and Effegen is the truest champion of those edicts. She believes the people can negotiate resolutions to their conflicts; she believes in the power of mercy, patience, and mediation. What does *whatever it takes* mean in a context such as theirs?

"I won't disappoint you, my Star."

Effegen places a hand on his chest, as if she were about to confer a blessing. "You have never disappointed me," she says. Her small hand is a warm, unexpected weight, and when her eyes flick from him to her hand, her brow furrows for a moment. She steps back.

"Thank you, Masar."

Clearing his throat, he bows over his open palms. "Thank you, my Star."

He thinks he's dismissed, but she asks, "Have you eaten yet? Bene is joining me for breakfast in a few minutes. Would you like to stay?"

The words startle him more than they should. It's not the first time that she has invited him to eat with her. It *is* the first time she's invited him to join her private meals with Bene. Jun Ironway's cousin is beloved by everyone who knows him in Farren Eyce, and that includes Effegen. The two of them have been friends from the beginning, and they share an unnerving ability to look at Masar as if they can see through to his heart.

Sitting in the presence of both of them feels like far too much to bear, today.

"Apologies, but I must get to work," he says, more stiffly than he means to. It's not her fault that thoughts of Bene make him go squirmy inside. It's not her fault that thoughts of them together make him even squirmier. She doesn't deserve him to be cold.

After a pause, Effegen nods. As she does each time he refuses her invitation.

"Of course. Thank you again."

He turns in relief, eager to go, but when he reaches the door, Effegen calls to him, "Masar." Wincing, he faces her again. "I thought you'd like to know. The construction guild has given *The Risen Wave* clearance to leave the system. Chono and Six will jump back to the Treble this morning."

CHAPTER THREE

1664

YEAR OF THE CRUX

The Risen Wave
The Black Ocean

Chono sits in the captain's chair, counting ships on the view screen. There are over a hundred of them, circling *The Risen Wave* like vultures around a fallen behemoth. Every minute or so the command ship transmits an automated message:

> **PREPARE TO BE BOARDED. ALL ACTS
> OF AGGRESSION WILL BE MET WITH
> LETHAL FORCE.**

STAND DOWN AND AWAIT FURTHER INSTRUCTION. THIS IS YOUR ONLY WARNING.

It's tedious. They invited the Kindom here; their docks are open and their weapons are cold. There's no need for histrionics.

Her eyes shift toward a casting view to her right, tracking in real time the dissemination of the data flood they released as soon as they entered orbit. Two hours ago it reached the mining station that circles the nearby gas planet, Locali. After that it was not long before it got as far as Ma'kess, and then Quietus, hitting farming stations and other outposts along the way. Ninety minutes ago it hopped through a jump gate and, just as Jun Ironway predicted, spread its fingers across the remaining two systems in the Treble. It took twenty minutes for the Kindom to realize what it was, to start jamming its signal. But already local casters have gotten ahold of the flood. Now they're doing the rest of the work, distributing the files via private comms. As Chono watches, a little township in the Teros hinterlands lights up. The package has arrived. Whatever else the Kindom tries, it's too late to stop the worlds from knowing what they've done.

Satisfaction moves like static over Chono's skin. She feels dangerous now, and vengeful. Her thoughts are full of the five thousand Jeveni who jumped back to the Treble eight months ago, innocent saan whose only crime was their determination to go home. Chono warned them. The Wheel warned them, but there can be no true freedom on Capamame if people are forced to stay there, and the five thousand did not want to stay. They had family, friends, lives they wished to return to, and unlike so many in their same position, they refused to wait to see how the Kindom would behave in the aftermath of the Jeveni's disappearance.

Now, they are in a labor camp, driven to fill the hole left behind in the sevite trade, when the vast majority of its workforce disappeared.

She knows that plenty of people in Farren Eyce blame the five thousand, call them shortsighted and naive, think they should have known this would happen: capture and imprisonment. But Chono doesn't blame them. Chono wants them back, with a ferocity that burns. If these people are unwitting pieces in a game, then she'll see that game destroyed.

She clenches and relaxes one fist, a meditative exercise that a Jeveni doctor taught her when she was recovering from complications to heart surgery. But it does little to cool her thoughts. She watches another array of casting screens, which record the various entry points for the cloaksaan who have boarded the ship and who are surging through the lower decks like a plague. With the flick of a hand, Chono could cut the oxygen and bar the doors, and the cloaksaan's military suits would eventually run out of oxygen. She could suffocate them all, and it would not even begin to be a fair return.

Six moves slowly from one end of the bridge to the other, head down. Silent. A common attitude, for them. At least there's plenty of space to walk. It's a large bridge, befitting a generation ship that, a year ago, was no more than a museum piece. But lots of things changed their function a year ago. *The Risen Wave* became an escape hatch for seventy-six thousand Jeveni. Chono's identity as a loyal Kindom cleric met its final test, and failed. And Esek Nightfoot, brilliant, beautiful, terrible Esek Nightfoot—turned out to be dead.

Her murderer paces the deck. Chono watches them.

PREPARE TO BE BOARDED. ALL ACTS OF AGGRESSION WILL BE MET WITH LETHAL FORCE.

STAND DOWN AND AWAIT FURTHER INSTRUCTION. THIS IS YOUR ONLY WARNING.

"How far has the data flood gone?" Six asks.

Chono glances to the view at her right. "Everywhere."

"Any chatter?"

Chono makes a few quick gestures, and new skeins of data unfurl, messages pinging off a thousand signals, growing exponentially as people view the data flood and exchange their thoughts on its reliability. Here and there are the signs of Kindom operatives trying to cut these conversations off at the source, but for every exchange they silence, a new one pops up. The messages are full of incredulity, questions, vindication. She keeps looking for the theme of outrage, but so far surprise and distrust seem paramount.

"Yes," says Chono. "Lots of chatter."

"Any friends, in the Black?"

Chono watches the data on her view. "Not yet."

Certainly not in the Kindom. She has a fleeting thought for Ilius Redquill, a secretary in Riin Kala who has been her friend and information broker for a decade. But even if he was still inclined to help her, she doubts that there's anything he can do. As for Aver Paiye, the powerful First Cleric of the Righteous Hand, Chono has well and truly burned that bridge.

No, she returns to the Treble a fugitive and traitor, and her first act is further treason. Esek, if Esek were here, would be proud of her.

Chono watches Six continue their pensive circuit. She takes in the cut of their cleric's coat, the shine of their boots, the perfect smoothness of their dark braids, coiled in a crown. And of course, the disfigured helix of their left ear. Over the past months, Chono has grown used to seeing them in the borrowed attire of Jeveni civilians, clothes that Esek would never have worn. That dissonance helped. Watching Six among the Jeveni, working with them to build up their colony—if Chono squinted just right, she could almost believe they looked nothing like Esek. Now, resplendent in the uniform that Esek wore so beautifully, they are once again a strange and horrible contradiction. The face and body of her dead mentor. The mind of her schoolkin.

"How close are the cloaks?" Six asks.

Chono projects the answer onto the main view. Six watches with her as one of the nine invading clutches surges onto the bridge level. The cast predicts they'll arrive in less than ten minutes. A familiar figure leads the way.

"Is that—" Six asks.

"Yes."

They chuckle. "Good of her to stop by."

Gooseflesh ripples down Chono's spine. That chuckle sounded *just like* Esek. She tries to see past their appearance itself, to see their energy, their mannerisms. A stricter posture than Esek had. None of her lazy grace, but rather a pristine bodily command, like a dancer. As a child, Six had the skinny muscularity of a wild rabbit, their body already long, their skin darker than Esek's. Esek was probably a gorgeous child; Six was stark-featured, intense. Angry.

"Can you tell how many of them have viewed the data flood?" Six asks.

Chono shakes her head. "These reports aren't that detailed."

Six paces. Chono watches. They look like her broody schoolkin again, just as grim and taciturn as their child self, though far less known to her. She recalls how the other schoolkin feared them, all those years ago. Cold, unreachable, dangerous Six.

"Do you ever think about what we were like as kids?" she asks.

She doesn't know why she asks it. She doesn't know why she would expect Six to answer. The past few months have been . . . tense, the two of them not sure how to engage each other.

True enough, Six's gaze is flat. "What?"

This is the sort of unwelcoming response that she has come to expect. Six has shown no interest in discussing the fierce, devoted, intimate friendship they had as kinschool students at Principes. And now is hardly the time to begin the conversation, with the cloaks five minutes away.

Yet when Six asks, "What?" Chono can't give up the opportunity. She shrugs, gazing out at the sea of Kindom warbirds. "I was just trying to remember at what point you stopped being scary to me."

Think of Six as a child. Think of Six's rare moments of vulnerability. Tie those moments to this creature before you, and maybe the illusion of Esek will fade . . .

Six doesn't react at first. Chono thinks they won't react at all, until they say blandly, "Perhaps it was the first time I hid under your covers during a storm."

Chono smiles, surprised and inordinately pleased by the self-deprecation in their voice. By the humanness of them.

"You told me not to tell anyone. And I didn't. And the other students went on thinking you were terrifying."

Six snorts. "That is cute, coming from you."

She frowns at them. "What do you mean?"

Six gives her a droll look, too much like Esek. "You terrified everyone, too. Even the older students stayed out of your way."

This is . . . not how she remembers it, and she tells them so. Six clicks their tongue, looking out at the Black.

"Student Four," they hum. "Quiet and terrible."

Chono scowls at the use of her kinschool moniker, which she abandoned when Esek took her for a novitiate. She was quiet back then, but terrible? Yes, she avoided the beatings that other children often took from older students, but that was because of Six. Always a malevolent, protective presence.

"How close are they?" Six asks again.

Chono doesn't answer right away, distracted, remembering—

"Chono?"

"Two minutes."

A firm nod. "You will stand behind me. Let me take the brunt of the violence."

They are a great contradiction. Chono nearly died in the battle of *The Risen Wave*, and Six saved her life. *I told you we weren't going to die*, they snarled at her, *and I* fucking *meant it!* They gave her their blood. They threw themself between her and the threat of the cloaksaan Medisogo. After she survived, they followed her recovery like a gambler on their last mark, watching a game of tiles. Yet now they are also cold toward her. Which is a far cry from wanting to protect her.

"I'm as fit as you, Six," she says. "I can take a punch."

A punch is the least of their worries, but Six glowers, tension ratcheting between them.

> *PREPARE TO BE BOARDED. ALL ACTS*
> *OF AGGRESSION WILL BE MET WITH*
> *LETHAL FORCE.*

> *STAND DOWN AND AWAIT FURTHER*
> *INSTRUCTION. THIS IS YOUR ONLY WARNING.*

The clutch is only thirty or so feet away, just a single door separating them, and Chono has no interest in playing coy. She casts a command, and the door irises open. She walks over to Six. Esek's face was always so expressive, full of humor and cruelty, but Six has a quietness about them. Not peaceful, not *calm*. They radiate emotion, but all so carefully contained. Deadly currents under a placid surface.

"Are you ready?" Chono asks.

She would never have asked Esek such a thing. But she asks Six because it's a way to ask herself. Is she ready? For what will happen now? For what Six will become?

Six responds by pulling a deep breath into their lungs—and releasing it. With it goes the vibrating silence of their ordinary affect. Suddenly, a ghost floods their face. Their body relaxes into a posture both arrogant and feline. Their full lips twist with that smirk that Chono knows so well. Their diamond-hard jawline flexes, and their eyes are worst of all. Glittering mockery that dares Chono not to flinch. It's bad enough they had themself modded into a physical copy of Esek. Learning to re-create her mannerisms with such precision—that is the real horror.

"Oh, Chono," they drawl, and their voice is a clever, animal thing, raising the hairs on her arms. "The real question is, are *they* ready?"

Sudden, pounding feet, and a voice calling out, "Targets sighted!"

And another booming, "Get on the ground! Get on the ground right now!"

Nine cloaksaan surge into the room, all in black combat armor with the face guards down. She sinks to her knees. Six does the same, both of them with their hands raised above their heads. Rifles wave angrily at them.

"Get down—put your face on the ground—do it!"

They lower carefully onto their stomachs, heads down.

"This is overkill," says Six, with all of Esek Nightfoot's scorn.

From the corner of her eye, Chono sees two cloaksaan grab Six by the shoulders of their coat, dragging them into a kneeling position. A split second later rough hands haul her up as well, touching her all over, searching for weapons. They strip her and Six's cleric coats, and like a javelin through her brain, Chono flashes on another time when someone ripped her clothes off. Her breaths turn thready—*Not now not now!*—and she can feel a fugue coming over her, but by some miracle her eyes shift toward Six—who is looking right at her, calling out to her with their eyes, *Look at me. Just look at me.* And there's no Esek in their look.

In the end, the cloaksaan do no worse than strip her coat. She's not naked, not cold and frightened and a child—

"What have you got on you?" a voice says at her ear. "Don't you fucking move; I'll shoot your legs off. What have you got?"

"I'm unarmed," says Chono. "We both are."

Though that's owed more to her than Six, who wanted to secure Esek's bloodletter somewhere on their body but finally consented to store it in their single pack of belongings instead. It seems pointless to Chono. These cloaks will take everything they have.

Case in point, the hands keep raking over her, digging for pockets and closures, squeezing under her arms and the small of her back and her ankles and thighs. Her pulse speeds up again; she tenses as they grope her breasts.

"If I find out you're lying to me, I'll peel off your eyelids, understand?"

Six makes a low sound of dangerous amusement. "This one's creative."

"Shut your fucking mouth. I don't care who you are."

"If you're done molesting us, I think it's about time you—"

Their words cut off with a grunt as one of the cloaks punches them in the face, snapping their head sideways and making Chono grit her teeth. Pretending to be Esek aside, Six could always just shut up. But they're trying to pull all attention onto themself, to make Chono look harmless by comparison. By the gods, what do they hope to accomplish?

"Put your hands on your heads," a cloaksaan orders. "Now!"

She obeys, and the mouth of a rifle kisses the back of her neck. She chances a look at Six again, sees the wet blood on their mouth and the gleam in their eyes. How many of these cloaks could Six kill before a lucky shot took them out?

A cloaksaan thunders, "All clear!"

And Seti Moonback strides onto the bridge.

The First Cloak of the Brutal Hand doesn't even look at them, her eyes scanning everything with lazy curiosity, as if she is a tourist in a museum. Though she wears the same close-fitting combat armor as her kin, there's no helmet, and her black cloak flows from her shoulders. The three-pointed star on her leather pauldron catches the light as she slowly walks the bridge. It's not unlike the pacing Six did, mere minutes ago, but whereas Six was lost in their own thoughts, there is something performative about Moonback's casual movements.

"So, *this* is the bridge of *The Risen Wave*," she says, grandiose. "I admit I've never been. It's a bit ostentatious, isn't it? I hear the command panels are inlaid with gold."

Her modded eyes, a glittering electric blue, land on Six, raking over them. Fear crackles through Chono. What if it doesn't work? The five thousand who returned to the Treble did not know Six's true identity—they could not have revealed it to Moonback under torture. But what if Moonback sees the truth anyway, sees that the person in front of her is not Esek at all, but her murderer and interloper?

But Moonback only looks pleased. She shakes out her blond hair, like a lion vainly rustling its mane, and says, "Put down your hands. You look ridiculous."

They let their arms drop to their sides. Moonback looks slowly back and forth between them. A white scar running from nostril to chin twists with her smile. Chono wonders what it means, that both Six and Moonback have chosen to hold on to the gruesome scars that they could so easily have modded away.

"What an interesting pair you are," Moonback remarks, sounding quietly fascinated. "The righteous, beloved Cleric Chono, and the selfish, capricious Esek Nightfoot, suddenly united in their desire to damn the Kindom for its crimes." She looks at Six. "I suppose you think the Nightfoots will be eager to welcome you home?"

Six grins, rakish. "Lost without me, I wager. Sevite trade in shambles. Matriarchy fallen to a child. You're an iron-fisted sort of person, Seti. You must agree that people need a firm hand."

Moonback looks amused. "It's interesting to me that you collaborated with the very people who left the trade in shambles, and now here you are, ready to save the day."

"Well, someone must. Gods know the Kindom can't do it."

Chono half expects Moonback to strike them for this. Nothing is more infuriating than an insult that's true. And it is quite true, that when vast numbers of the sevite factory workers jumped to Capamame, they left behind an industry ill-equipped to survive without them. From the safety of Farren Eyce, Chono has watched the Treble newscasts describe the steep decline of the energy trade over the past eight months. It had been balanced on a knife's edge even before the battle of *The Risen Wave*. Now, newly conscripted laborers and the dregs of the staff that never went to Capamame are scrambling to keep the trade afloat. The Nightfoots have floundered without the leadership of their recently dead matriarch, Alisiana, and the Kindom, for all its private sevite stores, has proved withholding. Unrest and desperation seethes in the Treble.

"And yet," says Moonback musingly, "your loyalties seem divided when it comes to the sevite trade. If you're really here to claim the matriarchy and help your family rebuild, I wonder why you wrote that curious little will of yours."

Six winks. "Pissed some people off with that, did I?"

"Conscripting Clever Hands to help you will your fortune to the Jeveni Wheel? Now *why* would that bother anyone?"

Chono imagines it bothers the Secretaries most of all, to know that saan among their ranks took payment from Six (who they thought was

Esek) and wrote the inviolable will. Would it relieve them to hear that the Wheel didn't want Six's gift? That they rejected it outright? Probably not.

As for now, Six replies, "What can I say? I'm an altruist."

They smirk at each other, as if they were insiders on a joke—as if Seti Moonback had not spent nearly twenty years hating Esek for her loyalists among the Brutal Hand, for her showboating and her irreverence, for daring to train cloaksaan novitiates even though she was a cleric herself. Chono, glancing back and forth between them, is hyperconscious of Moonback's hand, resting casually on the hilt of her bloodletter.

Suddenly Moonback's eyes snap toward Chono. "And you, Burning One," she says. "You are supposed to be dead. We told the whole Treble you were dead! What a fuss they've made over you. They say you were a great champion of the downtrodden. A defender of the defenseless. Tell me, from your hiding place in Farren Eyce, have you watched your star rise?"

Of course Moonback knows the name of the Capamame colony. She would have interrogated the five thousand for everything they knew, which in the end would not be much. The five thousand never left the fleet, never set foot on Capamame, never had insight into the colony or the motives of the Wheel. Still, it makes Chono sick to think of innocent Jeveni tortured for any scrap they might know, even if only that name, Farren Eyce.

As for her rising star...

"I am what I have always been. A servant of the Godfire."

It's Six who laughs, looking some combination of scornful and delighted that so perfectly evokes Esek, it's nauseating.

"Isn't she a treat?" Six asks Moonback. "Humble to her core. No amount of fame or veneration can crack that cool exterior." Chono marshals any reaction, though inside she feels squeamish and annoyed. She of anyone knows how little she deserves veneration. Six knows, too, and the thought that they are secretly thinking how unrighteous she is makes Chono feel mocked, and ashamed. Six says, "It's your fault though, of course, Quiet One. Saying she was dead made her into a martyr. People do so love martyrs. Do you suppose they sing songs about her in barrooms?"

Moonback sniffs, unimpressed. "But now it turns out she didn't die at all, but is allied to the very people who are responsible for the resource scarcity in the Treble. I doubt very much her heroism will stand the test of that."

Six clucks. "Then you haven't looked closely at the data flood we sent, have you?"

"I'm aware it contains so-called evidence that implicates the Kindom in criminal action. Surely you're aware that we'll be able to disprove all of it? Especially when we demonstrate that the notorious Sunstep created it. We've done quite a good job of poisoning the Treble against Jun Ironway since she left. A criminal. A con artist. Child of terrorists and lover to a cloaksaan defector."

Six says, "Sounds to me like you've only propagated her legend. People love a scoundrel just as much as they love a martyr."

"Give me two minutes in a room with Jun Ironway and I'll prove she's as pathetic a coward as the rest of you."

Moonback says it with sharp vitriol. Jun Ironway made a fool of the Kindom. She evaded their attempts to capture an incriminating memory coin in her possession. She jumped the Jeveni fleet out of their grasp. She has replaced the Jeveni casting corps that the Kindom assassinated shortly before the jump. She is doubtless a symbol to them of all they cannot control, and they would do anything to crush her.

But Chono and Six are symbols of that, too.

Chono says, "Jun Ironway is safe from you."

Moonback snorts. "The game's not over yet. I'll see her and your Wheel on spikes before this is over."

Quiet fury, like the wisp of smoke that presages a fire, crawls through Chono. Why did she think the Kindom would be cowed by its mistakes? Why is she still so naive?

"You're on the verge of millions of people blaming you for the Jeveni flight," she says, voice hard. "Rather than fantasizing about more destruction, perhaps you should think about how to attain some goodwill. Such as by releasing the five thousand Jeveni you wrongfully imprisoned."

Moonback laughs, blunt and mechanical. "Those little birds who sang every word they knew about you and your Capamame? I wonder why you want them freed at all, after the poisonous things they've said."

"People will say anything with a gun to their heads," Chono says. "And our data flood proves how many guns you've held to the Jeveni's heads."

"Your proof will collapse under scrutiny," Moonback retorts.

But all three of them know that the data flood will breed doubt, that it has the power to change public opinion and shift ire from the Jeveni to the Kindom.

"Perhaps before you dismiss our proof," says Six, "you should test the wares yourself. It's obvious you haven't even looked at it yet."

"I don't need to look at it to carry out sentence," Moonback says coolly. "You're both deserters and traitors to the Kindom. You've returned on a stolen ship, spouting lies about the governing body of the Treble. Perhaps I'll shoot you right here."

Six says, "The data flood is only going to make Chono more famous. Kill her now and you'll pay a price later."

Chono notices in irritation that they say nothing about sparing their own life, but they seem to have caught Moonback's attention. She says, "Famous?"

"Go ahead," Six says. "Search the flood for her name. You'll find she left you a gift."

Chono feels more of that squeamish annoyance, to be singled out and made important by Six's words, and by the Wheel's design. It was Hyre ten Grie who argued they should make her the voice and face of the data flood, to capitalize on her name recognition, and on the fact that she was not Jeveni herself. As Moonback's eyes shift, clearly searching something on her ocular, Chono grimaces to think of what the First Cloak is seeing.

She grimaces far more when Moonback projects something into the air.

It is Chono herself, standing in front of a nondescript gray wall in the newsnest of Farren Eyce. Staring into the camera that records her, she begins to speak.

"People of the Treble. Some of you know my name. You're probably surprised to see me alive, given that the Kindom declared me and Esek Nightfoot dead eight months ago. It was easier for them to put us in the grave than admit what happened on *The Risen Wave*. I have been a loyal servant of the Kindom for more than twenty-five years, but sometimes loyalty requires us to question and challenge our leaders. I'm here to challenge the Kindom."

"My, but that voice is compelling," Six taunts. "Ever heard her recite Godtexts?"

Moonback ignores them, watching the cast.

"I'm not a leader," Chono says. "I have no interest in power. What I am interested in is justice. The tragedy on *The Risen Wave* began when the Kindom spread lies to convince you that Jeveni labor unions were causing sevite shortages. The Kindom did this because they wanted to hoard the sevite for their own purposes. They wanted to turn you against the Jeveni so you would forgive the Kindom for crushing the labor unions. The evidence that accompanies me in this data flood proves that there was never a sevite shortage. More than that, it proves that this isn't even the first time the Kindom has lied about its treatment of the Jeveni. Seventy-five years ago, it blamed the firebombing of Jeve on a single man named Lucos Alanye. But this was just another deception. It was the Kindom that murdered over two million people on Jeve."

Chono watches herself swallow. She watches Seti Moonback watch the cast—but so far she looks unimpressed, her scarred lip curling.

Chono on the casting view says, "Maybe you aren't moved by genocide, or any of the oppression of the Jeveni. That's between you and your gods. But are you moved by how the Kindom has betrayed *you*? They've withheld gate travel from people who needed it. Just as they are withholding it now. Trade is down. Goods are more expensive than ever. Guardsaan and cloaks police your streets. The Kindom wants you to blame all this on the Jeveni, but has that made your lives any easier? Has forcing the remaining Jeveni in the Treble to work in sevite labor camps solved the crisis? And if the Kindom can justify genocide against one impoverished group, how soon before they justify it against you? Go and ask them. Ask Aver Paiye. Ask Seti Moonback. They, of anyone, know what has been done."

Moonback's nostrils flare. Six shifts restlessly, and Chono realizes that they are not watching the hologram—they're watching Moonback, like someone preparing to throw themself in front of a bullet.

"I am a Hand of the Kindom. I'm no more free of blame than any Hand. I have no right to ask you for anything except this: Take the evidence here into account. Assess it, evaluate it. Put aside your own prejudices and look at the facts with clear eyes. If you think I deserve punishment for what I've done, seek me and Esek Nightfoot in the custody of the Kindom. Find us at the mercy of our gods. I await your judgment . . . Gods keep you well."

The cast ends, but Chono's frozen visage hangs in the air, disquieting. Moonback stares at that image for a long time. It is silent on the bridge, the other cloaks waiting for a signal. Chono wonders, *Is it enough? Will the Treble care? Will the Kindom care?*

Moonback draws her gun with the speed of a viper. Six springs— and five cloaksaan tackle them to the ground. Chono eyes the barrel of the gun; she can almost *feel* Moonback pulling the trigger, the cracking report, the obliteration—

A sharp ping fills the air instead.

Moonback's eyes flinch back toward the casting view, where a green flash signals an incoming message intended for her. Green. That means it's from the Clerisy. Aver Paiye.

Gun still drawn, Moonback snaps the cast out of the air, stepping away from them to speak lowly with her back turned. The five cloaksaan have a snarling Six up on their knees again, their coiled braid loose, their face bloody. Chono barely breathes, waiting.

At last, the conversation must end. Very slowly, Moonback turns around. The gun at her side twists with the movement of her wrist, as if she is testing its weight—trying to decide whether to use it. Her eyes on Chono are full of black humor, almost impressed, and hateful.

"You clever thing," Moonback murmurs.

Chono listens to the pounding of her own heart and Six's ragged, furious breaths, and she thinks, *The Clerisy. The Clerisy. Aver Paiye. Aver Paiye has stayed her hand—*

Moonback says, "When we are done with you...your reputation for heroism will be a backstreets joke. The people you love so much— they'll clamor for the deaths of Chono and Esek Nightfoot. They'll want it long and drawn out and brutal. And you'll wish that I had done it quick on this deck. But it will be too late."

Chono keeps her expression flat, but inside she shudders with relief. Moonback said Esek Nightfoot. She won't kill Six, either. Six is safe. The data flood is like wings, sheltering them both. For now.

But Six-as-Esek can't leave well enough alone. "I'd have a care for *your* reputation first, Seti. Soon everyone will know you're no better than a thug."

Moonback's eyelid twitches. Her hand holding the gun strikes out like a whip, hard metal cracking against Six's head. There's a wet crunch; Six sways. Even so, they might have stayed on their knees, but Moonback kicks them over with a boot to the ribs.

"Stop!" Chono cries.

Moonback ignores her, aiming her next kick into Six's gut, and Six makes a terrible gagging sound. Chono lunges toward them—hands grab her. Pain bursts hot and throbbing in her eye and again in her temple. Great firecrackers of black and white distort her vision. Her neck wrenches, her skull throbs, and by the time the third punch lands, she is already passing out.

CHAPTER FOUR

1664

YEAR OF THE CRUX

Drae's Hope
Orbiting Capamame

The hallways of *Drae's Hope* spread outward from the docking bay like strange tributaries, emergency lights creating a sickly glow that puts Jun in mind of sewer systems, or the lonely networks of underground casting dens. She hasn't been on a ship in five months, and this one is particularly mammoth, and particularly quiet. To think that it was the generation ship that ferried the Jeveni forty light-years to Capamame. Now it is a cold husk, stripped for parts, and she is making her slow, careful way toward the third engine room.

She feels like a krill in the belly of a whale. It must have felt simi-larly bizarre and disturbing for Six and Chono, when they piloted the abandoned *Risen Wave* back to the Treble. Only the "whale" intent on devouring them was not the ship but the Kindom.

It's been a week since Farren Eyce lost contact with them. Hard to say, yet, if they've survived the devouring. Jun gave them many gifts to take on their way, but maybe they're already dead. Theories circulate among Farren Eyce colonists, who may not be able to communicate with the Treble but who have access to Treble information, same as Jun. Do they hope that Chono and Six have survived? Or is it only an entertainment, to help distract them from the troubles on Capamame?

Behind her, Luja moves with the tentative steps that Jun has come to expect from her little cousin. The young woman follows her into the farthest hallway on the right, carrying the long duffel bag they'll use to transport the cable back to Capamame.

"Kinda creepy, isn't it?" Luja says.

She has a soft voice, not exactly meek but wary, like she expects that every word she says might meet with a physical or verbal attack. She doesn't talk much at all, actually, so it surprises Jun to hear her make the observation. Jun left home when Luja was just five years old, her memories of her limited to a really cute kid with big eyes. She has far more concrete memories of Bene. And he has concrete memories of her. The twins do not.

Jun looks back at Luja, smiling reassuringly.

"There's nothing wrong with the ship. It's charged down to conserve energy. Like this, it can remain operational for at least a decade on the power it's already got."

Luja gazes doubtfully at the exposed wiring in the ceiling. Not a particularly pristine ship, it's nearly a hundred years old. But in its very age resides its value: The third engine room has over three hundred feet of electros cable running through its walls—the kind ships used to use for networking infrastructure. There are more sophisticated materials now, leaner and faster, which is probably why the Farren Eyce requi-sitioners left the electros cables behind. But Jun knows how to make a foot of electros do the work of ten down on Farren Eyce. *Drae's Hope*, it seems, is not done serving the saan it was built for.

As they follow the map projecting over their oculars, winding deeper into the ship, Jun wonders again if she should have left Luja behind. Luja and her twin, Tej, spent their entire lives on cramped space stations before coming to Farren Eyce, and Luja (if not Tej) seems to relish the feeling of being on a planet, even if they are mostly sequestered in an underground colony. It still feels more open and airy than any station or ship Jun's been on, and Luja especially likes to hang out in the upper levels, near the surface and the dome. Must feel like freedom to her.

She's been jumpy from the moment they got on the shuttle that brought them aboard. Jun spun up the gravity before they disembarked, but still. Maybe this is too much, too fast.

"Ya all right?" she asks, as they turn a corner and weave around some abandoned crates.

This time Luja's tone is droll. "You don't have to coddle me. I'm okay."

Jun grins to herself. Luja may be an antsy, traumatized kid built too small from years of malnutrition, but she's got some spunk in her, and even when her hands are shaking she doesn't back down from a challenge.

How's it going up there?

Bene's cast message amuses her. Of course he's feeling just as protective as she is.

We're good.

If she panics, remind her of her breathing exercises.

She's not gonna panic. Scram.

She can imagine his amusement. Nothing she does or says intimidates Bene. He's too easygoing, blessed with Jun's wit and irreverence but cursed by none of her unlikability. When he doesn't cast her back, she makes a mental note about that breathing exercise thing.

Up ahead, the hallway opens into the engine room. Jun can see the core from here, cold and still when once it breathed fire. Jun loves ships, she loves machines, she loves the living, breathing heart of tech, so much less likely to betray her than people, and she feels a little sad for *Drae's Hope*, put to sleep like an enchanted creature in a story.

When they enter the engine room, things look better than she's expecting. Eight months ago, she threw her cloak program, her Hood, over hundreds of Jeveni ships so that the Wheel could jump them through the gate to Capamame. Trouble was the existing colony of Farren Eyce was serviceable but unfinished—and had not been designed for over eighty thousand people. Making it ready for the Jeveni on the ships to migrate planet side has required a lot of new construction and technological infrastructure, and to that end they've stripped the fleet of almost every useful supply. Cots and kitchenware and sheet metal and piping—even the little bookcase where Liis keeps her Katish poetry—all come from the fleet.

Liis...

Thinking her name opens Jun up with restlessness, her body suddenly unsettled as she thinks about the weeks they've been apart. It's not as if they never went their separate ways in the Treble, but those separations rarely lasted more than a week. Jun made sure of it. When they go longer than that, something strange and uncomfortable happens inside her. She starts to worry that Liis might not be real. Like maybe Jun invented her. For Liis had been so alive, when they met—a person made of thunder, a focal point for all of Jun's nervous energy. What if she simply made her up, the thing she needed? And that would mean that the poetry books in the apartment don't belong to Liis. And that the green smell of Liis's body oil is a fabrication. And Liis will never come back from the expedition aboveground.

She snaps out of it with a jerk, blinking hard, berating herself. The fucking sentimentality of it; what is wrong with her? She knows better than to get distracted on a job, especially with Luja relying on her, waiting for guidance.

What was she thinking about before? Right. Yes. The engine room. It's been picked over pretty well, right down to the wall paneling. But with that paneling removed, the guts of the room are exposed, lots of wires and metal connectors left behind, and most important, the yellow electros cables, which wind the circumference four times over.

Luja shifts the duffel bag off her shoulder, dropping it on the ground and looking around curiously. When Jun meets her eyes, she's pleased to see a rare smile.

"It looks all right, doesn't it?"

Jun showed her before they left how to tell the difference between useful electros and the kind that's too old. The bright yellow of the cables and the lack of any fraying or visible cracks is a good sign, and she's proud of Luja for noticing.

"Damn right," Jun says, and unshoulders her own supply bag, rolling it out to reveal the tools they'll use to disconnect the cables. "You got your gloves? With the power down we should be okay, but I don't want you getting a stray shock."

"Yeah, I'm good," Luja says, pulling her gloves out of her pocket and yanking them on as she sets the duffel down.

They each take one side of the room, working carefully to disconnect the cables from their power sources, cut the ties binding them into the walls, and lift them out of their grooves to lay on the ground. Each piece of cable is around fifteen feet long. Jun shows Luja how to test the material for structural integrity before carefully winding it into tight coils that will fit in the bag.

They work in relative silence. Jun, as usual, is holding a line between herself and the Farren Eyce casting lab, watching for any sign of problems on the planet. Getting that lab up and running, and keeping it running in a colony bigger than it was designed to manage, has been like a never-ending game of tiles where someone keeps rearranging the pieces. She's got a good crew of casters down there, but most of them are green, like Luja. The Kindom murdered all the senior Jeveni casters a year ago, destroying their corps in a single shot, and this was why the Wheel recruited Jun in the first place.

Flicking a glance at Luja, seeing the way the tip of her tongue pokes out as she works, Jun thinks again of what an amazing caster her little cousin might have been. Jun has seen the aptitude tests Luja took when she still lived on K-5 station. As young as four, she showed real potential. Maybe she could even have been as good as Jun. But when Esek Nightfoot sent their family into hiding, Luja's access to the education she needed disappeared—along with every bit of stability she ever had. Now she's trying to catch up years later, and that would be hard enough for anyone, let alone someone with an anxiety disorder and insomnia.

She'll get there, Jun thinks. After all, Bene is thriving in Farren Eyce. Luja will, too.

Though as for Tej . . .

"Hey, Jun?"

Luja's voice is soft, a little tentative, like she gets when she thinks asking a question might be dangerous. Jun has learned at times like this the best thing is to not look at her directly, so she goes on working, throwing back a casual "Yeah?"

Luja hesitates. "Did you know any of them? You know . . . those collectors who died?"

Jun keeps working, processing the question. When she saw Masar this morning, he was in his head, all his focus now committed to this latest mystery in his long career of solving mysteries. Though this is worse for him. The collectors were his friends. She admits, "No. I mean—I met them, back in the early days, but I didn't *know* them. Why?"

Luja pulls down another length of cable and winds it carefully, and it's not until she's zip-tied it into shape and placed it in the duffel bag that she answers. "People are saying it wasn't suicides, you know?"

She doesn't have to add what people *do* think it was. Or that rumors have been circulating that the deaths may be related to other, unexplained events in Farren Eyce. But even if she doesn't say it, it's clear she wants to know if Jun agrees. Sometimes Jun's so grateful to have her family back that all she wants to do is Hood them from the universe. But Luja is twenty-one, and if anyone had babied Jun when she was twenty-one, they'd have woken up to find their network access corrupted and their neural link full of bugs.

"Yeah," Jun says. "I, uh . . . It probably wasn't suicide."

Luja nods, her expression distant. "Not an accident, either."

Jun thinks of Roq, shot in the head with a nail gun. "No."

"So . . . murder?"

Jun unclips one of the cables, using the tricky work of detaching it as an excuse to think this through. "Yeah, it looks like it."

They go back to work for a few minutes. Jun keeps thinking she should say something, try to offer reassurance, but that's easier said than done when there's some kind of serial killer loose in the colony.

"Does Masar have any idea why they're doing it?" Luja asks.

Jun waffles. Masar seems as in the dark as he was last week. He's combed over all the evidence of each of the murders, bringing Jun in at every opportunity to help him interpret what's happened, but neither of them has found anything that takes them in any particular direction. No suspects. No warning signs.

"Could be political," she says. "What with . . . so many people angry at the Wheel. Or maybe it's random."

Luja mutters, "It's not random." She yanks some cabling out of its fasteners, probably harder than she should, and Jun deliberately doesn't look, not wanting to rebuke her right now. Luja says, "Shit like this is never random. It's meant to scare us."

Jun snorts. "Yeah, well, I'm not scared."

"You should be."

When Jun turns again, she finds her cousin staring at her in reproach. Luja has deep brown eyes, almost black, and in the darkness her pale brown skin seems washed out, so that she's almost like a ghost on the other side of the room. She says, "People who do that, who just . . . throw someone off a railing like that, or make it look like you hanged yourself, they're not afraid of someone like Masar, or anyone else, looking for them. That's why they're targeting the collectors. They want the collectors, and everyone else, to be afraid. It was the same on Q-9." Jun says nothing, but her body tenses, like it does any time Luja talks about the farming station where she and Tej lived before the Jeveni rescued them. Luja goes on in her low, raspy voice. "We had a boss, she was in charge of squash fruit harvest. You know why they call it squash fruit? Because it bruises so easily. This boss, she used to walk around with a cane, really thin, like as thin as your finger, but with a heavy-duty metal handle. If we bruised a piece of squash fruit, she'd smack the backs of our heads with the cane. It hurt bad. But if we kept bruising the fruit, she'd hold us down by the wrist and use the metal handle to break our fingers." Luja's eyes fade out, as if she's back on the farming station. The room is so quiet. "Tej used to ask me why she did that. If she damaged our hands, it made it harder for us to work, so why would she hurt her own workers like that? But I know why she did it. It wasn't because it was a logical way to get the job done. It was so that people would be scared, too scared to complain, too scared to fight back. And anybody who did fight back—all they got out of it was a broken arm."

Jun can almost feel the pressure of the Black, squeezing the ship, squeezing her heart. She watches Luja closely, looking for signs of elevated breathing, sweat, pallor. *What are the breathing exercises again? Does she need the breathing exercises?*

Luja blinks, as if coming out of a fugue, and turns back to the nearest length of cable. She starts winding it into a coil, and Jun feels useless to think of what to say. She suffered her own calamities after Esek Nightfoot's attack. She went off on her own and survived by the skin of her teeth and the skill of her casting. Sometimes, it was real bad— but she never had a boss wield a switch at her, never found herself in a place where she couldn't at least run.

It was Six who rescued Jun's family and put Tej and Luja on Q-9 with their mother, Aunt Rozna. Hid them under false names and pristinely fabricated records. Supposedly it was a good place at first, 70 percent Jeveni but kind to outsiders. Rozna married Emos, a Jeveni man who adopted the twins. But Rozna died of a flu, and later that year, an industrial accident killed Emos. Then some oligarch from Kator bought the station, and things got bad. Jun will never be able to make up for what her youngest cousins went through. Neither will Six.

Something pings in her ocular, and she's shocked back into her body. It's a message from one of her casters. Jun's first worried thought is that there's been a significant power or comms malfunction, but they're only relaying an inquiry from the *Drae's Hope* facilities manager. Apparently she left a fifth of praevi in the toilet tank in her cabin, and since it's so close to Engine Room 3, would Jun mind grabbing it for her?

Jun rolls her eyes.

Is she serious?

I think so, boss.

Kata's tit. All right, we're halfway done here. Tell her I'll look for her damn praevi and she better hope I don't drink it on the way planet side.

Understood, boss.

Understood, boss? Jun thinks dryly. Don't these kids know that a real caster signs off by cussing you out?

She looks at Luja again, realizing she hasn't said a word about her story, but Luja is back at work, as if she never said a thing. Feeling awkward and ill-equipped, Jun tells her, "I'm ... gonna go check something. Can you hold things down here? I shouldn't be a minute."

Luja shrugs indifferently. Sometimes she actually seems to be warming up to Jun. Other times, she's as cold as the Black. "Yeah, sure. You don't need my help?"

"Not for this particular errand," Jun drawls, and strides out of the engine room.

Her cast map directs her down a new hallway toward a neighborhood of living quarters, and finally, to the right cabin. The door pulls on dregs of reserve power, crawling open at Jun's signal, creaking closed behind her. It's a tiny cabin, barely fit for one person. Farren Eyce is a paradise of open space compared to how the Draeviin lived during their long voyage. In the washroom, she lifts the lid off the tank, but there's no bottle inside. Someone must have snatched it. Sighing, Jun resets the tank lid, looking up at a mirror hung on the wall. There are words etched into it, carved through the glass. She uses her translator bot to translate it from Je:

> OUR HOME SHALL BE OUR SANCTUARY.
> AND OUR WEAPON.
> —DRAE SEN BRIIT

Jun reads it three times, intrigued. There's so much about the lives of the Draeviin, and the voyage of *Drae's Hope*, that she doesn't understand. So many decades of travel. So much purpose. So much at risk. Particularly strange to Jun is that the ship's namesake, Drae sen Briit, is a distant ancestor of Six's. Not that Six has ever expressed interest in talking about that. Or talking about much at all, the stoic fucker.

She leaves the washroom and pokes around the main cabin to see if there's anything that got left behind. A stub of pencil. A scrap of trash. A decaying piece of orange peel. She ponders Luja's story about the squash fruit. She decides to figure out whoever the boss with the switch was. There must be some way to ruin her life from the other side of the Black.

Feeling slightly better for this plan, Jun turns to leave. But instead of opening for her, the cabin door sticks.

Jun waves her hand at the lock pad. Not a quiver of reaction, not even an error beep. She rolls her eyes, exasperated. The thing doesn't have a doorknob. She tries casting into the security system, but it looks like the door operates independently of the network. Godsdamned battery-powered nonsense.

She comms Luja, who answers, "Yeah, what's up?"

"The door to this fucking room is jammed. I'll just be a minute."

"Do you need my help?"

"It's fine, keep working."

"Okay, I'm almost done on my side."

They cut the connection, and Jun reaches into her back pocket for the slender multitool she keeps on hand. Crouching by the door, she uses the tool to pop open the control panel. If she can get the door keyed back into the network—

A rusty, churning sound behind her makes her look over her shoulder. At first she doesn't know where it's coming from, but then she notices a puff of dust around the air duct in the ceiling. Standing up again, she squints up at it in time to see the slats judder open.

Luja pings her comm again.

"Yeah?" Jun asks.

Silence, and instead of Luja's voice, a message crosses her ocular.

I'm not Luja.

Jun stills. She checks the coordinates of the ping, realizing that what her neural link read as Luja's cast signature is actually a clone signal. Confused, she peels apart the layers of the identification, trying to find the real signature, but there's nothing underneath. The signature didn't exist until this very moment, until the cloning. Jun hesitates, wondering if this is some prank from a kid on Capamame, or even one of her own casters. She asks:

Oh, yeah? Who are you, then?

A worthy successor.

Something contorts in Jun's stomach. Like a diver, her mind tips forward, dropping down and slicing through the surface of the casting net, into the cool darkness. The cloned signature is like a little fish up ahead, darting through the waters in endless zigzags, obscuring its own wake and thus its starting point, as the signal bounces from location to location.

Successor, huh?

All giants need a successor, don't they, Sunstep?

Well, if I'd known I had a fan coming, I would have worn my fancy jumpsuit.

Several seconds go by, no response. Jun swims after the little fish, casting toward the ship's main casting hub. She images herself leaving the water and stepping into a room, full of buttons and levers and circuits, which, if she can align, will show her the origin of the signal. But in the dark corners of the room, a shadow flits past.

And another message appears.

You know anyone with any talent for casting would realize I was cloning their signature. Your trainees are shit.

Well, taking a shot at Luja is just petty. Jun works fast, watching the shadow from the corner of her eye, ignoring its obvious desire to piss her off. If this was some kid caster on Farren Eyce trying to show off, she'd be able to track down their identity pretty fast. This messenger— it's like a faceless avatar in a vid game. She hears it behind her and turns.

It's laying brick.

She watches, takes it all in with a dozen casting eyes, and though she still can't see its face, whoever it is, is building a wall around her, cutting off her connection to the casting net from multiple directions.

This is amateur. How many times has someone tried to build a firewall to keep her out? Getting around these kinds of blocks is the bread and butter of a talented caster, and Jun is like a gunslinger at a shooting range, picking off one brick at a time. She sends a message:

I take it you've got some issue. Wanna talk like grown-ups?

Is it possible to imagine a shadow chuckling?

We're not grown-ups, Jun Ironway. We're far more ancient than that. We are archivists.

Now Jun is really annoyed. She blows the crap out of a dozen or so bricks, securing her comm line so she can message Luja.

"Jun?" Luja sounds anxious.

"Yeah, I'm okay. Are you okay? Where are you?"

"I'm in the engine room still. All the doors closed; I can't open them."

Jun's chest squeezes.

"Look, just sit tight, okay? I'll take care of this."

"Jun." Luja's voice sounds suddenly even warier than before. "The ventilation ducts. There's . . . there's something coming through the ducts."

In two places at once, Jun watches the avatar build, the bricks going up faster than before. But Jun also turns to look up at the duct in the ceiling and sees a whitish smoke tendril into the room. She smells it next, the unmistakable odor of fuel exhaust.

"Luja, there are masks in my pack. Get one and put it on right now. Do your breathing exercises. I'll be back—"

The comm cuts. Jun throws all her energy back into the room with the climbing brick wall, and fuck if she isn't done with this shit *right now*. She gathers her cast connections to her like the Godfire shaping a globe, and between her hands she grows a cannonball as big as her own body. She hurls it at the bricks, and they blow apart in a smashing, smoking uproar, hurling the avatar back. The force of the explosion thunders in Jun's ears and tears at the avatar's clothes, exposing its face for just an instant, but—

"Jun?" Luja's voice comes back, but glitchy. "You—ere? Jun, it—talk—"

The avatar's message hits her vision with a stinging slap.

Very nice. Let's play again.

Ignoring it, Jun flings her cast through the wreckage of the brick wall, charging toward the maintenance quarter of the ship. Her head is starting to throb, and a hit of dizziness makes her body sway forward, hand bracing against the locked door. She ends up with a visual of a generator room one level up. The gas-powered generators are awake.

Rumbling. She examines the readouts on the generators, finds them ancient and malfunctioning. *Drae's Hope* probably only used them as backup, depending instead on its jevite-fueled engines. Jun watches the exhaust from the generators, thick and gray and pouring outward, into the ventilation system.

Nausea climbs up her throat. Blinking, she forces herself back into her body, taking stock of the room around her. The exhaust creeps in. She rises on tiptoe to try to close the slats in the vent, but the ceiling is high, she's short as fuck, and there isn't even a chair left to stand on. Blinking rapidly, she pulls out of the cast altogether, brandishing her multitool and going at the lock pad again. It's okay, Luja has a filtration mask, she'll be okay. And if Jun can get out of this tiny coffin, she'll have more time to—

The lock pad explodes. Sparks fly at her, stinging against her hands and face as she staggers back. Staggers, and stumbles, her headache worse than ever, her breathing fast and thready now. Her chest feels like she's pinned under a boulder, and for the first time she recognizes through cloudy thoughts that she should be afraid.

Liis, she thinks, the word a glimmer of hope that can't help her now.

What will your poor, defenseless cousins do without you to protect them, Jun Ironway? You couldn't protect the collectors from me, could you? What makes you think you can protect your family?

The avatar's ridicule gives her a hit of clarity. It's so natural, so second nature to slip into the cast again, to watch the shadow figure building up its brick wall, entombing her. She gets upright, but staggers again, her vision fuzzy. She throws a clumsy program at the brick wall, but her head is spinning, and she hardly chips the edges. She falls out of the cast altogether, unable to hold the connection. The smell of the exhaust and the faint haze of it filling the room remind her of smoky lounges in gambling halls, like the one where she ran a con that went bad and nearly got her beaten to death. The one where Liis saved her. But Liis isn't here.

Bene is weak. Tej is a drunk. And Luja? Why, the caster pirates of Farren Eyce would eat her alive.

Confused and dizzy, Jun throws the last of her mental acuity back into the cast, hammering her way through the brick wall toward a glowing exit point. Wait, or is that a furnace? Is she walking into a furnace? Why is she so hot? No, it's not real. It's just in her head, it's not real.

Words dart across her vision:

I really thought you'd be more of a challenge.

She's on the ground again. She can't breathe and her chest is tight and she can't see and she can't die because Luja is out there, she can't fail Luja, not again, not after everything.

But the great cloaked body of the avatar spreads its wings, swooping down and covering her in darkness.

The governing body of Quietus takes as sacred that our god, Capamame, is the dear friend of all and shall reject no person for their past crimes or poor circumstances. To that end, all people are welcome on Quietus, and all people are expected to swear the oath of the friend: To do no harm, to voice no evil, to plan no cruelty, and to honor all life.

excerpt, the Unifying Constitution of the Floating Cities of Quietus, Article 1. Dated 201, Year of the Claim.

CHAPTER FIVE

1650

YEAR OF THE KINDLING

The Honor
North Seas
The Planet Quietus

Six stood on the deck of *The Honor* watching a storm roll in from the east. The clouds out there were a confused mixture of slate and black and blue, with white edges and shades, and they were coming in fast. Though the ship at this moment floated under a bright sun, that wouldn't last long. Quietans liked to call storms like this "a grumpy Capamame," their water god venting his frustration. How satisfying it must be, to make one's anger into storms.

A tug at their shirtsleeve brought them back to the deck. They looked down to find a girl staring up at them, her gendermark pink and new, her eyes arrestingly dark. She was short, stocky, with black locs framing her serious face. A clone of her father, practically, though Six thought her facial structure would mature into something sharp and pretty, like her mother's face.

"Mama says to ask if you've battened down your cabin yet."

Their cabin was a closet-sized room with a cot and a chest bolted to the floor. Six had little in the way of possessions.

"I have, thank you."

The girl looked doubtful. "You don't have to be scared, you know. We have these storms all the time. Papa says it's not even a bad one, and anyway, we'll be underwater for all of it."

Six's lip quirked. "Do I seem scared?"

A shrug. "I guess not. You're just standing here staring. I thought you were scared."

"I appreciate your concern. But I am not scared of the storm. I was thinking."

"About what?"

Six regarded her for a long moment. She was, what, ten years old? Not much older than Six's youngest cousin, who had died three months ago. And not much younger than Jun Ironway, who would not live long. Esek Nightfoot had slaughtered both their families, excusing it with the lie that they were political radicals who had attacked her first. Clever, brutal Esek.

Six answered the girl flatly, "Revenge."

She gave them an unimpressed look, which they couldn't blame her for. A voice boomed across the deck, "Graisa, stop bothering Sa Enye. Get along and help your siblings."

Graisa threw a rebellious look at her father, then squinted up at Six again. Six was unblinking, and after a second she sniffed and darted away. Her bare feet slapped on the deck as she ran for the stairs that led below. Then Yantikye was beside them.

"I'll thank you not to frighten my children with your creepy stoicism," the Quietan said.

"Your children belong to the Endless Sea. I do not think I can scare them."

Yantikye smirked, full of pride. Like a lance, Six remembered Ricari Ironway talking about his great-grandchildren, saying how Jun was a genius and Bene wasn't afraid of anything, and the youngest, the twins, were clever and happy. Six tried to remember their own little cousins, who they'd met only once. Were they brave or clever or happy? No. They were dead.

It had all gone terribly wrong. Six had gone to Braemin to learn more about Lucos Alanye, their ancestor and the man responsible for the Jeveni Genocide—the man who might give them clues on how to impress Esek Nightfoot. Six's relatives on Braemin had told them, among other things, that Six could seek shelter and information from Ricari Ironway on K-5 station. Six had not known at the time that Esek was already hunting for the Braemish Alanyes. Nor had they known, when they went to K-5 station a few months later, that Esek would hunt the Ironways, too. It was the biggest failure in judgment of their entire, carefully plotted life. Now, the last members of their bloodline were dead. And though they had managed to save some of the Ironways, Ricari was dead, as were two of his grandsons.

At least Six had avenged them by killing Esek's novitiates. Well, most of Esek's novitiates.

The past few months dragged behind Six like a train of blood, and they could never make it clean. Yet somehow, what tormented them the most was the question of Chono. Chono did not witness the murder of the Ironways. Did she witness the murder of Six's family? How culpable was she for the crimes that Esek was committing? And why hadn't Six killed her, too?

Yantikye asked, "You thinking about those Ironway kids again?"

His insight annoyed them. They cleared their throat, unwilling to confirm or deny. They glanced up, past the gathering cloud cover, imagining the limitless Black and the farm station that orbited Quietus. On clear nights, it was an overlarge star, visible from the deck of *The Honor*. Two of Ricari Ironway's great-grandchildren were there now, with their mother.

"They're safe, you know," Yantikye said. "My people set them up perfectly. It's a quiet station with a good governor—hates Kindom interference. No one will hurt them."

"I am sure that is true," said Six, and gave him a slow look. "I paid you well enough."

Yantikye flashed a grin, and they were back in that alley in Barcetima, where they'd met. Two years had changed Six quite a lot, but Yantikye remained bright and cheerful and, at times, unnerving. A jolly shell that contained a deadly actor. After they met, Six had researched him, uncovering a history of dangerous jobs, ruthlessly executed. And while Six had determined that they themself would not be Yantikye's tool, Yantikye could certainly be theirs.

"I am leaving you after the storm," Six told him.

Yantikye pushed his bottom lip out. There was a wind now, salty and aggressive; it whipped at their bodies. Six felt it in their hair and needling under their clothes. They thought of the factory town on Kator where they had left Jun Ironway. A gray, cold, unfriendly town whose main recommendation was that it was an easy place to get work. Jun Ironway was studying in Riin Kala when Esek attacked her family, and her education would serve her well in the factory town. Six had been supposed to take her to her grandmothers and cousin, but the girl refused. She was a stubborn child, determined to go off and seek redemption for her scattered family, all in hiding now. She was irrational. Naive. But Six believed in self-determination, so they gave her a little money and let her go.

It was a mistake. The whole thing was a mistake. Going to K-5. Trying to save the Ironways at all. They had exposed themself in doing it, put themself within a few feet of Esek's clutches. And for what? What had they gained? It was better, everything was better, when they worked alone and banished sentiment.

Yantikye asked, "Where will you go?"

"That is not your concern."

The Quietan clucked his tongue. The wind flung back his locs, making him a dramatic portrait of the wild sailor. "Just looking out for you. Wouldn't want you to get shot again."

Six was annoyed. "I still wonder if it was *you* that shot me."

"It was fate, little killer!" sang Yantikye. "What are the chances you get shot so close to my friends, and come back into my orbit like a planet rotating round a star?"

"Are you the star in this analogy?"

"I'm the damned bastard that saved your life, nah?"

It was not exactly a coincidence. And they refused to consider it fate. A job gone bad, a bullet in their side, and they had had nowhere to go, no means to save themself—except they were in Riin Kala. They knew that the Quietan neighborhood in that city had connections to Yantikye. A gamble, to seek his help. But a gamble that had kept them alive.

"You have had all the gratitude you will get, on that front."

"You god-defying mongrel. Capamame brings us together again, and now you want to run away from me. Haven't I been a good partner so far?"

The clouds loomed closer. Six said, "It may have escaped your notice, but I have been bad luck on families. I like your wife."

"You like her too much."

"She is too beautiful for you."

"Fuck off."

"I do not want the Honors to be Esek's next target."

Yantikye snorted. "So this exodus is for the sake of my family? Be careful, Sa Enye. I'll think you have feelings."

Every time Yantikye called them Enye, they felt little pinpricks on the back of their neck. Not because they weren't used to handing out aliases, but because Yantikye was one of very few people who knew it was an alias, who knew their Alanye heritage, and he only knew it because he'd extracted it from Six in exchange for the medical care they needed. When they recovered, Six had fully intended to kill Yantikye to protect their secret, only they woke to find themself on Yantikye's ship, surrounded by his children.

"They're awake!" the youngest one had yeeped, and the middle one ran from the room.

Graisa the Honor, not yet gendered, had narrowed their eyes shrewdly. "You gonna live?" they asked in that lilting Quietan accent.

Six, utterly baffled by their audience, said gruffly, "Long enough to box your ears if you do not get out of here."

The youngest one tore off. Graisa folded their arms, imperious. "You box my ears and Papa will shoot you again."

Papa. Oh. Well, Six could hardly kill him now. In annoyance, they forestalled murder, but made Yantikye swear to call them Enye. Enye was the name of the arms dealer to whom they'd apprenticed in the years after fleeing their kinschool. She was an irascible, brutal master, and she had trained Six to find the lucrative deal in every circumstance, to foster connections and opportunities in the Treblen underbelly. Though Six had found it expedient to kill Enye when they left her service, they still appreciated her lessons. Survival, after all, was a muscle group that must be exercised, and Enye had made Six very muscular.

They told themself that letting Yantikye live was a business decision. The Quietan trader had many connections. This had paid off just a week ago, when Six needed a place to hide the Ironways. And when they needed a place to hide themself, afterward. Thus had they returned to *The Honor*, a year after that bullet wound.

Six said, "This is not sentiment. It is the rejection of sentiment. You treat me like a street urchin you want to adopt. I do not need a father. I prefer my relationships to be transactional."

"You ungrateful shit," said Yantikye, without bite. "We could be transactional, nah?"

"No."

"Don't be like that. I'm not sentimental, either. I know you're a weapons trafficker and I could use one of those."

That was the problem. If Yantikye had simply wanted to buy weapons, they might have been able to do business. But Yantikye was a political dissident. He wanted weapons for reasons that drew too much attention.

"I am not interested in your causes," Six said.

"And I'm not one of your naive cousins."

Six tensed. The thought of their cousins, so warm, so welcoming, made their stomach sour. They had been good, kind people, full of optimism about the better, more just Treble that could exist, if the worlds would demand it. They had told Six stories about the corruption of the First Families and the Kindom Hands. They had offered Six a cache of Lucos Alanye's effects, including image stills and records—all evidence that Alisiana Nightfoot was Alanye's investor on Jeve. How greedily Six had seized on the photograph of Alanye and Alisiana together. How eagerly they'd sent it on to Esek, their first effort to impress her, to show her what they could do, after their failure in Barcetima. They had intended it as an opening salvo, a way to show her that they were alive and had not forgotten her deal.

Why hadn't they guessed what would happen? Why hadn't they done more to protect their cousins? Their cousins thought Six would use the records to pursue the same justice that they themselves longed for. Why had Six let them believe that?

"Is that what you think of them?" asked Six woodenly. "That they were naive?"

"You think different?" asked Yantikye.

"Naive for trusting me," said Six. "Naive for welcoming me into their home." They looked at Yantikye seriously. "If Esek ever finds you, tell her the truth. Tell her everything you know about me. Do not try to protect me."

Though of course they knew it didn't matter. Esek would kill the Honors anyway.

Yantikye snorted. "If Esek ever finds me, she won't have to make up lies about a firefight."

Six thought Yantikye was a good fighter, a smart tactician. But he was not equal to the force of Esek and her novitiates. It appeased Six that ships were hard to find on the Endless Sea. Being able to hide underwater was an advantage that Esek didn't have.

"I'm serious about us working together," said Yantikye.

"I will give you one of my contacts. Someone discreet. You can work with him."

It was a self-serving compromise. Six would take a referral fee but wash their hands of anything that came after. If Yantikye got himself killed, that was his problem. And if Six chose to use Yantikye in the future, it would be a separate matter.

Yantikye, looking satisfied, asked, "What will you do now?"

Six answered, "Kill Esek Nightfoot."

It was two years since they'd flipped a coin in that Katish bar—two years since they'd been uncertain about the choice to serve Esek, or murder her. They felt no uncertainty now. It was one thing for her to destroy Six's life. But those little cousins...

Yantikye snorted with laughter. Six scowled. "You do not think I can do it?"

"No, I suppose you can. And Godfire speed you on your way."

He spat on the deck. Six hummed. "I did not know you held anything against Esek Nightfoot."

"Nightfoot, Moonback, Khen. They're all the same thing. They tussle with one another and step on us in the process, and the Kindom lets them. I pray to Capamame the Black Ocean opens up and swallows them all."

Six said, "You'd be better off praying to a different god, Yantikye. Yours is too passive for the bloodshed you want."

"Peaceful. Not passive. In the name of peace, some bloodshed is worthwhile."

Six said nothing. They had little use for gods. Since learning of their own Jeveni heritage, they had considered whether they should take up any kind of practice, but whatever their ancestral connection to Sajeven's people, their heart was utterly cold to the goddess.

Yantikye said, "Killing Esek Nightfoot seems a waste."

Six looked at him, their lip curling. "Waste?"

"I realize you have very bloody fantasies of fighting Esek to the death somewhere, but you shouldn't let that stop you from a more creative approach."

"I assure you I will find creative ways to kill her."

Yantikye laughed. Then he turned pensive. "Is it enough, killing people like that? Wouldn't you rather make her consequence equal to her crimes?" Six said nothing, wishing that the Quietan had not intrigued them with the question. Wishing that they were immune to these kinds of emotional manipulations. Chono had always been good at faking immunity, and Six had tried to model themself after her, these past few years. But Chono had also become Esek's creature since she left the kinschool, and Six recognized that she was no longer their schoolkin.

So why hadn't they killed her? Why couldn't they kill her?

They repeated flatly, "Equal to her crimes?"

Yantikye was pleased to have hooked them. "How does the Kindom control us, after all? With the cloaksaan, it's threats of death in the dark. With the clerics, it's fear of vengeful gods. These are both effective methods, but they're child's play." Six said nothing, waiting. Yantikye crossed his arms against the wind. "The Kindom is powerful because it has wealth. It's powerful because it controls the law. The Secretaries—they have *always* been the most powerful of the Hands. Economics and law. The vicious arts. That is how the Kindom tortures us. What better revenge than to torture them in the same way?"

"With economics and the law?"

"Yes. Take their money. Take their wealth. Turn the law against them."

"I am not trying to go to war with the Kindom."

A tsking sound. "All right, then, leave that to the rest of us. Turn the law against Esek Nightfoot. Turn the money against Esek Nightfoot. Use knowledge, use information. You can only kill a person once. But you can strip their power from them over and over again, in tiny bits and pieces, like fish nibbling up a corpse."

Six considered. On the one hand, they felt a delicious and slightly queasy sensation of inspiration. On the other hand, they were suspicious. Did Yantikye know about the records the Alanyes had given Six? Had he snooped through Six's things? Was he trying to manipulate Six into pursuing more evidence against the Nightfoots, more proof of their complicity in the Jeveni Genocide? If so, it would be for his own purposes, not Six's.

"I am a very talented investigator," Six said musingly. "But such a task would require me to rely on other investigators. To work with others. That is not my preference."

"That's just your ego talking," said Yantikye.

For some reason, these words went through Six like a blade. They fell silent for some time. They were thinking of Esek on K-5 station, how easily they had manipulated her and how they might have killed her, too. It was Esek's ego that had laid her open to Six's trap. It was Esek's ego that had prevented her from making more progress in her effort to track Six down. If Esek were wise, she would leverage her cloaksaan loyalists to help. She would find the right person for the job and put aside her pride in the interest of her aims.

Six, too, was prideful. They were full of ego, full of arrogance. But more than this, they were determined, utterly determined to destroy Esek. Which meant they would have to reevaluate their policy on working alone.

Though they swore it would be them, and no one else, who killed Esek.

Yantikye pressed his suit again. "You could work with me." But Six's silence said *No*. He chuckled. "Well, I suppose you'll find someone. The worlds are big. And life is long."

A Quietan adage. But, *No*, Six thought. *Life is short and pitiless.*

Just then a voice shouted to them from the other side of the deck. It was Yantikye's wife, Martise, standing at the door that led belowdecks. "Come in, you fools. Let's have our dive and then we can eat. The children are hungry."

She disappeared again. Yantikye clapped Six on the shoulder and said, "Come on."

Six didn't like to be touched, but they followed him across the deck, and together they went into the cockpit. Yantikye cast a comm into the wider ship. "Everybody strap in."

Six settled into the second command chair and belted themself in just as Yantikye threw a switch on the wall. Immediately, the deck began to transform. All the sails were already down, but now the mast itself retracted, and the storm doors slid into place, enclosing the cockpit and shuttering the belowdecks entryway.

Martise's voice came through the comm. "We're secure."

Six heard the sucking and rumbling of the engine. They braced their feet, watching Yantikye turn switches and pull a lever, and at his guiding touch the ship began to sink. It went down slowly, the black storm clouds in the distance disappearing under a curtain of water. The air around them thickened, pressure tightening as Yantikye manipulated the controls again, and they began a gentle dive. *The Honor*, now become a submarine, sailed deeper and deeper into the Endless Sea, where it was cool and dark and sublime.

Six had trained themself in their short life to be indifferent to things that frightened other people. Heights. Darkness. Close spaces. Fire and drowning and spiders. Once, they had paid someone to bury them alive for twelve hours so they could overcome a lingering fear of suffocation. Once, they had untethered themself during a spacewalk and floated off, just to cure themself of the fear of dying alone. In both those instances, the solitude was so deep and silent that they had no choice but to embrace it, or panic. So they embraced it. They absorbed it till it was a part of them. And now, with so much of their life loud and chaotic and trending toward disaster, they longed sometimes for the perfect still solitude of that box underground, or that spacesuit drifting in the Black Ocean. *The Honor* underwater gave them a taste of that.

Yantikye grunted in satisfaction, unbuckling from his chair and getting up to grab the door that led belowdecks. Six followed.

The Honor was a good-sized ship, a family ship, and as they walked down the steps into the hold and passed the family bedrooms, Six heard Yantikye's children squabbling. In the kitchen, the three of them were running around, and Martise was yelling at one of them to help bring the plates to the table. Martise was a tall, broad-shouldered woman, beautiful and strong. Six rarely noticed beauty, except as a tool.

"Ah," Martise said when she saw Six. "So, you're showing your face, are you?"

Six had often taken their meals alone, this past week.

"Sit by me!" cried the youngest one, who had overcome their fear of boxed ears and who thought Six was a warrior. "Sit by me!"

Six let themself be crowded toward the table, made to sit between two of the children and across from the third. All the children, even wise-eyed Graisa, were fascinated with Six. But when Six looked at them, all they could see were the kinschool students they might have been, heads shaved and barefoot. Forced into one of three molds. *Righteousness. Cleverness. Brutality.*

How grotesque that would have been. These children were wild, seafaring creatures, their bodies tight and muscular from play. To make them into Hands would be worse than sticking fish in a bowl.

Yantikye and Martise came to the table. One of the children picked up his fork, but Martise made a clucking sound at him, and then they were all looking seriously at their mother. There was a little bowl of salt water in the center of the table, and Martise dipped her fingers in it, flicking the water at each person at the table, though not Six.

"Let us pray to Capamame," she said.

Five voices joined in a single prayer, which was the same prayer that Six had heard them praying in the morning, over their breakfast:

> *Dear friend, kind heart,*
> *Give us the sea full of life and depth,*
> *Give us fins that will carry us through the stars.*
> *Bless us to be holy and just,*
> *And we will change the currents of the world.*

The prayer was a short one, simple. Afterward, everyone began eating, talking, laughing. Martise chatted about the navigation system and Yantikye told a story about a squid that ate ships. Even Graisa was enthralled. Six looked around at them, leery of their happiness, and could not stop thinking of Esek.

CHAPTER SIX

1664

YEAR OF THE CRUX

Farren Eyce
The Planet Capamame

Sat in a threadbare armchair, Masar watches Jun weave a web of casts, her movements steady, her attention absolute. The first time he saw her like this, it creeped him out. She seemed so alien, disconnected from the real world. Now, he's used to it, though she still looks like a freak. You'd never know she almost died yesterday, and she's refused to rest. How well Masar remembers another time when Jun tried to ignore her body, walking around like she hadn't been shot. Liis hit her with a tranquilizer. Masar sort of wishes he had one now.

"How's the headache?" he asks.

From behind her wall of casting views, Jun mutters, "I'm fine."

Near death would make anyone surly. There were rudimentary medical supplies in the shuttle she took to *Drae's Hope*. Luja showed quick thinking once she reached her, dragging her from the hotbox of the cabin and treating her with oxygen—then flying her back to Capamame. Thank Sajeven for autopilots, and for the doctors planet side who flushed her body clean. Her voice is raspy from inhaling the generator fumes, but otherwise she seems to be herself.

Asshole tendencies and all.

"Shouldn't you be resting?"

"What good would my resting do?"

He pauses. Ventures cautiously, "What about Liis? Have you comm'd her?"

Jun tenses even more, eyeing her casts. The expeditioners exploring the planet and searching for potential resources are working on the ground rather than from the air. Aerial scans have proved less dependable than they hoped. But on the craggy, icy stretches of Capamame, communication with Farren Eyce gets spotty. From what Masar's gleaned from Bene, Jun and Liis have only found a handful of short opportunities to talk.

Now Jun says woodenly, "And scare her for nothing?"

"Uh, well . . . It wouldn't exactly be for *nothing*."

"Just—just—*be quiet*. I'm working."

He huffs, rising from the chair to lean against the wall, arms crossed. He misses his shotgun, not because he'd like to use it, but because its weight on his back always gave him a sense of security and completeness. Not that a shotgun could have protected Jun from the cast attack of this . . . avatar, as she's calling it.

In fact, the only person who could have protected Jun from the attack—was Jun herself. But some untraceable predator got the jump on her, poisoned her so she couldn't cast properly, brought her to the verge of death, and then, with fickle mercy, let her live. Even the story about the bottle of praevi in the toilet tank was a fabrication—the avatar tricked Jun's casters into thinking they'd had a message from the facilities manager, but the facilities manager doesn't even drink. Jun was lured into a trap—and it makes her furious.

This is Masar's lead, same as Jun's. But she won't let him in. She is as fixated and unreachable as he has ever seen her, and he feels lost. He's had no success finding out who killed Uskel. If some evil caster genius is involved, then he needs Jun to work with him more than ever. But Jun is far away, playing the solitary gunslinger. He forgets that he has years of experience working in teams. Jun has only ever worked with Liis.

Out in the larger apartment, the sounds of the other Ironways filter through. They used to be divided between two places, but when Grandmi Hosek died a month after the jump, Bene insisted that they all house together. Masar isn't sure it was a good idea, with tensions so often running high among the cousins. But there is something comforting about the sound of someone in the kitchen, preparing dinner. Probably Bene. And Tej is playing his mandola, which he only does when he's trying to soothe Luja's anxiety—a rare gesture of tenderness. The plucking of the strings is calming. When Masar showed up at the apartment half an hour ago, he could tell as soon as he laid eyes on Bene and Luja that they needed a lot of calm.

"You should go out there," Masar tells Jun. "You haven't left this room since the hospital released you. Luja is still shook up. It would do them good to see that you're all right."

Perhaps unsurprisingly, this is the thing that breaks Jun out of her trance. She scowls, looking up at him for the first time, eyes fuzzy. In an abrupt, irritated way, she disconnects from her casting views, which wink out around her like stars going dark. She blows a breath out through her nostrils and stomps over to her closet. The whole room is a mess. Laundry everywhere. Bed unmade. Liis's books of poetry overflow the bookcase. A stack of laminate records sits in the corner, with Drae sen Briit's name stamped on the top, which gives Masar pause. Are they records about Drae herself or about the ship she helped to build?

He refocuses on Jun, rummaging for fresh clothes. Her undershirt is soaked under the armpits and across her back. She yanks it off without modesty, wiping down her face and chest. He's never seen her sweat through her clothes from the exertion of casting.

"I'm gonna find this shithead," Jun says.

"You will," Masar agrees.

Her body is nearly vibrating. "Luja could have died."

Masar nods, though she can't see it. "I know."

She finishes changing, and the fury of helplessness radiates from her. Masar wishes Liis were here. Liis would know how to help her, how to rein her in. He's not particularly adept at emotional support. It's why he's pulled away from the other collectors in the past few months. There was so much memory and grief and trauma among them; he couldn't stand to be near it. And now most of them are dead. If Jun had died on *Drae's Hope*, what would it have done to Masar, to his walls of self-control? He doesn't want to guess.

They walk out into the living space of the apartment. Instantly, Tej sets the mandola down. In the open kitchen, Bene is cooking. He looks at them as they emerge, smile warm and hopeful—but worried. Masar's not used to seeing him like that. Of all his family, Bene is the calmest. He has a friendly sense of humor. He's cheerful and good-natured, and he seems to have embraced his life on Capamame with fierce gratitude. Masar meets his gaze, and the intimacy of it makes him nervous. Bene's eyes, a dark gold, soften with affection.

Masar glances toward the couch. Luja sits with her knees hugged to her chest, big dark eyes distant but also hard, like she's plotting revenge on whoever did this. Tej alone looks indifferent to what has happened, carrying the mandola to the closet, never acknowledging Jun.

"When's dinner ready?" he asks.

"Almost," Bene says, pouring boiled noodles into a colander.

Jun goes into the kitchen to help. Masar sits down next to Luja, patting her thigh. She jerks in surprise, looking at him, and he's sorry for startling her.

"How you doing?" he asks.

She blinks a couple of times. Masar recognizes it as the look of someone pulling out of a cast. "I was checking the forums," she says. "It seems like all people know is Jun got injured on *Drae's Hope*. There's nothing about . . . who did it."

Tej blurts a laugh. "That won't last."

Masar looks sharply at him. "Why? You planning to spread it around?"

The warning is obvious in his voice, but Tej shrugs. "I just mean someone's gonna claim responsibility. You don't slap down a boss and not brag about it."

In the kitchen, Jun's expression is flat, but her shoulders are tense. Bene, on the other hand, frowns at his cousin. "Nobody slapped Jun down."

"Sure they did," Tej says.

"Tenje, don't be such a—"

"Don't call me that!" Tej snarls.

The room goes still; the air itself seems to have knives in it. Tej looks furious, his body tight. When Tej left K-5 station, his name was Tenje Ironway. On the farming station where Six relocated him, he became Tej Redcore, just as his sister became Ujan Redcore. Luja chose to reclaim her family name when she came to Farren Eyce. Tej did not.

Bene, realizing his misstep, raises his hands. "I'm sorry. You're right. I'm sorry."

Tej keeps scowling, and the knives in the air stay sharp. Masar knows he should feel sympathy for Tej after what he's been through. But when he looks at him, all he sees is a posturing little malcontent. Short and skinny, tiny brown eyes, a narrow face constantly pinched. Usually Tej gets along with Bene and Luja, but he's entirely cold toward Jun, and he never showed the slightest affection to Hosek before she died. Masar was raised by his own grandmi, a woman who died two years ago. How many times has he wished he could have her back, tell her again that he loved her? Tej would rather run around getting into trouble than build a life for himself.

Finally, looking very satisfied by the effect of his anger, Tej goes over to the kitchen table and sits down.

"Anyway," he says, puffing up, "the point is that whoever attacked Jun is bound to tell people. They'll probably even do it again."

"Jun will stop them," Luja interjects, reassuring herself.

"How?" Tej scoffs. "Whoever it is, they're clearly a better caster than her. No offense, Jun."

"Thank you, Tej," Jun drawls. "I assure you I am utterly crushed by your opinion."

"And if it gets out that some random caster can take you out, how do you think the colony's gonna feel? People already hate how things are going. They don't trust the Wheel or anyone else in charge. Right, Luja? I mean, you've seen it on the casting forums, same as me."

Luja looks embarrassed. Masar has gathered that after their mother died on Q-9, Luja took over caring for Tej—even though they were the same age. She loves him fiercely, but it's obvious he makes her uncomfortable.

"It's not everybody," she says. "It's just, you know...people don't like feeling like they don't have a choice."

Tej snorts, putting his feet up on the table. "I can relate."

Jun gives him a scathing look. "You can go back to the Treble tomorrow if you want, Tej. Just be prepared to have them throw you in a cell."

"Wouldn't even be in this position if you hadn't jumped us here."

"No, that's true. The Kindom would have killed you already."

He looks at her hatefully. Luja reminds him, "We all made the choice together. We decided to stay, as a family. You agreed, Tej."

He retorts, "Only 'cause I couldn't just abandon you."

Luja flinches. Masar is ready to murder him.

Bene pours the drained noodles into a pot of vegetables and sauce, saying, "It takes time to get used to the idea that you've left home, and your life isn't what you expected. We know that better than anyone, don't we? But once people work through their fear and grief, they'll see that we're truly free on Capamame. We didn't have that before."

"The home I left was K-5," Tej says. "And the place they sent me to turned out to be Som's own shithole. Sorry if I don't think this ice rock is any better. I mean, what have we got here? Work for no pay. The same measly rations as everyone else. Fucking Je bastards who think they're better than us."

Masar's head goes hot, eye glitching. Jun comes out of the kitchen before Tej can finish his sentence, snarling at him, "Don't you fucking say that shit ever again, do you hear me?!"

Tej blinks, flicking a nervous glance at Masar as he remembers his audience. Bene asks disbelievingly, "Tej—how can you say that? What about Emos?"

It's the name of Tej's Jeveni stepfather, long dead now. Tej looks startled, then defiant. He ignores Bene to sneer at Jun, "What are you gonna do? Hit me?"

"No, you get enough of that in the bars, don't you? No wonder you can't find any purpose here. All you do is waste your life getting drunk and starting fights and trying to fuck people who don't want you."

Tej blanches white. He storms to the closet, snatching his jacket from inside. Jun says, "Running away, huh? Just like always?"

"Fuck you!" he shouts, yanking open the door.

"*Tej*," pleads Luja.

But he's already gone, slamming the door after him. In his wake everybody seems frozen, and Jun wears a look of rage and humiliation. She looks at Masar, eyes full of apology, but it's Bene who says, "I'm so sorry, Masar." His voice is soft, his eyes entreating. "Tej... There's no excuse for him saying that."

Masar clears his throat. He's had plenty of practice with Jeveni slurs. But he hasn't heard them in Farren Eyce before. Among the non-Jeveni, it could be common.

Strangers, whispers the farmer in his ear.

"It's not your fault," Masar says, encapsulating in those words all the hatred for all the Jeveni in all of history. It's not Bene's fault. It's not Jun's fault. And yet they grew up immersed in the same beliefs. It's somewhere in them, he knows it—even if they've fought to stomp those words out of themselves.

Nobody seems to know what to do. Luja is watching them all with a blank expression she gets sometimes, when her thoughts are far away.

Bene sighs. He brings the pot to the dining table, where the bowls are already waiting. He spoons out heaps of noodles.

"Come and eat," he says.

Later, when some of the worst tension has bled out of them all, when they have the benefit of a good meal and Tej's poisonous energy has dissipated, Luja says, "It was hard for him on Q-9. He had to act tough to get by. We both did."

Jun lifts her eyes from her bowl. "You don't owe me an apology for anything. I thought I had a handle on what things were like for you there. If I had known, I would have found a way to get you out. I just...thought it was better to wait until I had enough money to get us to a frontier station. I shouldn't have waited, and I'm sorry."

It has the tenor of a speech she's made before. Luja looks at her for a long time, her expression unreadable. Not accusing, not angry, but shuttered, like she doesn't know how to say everything she feels. She turns back to her bowl, mumbling, "Tej is worse since we got here. I think it's the people he hangs out with."

Jun sighs, clearly hurt that her apology got no acknowledgment. "That's how it goes."

"He's started hanging out on Level 2 a lot," she adds, like that will explain everything.

In a way, it does. Two is a residential level, and it has the largest population of lifetime stationers in the colony—people like the Iron-ways, who grew up space side. Farren Eyce is harder for them than other people. Some of them, like Luja, seem relieved to be on a planet. But most are disoriented by their distance from the stars. Even if you go up to the surface level at night, and stand under the clear holo dome that protects them from the worst of the weather, cloud cover usually obscures the Black. Stationers like Level 2 because it's deep underground, tightly contained, familiar. It's also where they've had the most success running the black markets that, while not illegal, form an epicenter for Farren Eyce's rare instances of crime.

"Bunch of crooks," Bene says.

Jun chuckles. "Remember who you're talking to. I probably have more in common with the people on Level 2 than I do with the Wheel. No offense, Masar."

"None taken. You're an acknowledged reprobate."

Jun grins. "There's nothing wrong with people challenging the Wheel. Every civilization needs that."

"The people on Two aren't just antiestablishment," Luja says. "They're using the immaturity of the colony to try to set themselves up to control energy and information going forward, not to mention supplies. The way they run the black market is exploitative. I wouldn't be surprised if they're the ones who started the fire in the market, hoping to drive business down to them. There's even a group of casters down there who call themselves pirates."

Jun's and Masar's heads swivel toward her, sharp, but Luja is looking glumly at her bowl. Masar's chest thumps hard, a hit of adrenaline.

"Caster pirates?" Jun asks. "Where'd you hear that?"

Luja shrugs, listlessly twisting her noodles around her fork. "From Tej. Bunch of casting lab rejects, I think."

Not for the first time Masar is struck by the fact that he and Jun don't have the same connection to the average saan of Farren Eyce as the younger Ironways do. His position as a leader of the collectors and a direct confidant of the Wheel disconnects him from conversations that would give him better insight into what people think. He and Jun keep an eye on the public forums, of course—but there are private forums, too, and surveillance is not permitted in Farren Eyce. Perhaps if it was, they would have heard this phrase "caster pirates" before.

Perhaps he would know who killed the collectors.

Masar looks at Jun, and she looks back at him. He's read the full transcript of her exchange with the avatar. Its threat comes back to him: *And Luja? Why, the caster pirates of Farren Eyce would eat her alive.*

Jun's eyes blaze.

He's about to ask Luja to tell him more about Level 2, when a comm from Fonu sen Fhaan reaches him. He answers, and the River's voice is typically flat in his aural link, "I need you on Four. Someone has vandalized a shrine to Kata."

Aware of the Ironways watching him, Masar asks, "We don't know who it was?"

"People seem to have their theories. I need you to talk to them and look into it."

This is the second act of vandalism against a non-Sajeven shrine in as many weeks. The last one was aimed at Makala and left her covered in graffiti. This would seem to point a finger at the Draeviin, who abhor other gods than their own—but the Draeviin respect the colony too much to vandalize it. Masar looks regretfully at his unfinished bowl.

"All right, I'm going."

Fonu cuts the comm, and Masar shovels down a few mouthfuls before standing.

"I've got to head down to Four," he says.

Jun asks, "Everything okay?"

"It's fine. I'll cast you later. We can talk more?"

He doesn't have to say what about. Jun's tight nod confirms that they'll be making plans about Level 2. He'll need to make a report to the Wheel, as well. No doubt they'll have opinions about the next move. Tomesk and Fonu are particularly disapproving of the black market. Masar hopes they don't float some ridiculous idea like shutting it down.

Bene stands. "I may as well go with you as far as Five. My shift starts in half an hour."

Masar studiously ignores Jun's eye roll. So does Bene, grabbing his work boots from their spot by the door and yanking them on. Bene was a miner in the Braemish city where Six sent him and Grandmi Hosek. His life of physical labor makes him an ideal member of the construction crew. For most of the past two months, he's been working on the development of the Market District, which is nearly complete. Fixing up the residential levels has been a higher priority, but building out the infrastructure of the Market District will give the people another communal center.

Finished with his shoes, he looks at Masar expectantly. Masar squeezes Jun's shoulder in passing, gives Luja a wink, and follows Bene into the hallway.

They walk in silence, moving through the residential grid toward the central courtyard and the staircase. Some people have set up chairs in the hall, chatting together, and children run and play in the early evening. Masar notices a few curious looks for him, but also smiles and waves. Maybe more than usual, since Bene is with him. Bene is popular with everyone, everywhere. When Masar was a collector, he knew how to charm and bluff his way into the places he needed to be, but whenever he stayed somewhere for a length of time, his bosses and coworkers tended to view him as an outsider. Probably because he *was* an outsider, dreaming of leaving the Treble, of going to Farren Eyce. But no one treats Bene like an outsider. No one treats him like a stranger.

An old woman sees them coming and greets Bene with a Je blessing. She urges him to wait and darts into her house, coming out with a plate of fried dough tossed in sugar. Bene grins. "Thank you, Auntie," he says, taking a piece and, when Masar doesn't reach for the same, rolling his eyes and grabbing a second. As they walk on, Bene pushes the fried dough at him.

"Don't insult them. Eat."

Masar obediently eats, and Bene smiles up at him, amused. Not for the first time, Masar gets distracted by how beautiful Bene is. Only a little taller than Effegen; the same round face. A stocky build and impish golden-brown eyes. His male Braemish gendermark has a linguistic insinuation of femininity. For a few years as a teenager, Bene had a female gendermark. Masar doesn't know why he changed it, though of course people often do. He seems happy as he is.

"You know," Bene says, snacking on his treat, "you don't have to walk around like you think everybody hates you."

Masar balks. *"What?"*

"You always look so guarded around people, like you think they hate you. But they don't hate you. You're a hero."

Masar grimaces. He has a memory of standing in Effegen's office on *The Risen Wave*. Cleric Chono and Six were there, and Effegen was showing Chono another round of casts from the Treble that were painting her as a fallen martyr. Masar doesn't particularly like Chono or Six, unable to cast aside his suspicion about their pasts and their motives, but even so, he felt sorry for the cleric. She was so clearly unsettled by the idea of anyone lionizing her.

And now he knows how she felt.

Bene chuckles. Masar feels embarrassed. Bene finishes off his piece of fried dough and nudges Masar with his elbow. "You know when I met you, I never thought you'd be so modest. You didn't seem to have much to be modest about."

Masar is terrified he's going to blush. With his fairer skin, there'd be no hiding it. When they met, Masar was too busy with the afterward of their jump to Capamame System to give Bene much attention. He recognized that Bene was a beloved of Jun's and he was happy to reunite them, but aside from a passing realization that Bene was a beautiful young man, he gave him very little thought in the first couple of weeks. It was only later, when Masar started going to Jun's place for meals in between work shifts, that he got to know Bene, whose cheerfulness and optimism annoyed him at first, and then reeled him in against his will. This, too, reminds him of Effegen, of her relentless determination to be Masar's friend, rather than just his Star.

He doesn't realize they've been walking in silence for almost a minute until Bene says, low and slightly hesitant, "I haven't seen you in a while."

They see each other a lot, actually. But that's not what Bene means. He doesn't mean shared meals in the Ironway home or afternoons in the gymnasium playing Som's Catch in teams of other Jeveni. He means their occasional evenings at the bar on Level 7, or that time Bene ran into him in the Market District and made him help with some shopping. He means that one frantic half hour when Masar found Bene alone at the apartment, and pushed him against the wall and kissed him with melting intensity, the younger man holding him tight against his body. It was only when Bene tried to slip a hand inside his trousers that Masar came to his senses, remembered who this was, and left with barely a word of excuse.

Since then, he's made sure not to be alone with Bene. Though it's obvious Bene would like things to be different.

"I'm sorry," Masar says. "There's a lot going on."

Bene is quiet, and Masar thinks he's going to push back in some way, but they've made it to the courtyard. There are dozens of people around, enjoying the communal space and coming and going on the stairs. Masar appreciates that Bene has enough tact not to talk about it with so many ears around them.

"Don't just cast Jun when you're done with whatever happened on Four," Bene says. Masar gives him a confused look, and Bene shrugs. "She spends too much time in her casts. Go back to the apartment. Talk to her. You're her closest friend in Farren Eyce."

Masar snorts. Yes, of course, he and Jun are reluctantly and grumpily aware that they are friends, but does Bene have to *talk* about it? Masar says, "Even if I told her to stop casting, she wouldn't listen. She only listens to Liis."

Bene chuckles. "Yeah." He tilts his head, contemplative. "What about you? Anybody you listen to, when it comes to taking care of yourself?"

Masar thinks of Effegen a few days ago, urging him to take a day off.

"Not presently, no."

"What about Dom? Do you take care of each other?"

For a split second Masar misunderstands the question, is about to remind Bene that Dom has a wife, but—

"Have you talked much, since you found Uskel?" Bene asks. "Seems like the two of you would have the most to talk about."

Masar, still embarrassed by his misunderstanding, grunts. "We've been working together ever since it happened. We talk all the time. About work."

They reach the staircase, with the elevator bank on the left. Bene asks, "Wanna walk?"

They start down together, the stairs a little less crowded than usual. With tens of thousands of people in Farren Eyce, there's rarely a time when the levels or the stairs aren't crowded. Whoever threw Uskel over the railing would have had to find the perfect moment. They would have had to study the pattern of traffic on the stairs and waited until everything was abandoned to make their move in the early-morning hours.

Bene says, "I know you don't like people being protective of you. I guess it's just worrying to know that you and Jun are targets."

Surprised, Masar says, "I'll protect Jun."

Bene gives him a fond look, seems about to say something, but a sudden flutter of the overhead lights distracts them both. They pause on the stairs. Many people do, and wait for the fluctuation to pass. Masar feels like his skin is crawling, but Bene nudges his elbow, and they continue on as if it hadn't happened.

At that moment, a group of about five Draeviin come up the stairs, passing them on the right. They give Bene a cool perusal, clearly noting the absence of a Jeveni tattoo. Masar wants to smack them for their turned-up noses, but Bene seems unaware, and soon afterward they have reached the Level 5 landing.

They stop, regarding each other. Masar doesn't know what Bene sees on his face, but he says with soft assurance, "You'll find the avatar, Masar. I know you will."

There's a touch of worship in his eyes, as unnerving as the memories of their passionate kissing a few weeks ago. When Masar signed up to be a collector, he had some idea of becoming a hero—the way Nikkelo was a hero. Nikkelo was the first member of the Wheel he'd ever met. A figure out of lore, a warrior giant in the body of a slender gentlesaan, always wearing those tailored suits, his blue eyes vibrant, the white crest in his hair like the touch of a god. Masar knows very well that in the early days he looked at Nikkelo exactly as Bene looks at him now.

It makes Masar nervous. He risked everything for Nikkelo. He did it again and again, driven by love. Could Bene's devoted admiration be similarly dangerous? Especially if Masar is indeed in the crosshairs of some collector-murdering avatar? He can accept any level of consequence for himself. But not for Bene.

"I've got to get going," Masar says. "I'm already late."

Bene looks like he's going to say something else, and Masar's chest tightens. But he just smiles, and his smile is so beautiful it aches.

"Okay. I'll see you later."

Masar nods gruffly, and walks on.

CHAPTER SEVEN

1664

YEAR OF THE CRUX

A prison in the Treble

Chono has had this dream before. Sometimes she's standing with Six on the cliffs of Principes, rolling sable hills behind them and the sea a flat gray slate below. Sometimes they're on the floating city of Pippashap, perched on the gunwale and holding a cup of temple tea. Most often, they're in Farren Eyce, and Chono finds them on the rail of the great staircase, open air plummeting beneath them. In every version, Six's back is to her, and when they turn around they don't look like Esek at all, but like some other person, alien and strange. Yet their voice is always Esek's voice, drawling, resonant.

"I have chased you all my life," they say in the dream, not like a lover, but like an accuser. Then they step off the edge of the cliff or dive from the gunwale or tumble over the railing, and just as Chono starts to scream, "Don't!" she wakes up, sweat-drenched, alone.

This time, though, she's not alone. She can feel the leftover shout in her throat, she can feel the moisture on her body, but she can also feel someone else in the room.

She's seated in a plain metal chair, her upper body resting on the table with her arms for a pillow. Her wrists are shackled to a metal ring, and this is the dozenth time they've brought her here and interrogated her and then left her for hours, till finally she fell asleep. She thinks it's been ... three weeks? No, longer than that.

She doesn't raise her head. She pays attention to the quiet electricity of somebody new in the room. She would know if it was her main interrogator, for he wears a distinctive rose perfume that is notably absent from the air. Still bleary from her dream, from weeks of exhaustion and uncertainty, Chono has a fleeting memory of what Esek smelled like. No perfumes or colognes, but she did have a scent. Something full of heat.

Chono listens for the sounds of her visitor, remembering the game Esek used to make her novitiates play: Hunter and Prey. She would pick one of her novitiates to be prey but not tell them. They only found out when the other novitiates, the hunters, attacked. It was an efficient game, not only because it taught the students to be ready for anything, but because it prevented them from developing a loyalty to one another that might supplant their loyalty to Esek. Which, jealous creature that she was, may have been Esek's primary goal.

The first time Chono was prey, they got her at night. She was sleeping in her bunk when she woke to the sound of an ill-placed footstep. She and Six had older students as enemies at the kinschool, so she was already familiar with nighttime attacks. She sprang out of bed. At the end of it she was mottled all over with bruises, three broken ribs and a fractured scapula, but she'd given back as good as she got. Six would have been proud. She remembers reveling in the way Esek looked her over after the bout, looked at the other, badly bruised novitiates, and smirked.

Now, years later, she wonders what new pack of wolves has come to set upon her. More cloaksaan, eager to dispense a beating? More interrogators, not violent yet, but withholding of food, water, sleep? Aver Paiye, come to metaphorically strip her cleric's coat? Or maybe, at last, an executioner...

Done with waiting, she steels herself, and sits up.

But the wolf she imagined is Secretary Ilius Redquill.

Chono looks at him in blank incomprehension. In the past month she has not traveled farther than the space between this interrogation room and her cell. No windows. Nothing to tell her where she is. But she knows that Moonback jumped them away from the Ma'kess System, and Ilius lives on Ma'kess, in Riin Kala. Which means he would have had to jump to her location. Why would the Kindom take him away from his lowly appointment in contract law? Is this some new tactic? Spice things up by bringing her a friend?

If he is a friend, anymore.

He looks exactly the same. She saw him in person less than a year ago, and she's known him for a decade, and in all that time he's always kept the same short, curly haircut, always looked just a little underfed, always worn small round spectacles over milky-brown eyes. In his secretary's uniform, all blue with the white tippet, and wearing finger bracelets on one hand in homage to Kata, he is everything that she remembers. With so much changed, with Esek dead, with Six made into her doppelgänger, it seems bizarre that anything should look the same as it did before she left the Treble.

"Hello, Chono," he says, smiling a small, uncertain smile. He's seated across from her at the table, and there's a cast camera in the wall behind him. No doubt others are watching them.

"Ilius," she says slowly, like his name might be a bomb.

He smiles again, tense. "How are you feeling?"

How is she feeling? Those fucking cloaks broke her eye socket. The guardsaan of this prison gave her nothing more than a regenerative patch to heal it. No painkillers. Nothing for her bruised ribs and hip.

Instead of answering, she says, "You're far from home."

He shifts in his chair, looking awkward. "I was transferred a few months ago. I don't work in Riin Kala anymore."

Chono supposes she could have run a search on Ilius before leaving Capamame, to confirm where he was, but he has been the last thing on her mind since the jump. Why would he transfer from Riin Kala? He loved Riin Kala. She takes him in more carefully, and that's when she sees it. On the left shoulder of his tippet, there is a new appliqué. Ilius has always been a talented secretary but never high-ranking. The appliqué says otherwise...

"That's a notable promotion."

Her voice is calm, but her thoughts are not; her surprise comes second to a blazing sensation of betrayal.

Ilius looks squeamish. "It's a recent development."

Yes, it must be. The First Secretary of the Clever Hand, a man named Ostiver Ravening, holds the same pride of place as the First Cloak or the First Cleric—but he also has two lieutenants, nearly as powerful as him: the Major Advocate, and the Minor Advocate. Together, they form the Secretarial Court, and to Chono's amazement, Ilius bears the mark of the Minor Advocate. If she had been in Farren Eyce when this happened, her newscast access to the Treble would have alerted her. Which means it's a very recent development indeed. Her humble friend is now in the upper echelons of Kindom power.

"Are we in Praetima?" Chono asks.

Ilius pauses and nods. Praetima is a small city on an island in the north Katish seas, and houses Nikapraev, the headquarters of the Clever Hand and the Secretarial Court itself. It's also renowned for its prison, where traitors and terrorists receive a cursory trial before execution. Is Ilius here to escort her to the famous gallows? Is Six already dead? *I have chased you all my life*, she thinks. *Don't you fucking dare be dead.*

Ilius must see something telling in her expression because his brow furrows deeper and he raises his hands. "Chono, I'm here to help you."

She feels her preternaturally stoic face flatten even more, hiding emotion and intent. So, he *is* a new interrogation technique. Maybe this is even a test for him. Can he get the traitor cleric to talk when no one else can? She supposes this will be the last step before they move on to physical torture.

Chono says, as she has said to all of them day in and day out, "I want to see Esek."

For every question about Farren Eyce, about the Wheel, about Jun, for every demand to know when she turned traitor and when Esek allied with the Jeveni, she has responded with the simple request for proof that her friend is alive. She expects Ilius's expression to fall, to see frustration or helplessness as he prepares to tell her, as the rose-scented interrogator has told her, that she can see Esek when she cooperates.

Which is why it almost shocks her into a reaction when he nods.

"All right."

The door to the room shrieks open, and a guardsaan steps inside. Behind them comes Six, trailed by two more guards. Six's head is high, their mouth quirking in a familiar way. No signs of injury. Perhaps some weight loss, but—

"My gods!" Six, radiating Esek, laughs at the sight of Ilius. "What a stunning twist!"

Ilius still wears that uncomfortable wince. He stands from his chair, and the guardsaan take Six and put them in it. They seem about to shackle Six to the metal rings, but—

"No," Ilius orders. "Leave those off. And release Cleric Chono as well."

Chono blinks confusedly as the guardsaan obey, and only when she is rubbing the soreness of her freed wrists does Six finally meet her eyes across the table. To have them so close after wondering if they're dead for almost a month is...disorienting. It brings relief and fear at the same moment. If the Kindom is letting her see "Esek," it must be part of their strategy to break her.

"You look all right," Six observes. "There's the stench, of course, but I don't suppose I smell very good, either. What do you think, Ilius? Does Chono smell good?"

Standing at the head of the table, Ilius asks, "If I dismiss the guards, will you attack me?"

Six laughs. "Why dismiss them, Prudent One? To give some illusion of privacy? We all know you've got a court of observers somewhere nearby." They jerk a thumb over their shoulder at the camera. "Ravening, I presume? And the Major Advocate? Maybe Seti Moonback as well? But yes, go ahead and make your symbolic gesture. I dare say if I try to attack you, Chono will stop me. She remains confoundingly moral."

Ilius nods at the guardsaan, who leave. He drags over a chair from the corner of the room, sitting between them with his hands folded, finger bracelets tinkling. Chono looks between him and Six. Ilius always showed distaste for Esek Nightfoot, though he claimed to know her only by reputation. The way he avoids Six's eyes may simply be a function of that distaste, and yet there is something about the way that Six looks at him, the way that Six-as-Esek looks at him, that breathes with mocking familiarity.

Chono asks Six, "Are you all right?"

How badly she wishes she could ask the question in private. How much she longs to cast them other questions. But her access has been shut off. Before they left Farren Eyce, Jun Ironway equipped them with a number of "gifts" meant to help them move and communicate in secret: the Hood program, for one. A scrambling tech that prevents audio recorders from picking up their voices. A secret comm link to Capamame itself, undetectable by Kindom casters. All these gifts would be useful to Chono now. Instead, she is in the dark.

Six rolls their gaze back toward her, smile thin, eyes sweeping over her in assessment. "Perfectly well," they say. "What about you, old friend? You're looking thin."

In Esek's voice the words lack all concern, but there is a tiny chink in Six's mask, and if Chono looks just right, she can see through the peephole into a dark, malevolent energy that says if she is not all right, they will kill everyone.

"I'm fine," she says, trying to imbue her own flat affect with the reassurance that Six needs. Their protectiveness is bizarre, but she feels protective, too. She wants to search them for bruises and scrapes, to scour their very bones to see what was broken and what has healed.

"And how has your morning gone?" Six asks mildly. "Has Ilius pried all your secrets out of you? Talented little fucker that he is, I didn't take him for much of an inquisitor."

"He just arrived," Chono says, annoyed by the implication that she would talk.

Six winks at her. "Very good. Then I suppose we can begin."

Ilius has been quiet during their exchange, but when Chono and Six look at him expectantly, he clears his throat. "I know you've had a difficult few weeks. At the end of this conversation, you will be freed."

Chono gives no reaction beyond a flicker of eye contact with Six, who smiles slow and lazy. "By the gods. What a turnaround! Do you hear that, Chono? The Godfire has delivered us!" They shake a finger at Ilius. "Or perhaps the data flood has its teeth in the Treble, and people are clamoring for proof that Chono is alive? It did move them so much, to think she was dead."

Ilius's pained look is plenty confirmation. Chono says, "Releasing us must come with some condition."

"There's no condition to your release. We do hope to work with you, though."

"You mean tell you everything about the Jeveni and their colony?" Chono says. "You may as well bring in the torturers now, Ilius."

His eyes widen, startled and wounded.

"I'm your friend, Chono," he says earnestly, as if he can't believe that she would forget.

But that only makes it worse. The stab of pain in her chest, just beneath the bullet scar, only hardens her. There are years of warmth between her and Ilius, years of correspondence and alliance. He was her first friend, after she left Esek's service. But now he is the Minor Advocate. He is in the command post that drives the Kindom's machinery. He is complicit in the imprisonment of the five thousand.

Six, for their part, chuckles. They link their hands behind their head, leaning their chair back in a graceful balancing act. "Friendship doesn't pay the bills, Ilius. And there are some pretty high debts on the table. As you may remember, I don't forgive debts."

Ilius's lips thin, all the entreaty he showed Chono turning to dislike. What does Six mean *as you remember*? Chono glances back and forth between them. Do they know each other?

Ilius says, "We've exhaustively reviewed the contents of the data flood. In the face of the evidence, we are law-bound to pardon you both. Therefore, the letter of Alisiana Nightfoot's will restores you as matriarch of your family, Sa Nightfoot. Perhaps access to your fortune will mollify you?"

Chono's pulse quickens. It's one thing that they're not being executed. But *pardoned*? Fortunes restored? If Six is the matriarch, their will and testament is the law, and that will declares that on Esek's death, the sevite empire becomes the property of the Jeveni Wheel. Why in the worlds would the Kindom let Esek become matriarch if it could result in the sevite trade moving outside the control of the Nightfoots? Outside the reach of the Hands?

Seeing that Six will not speak, that Six is merely looking at Ilius with the intensity of a solar storm rolling in, Chono says, "If Esek controls the sevite, then—"

"She doesn't," Ilius interrupts. Six's eyebrows leap up. Chono frowns. "Riiniana Nightfoot has been serving in Sa Nightfoot's stead these nine months. She's a righteous and loyal girl. She agreed last night to formally turn the trade over to the control of the Kindom, for a temporary period. It's the best way to protect the economy from upheaval, given Esek's... reemergence."

Chono has a searing memory of Liis Konye, who warned her once, *The Kindom will seize the trade. There will be no check on their power.*

Six laughs. "How efficient. Pardoned us and stole the trade in one shot."

"This is a matter beyond the scope of a single family's power," Ilius says, sharpness bleeding into his voice. "It's about the survival of the Treble." He looks at Chono, growing gentler but no less urgent. "Unrest has doubled this past year, and since your return, things are worse. We have an obligation to protect the systems from anarchy and revolt. This is the easiest way to do that. With control of the trade, we don't have to rely on our own reserves of sevite. We can relax gate travel restrictions and amp up supply runs to the places that need it."

Chono has an image of the figures behind the cast camera leaning in, waiting to see what Esek will do. She says, "If things have been so bad, why are you just now taking over the trade?"

"Stealing the trade," Six repeats.

"We can't *steal* it," Ilius insists. "We're not Black Ocean pirates. Riiniana wouldn't cede the trade to us before. Now she has."

"Ahh," Six croons. "And on the eve of my ascent. It's beginning to make sense."

It makes sense to Chono, too. The Nightfoots are jealous monopolists of the sevite trade, a trade they created and have controlled for centuries. But with Esek pardoned, the trade would fall to her. And Riiniana's keepers would rather let the Kindom have it than see it in Esek's hands. If the transfer of power to the Kindom really is temporary, the Nightfoots must hope that they can get rid of Esek before reclaiming the family business. They must think they can find a way around her will. Which, if Six's secretaries were as good as Chono suspects, seems unlikely.

"So I've got my wealth but not my income," remarks Six. "Tell me, Ilius, how does First Cloak Moonback feel about that? She ordered her second-in-command to assassinate me nine months ago. And she very much wanted to shoot us when last we met."

Ilius pushes back that silly curl of hair, rattling his finger bracelets. "Seti Moonback's opinion doesn't rate at the moment, Sa Nightfoot."

Chono and Six glance at each other, weighing the tiles on the board.

"And Aver Paiye?" Chono asks. "Does he not rate anymore, either?"

"Aver Paiye has resigned."

He may as well have said that the temple at Riin Cosas has collapsed. Aver Paiye has been the First Cleric of the Righteous Hand for almost thirty years. He has ushered in some of the most popular religious policies of the century. He is universally beloved and politically powerful, a giant in the Kindom. How does a giant resign?

"You look surprised," says Ilius to Chono.

"Of course I'm surprised."

"How can you be, after what you've done?"

"*What* have I done?"

"Chono," he says, gentle but chastising. It's a voice that recalls their long friendship, their fluctuating intimacy, and the tenderness of it embarrasses her. "You flooded the Treble with evidence of Moonback's and Paiye's crimes. You proved that they attacked the Jeveni without provocation. Aver Paiye ordered the destruction of a civilian vessel, and Moonback broke the laws of the Anti-Patriation Act. Not to mention she accepted a contract to have Esek killed. You've come back here demanding justice and provided all the evidence necessary to prove your case. Didn't you hope it would work?"

Six says, "Come now, Ilius. I'm sure that's the party line, but if you believe it, you're more naive than I thought. And if you don't believe it, you'd best not sit there and lie to us."

"It's not a lie," Ilius says, clearly battling his temper. "The Clever Hand had nothing to do with this scheme against the Jeveni."

"Not one we could prove," Six purrs, like a threat.

"We've moved swiftly to make it right. We've publicly condemned our role in the Jeveni Genocide and we've removed corrupt leaders from power."

"What do you mean *you've* removed corrupt leaders from power?" Six asks. "How exactly have you managed to depose Paiye and Moonback? The Secretaries have no authority over the other Hands, and yet you talk as if you're running the whole show."

Ilius draws himself up a little taller. "We have implemented the Rule of Unification."

Chono's brow furrows, confused. A memory peeks out from her kinschool days. She was never interested in being a secretary herself, but she threw herself into her lessons on law and economics as rigorously as she threw herself into sparring. She had to work harder in that area. She wasn't naturally brilliant, like Six, who barely studied but knew everything and disdained most of it. Now, she recalls a lesson about the early formation of the Kindom, the ultimate justification of three independent bodies, and a contingency called the Rule of Unification, whereby one Hand could take leadership over the others. Dread flashes through her.

"No one has implemented that rule in centuries," she says.

"We're aware."

"It led to martial law. It led to war."

"The Rule of Unification is a temporary measure while we restore order."

"*We*," Six says. "How did the Secretaries get the crown?"

Ilius flicks a scathing glance at Six. "We proposed it, and the Righteous Hand seconded us. The rule only needs a two-Hand majority."

So Moonback was betrayed.

"Did you do this before or after Paiye resigned?" Chono asks.

"Before. He agreed to it. He wants peace, Chono. Bringing the Hands together under central leadership will help us root out any further corruption and lay the groundwork for renewed trust between the people and the Kindom."

He sounds like an official proclamation. Chono barely controls her voice. "The independence of the Hands is a *check* against corruption. An imperfect one, yes, but—consolidating all Kindom control won't make the people trust you. It'll make them fear you for powermongers."

Ilius exhales through his nostrils. "That's why we need your help."

Chono doesn't know what to say. He takes advantage of her silence, leaning closer, speaking urgently. "Look—I know this is dangerous. We all know it. Moonback has gone missing and there's every possibility she'll create a schism in the Brutal Hand. There will inevitably be more uprisings. But we have to be strong now so that everyone can be safe later. Chono, I know you don't have any reason to trust the Clever Hand, but can't you trust me? There are groups across the Treble who are holding you up as an image of rebellion and anarchy. They're wielding you like a weapon, using you to excuse things I know you would never want. Murder and looting and desecration of the temples. If you work with us, you can persuade people to stand down. You can save lives."

It is often said that the motto of the Clever Hand—*to prove prudent*—is dishonest; that the motto ought to be *to prove vicious*. What are the Secretaries if not vicious executors of their own desires and will? But in the years that she has known him, Ilius has always seemed so prudent, so committed to what's best for the Treble. He's believed in the law, not as a tool of oppression but as a means for ensuring justice.

"Please," he says. "You know I'm right."

"What's *right*?" Chono retorts, her desire to trust him slamming up against the actions of his Hand. "You admit to crimes only because we force you to, and now I'm supposed to believe in your goodwill? What about the five thousand Jeveni you imprisoned, Ilius? Have you done what's right by them?"

Ilius, already fair-skinned, loses a shade of coloring, and for the first time his eyes dart toward the cast camera, as if looking for help. That's how she knows—

"I'll take that as a no." Her nostrils flare. It's much harder to control her anger than she remembers. "I swear by the gods, Ilius, you *will* free them."

"Chono, please—"

"You think I've been a symbol so far? You think I've been a threat to peace? You *will* free the five thousand." She turns toward the camera, voice rising for her invisible audience. "You'll free them now, or I'll speak so loud against you that you'll *have* to kill me."

Ilius stutters. "We're going to free them! Chono, I swear, we will. There's just some question of…well, you see—the factories. The Jeveni had so much institutional knowledge, and with them gone, the trade can't thrive on its own. We need Jeveni to work the trade. We can't keep it going if we don't—"

Six is out of their chair so fast that neither Chono nor Ilius has time to react. With the quick efficiency of a striking snake, they grab Ilius by the shoulders of his tunic, yank him out of his chair, and slam him down onto the table as easily as if he were a sack of grain.

"Esek!" Chono shouts, jumping to her feet, distantly grateful she said the right name.

But Six ignores her, looming over Ilius, holding him pinned and hissing close to his face, "Factories need laborers? Slaves, you mean."

Ilius stares up at them in frozen terror. The door to the cell flies open. Half a dozen guardsaan flood inside, rifles raised and shouting orders.

Chono's hands dart into the air, and she cries again, "Esek! Esek, *stop!*"

"Get back!" one of the guardsaan thunders. "Get back or we shoot you both!"

But Ilius yells shrilly, "No! Stand down! Don't shoot them!"

The guardsaan look at one another, never relaxing their aim but clearly bewildered at the order. Chono's heart races out of control, and Ilius gapes up at Six with a combination of terror and entreaty. Six is the only one who seems at ease. Their hands fisted in Ilius's clothes look unbreakable. The coldness of their smile is distinctly different from Esek's. It is *Six*'s smile, *Six*'s fury, that fills the room with crackling heat.

And Six's voice that whispers, "You speak of justice, of making things right. And in the same breath you admit the five thousand are your slaves. You pretend that the Brutal and Righteous Hands have acted apart from you. But your secretaries have known our innocence for months. And now you want credit for realizing that we have backed you into a corner." They lean even closer, as if they would kiss Ilius— or bite off his ear. "I have never had a problem with hypocrisy, dear Ilius. But you have to be able to bring it off. And this... this is sloppy. You are the same transactional little cretin you have always been. Do not try to lie to me."

Their voice is losing all hints of Esek's affect, and in a panic Chono shouts at them again, "Esek! Esek, look at me *right now!*"

Two seconds pass. Three. Never relaxing their grip, Six raises their eyes to her with an expression of perfect composure. With her whole soul Chono begs them to recognize the warning in her face, to realize that they are on the verge of exposing themself to a roomful of Kindom operatives. She begs them to be the calm and temperate Six who haunted Esek for years, a patient ghost waiting for its moment.

Yet there is something in Six's face that makes her realize that this was not a loss of control. Their liquid gaze, their cool smile—they have played a move in a game, and she is the fool for not remembering that everything they do is strategy.

Abruptly, they lift Ilius off the table. They let him go—patting down his rumpled clothes and stepping back. They grab the chair that he was sitting in, set it against the wall, and sit.

"Now," they say, a dangerous chirp. "It seems to me that all of this has just been . . . opening negotiations. You could hardly have expected us to come to an accord at once, could you? Secretaries. You're smarter than that. So I for one would like a bath. Consider it my first demand . . . and you know how demanding I am, Ilius."

Up to now, Chono's anger has had a steady focal point: the Secretaries. But now it redirects like a missile sighting a new target. The way Six speaks to Ilius confirms that they knew him before this— knew him, and hid it from her. Six and their secrets. Endless, churning mazes, and her lost in the center.

"You know each other," she blurts, as if that is the thing that matters right now, as if her own pride and anger at being held in the dark should have any say in this moment.

But the way Ilius looks at her, still flushed from fear, and now embarrassment—and the way Six tips their chin up, arrogant in the face of her revelation—

"Of course," Six says breezily. "Why, Chono, you knew I had secretaries in my employ. Clever fish who carved my will into stone. Allow me to introduce the best of them."

Chono feels sick, more so when she sees the shame on Ilius's face. Even with a thousand guesses at her disposal, she would never have thought Ilius was one of Six's pawns. He spent years telling her he had nothing to do with Esek or the Nightfoots. He spent years insisting that his information trafficking and research skills were in service of Kindom justice, principled and correct. There's no way he could have thought it principled to help "Esek" write the Jeveni Wheel into control of the trade.

As for Six—they knew that Ilius was her friend, and they've never said a word about it. This is what Esek would have done. Kept a secret she knew would hurt Chono, not because she *didn't* want Chono to hurt, but because it satisfied her to hold a weapon in reserve.

Focus, Chono tells herself. Wasn't that what serving Esek taught her? To focus, in the face of that arbitrary cruelty. What else could a fickle and brutal master do but teach someone to focus—even if only in the hope of protecting herself?

She looks at Ilius again, putting aside all talk of wills and secret alliance, and repeats, "I want the five thousand freed."

Ilius looks desperately grateful that she will not question him about the will. "We'll begin the process. But . . . my kin want something from you as well."

Of course. The bargaining game of the economist.

"What?"

"We want you to speak in favor of the Rule of Unification. And to call for an end to the violence happening in your name."

"You mean you want her to be your lapdog," says Six.

"Our ally. A loyal cleric."

"I wasn't aware I was a cleric anymore."

"Don't you want to be?"

The question is uncomfortable. Despite everything, her devotion to the Godfire, to what the Godfire represents, still runs through her like a hot river. Her desire to minister to the people of the Treble, to offer them the comfort of a conduit to their gods, is deep. If she tears that out, if she denies that part of herself, she will leave great gaping wounds behind.

But she can't be anyone's instrument but her own, now. And it's her own ends that matter to her. The protection of the Jeveni, in Capamame and here. The freedom of prisoners.

"I'll call for an end to violence," she says, deliberately omitting mention of the rule. "And in return, you'll release the five thousand."

Hope flares in his eyes. "Yes. You have my word."

His word. She doesn't know what that means. She always thought he was an institutionalist, devoted to the letter of the law, to the good of the people. And yet he's the Minor Advocate of a Hand now poised for tyranny. He's the jailer of five thousand innocent Jeveni, to say nothing of the Jeveni who never went to Capamame. Whoever helped Six draft that will was not interested in the good of the people. What were they interested in? What did Six offer them in exchange? Money, power? No, Ilius would have had a different motive. He would have wanted something else. What is the something else that Ilius wants? And how dangerous does it make him, this shy, bookish man, who she thought was an ally till now?

CHAPTER EIGHT

1660

YEAR OF THE SURGE

Ycutta
Ka'braevi Continent
The Planet Braemin

The blast from the explosion lifted them off their feet to smash into the back wall. Without their armor, the impact would probably have broken their spine, or left them a pile of shattered bones. Ears ringing, disoriented, they lay in the rubble at an awkward angle for several seconds, trying to get a grasp on how badly hurt they were. It didn't help that they were only six months out from the most recent surgeries. Every time they took on a new change, adapting to the result was like learning to be a body all over again. Esek's narrower shoulders, her slim but muscular torso, had changed their balance and weight in inconvenient ways. Snarling, they climbed to their feet again—and flung themself out of the trajectory of a shotgun blast.

Fucking fires.

They crouched behind the half-destroyed wall as someone fired back at the shotgun, then Six heard a strangled cry perhaps twenty feet away, and nearer by, the sound of a body hitting the ground. Everything fell silent. Six peeked around the wall and saw a body. It was one of Redquill's contracted guardsaan, their faceplate and the face behind it blown open. Six listened for the sound of more gunshots and heard instead a weighty silence, like the center of a cyclone.

This was not what they had wanted.

Several seconds passed, until it had been over a minute since the end of the gunfire. Six ran a quick cast of the grounds, searching for heat signatures—but the ones they found lay still. The crowds had fled the galleria when the fighting started, and the city guardsaan were yet to arrive. Rising, Six came around the debris and stared into a field of dust and smoke, punctuated by gory black heaps. Whoever had the brilliant idea to set off an explosive deserved to be disemboweled. Six had no way of knowing yet if there were civilian casualties.

They walked onto the field of carnage. They saw more dead guardsaan, armor ruptured by blast rifle fire and by the—had it been a bomb? A crowd-killer grenade? They approached what had been a doorway into a shop five minutes ago. The scorch marks and debris of the explosion centralized there, and Six realized that one of the guardsaan had been trying to neutralize the fighters on the other side. But the guardsaan had underestimated the strength of—it had definitely been a crowd-killer. Now multiple people were dead.

Six moved into the shop behind the door, which was a cavern of debris now, sparking wires dangling from the ceiling. There were three bodies on the ground, and one person still alive.

Six picked their way through the wreckage toward the quivering, rasping figure that lay on their back about seven feet away. A shotgun lay beside them, and Six sensed intuitively that they were the one who had made the final stand against the guard a few minutes ago. When Six knelt beside them, they saw a woman's face, eyes blinking rapidly but blind, shoulder hanging loose where a bullet had destroyed the joint. Her chest was a bloodbath of shrapnel. Yet somehow, she was still alive. How had she found the strength to fire at the guardsaan? Well, her strength was gone now. She lay quivering in her death throes, and then, seeming to recognize Six was there, she gasped and flinched back.

"Shh," Six said. "I will not hurt you."

They used a gloved thumb to wipe away some of the blood on her face, revealing what they'd feared: a Jeveni tattoo. The weight of it hit them harder than the sensation of being thrown into a wall. The woman made a gurgling sound, and rasped, "Roq...?"

"No," Six said. "I am not Roq. But I will not hurt you."

The woman's body tightened, and panicky whimpers escaped her mouth. Six withdrew a syrette of morpho from their field kit and saw the moment the relief bled through her, softening her expression but doing nothing to save her life. Six had nothing that could save her life. She would be dead very soon.

A voice crackled in their aural link.

"Sa Penrider? Are you there? Sa Penrider!"

It was Ilius's voice. Ilius, who was holed up somewhere in the city, maybe just now beginning to understand that things had gone wrong. How promising Ilius had seemed.

Six ignored him, speaking to the woman. "I can help with the pain. I cannot save you."

Blind eyes dilated, the woman was still present enough to nod.

"Did...Who got out?" she whispered. "How many got out?"

"How many were there to begin with?"

A furrowed brow, a sudden clenching of the teeth. "Who are you? I won't tell you."

Of course she would not. Loyal to her last breath. Six did not want to upset her, so they said, "There are three other bodies here. That should tell you if any of you survived."

Tears that had been rimming the woman's eyes leaked out, and Six didn't know what that meant—if all her kin collectors were dead, or if some had escaped. What had happened to the one called Roq? they wondered. But whatever the final number, their deaths lay at Six's feet. Six had let Ilius set up the meeting with someone who claimed to know the names of the Jeveni Wheel. Six had known that Ilius kept a protective detail, but they had assumed the detail would stay with Ilius. It never occurred to them that Ilius would send guardsaan to scout the galleria for threats, or open fire on the Jeveni who had been scouting them in turn. That was Six's mistake. In the end, all of this was their mistake, their crime, their unredeemable error.

"Sa Penrider," Ilius said in their ear, sounding a little shrill, clearly afraid he had gotten a Nightfoot ancillary killed.

Well, he should sound shrill. When he got here, Six was going to murder him.

Six put the thought aside. They took off one of their gloves and laid their Esek-colored hand on the woman's forehead. She flinched again. She was shivering badly. Six leaned close to her, voice soft. "I know the death prayer. If you want, I can say it for you."

The woman's brow furrowed again. "You're a Jeveni?"

Six felt their jaw lock, body resisting like a stubborn animal that doesn't want to be led to water. For her sake, they forced themself to say, "Yes. If you give me a name—it does not have to be a real name—I will say the prayer."

But when the woman said, "Ademi," Six knew that it was her real name. They saw her for who she truly was: a Jeveni warrior, a collector of the Black. She had spent her life in service of the Wheel, of goals that Six had yet to uncover. How badly Six wanted to ask her for the names of the Wheel—how badly they wanted to know what the Wheel was trying to do. But they would not do that to her now. They would let her die with her secrets and honor intact.

Six bent to the woman, murmuring, "For when you die, Ademi, you shall return to that which matters most, to that which is the core of yourself. And you will see what you are, laid out before you as a banquet." They saw her lips moving soundlessly, saying the words with them. "In your death, you will eat the fruits of your life, and whatever ripens them shall ripen your death—either with joy, or regret. And your loves and your hates will gather to you, and you will dine with them at the long table of your life. And thus, Ademi, is all death a return."

They had always thought it was a strange prayer, as likely to torment the dying as reassure them. In their own death, Six feared, they would find a table overflowing with the rotten fruit of regret. But when they finished the prayer, Ademi seemed calmer. She asked in a raw whisper, "Did we stop them? The one who was buying the names? Did we stop them?"

"Yes," Six told her. "Your Wheel's names are safe."

She exhaled shallowly. If Six had known the collectors were coming, they would have called the sale off. It was their fault. But it was not only their fault. It was the fault of the guardsaan who had thrown the crowd-killer. It was the fault of Ilius for sending his guardsaan. It was the fault of the Kindom, which nurtured Ilius's distrust and disdain for the Jeveni.

"I will make recompense," Six promised her. "I will have revenge, for all of this."

But she did not hear them. Her eyes stared fixedly upward, her body limp and unmoving. Six closed her staring eyes and committed her face to memory. Only now did they notice the machete at her hip, with the twine-wrapped handle and curve that signaled it for a Quietan weapon. Quietans passed their blades down through family. Now that Six knew her name, and that she was Quietan as well as Jeveni, they could find her family and return the machete. They released the scabbard from her side and rose to their feet. In that moment they heard tromping boots and voices calling out. They went out to the galleria as three guardsaan appeared. With them came Ilius, his face twisting in horror as he stumbled to a halt.

It was Yantikye who had suggested they make contact with Ilius Redquill. The idea was to use him as a tactical exercise by sending him documents that Yantikye's best forger had written up. If the documents passed muster with Ilius (a man flush with resources, a scheming man, with forgers of his own), then Six would know that Yantikye's forger was impeccable. An impeccable forger of neural links and identification would be crucial when it came time to take over Esek's life.

Six had floated to Ilius the name and history of a Ma'kessn mercenary called Penrider. The forgeries worked. Yantikye was very smug.

But Ilius Redquill's value as a test subject proved insignificant to his larger value as an information contractor. Six had been slowly accumulating those over the years, using them to track down Nightfoot secrets. Building up a network that would bear the fruits of all their plans. Six convinced Ilius that they worked for the Nightfoots—that they were tracking down the Wheel's names on behalf of the Nightfoots. That if Ilius ever breathed a word of their mission to anyone, even to Alisiana herself, the Nightfoots would have him killed. And Ilius, for proper pay and the conviction that he was ultimately serving the Kindom's best interests, had found them a seller of the names. Surprising, useful Ilius.

Then, of course, there was Six's other interest in him: his long friendship with Chono. Their peculiar attachment to each other. Ilius's obvious infatuation, which always made Six disgusted and angry.

They put aside the thought. They looked at Ilius now. They had never shown him their face, but they would do it now. They would meet him eye to eye before they killed him. Six raised their faceplate first and removed their helmet. They still had much of their original facial structure—though not their original nose, their original ears, their original skin. All that changed, after the bombing of Soye's Reach burned them alive. Since then, they had become a macabre mixture of themself and Esek.

Ilius was a smart man, an intuitive man. They expected him to understand what removing the helmet meant. They expected to see his already pale face wash white in the terror of realization, that his time was up.

But to their surprise, Ilius was not even looking at them. He had rounded on one of the guardsaan with a look of confusion and despair. "What happened here?!"

The guardsaan, a captain, lifted his faceplate. "Prudent One—"

"I ordered you to stay back unless Sa Penrider called you in! You were meant as a last resort, as backup! This—" He looked around at the field of carnage. "This was avoidable!"

"We realized there were Jeveni observing the scene. They were an obvious threat to Sa Penrider. I ordered my people in to neutralize the threat."

"Who told you to neutralize them?" Ilius cried, looking like a boy whose illusions had shattered. "We could have captured them! They could have given us information. Now all we have are dead bodies, and if any of them escaped, they know that guardsaan are hunting them. They'll be more cautious than ever!"

Six, watching the exchange, was intrigued. So Ilius had not ordered the guardsaan to attack. Ilius even recognized that the attack was a blunder. And yet Ilius had failed to control his people, and that made him responsible.

But no more responsible than you, Six thought grimly.

"Ycutta is surrounded by checkpoints," said the captain impatiently. "We'll catch them when they try to leave the city."

"We have an explosion and bodies to answer for! The governor will be apoplectic. Do you think I hired you to invite scrutiny on my operations?!"

The captain's face twisted, and suddenly one of his comrades raised her own faceplate. "This is a lot of fucking grief over a few dead Jeveni. They killed six of us! We had every right to fight back and to defend Sa Penrider from these animals—"

"Do you believe I need your defense?" interrupted Six quietly.

Eyes shifted toward them. There were looks of surprise, but also irritation and contempt. How undisciplined these guards were, compared to cloaks.

Six, still holding the machete in its scabbard, moved closer. "Your interference neither protected me nor achieved my aims for this operation. I am more than prepared to respond to an ambush, if it had come. Which I doubt it would have, given how long I have been here waiting for the seller. And if that seller saw what happened, they are gone now, permanently, and I have nothing to show for it. Nothing but needlessly slain Jeveni."

The woman guardsaan leered. "You seem pretty worried about the Je. What about our people? They died protecting you!"

"They died for nothing. The Jeveni, at least, died to protect what they love."

The third guardsaan yanked off his helmet. "You some kind of fucking sympathizer?"

Six ignored him. The captain turned on Ilius. "Who the fuck are you working with? What were they hoping to buy in the first place?" He narrowed his eyes. "What's all this about?"

"I'm paying *you*," Ilius exclaimed. "I don't owe you any details beyond your mission brief. And you failed that mission."

The captain's sneer put Six in mind of a hundred people who had looked at them with disdain over their life. He said, "You won't make me regret killing a few factory rats. Keep my pay if you want. Bet I can get twice as much when I tell the Cloaksaan what you're up to."

With a whisper of movement, Six was on them.

They had planned to kill them anyway. This only provided them their stage entrance.

The one who had taken his helmet off was the first, easiest target. Six slashed out with the machete, slitting him open at the throat. Even as he grabbed uselessly at his wound, already collapsing, the woman guardsaan drew her sidearm. The machete was sharp and well cared for, and went through her wrist like it was butter. She screamed, and the captain was also drawing his gun, but Six flattened him with a dropkick, still focused on the woman. They grabbed her by her face-plate, wrenching her helmet off of her and stomping into the back of her knee. She buckled to a kneel, and Six flipped the machete into a reverse grip and drove down into her left shoulder, through the muscle and then her heart.

They slid it out of her as the captain recovered from his fall, gun drawn, but Six used their free hand to grab his forearm and the gunshot went wide. As he brought up his other arm to try to strike their head, they ducked under it, rose again, and put the machete through his eye.

The furious sounds of the fight turned to a quivering silence, and the three bodies lay at their feet like a corona.

Six flicked the machete and heard the wetness of blood sluicing off its edge. They turned to look for Ilius. He was standing exactly where he had stood before, frozen and ghost pale. Six wondered what he had been like as a novitiate. How he had endured the brutal sparring court, or if the masters had delivered him from that early. It happened, sometimes. A particularly gifted young person, bound for the Clever Hand, was wasted on stave drills. Perhaps that had been Ilius, and this was the closest he had ever been to real bloodshed. Six advanced on him, until they stood almost toe to toe, and they could feel his ragged breaths.

"Are there any other guardsaan you hired for this?"

Ilius's throat bobbed. He shook his head. "No. No, they're...all dead."

Six nodded pensively. "Why hasn't security arrived?"

Another swallow. "I have the governor in my pocket. I ordered him to keep his people back until I could...confirm what had happened."

That was smart. Ilius was smart. Six wondered if this was why Chono liked him.

"You are only as useful to me as your results, Ilius Redquill," they said.

They raised the edge of the machete. Ilius froze, too terrified to move. Six tapped his cheekbone with the machete, leaving a spot of blood behind. Ilius trembled but dared to say, "I found your seller in the first place. I can still be valuable to you."

Six smiled thinly. "And yet...you think no more highly of the Jeveni than these, do you?" They gestured at the bodies. "I know you, Sa. You disdain the very idea of the Wheel."

Ilius looked a little confused, and still very frightened. He said, "I didn't know that... *liking* the Jeveni was part of the mission. Surely the Nightfoots aren't hunting down the Wheel because they *like* the Jeveni."

"They rely on the Jeveni," Six said. "They *need* the Jeveni. Do you know what would happen, if the Jeveni disappeared? You ask a random person on the street, and they will tell you the Nightfoots would simply begin hiring more deserving laborers. Treblens misunderstand the Jeveni's value. But you do not misunderstand it, do you, Ilius? Tell me. What is their real value?"

Ilius looked as though he didn't understand this course of conversation, but he said warily, "They have... institutional knowledge. They're scientists and engineers and uniquely qualified factory workers."

"Exactly. Which means that every one of them is worth ten times their weight in jevite."

"They're not *all* factory workers. The isolationists don't know anything about sevite. Whoever these fighters are, they don't work the trade." He said it with barely contained scorn. "They're hardly valuable."

"And yet assimilationists and isolationists alike are bound by common cause. The survival of their people. Which makes them potential acolytes of their Wheel. The Wheel could devastate the entire trade. And I still don't know their names. Every Jeveni death I cause makes finding those names harder."

Ilius was wise enough not to argue this point, and Six thought suddenly of Esek, who had destroyed Six's life on a whim so many years ago, simply for the satisfaction of it. The *pleasure*. Six could kill Ilius now, and that would be pleasurable, because Ilius's Kindom devotion and contempt for the Jeveni crawled over Six's skin like flies. But Esek's impetuous choices had served her ill. Six must not be impetuous. Their plans must be flexible, and patient.

They sighed, as if all this had been merely irritating, and looked around at the bodies. Time for a lesson. "Why did you hire these guardsaan, Prudent One?"

Ilius hesitated. "I—for protection."

"You don't seem very protected to me," Six said. Ilius swallowed. "You brought a battering ram to this mission, when what it called for was a lockpick. You have notable talents, but your instincts need work."

Ilius said, "I agree with you that all this was...unsubtle. But I can be very subtle, Sa."

"Oh, yes, I know. That's how I found you in the first place. Your subtle machinations."

"I am a better wielder and collector of information than ten Jeveni collectors put together," Ilius said. Six liked that he could be arrogant at a time like this. "I can only assume the Nightfoots agree, or they would have asked you to contract some mercenary player or some underground caster with half my resources. I know more and I control more than—"

"So you are like Terotonteris," they interrupted. "A hoarder of shiny things."

He didn't answer. His gaze flicked down to the machete. Six raised it, nudging at his chest with the bloody blade. Ilius sucked in a breath but held his ground. Was this courage? Or merely the pride of the Secretaries, who thought themselves beyond the reach of the Treble's most violent actors?

"You are not so big as him though, are you?" Six went on. "Did you know there is a little Braemish bird named after him? It is called a tero. It takes valuables back to its nest and builds an exquisite palace. Children and poor people go into the jungles hunting for these nests, hoping to find treasure. But it is a dangerous job, because they are not the tero's only predator. You know about the jaw spider? It catches and eats the teros, and uses their nests as scaffolding for its elaborate webs. It lies in wait, to see if someone else will come after the shiny things."

To their surprise, Ilius said, "Sometimes the jaw spider doesn't kill the tero bird. Sometimes it leaves it alive because its singing attracts potential victims."

Six chuckled, and they knew that very soon they would have to change the sound of the chuckle, the sound of their voice, their every inflection and verbal instinct, to mimic another. But that time had not come yet.

"Is that what you want, Ilius Redquill? To sing for me?"

Ilius declared, "Your seller isn't the only one I lured into my nest. I have people all over the Treble, embedded in Jeveni communities. I have casters in the Silt Glow Cliffs, and traders on Ar'tec Island. I have cloaksaan who will answer to me, if I want them to."

Six tsks. "No, no. Not that, tero bird. Never that."

"But if the Nightfoots are willing to work with a secretary, then surely they're willing to work with other Hands who—"

"Let me tell you what is going to happen," they said. Ilius flushed at the interruption. He must have decided that his life was safe. Well, let him think it for a few more moments. "We are both going to go away from here. Your pocketed governor will dispose of these bodies and do nothing to hunt down the Jeveni. *You* will do nothing to hunt down the Jeveni, or the Wheel, ever again. Your little inside agents? They will desist, now. I can't have your spies threatening my work, tipping the Jeveni off, grabbing attention like you did here. No. If I find a single one of your people lurking like a snake among the Jeveni, I will hold *you* responsible. I will open my jaw and bite you into pieces."

The edge of the machete slid down his chest, slicing cleanly through the front of his blue suit with a whisper that left Ilius bug-eyed.

"But do not worry, Ilius Redquill. Our time is not over yet. The Nightfoots may have no use for cloaksaan, but they do have use for a secretary of your...flexibility. Which is why I am going to introduce you to someone soon."

Ilius's brow had furrowed when Six said *flexibility*. Nervously he asked, "Who?"

A slow smile. "Esek Nightfoot."

Six may as well have said that they would be introducing him to Som, the Blade's Edge, the Devourer. What little color had come back into Ilius's face drained away.

"What?" he whispered. "No..."

"You have some objection to meeting Esek Nightfoot?"

"She's *deranged*. She kills people for sport, and everywhere she goes she draws attention—no! A person like that could expose everything I'm doing!"

"She is…eccentric," Six allowed. "But we do not always get to choose our employers. My own fate is tied up with Esek Nightfoot. And now your fate is tied up with me. So this is an inevitable intersection. And though I had thought until a few minutes ago to kill you and find another secretary, I am persuaded to give you another chance."

Ilius seemed shocked to discover that his life was on tenterhooks. But then perhaps a breeze moved through him, reminding him of the open pieces of his sliced shirt, which had revealed a pale, narrow chest, framed by the white tippet. He must realize that with another swipe of the machete, Six could open him up like a fishersaan shucking an oyster.

Voice raw, he asked, "What does Esek Nightfoot need from me?"

Six bent and retrieved the sheath of the machete, which they had tossed aside when they drew it to kill the guardsaan. Now they sheathed the machete and faced him again. "From what I understand, she needs your help drafting a will."

"A will?" Ilius said.

"Yes, apparently it will be a very strange will. It is yet another trap for the Wheel."

They must say this. They must make Ilius go on thinking that everything they did was in service of the Nightfoots and to the detriment of the Wheel. They must make him believe it so much, both as Sa Penrider and as Esek Nightfoot, that he created an infallible, perfect document. One so ironclad that by the time he learned its true intent, even he would not be able to undo it.

"And what about you?" Ilius grimaced. "Will I—are we going to work together again?"

Six picked up their helmet. Ilius had seen their face, but that was all right. It would not be their face for long. They thought of the months and years of surgeries, the *agony* of it, the sweat-drenched nights and morpho-addled thoughts, and only one thing to focus on, to keep their purpose alive: *Esek. Esek. Esek.*

Donning the helmet again, they told him, "I am the jaw spider, tero bird. I will never be far from your nest."

Okay, fuckers, here's the rules. You don't poach other people's juice or interrupt their casts, and if you want in on a job, you prove you're worth it first. You respect everybody's handle, and if I catch you trying to track down real idents, I'll bounce you out and good luck finding another den that wants you. Biggest rule of all? This is my fucking den, and I'm the last word. You don't like that? Build your own house.

excerpt, Conduct Code, Casting Den 12A4756 community
forum. Dated 1639, Year of the Stones.

CHAPTER NINE

1664

YEAR OF THE CRUX

Farren Eyce
The Planet Capamame

"I still think that Masar should go with you."

Jun waits to a count of five, tells herself that she will speak to Fonu sen Fhaan in a polite voice. Instead, she's icy as Capamame. "If Masar is there, the saan on Two will assume he's spying for the Wheel. The den will never let us inside and no one will talk to us. Me and Bene going on our own will make it look like a—a *family outing*. I've been to the black markets before, anyway. I'm less suspicious."

Fonu, clearly annoyed at her reveal, throws a skeptical glance at

Bene. He stands beside Jun with his typical good-humored expression, as if he can't sense the tension in the room. But of course he can. It's thick and dark as storm clouds.

"You're interested in subterfuge. I'm interested in success," says Fonu. "Masar can protect you if there's trouble on Two. Your cousin is a liability."

Jun nearly snaps at him that subterfuge is *essential* to their success, but Bene says in a bright voice, "Oh, don't underestimate me. I can throw a punch."

From the corner of her eye Jun catches Effegen's small, amused smile. The Star is sitting at her desk, hands folded. She spreads them apart in a decisive way, her jevite rings glinting. "I don't want Masar going down there. If these caster pirates are responsible for murdering the collectors, sending him would be like dangling bait."

Masar, already the biggest and tensest person in the room, hardens into a boulder. His arms are crossed, one of his fists clenched against his chin, and the knuckles whiten as he tries to control his reaction. His silver eye twitches. Of course he wants to throw himself into the fray even when he's not needed. Big, self-sacrificing fucker.

Bene makes it worse by saying, "I agree."

Jun's eyes roll upward in exasperation. "Yes, we're all very protective of poor, helpless Masar. But this isn't about what's safe, it's about what's effective. Masar keeping away is the best thing he can do for the mission. Let's not forget, this is the only fucking lead we've got."

Even Fonu can't argue with that.

Masar says, "I'll be on Three. If there's trouble, Jun can cast me, and I'll be down there in minutes. Dom and a couple other collectors are down there already."

This doesn't actually reassure Jun. Dom ben Dane has been a wreck since the deaths of his friends, and he's clearly afraid he's going to be next. Sending him down to Level 2 ahead of her and Bene was only a reasonable decision because he's got family on that level, which will explain him being there. But if he's twitchy, it'll draw attention.

Effegen says, "Yes, well, I'm not happy with Dom being exposed, either."

"He's not alone," Masar grunts. "And can we all just take a moment to remember that collectors are the best warriors in Farren Eyce?"

"We should get moving," Jun says.

But Effegen raises a hand for them to wait. They all watch her. For how young she is, she nonetheless has an impressive command of those around her. Jun had nowhere near that level of composure when she was twenty. Come to think of it, she still doesn't.

"I want us all to remember something," Effegen says. "It was this avatar who told us about these pirates. The avatar planted the clue. We've seen tricksters in action before, and tricksters lay traps."

Six, of course. Still no word on them or Chono, though the Treble is flush with rumor and unrest, not to mention Chono's devotees, shouting to know what has happened to her—the woman who, from their perspective, has come back from the dead.

"We should assume that this is also a trap," Effegen says.

Fonu jumps at their opportunity. "All the more reason to send Masar."

"Masar is useless against a cast attack," Jun says.

"And you were useless against the avatar. Moon arise, it nearly killed you!"

"Jun wasn't useless," Bene intervenes, with a rare hint of temper. "She was taken off guard, and the avatar attacked her physical body. That won't happen this time."

"It may, if this is a trap," says Effegen.

"Then give me a gun," Jun suggests, fingers itching for the stock of the Som's Edge that Great Gra left her.

Effegen gives her a chastising look. "No."

Of course not. No weapons in Farren Eyce. How long will that last?

Jun turns aside toward Bene, murmuring, "Maybe it would be safer if you stayed—"

"I'm going."

"If it *is* a trap—"

"Then you'll need backup."

Jun grumbles, angry that he's right. She's no hand-to-hand fighter, and Liis isn't here. Whatever Fonu may think, Bene grew up in the eat-or-be-eaten mining town of Najic, and it taught him hard lessons about self-defense. She trusts him to have her back. But Masar and Effegen look stormy, clearly upset about him going. The three of them are fucking ridiculous.

"All right," Jun mutters. "We're on guard against a Six-wannabe asshole and we've got our contingencies in place. Now, this motherfucker tried to kill my little cousin. Let's go."

People notice them as soon as they step off the elevator.

The open courtyard of Level 2 is busier than most, a market district unto itself, with over a dozen little shops working out of pop-up tents and bicycle carts, most dealing in black market goods. There are also tables and sofas and chairs that people have obviously taken out of their homes to create a bigger communal space, and as she and Bene walk into the crowd, she sees a wide array of Draeviin, Treble Jeveni, and non-Jeveni saan, of all planetary origins. Shops proudly display symbols of their gods—Kata with their single large breast and scarred stomach; wily Terotonteris, his many arms casting tiles and hefting tankards. And of course, Sajeven, five eyes and a mysterious smile, the patroness of Farren Eyce.

Jun nods her head toward a wide hallway that leads into the western residential block. "The den is in that neighborhood," she says.

"We should mingle first," Bene says. "Take our time."

Jun chuckles. When she mingles, it's an act, a costume that doesn't fit her right. But Bene is a naturally friendly and sociable person. He strides off and she follows. They end up in front of a drinks cart with a punch bowl full of something pink. When the vendor looks up, startled to see Jun, Bene smiles amiably. "Can we try some?"

The vendor clearly expects trouble.

"Sa Ironway," he says, gaze flicking from her to his drink to her again. "Now, it's nothing sordid. Just a bit of stimulant in it. Gives people a kick."

"We'll have a cup each," Jun says. "Ration credits okay?"

She pings a reasonable fare at the man's neural link, and slowly he reaches for his ladle. "That's more than pink juice is worth," he says.

Charmed by the name, Jun shrugs. "Call it a tip."

Suspicion fading, the vendor starts ladling up a cup, when someone says, "I wouldn't take those credits, Sa. Probably got some virus on them to track your movements."

The vendor blinks in startlement, unsure again, and Jun rolls her head in the direction of the speaker. A Quietan woman is reclining in a nearby chair, legs crossed and lazily twirling one of her long dark locs. Her smile is cool and fine as a razor blade, eyes accentuated with dark cosmetics. No Jeveni tattoo.

"Now what's this," says Jun, returning a similar smile. "What have we done to make you so suspicious?"

The woman chuckles. "Nothing yet, sweetheart. But there's time, nah?"

Bene tells the vendor. "There's no virus on the credits. We just want a drink."

Finally, slowly, he hands them their cups. The Quietan woman cautions, "Better be careful. It's strong stuff."

"You're just full of advice, aren't you?" Jun says.

She and Bene sip together, Bene's brows shooting upward in surprise and appreciation. Jun can instantly feel the stimulant hit, sharpening her senses even as the sweet berry flavor rolls down her throat. Nodding her compliments to the vendor, she and Bene move on, but the Quietan woman rises smoothly from her chair, a full head taller than Jun—and joins them. Eyes watch them continue through the black market, plenty of whispers on their tails.

"Aris the Beauty," the woman introduces herself.

Jun huffs. Of course there'd be a Quietan ship called *The Beauty* and of course one of its people would be this tall, curvy woman with her dramatic eyes.

"Nice to meet you, Aris," Jun says. "You know who we are, obviously."

The woman flicks an appreciative glance from her to Bene, lingering on Bene—and no wonder. Jun is a skinny little tech head. Bene is beautiful. But she looks at Jun again. "Sure, I know who you are. Don't know why you're here, of course."

"We're just looking around," Bene puts in.

Aris the Beauty ignores him, eyes on Jun. "We're protective and private people, here on Two. We like to keep an eye on our visitors, make sure no one causes trouble for us by trying to be clever. And the colony sings with stories of your cleverness, Jun Ironway."

"Well, I can't help that. But I'm not here to make trouble, Aris the Beauty. I heard about Level 2 and I'm curious to learn more. Curiosity is the affliction of the clever."

"And what'd you hear about us, sweetheart?"

Jun stops walking and turns to face her.

"I've heard there's a casting den down here."

She can feel Bene's surprise. She hadn't planned to state their business so openly, but she can see that Aris is a shrewd character. It doesn't seem worth it to play games with a woman whose manicure is sharp enough to cut your throat.

Aris smiles in a pleased way that makes Jun think this was exactly what she expected her to say. She leans down to Jun, lips near her ear. "Now, why waste your time in a stuffy place like that? There are other things to do in Farren Eyce. I hear your girl is off being an explorer. Must get lonely, living inside simulations." One of those claw-tipped hands rises up between them, fiddling with the top button of Jun's shirt. Aris's nose skims her ear like a promise. "And there's nothing wrong with a little recreation."

Jun doesn't relish being pawed at in front of her cousin, but she's more intrigued by the tactic than anything. Far from immune to the ill-intentioned seduction of a beautiful, obviously dangerous woman, she nevertheless takes Aris's hand, guiding it away. She pulls back to look into Aris's sparking eyes.

"With those nails?" she drawls. "No thank you."

A laugh. "I could trim them."

"That's a scintillating offer. But I'm afraid my girl is a bit..." She considers her words. "Protective."

Aris's grin has teeth, but she doesn't try to touch Jun again. She shrugs one shoulder. "Bring her with you when she gets back. Share and share alike."

"She would eat you alive."

Aris laughs, full of delight, but not for a moment does Jun think this flirtatious front is the *fun* kind of predatory. She has the distinct sense she is being tested for weaknesses, and Aris's next words confirm it.

"I know another Ironway. Little Tej with the angry eyes." Her smile curls. "He doesn't mind my attention."

The strategy is obvious. If Jun isn't weak for these advances, will she be weak for mention of her wayward cousin? For shots at her family? Beside her, Bene radiates disquiet, and Jun knows they are both thinking that they haven't seen Tej since he stormed out of the apartment last night. Aris the Beauty dangles him before them, another distraction. Jun thinks of Effegen warning them all that they are dealing with a trickster. What are Aris's movements if not distinctly... tricksy? Could *she* be the avatar?

Jun smiles thinly. "Tej is his own man. I'm sure you showed him a good time. Now, come on, Beauty. Either you want to show me the casting den, or you don't. But I'd hate to think this conversation is a waste of both of our time."

Into these words Jun layers the faintest touch of warning: *Don't fuck with me.* Aris flicks her gaze into the crowd and toward the western residential block. She winks at Bene, then waves a hand in that direction. "Trouble finds trouble," she says. "Let's see if they let you in."

She strides away, and they follow her.

"She's been waiting for us," Bene says quietly. "It *is* a trap."

"Yes," Jun agrees. "But I'm not sure what kind."

Aris the Beauty leads them deep into the western quarter, walking ahead and never looking back. They pass dozens of private homes, periodically glancing over their shoulders to see if they're being followed. The residential levels in Farren Eyce are grids, tightly constructed to create the most comfortable homes possible for the most people possible in the least space possible. With so many hallways and turns, it would be easy to tail them.

They end up at a door at the end of a barren hallway, where Aris grandly gestures them forward, her look coy. Jun ignores the performance and knocks.

In her ocular, a message pings.

Everything all right?

Masar's cast bleeds paranoia.

Ask me again in ten minutes.

The door snaps open—though not more than a foot. A hunch-shouldered, whip-thin boy appears, wearing oversized casting goggles and a dirty thermal shirt. Jun thinks of a disgraced archivist she and Masar spoke to months ago. This boy has the same buggy movements, his obscured gaze jerking from Jun to Aris to Bene—to Jun again. With a wince, he pushes the goggles up to rest on top of his head, looking at her with red-rimmed, pale eyes.

"Sunstep," he says, and if this is a trap, he seems not to know about it. His expression is astonished. "How'd you find us?"

Aris raises a finger, smirking. "What can I say? She's cute. I was persuaded."

Jun scoffs. After a long hesitation, the caster opens the door wider, giving a glimpse of darkness dotted with points of light behind him. "You wanna come in here?" he asks, disbelieving and clearly excited.

"Sure." Jun shrugs. "I've heard good things."

His pale cheeks pinken, like a kid meeting their idol. Then, straightening up and clearly trying to look professional, he announces, "It'll cost you."

Jun nods, amused. "Naturally. What's your fare?"

The caster licks his lips, which are chapped with sores at the corners. After considering her question, he makes a curling gesture with his fingers, like running them through a curtain of beads. Through her own cast connection, Jun sees the query, a *knock, knock* against walls of data that she keeps under lock and key. What he wants is innocuous enough: surge credits, which colonists use to excuse uncommonly large drains on the electrical grid. The amount he's asking for is high. She parries with an offer of half as much, testing his mettle, but he accepts right away. Jun wonders what his life was like before the jump. A true built-in-the-Black caster would haggle much harder than this. Maybe he's intimidated.

She transfers his fee, and he waves them in.

The room is a studio apartment. Someone gave up their private residence so they could build a den. All the furnishings have been stripped, and the counter space and cabinets that once divided the main room from the kitchen are gone as well. The appliances have been replaced with tech. The only light comes from view screens and other holograms that flitter around the assembled casters like hovering birds. Jun's eyes adjust quickly as she takes everything in. There seem to be about ten casters, each of them sitting in a little nest of their own making, mostly pillows and blankets. Another figure is sitting in the back, knees to their chest and head on their crossed arms, like they're asleep. No figures emerge from the shadows to attack them. No one seems to even register that they've showed up.

In the middle of the room stands the den's casting hub. It's big enough to have come from a trade vessel or transporter or private luxury ship. It ought to be in Jun's casting lab, or stored away to serve as a future replacement unit. How did these saan get it?

The boy, goggles still on top of his head, juts his chin at the room. "This is all ours," he says proudly. "We built it ourselves. Nothing in the charter that says we can't. Don't know why it would interest you."

He sounds wary but also curious, and Jun can read the fascination in him, just shy of starstruck. She's about to answer him when a new voice cleaves the room.

"What's *she* doing here?"

Jun turns to find that one of the casters has clamored to her feet, glaring. A Braemish Jeveni, she has geometric tattoos on her chin and cheeks, though none of the braids that indicate a kill count. She glares at the goggled boy. "Fuck's sake, are you trying to get us shut down?"

The boy points an accusing finger at Aris. "*She* brought them here."

All around the room, the other casters pull their awareness out of the net, refocusing on the physical world with fuzzy expressions. The figure in the back raises their head, another young man. His red hair makes Jun think of Uskel, and she looks away from him, refocusing on the Braemish woman. Jun's been in enough dens to recognize a leader. She bows over her open palms in a disarming manner. "I'm not interested in shutting you down, Sa. I heard about you, and I wanted to check it out. Call it professional curiosity."

The woman glowers. "Expect to be welcome wherever you go, huh?"

"Expect to be welcome when I pay for it," Jun replies.

The Braem glares at the goggled boy, who ducks his head. She tells Jun, "You can't bully us. I was chief caster of *The Brute Crane* before you jumped us into an ice age."

"Sorry to hear that. Were things going well for you in the Treble?"

"Look, fuck off. People of your profession aren't welcome here."

Jun pauses, considering again that if this is a trap, the reception doesn't bear that out. She asks, "What profession is that?"

"Effegen's lackeys. Wheel spinners."

Jun raises her eyebrows. "That's cute. You know you could confine me to a private gaming hub and I'd still be able to take over this den in under five minutes?"

The woman's nostrils flare. "What's your point?"

Jun leans in. "If I wanted to shut you down, I would have done it from the comfort of my home. Look into my eyes, chief caster of *The Brute Crane*. I'm not lying to you."

They hold the stare like a couple of dogs vying for control of a pack. After what feels like too long, the Braem makes a grumbling sound, not coming around, but not pressing her aggression, either. "Can't blame us for being careful. We built this up as a place for ourselves. We won't have anyone stealing it."

Jun lifts her eyebrows. "Has someone tried to steal it?"

A grimace. "People sneak in uninvited. Everybody's gotta pay for what we find here."

"Ah, commerce," Bene says.

The Braem gives him a *Who the fuck are you?* look, telling Jun, "Well, you paid, so what do you want?"

"Just to look around."

A jeer. "Haven't you got better tech to play with?"

"Come now, we're all casters here. Well, most of us." She nods at Bene, nods again at the redhead watching from the back. His surprised look confirms her theory. He's not a caster. So what's he doing here? She deliberately does not try to label Aris, continuing, "It's not always about the best tech. Novelty has its own draw."

The Braem looks skeptical, but the goggled boy ambles forward. "Could be fun to see her work, boss."

A murmur of agreement goes through the room. Someone says, "She's Sunstep, anyway. She's one of us at heart."

The Braem retorts, "Maybe once she was. Probably can't even work outside the lines anymore, now she's doing what the Wheel says."

This fucking amateur, Jun thinks. *I should crash her system just to teach her manners.*

Bene pings at her neural link:

Steady. Keep your cool.

"Give her a chance," another voice urges. "Who knows? Maybe she'll have ideas for us."

Their leader squints at Jun. Then, apparently deciding it's no use arguing with her den, she waves an arm at the room. "Go on, then. Have a look."

Jun smiles, hums, "Don't mind if I do."

And she drops down into the net.

It's like opening a window in a pitch-black room. A sudden, disorienting brightness of energy and power that nearly makes her cast form drop back on its heels. Working on instinct, she rearranges and images the data into an arena. The threads of the den's casting net glitter gold, spun through the air like a spider's silks. The hub in the center of the arena throbs, full of startling power. She expected an anemic little candle glow, bits of connection pilfered from the larger net to create a comms center, or a media hub. This radiating star—this is not that.

Jun spreads her awareness through the arena, sees the figures in the stands, the other casters who have showed up to watch her. Seeing them like this, she can better read the skill and clarity of their casting. They're not amateurs at all. Not as good as her, no—but she understands with a grim feeling why the avatar said they could take Luja out. There's raw skill in this room, ingenuity and imagination, with which they've built a den worth fighting for. Why don't they work for her? Do they work for the avatar?

She faces the burning hub again. Something tiger fierce snarls from within it, and she sees teeth and swishing tails. She wields a whip, flicking the tip with a crack and striking at the heart of the hub. She catches something at once, hauling it out two-handed, until what surges into view stuns her movements.

It's a cast connection to the Treble.

She stands amazed. The connection allows the pirate casters to access information directly from the Treble—an access she thought she alone controlled. Sudden panic burns through her. She drags the tail-swishing cast connection into reach, and plunges her hands inside it. She doesn't rip it apart, too impressed with the mechanics to destroy it outright, but she peels and pushes and manipulates what's inside, scouring for evidence that the connection would allow colonists to not only access data, but send communications back to the Treble. It shouldn't be possible. Jun has built firewalls that prevent anyone from sending comms outside Farren Eyce without her permission. It's a crucial safeguard. An average laysaan communicating with the Treble could easily give away dangerous information. Details on their security, their location. Insight into their political unrest.

Six's true identity.

She sifts and searches, aware of the figures in the stands leaning forward and watching her, and yet no comm connection reveals itself; the den seems more preoccupied with pirating media signals from the Treble. Things they can sell. But they don't have the means to talk to anyone on the other side. She feels a slow, flowing relief and wonders at herself for fearing it in the first place. These people—what they're doing here is impressive, but it's not dangerous.

Then she looks again, and sees it.

It's *tiny*. Smaller than a peephole. A pinprick, the most minuscule communication link she's ever seen, spearing a sliver of negative light through the center of the tiger thing. Her stomach drops. The signal is no good for anything more sophisticated than text comms, but it's strong and flexible, like a wire. With gritted teeth, she looks at the casters in the stands, flicking her whip at each of them. She feels their shock as she reels them in, pawing through their bodies for signs of access to the pinprick signal, ready to sever each one with clippers.

But none of them is even aware the signal exists. It's like the comm connection is Hooded from them, like someone put it there without them knowing and they aren't *quite* good enough to have found it on their own. So if none of them created it, then who—

She feels it behind her, a thick, icy presence. When she turns, it's standing about ten feet away, a warbling shape, an outline of electric signals, with emptiness inside. The trap, springing.

Its words come at her next.

Hello again.

Jun is arrogant, but she's not a fool; she expected this. She dons thick leather armor, shields of firewall and virus protection. The avatar creeps closer. Jun says:

Something tells me you won't try to asphyxiate me this time.

What makes you so sure?

These casters are keeping the den alive. And the den is valuable, isn't it? Like a banquet you can rob from under the table. You're not going to kill them.

Yes, but you've rumbled this den, haven't you? It's useless to me now.

Jun finds herself sniffing the air for exhaust fumes. She notes how close the avatar is to her now. Stalking her. But it's Jun who strikes out, her whip a lightning bolt. She means to coil it around the avatar's body, reel it in, and split it open. This fails, but the razor tip still lashes across the avatar's body, opening up a sharp wound of light with data hidden inside. The avatar drops back, and Jun goads—

Careful. You're not bulletproof.

It strikes back, lobbing grenades. Virus-infused explosives burst against her shield, shattering. She hurls her own virus, a locater program that sails straight as an arrow into the center of the avatar, and in satisfaction she begins scoring it open, raking her nails through the wound as she traces its cast signature toward an origin—

The avatar recovers, the virus leaking out of its form like toxin-rich sweat, and Jun barely has time to raise another shield as it lobs more grenades at her. She blocks all but one, which strikes her with a percussive force she barely manages to contain. Nonetheless, she feels sticky shrapnel burrowing inside her. What is it? What is it?

Even as she works to rid herself of the fast-acting tech, she warns—

Somewhere out there you're flesh and blood, and I'm going to find you.

The avatar's outline crackles, and it puts her in mind of laughter.

What makes you so sure I'm in the colony?

Jun thinks of the communication thread between Farren Eyce and the Treble. Surely it's not robust enough to allow someone in the Treble to cast attacks through? Then again, does she really know what she's working with here?

She images herself a body full of disease and floods that body with medicine, white blood cells attacking the virus like creatures with teeth. But in the real world, in her real body, a stinging pain starts up in her head. It's localized to her left ear and eye. Sharp as needles, and unprecedented. Headaches and muscle aches are common enough, but this sharp sting takes her breath away, jerks her like an electric surge. A very distant voice cries, "Jun?!"

The virus is in her aural link and her ocular. It's overheating her tech, burning her up from the inside. She puts all her energy into shutting the virus down, abandoning all plans of assault to focus on defending herself. In the cast she can still see the avatar, prowling around her.

Think you're smarter than everyone, don't you? Smarter than the caster pirates. Smarter than the Kindom. That'll come back to bite you.

Jun finds enough energy to scoff.

You some kind of Kindom Hand?

The avatar somehow transmits contempt.

I'd rather rip out my neural link than belong to the Kindom.

Jun ignores this. Her white blood cell monsters are chomping the virus up. But her head is on fire. Her body has started shaking. She thinks of what the academy teachers taught her, before Esek Nightfoot forced her to flee. *Do not be your body. Be a creature in the cast. Believe that the cast is more real than your body. Manipulate it to your will.*

The avatar goads her—

Not working fast enough, are you? Imagine if this virus was in your
neural link. I could blow up your brain and you'd never stand a chance.

The pain is immolating now. The white blood cells are spitting the virus out onto the arena floor, purging her of the disease, but is it too late? No, it's not too late. She's not letting this happen again. Not this fucking cocky little shit of an avatar.

All around, the watching casters glitter, observing but doing nothing to help. Jun sets her teeth so hard she nearly cracks one of them, and in the open air of the arena, she gathers a storm, gathers the lightning—and brings a bolt of it down on the avatar like a hundred-ton weight. There's a vibrating crack, and a sonic boom, and the avatar winks out, hurled from the net. In the instant before it vanishes, she senses its shock and alarm, but has little time to gloat. She yanks herself back into her body.

The moment she's free, she weaves on her feet, stumbling back. Bene's there to brace her, barely restrained panic in his voice. "Jun? Are you all right? What happened?"

"I'm fine," she gets out, trying very hard not to faint. Her legs are watery, her head is throbbing, and there's something wet on her neck. She raises trembling fingers to the slickness leaking from her ear. It's blood.

"Fucking gods," Bene whispers.

Jun breathes hard. She tests her links, and though both the aural and ocular are glitching, she's still got connection. And her eye isn't bleeding, at least. But whatever that virus was, she's never encountered anything like it.

Blinking, she looks around the room. Everyone is staring at her, just as they did in the arena. The goggled caster looks wide-eyed and shocked. Even the redhead in the back has stood up, staring at her with an unreadable expression. As for Aris, her relaxed posture is inconsistent with someone who just had to fight a battle in a cast. Her smirk, on the other hand...

The den boss, the Braem, says accusingly, "You could have hurt my den!"

"Did you know it was there?" Jun shoots back. "Did you know it would attack me?"

A curled lip. "It doesn't answer to me. Never had a problem with *us*."

So she knows about the avatar, but not what it is or who it is. She just neglected to mention that there was something dangerous out there. *Fucking asshole.*

"But it does have a problem with *me*?" Jun presses, as if that weren't obvious.

The Braem shrugs. "It's not the only one. Colony is full of people saying we should raise hell for the Wheel spinners." Her face suddenly blanches, no doubt remembering that there *are* people, unknown people, causing plenty of hell in Farren Eyce with their power surges and their vandalism and their market fires. She quickly backtracks, "We're just running our own thing here. We don't want trouble."

Jun smiles coldly. She wants to ask them if they have reason to believe the avatar comes from outside Capamame, as it seemed to suggest—but that would alert them to some connection to the Treble, and she doesn't want them to go looking for that little comm signal. She'll have to destroy it, but she fears it'll crop up again. If not here, somewhere. And this avatar...If it's forced its way in from the Treble, how? What's its plan? And what the *fuck* did it do to her tech? She wipes at her neck, relieved the bleeding seems to have stopped. Liis is going to be so pissed when she hears about this.

"What now, Jun Ironway?" Aris the Beauty asks. "You going to shut them down?"

The boss objects. "You said you wouldn't! It's not right to punish us just 'cause you're not as good a caster as you want the colony to think."

In a fit of spite Jun swipes a cast at the pirate casters, like a scythe cleaving the air. It slices all their connections to the net—nothing permanent, but enough to shock them. They cry out, as startled as if she had stripped their clothes off, and Jun demands, "You looking to test my skill?"

Wisely, the woman backs down. Aris watches with glittering eyes.

"I won't shut down your den," Jun says. "But if I find out any of you are helping that thing, I'll have your neural links gouged out."

She doesn't actually think that Effegen would agree to that, but it's worth it to see the flashes of fear across their faces, to remind them that she is ten times their equal, even if she may have a worthy opponent in the avatar. No, they weren't part of this trap. They're tools of the avatar, but not its aides. If it is in the Treble, who are its agents in Farren Eyce? Who is killing the collectors? And what, ultimately, is it trying to achieve?

Suddenly, like a last shot across the bow, a message flashes in her spotty ocular:

See you soon.

CHAPTER TEN

1664

YEAR OF THE CRUX

Praetima
Nikata Leen, an Island
The Planet Kator

Chono stands in an opulent washroom that's bigger than her Prae-tima prison cell. True to their word, the Secretaries have released her and Six, and relocated them to an ostentatious hotel called Blue Spire, right in the heart of the city. Their suite is splendorous, befitting a Nightfoot or a high-ranking Hand. Six made much of it to Ilius, crowing over the amenities in a way that still managed to sound threatening, as if a failure in interior decorating would have unleashed more violence. Ilius hung back from them, eyes following Chono, but she would not speak to him. He finally left with promises to bring them to Nikapraev tomorrow.

Nikapraev, where Chono will give her formal statement in support of the Secretaries and the Rule of Unification. In exchange for which he claims they will release the five thousand.

The ground underfoot is a knife's edge, and she wears soft shoes.

But for now, she is alone—surrounded by marble walls and tiling, the perfumed air still a little humid from her shower, the silver fixtures gleaming. Chono watches herself in the mirror over the long vanity. The sink is full of clumps of dark hair, a pair of scissors and a razor laid beside. She puts her hands on the vanity and leans forward, inspecting herself. She can see the effects of her imprisonment on her naked body—she's lost weight. There are dark circles under her eyes. Above her right breast stands the puckered pink scar of her bullet wound.

She runs a hand over her shaved head, taking some pleasure in the sensation. She looks...stark, like this. She has a boxy body and a stern face, and what little softness her fine hair afforded her is gone now. But Chono has never wanted to be beautiful. Now she looks exactly as she wishes to look: like a Teron in mourning. Mourning as indictment.

She dresses. Her cleric's uniform was waiting for her in the Blue Spire room. It all fits perfectly, but the sight of the coat on her tall body, the sharpness of the red with its gold threadwork, is unnerving. She thought she would never wear it again, and yet there's a comfort in its familiarity. A comfort she doesn't want. She leaves the coat on the bed.

Out in the main room, the doors to a wide balcony are open, and Six stands near the railing. She thinks of her dream of Six throwing themself off the staircase in Farren Eyce—shunts the dream aside, and joins them. A sharp wind greets her, as well as the shifting gray cloud cover that defines northern Kator in its rain season. From the height of the tenth-story suite, Chono regards the city below and the high stone walls that surround it. There are rambling networks of roadways and alleys, everything paved in blue-gray stone. There are brick-and-mortar buildings with thatch roofs and chimneys. The city gates are tall, wide arches with carvings of faces that represent Kata's Many. Vines crawl over everything, a radiant green maze made brighter by recent rain.

But these archaic trappings conceal cast cameras in every window frame, explosive triggers in the city walls, and guns in the turrets. A guard of warcrows periodically zips across the skyline, as if to ward of predators.

Beside her, Six flits her a glance, looks at her more seriously, and mutters, "You fool."

Knowing they're referring to her shaved head satisfies her in some petty way.

"All Terons mourn like this," she says. "It's a signal to Terotonteris that we want recompense, for our dead."

She uses that word with intent. In one of Chono's earliest conversations with Effegen ten Crost, the Star told her that Six had declared their desire for recompense from the Kindom. To that end Six was willing to change their entire person into someone else. Yet they begrudge her a haircut?

"Are you trying to antagonize them?" Six asks.

Chono leans forward on the railing. "You're one to talk."

"It is expedient for me to antagonize them. That is what they expect me to do. I thought we had agreed that when the blows came down, you would stand behind me."

"We never agreed to that. You . . . *commanded* it. But I'm not your novitiate."

Emotion rolls off Six like a heat signature. Anger? Agitation? Concern? As schoolkin, she sometimes thought she could feel their emotions as her own. There was a connection between them. They need only share a moment of eye contact, and she knew what they wanted. She had the same instincts with Esek, though those were more self-preservative than intimate. Of course, the connection to her mentor seemed very intimate, at times. All these months later, memories of

Esek continue to hit like arrows, bringing a throb of grief and shame and remembered loyalty.

"If you were my novitiate, I would box your ears," Six remarks.

That feeling of grief, and the knowledge that Six killed Esek, makes Chono antsy.

"If you tried, I would box yours back."

A snort of humorless laughter. Abruptly, Six activates Jun's scrambling tech, tossing the program over them both like a cloak. A clever little gift, it masks their voices from any recording devices within fifty feet of them.

"Can you reach Capamame?" Six asks.

Chono shakes her head. "My neural link is working, but I can't access anything beyond Praetima. They've put a leash on us."

Six grunts an acknowledgment. They had made an agreement with the Wheel to send back reports, but though Jun's comm program is invisible to the Kindom, it's also useless if their neural links can't reach beyond the city. What do the Jeveni think has happened? Does the wider Treble know that Chono and Six are free? If so, that at least will have reached the Wheel.

"I wish I had my bloodletter," Six says, almost absently. Esek's bloodletter, that is. Which Seti Moonback is probably holding like a trophy.

"I wish I had my chest of letters," Chono admits.

Six tenses. She last saw the chest of Six's letters (the letters they sent her over the years of the hunt between them and Esek), on *The Makala Aet*, just before she and Six boarded *The Risen Wave*. She has wondered, often, what happened to those letters, concealed in their box, protected by a self-destruct mechanism. They are just as deadly as a bloodletter, she thinks.

"What are you going to say tomorrow?" Six asks, not acknowledging her words.

She doesn't answer right away, looking east instead. Up on a hill within the city walls stands a wide nine-sided building of blue glass and stone. Narrow windows mark the facade, and the flat roof boasts a loggia, three great pillars that bend inward and connect at the center, like a crown. Nikapraev, the headquarters of the Prudent Ones. Tomorrow it will be full of secretaries, and full of newscasters, slavering for her statement.

"I'll say what I need to say to get the five thousand released."

Six stands like a pillar of ice. It remains disorienting to see Esek's restive body so still. Six asks, "What does that mean?"

"It means I'm going to demand their release."

"Chono," they growl.

Something growls in her, too. A deep, ferocious anger. A desire to make the Kindom suffer. How easy it would be, with all the systems watching her on cast, to do the opposite of what she promised the Secretaries she would do. To call for the freedom of the five thousand and condemn the Rule of Unification in one breath. It would force the Clever Hand to do as she says, or risk more uprisings. Certainly it would satisfy her, to say once and for all that she is no longer a creature of divided loyalties. Her path is clear.

Though, is that true?

"You cannot make public demands of the Kindom."

Dryly she says, "It's what Esek would do."

"Since when does the beloved Cleric Chono behave like Esek Nightfoot?"

Chono's nostrils flare, her anger redoubling, but she controls it, contains it, like a hot ball of energy squeezed into a cage inside her.

"Chono." Six's voice is a low entreaty. "You must play the game. You must think long-term. Making the Secretaries believe you are willing to work with them now will give us more options in the long run. You must trust me on this—"

"Trust you?" she repeats, and chuckles coldly. "How should I trust you?"

Six pauses for long seconds, clearly assessing the question. At last they say in a sharp-edged voice, "I did not know that it mattered, my work with Ilius. I did not know he would be important here, or that we would encounter him."

This, of course, is worse, because it means that Six would have kept the secret indefinitely. Who knows what else they should have told her, that will come out in some inconvenient way?

"Say your angry things, Chono. Get it out so we can focus on what matters."

The impatience in their voice makes her shoulders tighten. She forces herself to stay calm. "My anger means nothing to you. If it did, you would have told me that you had a secret alliance with my lover, regardless of whether we ever met him again."

Their eyebrows shoot up. "Lover? I thought he was no better than your bed warmer."

She recalls nine months ago, when she thought Six was Esek, and they said some cruel thing, and she punched them in the face.

"You want me to play the Kindom's long game. But where do you fit into that? What's *your* long game?" She flicks her eyes over them, lip curled. "I know you have one."

They hesitate, and she waits for the lie. "My game is protecting you."

She snorts, eyes on the city again. Does Six think sentimentality will fool her?

Abandoning that line, Six says, "I want the five thousand released, as you do."

Yes, she believes that. But she also knows it's not *all* they want. It can't be. "Any other secret alliances I should know about?"

"It would be impossible to tell you about every person I have worked with. And calling them alliances is...a misnomer."

"You said you worked with other secretaries to craft Esek's will. Where are they?"

"They were footnotes compared to Ilius. They are dead."

Six doesn't have to say who killed these secretaries. They don't have to say that they neither regret it nor think about it very much. Gods, how different are they, really, from Esek?

"I'm going to my room," she says. "I need to think over tomorrow's statement."

"Chono."

"I need to think."

"That is not what you need. If there is a gap between us, do not drive it wider."

"I didn't make the gap," she snaps.

"You cannot do this alone. You have influence in the Treble now, but that means you are more vulnerable. You cannot go out alone. We must work together."

Inside her, inside that flaming ball of barely contained anger, pettiness begins whittling at its cage. She wants to walk away, to reject their help purely in the hopes that it will hurt them. She recalls a time when she and Esek were on their way to Kator, following a lead on Six. Esek wanted to storm an inn where informants had suggested Six was staying. Chono had urged her that Six would see the attack coming a mile away.

Ah, Chono, Esek had purred, looking her over as if assessing an expensive racing horse. *Stoic, rational Chono. Aren't you afraid all this self-control will strangle you someday?*

But it was not self-control that motivated her. She knew that if they attacked the inn, innocent people would die. Protecting them was more important than catching Six. She was playing a long game.

The five thousand, the Jeveni, are her long game. To free them, she'll need all the help she can get, which at this moment seems limited to Six. She cannot let ego derail her. She must be the stoic, rational Chono. Even if it feels like being strangled.

"We should have guessed that Ilius would be here," she says quietly. "He's connected to both of us. He's the only secretary that I was ever friends with. He fed me information for years and apparently he thought he was working for Esek at the same time. Of course they brought him in. Once your will became public knowledge and he knew you were a traitor, he would have come forward and confessed his involvement. He's . . . honorable, in that way."

Six chuckles, clearly unconvinced of Ilius's honor. "I wonder if he expected to end up in the prison at Praetima. Instead, they promoted him."

"Yes. That is . . . strange."

"Not really." Six shrugs. "They did it as a gesture, to you. They want you to think they are installing honorable saan in positions of power. They are trying to woo you, so you will use your influence to quell the uprisings."

Chono had suspected this already, but hearing Six say it feels like a confirmation.

"It has backfired though, has it not?" Six continues. "Even if I did not already distrust the Secretaries, I would trust them less for such a bald manipulation."

Chono doesn't want to talk about it. She doesn't want to think of Ilius. "What should I say tomorrow, in your opinion?" she asks.

Six doesn't answer at once, but she senses their relief. Is her trust, her friendship, something they crave in the same way that she reluctantly craves it from them? Or are they merely pleased to be getting what they want?

What do they want?

Six says, "It is more than what you should say. It is what *we* should say, together."

Chono considers them skeptically. "What do you mean?"

A little smile curves their mouth, reminding Chono of Six's sly maneuverings when they were kinschool children. "I will tell you."

Esek would have enjoyed being the focus of attention in the Nikapraev meeting hall. Liking attention is an advantage Chono never enjoyed, and now here she is, seated at a table next to Six. They are in the Centrum, the central meeting room of Nikapraev. Secretaries fill the stadium seating, its rows over thirty deep, nearly as steep as a cliff face. There might be a thousand secretaries in the room, their blue suits and white tippets like the foam caps on a clear summer sea. But not so welcoming. Chono realizes that hundreds of them must have traveled in to witness the spectacle. Meanwhile, a corps of newscasters stands at the ready, already broadcasting. Little cast cameras circle Chono and Six like buzzing insects. How many millions of people are watching? Is Farren Eyce watching?

Chono puts it from her mind. She folds her hands in front of her and stares up at the dais not ten feet away, where the Secretarial Court are seated at a table of their own, their chairs high-backed as thrones while they confer. Ilius looks skinny and wan—far less confident than the regal secretaries to his right. Ostiver Ravening, the First Secretary, flicks Chono an appraising look, before murmuring something to the Major Advocate, Lalik Songrider.

"They look very grave, don't they?" says Six in Esek's mocking voice.

It's true that Ravening, a big-bellied man with white hair and fading Braemish tattoos, has the dour expression of a resentful schoolteacher. Songrider, younger than him but still graying, is delicate and birdlike; her eyes flit across the larger room like she is searching it for threats. As for Ilius, his finger bracelets jangle as he taps his fingers on the table, a nervous gesture he ought to know better than to let his kin see. She feels a pang of sympathy, wants to put her hand on top of his and warn him to stop it, but she squashes the thought.

Abruptly, Ravening picks up a round, fist-sized stone, knocking it several times on a square of stone beneath. It makes a clear, sharp sound, and the talk in the Centrum dies down.

"Let us convene." His voice is as sharp and resonant as the crack of the round stone. "Please commence the roll."

Every secretary in the room casts a hologram into the air above their heads, stating their ranks and names. The baubles of information zip toward the dais, gathering into a single blue glut of data above it. A formal record of the attendees. Ilius, seated beside Ravening, casts his own bauble, before looking at Chono with a tight expression, as if he wants to smile encouragingly but doesn't dare.

She watches the roll numbers accelerate. There are indeed *many* secretaries here today.

"Very good," Ravening says at last, all the numbers on record. He calls the session to order, speaking monotonous, ceremonial words about the prudence of the Clever Hand and the serious purpose of their office. He has gravity but no warmth, and he speaks of the Secretaries as if they are the narrow gap dividing peace from chaos. Only when he has finished his speech does he look down at Chono and Six.

No. He ignores Six. His attention is all for her.

Chono met him once, when she toured the Treble with Aver Paiye, but he barely noticed her then. She was nothing but a lowly cleric, an assistant to the far more important and powerful Paiye. Now, as he acknowledges her, his thin smile has a quality of disuse.

"Cleric Chono, welcome," he says, without any welcome in his voice. He looks at Six. "And welcome to you as well, Esek Nightfoot, Riin Matri of the Nightfoots."

Six pipes up at once, all luster and arrogance, "Don't forget: rightful executor of the sevite trade."

The newscaster cameras swoop in, flickering rapidly, and the secretaries make uneasy sounds. Ravening's lips compress, but there's a touch of cold humor in it, as if he expected this bad behavior and considers Esek a mere annoyance. Ilius looks pinched. Songrider, expressionless, writes something on a tablet in front of her. She lifts her eyes to Chono.

"Burning One," she says. "Welcome to Nikapraev. I believe you have been here before?"

The woman's voice is unexpectedly friendly, more natural than Ravening's smile, and she has a relaxed expression that Chono can only assume is intended for the cast cameras.

"Yes, I visited Nikapraev in 1662."

"In company with Aver Paiye, were you not?"

"...Yes."

The Major Advocate gives her a sympathetic smile. "From what I hear, you were quite beloved of Paiye. Isn't that true?"

This is not a tactic Chono expected. She inclines her head in a not-quite nod. "He was a good mentor to me. His crimes shocked me."

"No doubt you have shaved your head in acknowledgment of those crimes."

Chono pauses, impressed at Songrider's attempt to immediately point the purpose of Chono's gesture at something other than the Secretaries.

Chono says, "I mourn many things."

Voices churn the air like the eddies of a rising wind.

Songrider nods, grave. "Of course. We join you in that purpose. Though we Ma'kessn don't shave our heads in grief, I evoke my goddess on behalf of all those who have died. Praise to the goddess Makala, who comforts all children."

Throughout the Centrum, there comes the sound of other Ma'kessn echoing her blessing. When Ilius says, "Kata's Many protect them," he receives his own chorus of agreement.

Ravening offers no platitudes or prayers. Braems worship Som, the Blade's Edge, the Devourer. Death is the only comfort Som can confer. Ravening says, "In the wake of these tragedies, we should all be grateful to have removed corrupt Hands from power. Not only Aver Paiye, but the traitor Seti Moonback."

Dignified clapping fills the room. Six chuckles and answers the disapproving looks, "You're in for a treat with that one. She'll have all your heads if she can manage it."

The crowd turns on them, a susurration of displeasure.

"We have secured control of the Brutal Hand," Ravening says.

Six's grin shows their eyeteeth. "Can anyone control brutality?"

"The Cloaksaan are as loyal to the Kindom as any other branch," says Songrider. "This is why we were forced to remove Paiye and Moonback. When we elect a new First Cloak and a new First Cleric, they will be loyal, unselfish people. The self-interested actions of any Hand must be squashed. We can only trust a Hand who acts in the interests of the Treble."

Chono thinks that edict allows for quite a bit of subjective interpretation.

"It must comfort you, Chono," Songrider continues, "that Aver Paiye at least saw the error of his ways, repented before the Godfire, and resigned."

Chono senses a trap. "May the gods keep him well."

"Very good." Songrider smiles approvingly. "Very good. As everyone here knows," she addresses the whole room, and the Treble itself, "Sa Chono exercised great bravery a month ago by returning to the

Treble with evidence against the traitors in our midst. She nearly died in Seti Moonback's custody, and she has been very patient these past few weeks as we concealed her from her enemies and confirmed the details of the data flood."

Concealed her from her enemies. So that's how they'll play it. Chono's linked fingers whiten at the knuckles, and under the table Six presses their thigh against hers, a warning. She loosens her grip, keeping her expression flat.

Songrider says, "And now, with you as our witness, Cleric Chono, we wish to put it on record what we have done to redress the wrongs you uncovered."

With an indulgent smile, she turns to Ilius, bowing her head in a signal for him to take the reins. To his credit, he looks neither nervous nor out of his element as he begins to speak. But nor does he have Songrider's charisma, or Ravening's ponderous solemnity. Chono listens in silence as he gives a report on the recent actions and proclamations of the Secretaries. The rooting out of disloyal Hands. More dispensations for jump gate travel. Humanitarian relief for the most vulnerable quarters of the Treble. Harsh punishments for the guardsaan and cloaks who have overstepped their authority these past nine months. As he speaks, the Centrum radiates self-satisfaction.

Ilius says, "It is because of the Rule of Unification that we are able to take these steps. The things that Seti Moonback would not do to create peace, we are doing now. The humanitarian resources that the Righteous Hand has hoarded, we are releasing to the people. And now that the Kindom controls the sevite trade, we can decide with one voice how to meet everyone's energy needs. This will mean true peace, under the Kindom. And unity, in the Treble. By reinstating Cleric Chono, we mean to signal to everyone the kinds of clerics and Hands that we value. Only the worthy will rise to leadership, after this." He looks at Chono for a long moment. "We are sensitive to the distrust and uncertainty in the Treble. We know the Rule of Unification is unpopular with many, but Cleric Chono, you of all of us can attest that what we're doing under its banner will only make life better for everyone."

He has not mentioned the five thousand. Of course he hasn't. This meeting, this whole performance, is about ransom. She must make her payment first, swear her loyalty and bind her reputation to the actions of the Clever Hand. She opens her mouth as if to do it—

But Six asks, "And what about the five thousand?"

They speak with such bright, cheerful accusation that Chono has to control her smirk. Everyone is staring at Six, the emotion in the room swelling like a breaker. Remembering her performance, Chono throws Six a startled glance, as if she had no idea they would do this—as if it was her intention, all along, to play the Kindom's game.

She looks up at the three secretaries, saying quickly, "I can only assume the Clever Hand's determination to protect the Jeveni extends to the five thousand in labor camps. It seems to me that the wisdom of the Rule of Unification includes our determination to treat the Jeveni better than they have been treated historically. This would preclude imprisoning anyone. How could I reject the rule, when that is its goal?"

A gesture of support, they required of her. And now she has given it—with a price.

The crowds are rumbling again. The cast cameras seem in a panic of activity. Up on the dais, Ilius looks slightly green and Songrider's smile is frozen. Secretary Ravening, big as an ox and similarly dangerous, purses his lips.

"Yes, of course," he says. "Gods know the Jeveni have suffered too much. Especially when we consider their mistreatment in a prior age. As your data flood proved, Cleric Chono, the Nightfoots themselves sparked the Jeveni Genocide—though they blamed it on Lucos Alanye. Why, Alisiana Nightfoot was the engineer." His eyes move like the sights of rifles, targeting Six. "Given this, I wonder how you can claim authority over the sevite trade, Sa Nightfoot. It's obvious that your family doesn't deserve to wield it."

Six smiles. "Well, I intend to wield it rather differently than my predecessors."

"Yes," remarks Songrider with a slit-eyed smile. "I admit you confound us all, Riin Matri. Who would have thought that Esek Nightfoot would want to raise the Jeveni so high?"

Six gestures dramatically at Chono. "What can I say? Chono's righteousness moved me over our many years together." Their voice drops to a croon. "We all know how effective she can be at persuading people."

Songrider continues smiling. "Indeed." She looks at Chono. "We hope to avail ourselves of your persuasiveness again. Now that we have proved we are no threat to the Jeveni, surely you will be our ambassador, in opening up communication with Farren Eyce."

Chono's heart kicks. This . . . she didn't plan for. The glint in Songrider's eyes is of someone who has played a particularly good tile.

"The five thousand, who you champion so righteously, have told us that many, many people on Capamame wish to return to the Treble, but have been afraid. Their return would be invaluable to the struggling sevite trade. They will certainly listen to you, if you assure them that they are in no danger from us anymore."

Fuck.

Chono tries to look at ease. "I am humbled by the confidence of so many, but I think you overestimate my influence on Capamame. I don't even have a means to contact them."

"But I understand that they have access to our casting networks," she replies. "Which means they can watch these proceedings. Everything we have done to redress the crimes in the Treble has been a message of apology and friendship. Surely if you encouraged them to speak with *you*, they wouldn't refuse. You have done *everything* you can to protect and empower their people. Why not this?"

So. Either Chono uses this quorum to ask the Wheel to contact the Kindom, or the five thousand will not go free. Either Chono collaborates with the Kindom to open negotiations with Capamame, or all her goals are in danger. Her support for the Rule of Unification is not payment enough. She will have to pay again and again.

Her only consolation is that Effegen ten Crost is far too clever to be taken in by this.

"There is wisdom in what you say," she lies. "If the Wheel of the Jeveni are listening, I urge them to take your offer to heart, and to trust in my friendship."

Songrider nods graciously, but there is a cutlass in her smile. They both know it was too carefully worded a concession.

"Thank you, Burning One. This is an important step in reopening lines of communication, and in protecting the long-term serviceability of the trade—on which we all depend. You are a wise and righteous cleric. In fact, we hope that you will remain in Praetima, and minister at our temple, until the time comes to install a new First Cleric. The holiday of the New Sun is nearly upon us. It's an important time for the people to seek the guidance of clerics like yourself. Surely you will accommodate us?"

Chono bows low over her hands, mostly to give herself time to control her expression, and rises with a vague smile. Songrider takes it as acquiescence and turns to Six. "As for you, Sa Nightfoot. Your choice to become Riin Matri is a repudiation of your vows to the Clerisy. It is...unprecedented but not against our laws. I can only assume you will be returning to Verdant to serve your family's interests."

It's a clear invitation to pack their bags. But Six feigns unawareness. "I think I'll rely on your hospitality a little longer, in fact. I've never spent a New Sun in Praetima! And dear Chono." They give her a mockingly affectionate look. "She is quite dependent on me. I can't imagine us parting so soon after our return."

The Centrum swells with displeasure, and Ravening looks as though he would like to have Six dragged off in chains. Will he make such a scene?

No. He smiles his bad smile, saying, "Very well. Since you are determined to be Chono's companion, we can only assume that you are also in favor of opening up talks with Capamame."

Six raises amused eyebrows. "So eager to talk to the Jeveni. A year ago, you would barely acknowledge their union leaders."

"As today's conversation proved, we will do things differently from now on."

"Today's conversation proves you know how to make promises. Get back to me when the five thousand are freed."

Six may as well have fired a gun. Chono waits for return fire, but Ravening's expression doesn't change, doesn't give Six the satisfaction of a reaction. Instead, he sits back in his chair. "I consider our conversation today to have been a great success, and I won't hold the room any longer. Cleric Chono, I hope you are open to speaking in private with the newscasters. They have many questions, and it will give you an opportunity to further reassure the Treble's people."

Chono expected them to push her harder on supporting the Rule of Unification—especially after Six's last salvo. But the Secretarial Court seems eager to withdraw. It's as if the real point of this meeting was to lay out a series of subtle threats and outline more specific demands than Ilius made yesterday. Perhaps he failed to be as aggressive as his kin hoped? Perhaps he is conflicted about what they're doing?

She notices that two guardsaan are standing behind her table, no doubt to escort her to the newscasters. She recalls Seti Moonback's cloaks attacking them and nearly flinches. Under the table, Six's thigh presses into hers again, a hard band of muscle holding her in the present. The Centrum is full of movement and voices as the secretaries disperse, most of them still watching Chono with the narrow eyes of predator reptiles.

A message from Ilius pings at her neural link.

Be very cautious with the newscasters. I'll come to you when I can.

A year ago, such a message would have felt normal from him. Even reassuring, though she never needed his guidance or protection. Now, it sours her stomach.

She stands, allowing the guardsaan to lead her and Six toward a doorway behind the dais. Nikapraev's interior is a square spiral three loops deep, full of interconnecting offices and hallways that produce a mazelike experience. Their escort to the Centrum an hour ago was disorienting. So she is relieved when the door only takes them to an empty room. No newscasters, yet. The guardsaan take up sentry by the door. Chono and Six move as far away from them as can appear casual.

"This is strange," Chono murmurs. The last thing she expected was for the Secretaries to risk putting her in front of newscasters. It's clearly another test.

Six says, "They will be starving, these newscasters."

"And just as dangerous as the Secretaries," Chono agrees.

"They will ask you about your shaved head. Be careful."

"I know that."

Six mutters at her, "Fool."

So they're still annoyed about it? Gods, they're as sulky as Esek sometimes.

A door opens. Chono expects a crowd of newscasters, or maybe even Ravening, furious. Instead, a smiling Quietan woman with newscaster credentials walks into the room.

"Cleric Chono." She bows over her hands. "And Sa Nightfoot." Another bow. "Thank you for your willingness to speak to my newscasters."

Chono thinks it is hardly a matter of willingness, but she nods nonetheless.

"I'll let them in presently. I simply wanted a chance to reassure you that this will be a friendly and respectful conversation."

"Oh, I'm sure," Six says.

The newscaster smiles back as if they are all in on a joke together. Then she turns to the guardsaan, raising her eyebrows.

"You will both be leaving, I'm sure?"

"We have no orders to leave," says the one on the right.

"This is the headquarters of the law," the newscaster says. "And the law asserts that guards cannot intimidate newscasters."

"We're not intimidating—"

"If I must, I'll appeal to the First Secretary to have you removed. I don't think he's foolish enough to antagonize us right now."

Chono feels like she is in the middle of a sparring bout, all lunges and feints. The Quietan woman is serene but implacable. Brave, when dealing with unpredictable guardsaan. It's true that the law is on her side, and eventually the guards realize it, too. They march from the room, looking surly, and the door snicks shut behind them.

"There," the newscaster says. "Much more comfortable."

"You handled them so beautifully," Six approves.

"I have some experience," she answers.

"I'm sorry," Chono says, "I'd love to know your name."

"Yes, I'm sure you would. But I'm afraid there's no time for it at the moment." Her eyes land on Six with finality. "I have a message for you. From Yantikye the Honor."

CHAPTER ELEVEN

1664

YEAR OF THE CRUX

Farren Eyce
The Planet Capamame

The smell of electrical fires and extinguisher mist brings Masar right back to *The Risen Wave*, eight months ago. He and Liis and Jun were surrounded by cloaksaan, and Masar had shot apart the power grid on a massive light fixture, knowing the smoke and sparks would bring the extinguisher mist and provide them a heavy cover to retreat. Those smells, noxious, inextricably connected to the memory of Nikkelo's death, are enough to make him feel sick. But the addition of burnt flesh, and Dom ben Dane screaming in the hallway, makes his chest constrict.

On the floor of the apartment sitting room, the medics have stopped trying to revive Dom's wife, and one of them went to talk to him less than thirty seconds ago. The terrible howling sound drives shivers down Masar's spine, and everyone in the apartment has gone silent. Just a few minutes ago, the room was full of the murmuring of the medics and their rushed movements, and the sound of Kereth ben Dane trying to breathe, and Effegen kneeling next to her, her prayers like a spell meant to keep the woman in her body—

"Sajeven, beloved, come here to us and create a path for our hope. Dissolve our weariness and shine a light to live by, we entreat you, Sajeven, beloved, come here to us—"

The prayer for survival changed to the prayer of death halfway through, and now, still on her knees, Effegen stares fearlessly at the ruined woman. Kereth ben Dane is a blackened husk of burns and shrapnel gashes. Masar glances toward the kitchen, where the oven has half detached from the wall, listed sideways and scorched. Cracks shoot through the surrounding plaster. A piece of ceiling panel dangles. Everything is doused in the sticky film of the extinguisher mist. Masar can feel it in his hair and the creases of his skin, gumming up his nostrils and mouth. His prosthetic eye, always glitchy, is harder to blink than usual. He tries to rub it clear.

Again, his thoughts swim back to *The Risen Wave*. He had one purpose that day: protecting Jun. He was fierce with determination, and sick with grief, because Nikkelo was dead in the shuttle bay—a different kind of explosion. A single bullet. Blood and brain matter. The River of his heart, for whom he'd fought his whole adult life. Dead.

Out in the hallway, Dom's wailing becomes a miserable whimper, harder to hear, and as if it releases them from their stunned silence, one of the medics says angrily, "We should have given her another infusion."

The other medic says helplessly, "We gave her five. Her chest is caved in."

"We should have taken her to the hospital!"

"There wasn't time!"

"Shhh," soothes Effegen. "Shhh."

"My Star, by Sajeven's own mercy, I swear—there wasn't time to move—"

Effegen holds up a hand to quiet him, not accusing but gentling. She lays her hand over Kereth's forehead, a gesture of infinite tenderness, her *shhhing* as much for Kereth as the distressed medics. She unwraps a fine golden shawl from around her shoulders and spreads it over Kereth's face and upper body, covering the worst. There are no eyelids to close. Effegen's lips are moving. More prayers. But Masar can't hear any words. His vision clouds, and with a swallow he looks toward the pitiful sounds in the hallway.

Fonu sen Fhaan comes to stand beside him. The River has watched everything in stormy silence, but now they give Masar a look and nod toward the kitchen. The two of them move carefully through the main room, picking through rubble until they're in the open kitchen. Masar looks up at the ceiling panel, squeaking a little where it dangles. The debris and damage show a clear shock wave that originated from the oven. It doesn't take them long to find the twisted piece of metal, cylindrical but flattened on one side, pocked with holes and looking as if it was torn off of something. Masar squats down, examining the remnants of the pipe bomb.

"Whoever made it would have stolen from the construction vaults," Fonu observes. "Our records will show who has been in and out. It will help us narrow down a suspect."

Masar grimaces. Fonu, leader though they may have been among the Draeviin, has no experience with these kinds of things. He doesn't want to belittle the River, but he must point out, "Thousands of people have been in and out of those vaults."

Fonu bristles. "We have to start somewhere. This focus of yours on the...*avatar*...has proven nothing but the weakness of our chief caster."

Masar's teeth grind. Before he can respond, Effegen joins them, her face seamed with extinguisher mist.

"We'll do our best with the information we have," she says. She looks at the piece of pipe bomb, saying in a distant voice, "I haven't seen one of those in a while."

Masar has heard about Effegen's birthplace. A little isolationist village that the local Ma'kessn terrorized for years, before finally burning it down and driving out the Jeveni that lived there. Effegen's entire family died before she was twelve. She was lucky, because the previous Gale of the Wheel adopted her. Four years later, she became the Star.

She looks at Masar. "We're in your way. Tell us what to do."

There it is again, her unbending faith in him. So undeserved. Fonu is right, after all—he is no closer to finding the people responsible for these deaths than he was when they found Uskel's body more than three weeks ago. He stands. "All this debris will need to be examined. We'll want Jun to do an apartment-wide sweep."

"I don't want her making theories before we have a chance to analyze the materials ourselves," Fonu says.

For just a sliver of time, Masar thinks he sees irritation cross Effegen's face, but her voice is placid. "Let's not forget, please, that *ourselves* and Jun Ironway are the same. Excuse me. I'm receiving a comm from Gaeda."

She steps aside, but Fonu follows her. Masar turns toward Kereth's body again; the scarf is wet and red. The medics have set up a float stretcher and are arguing in soft, strained voices about how best to move her.

"Here," Masar says, stepping forward. "Let's all do it together."

He and the two medics take up position and carefully lift Kereth. She feels insubstantial, like the wrong move will cause her already broken body to crumble into pieces. Once she is situated on the stretcher, the medics cover her with a thick blanket to hide the bloody shawl.

"Wait to take her out," Masar tells them. "I want to talk to Dom first, and there's got to be a crowd out there."

The medics nod. Effegen calls to him, "Masar, come here."

She and Fonu are in the farthest corner of the studio. The door to the washroom is behind them, a miniature mask of Sajeven placed in the center. Masar feels nauseated by how normal and untouched it looks.

Hanging in the air are holograms of the three remaining Spokes of the Wheel, obviously seated together in the council room.

Gaeda asks, "What do we know?"

Hyre adds, "We didn't want to get in your way."

"It was murder, yes?" Gaeda again. "Not some accident?"

Effegen explains what they know so far, and at the mention of the pipe bomb, Gaeda's lips thin. She, too, has seen pipe bombs before. They all have.

Tomesk demands in his brash way, "How did someone plant a bomb in an apartment without anyone noticing? What does Sa Ironway have to say about this? Is she incapable of defending us at all anymore?"

Masar bristles. "I'm going to see her in the casting labs after this. If the casts caught anything, she'll know it. In the meantime, I have other collectors on their way who will help examine the scene. We'll see if we can find any evidence of who was here."

"Ironway won't find anything," Tomesk says, as if pointing out a character flaw.

"What could she find?" Gaeda answers reprovingly. "She's not a magician. Whoever did this knew that there would be no cameras in the residential hallways." She looks at Effegen. "You know my position on this. We need better surveillance."

She may as well have placed a new bomb in the center of their circle. Every one of them grows tense, and Effegen most of all. Her normally calm presence takes on a craggy edge, those hazel-green eyes hardening. "Forgive me, Gaeda, but installing surveillance throughout Farren Eyce is the last thing that will make our people feel safe."

"Their feelings are less important than their lives," retorts Gaeda peevishly. "I'll endure their discomfort if it means we can catch these murderers before they strike again."

Tomesk interjects, "The bombing is only our latest problem. First it was power fluctuations and the fire. Then Ironway nearly died. Twice. Now it is vandalization of shrines and temples and *more* trouble with our electrical grid. These things are *connected*."

Masar grimaces at this unnecessary reminder.

Tomesk continues, "No reasonable person will object to protective measures. Those who do object will be revealing themselves as—"

"As what?" snaps Effegen, and Masar has *never* heard her sound like that before, has never seen such pure, tight anger on her face. "As enemies? As targets for further investigation? Is that what you mean? Shall we start building prisons now? Create our own Cloaksaan?"

Tomesk's nostrils flare, his expression unapologetic. Hyre speaks up. "Masar...you're the investigator here. You understand these things better than we do. Will increased surveillance help us find whoever is responsible?"

Ever since he received the report of an explosion in Dom's apartment, Masar has felt untethered, sick. He should have done more to protect Dom. He should have anticipated this. And now, this moment feels worst of all, like he is about to fail not only Dom, but everyone. He takes a long time answering and avoids Effegen's eyes.

"More surveillance could help us spot another risk in time to stop it," he says. "But I...don't know that that will make us safer, as a whole."

"Explain yourself," says Gaeda.

"Our people have spent their lives being surveilled. They associate surveillance with death and domination. We promised them things would be different."

"This colony is nothing like the Treble," Tomesk says acidly. "We have served our people a banquet of freedom. What more could we possibly do to assure them that they're safe here? Besides, of course, actually making them safe, by protecting them from terrorists?!"

"With all due respect, my Tree...after what they have endured, there may never be any efforts sufficient to make every Jeveni feel safe."

"By that logic we should despair of peace at all," Fonu remarks, their first contribution to the conversation.

"Or else treat our people with kindness and understanding," Effegen says.

Tomesk accuses, "You are being naive."

The Star raises her eyebrows. "Naive?"

"You have thrown your support behind a rogue caster whose

supposed genius has nevertheless failed to root out this threat. You have allowed recalcitrant citizens to say whatever they like, even when it erodes confidence in the Wheel. You sent Cleric Chono and that... *Six* back to the Treble knowing they will be tortured for information about our colony. These acts strike me as powerfully naive."

Masar gapes at him. Hyre says in an uncertain voice, "Tomesk, that's unfair."

"Tomesk is careless with his words," Gaeda agrees, her look sharp and considering. "But...he has the same motives as any of us. He wants us to survive. As the Wheel, that is our number one responsibility. Even if the necessary action challenges our idealism."

This is another shot at Effegen. To her credit, the Star doesn't balk. She seems to gather herself into a posture of exquisite self-control.

"I see." She looks at Masar. "Be straightforward. Do you or do you not believe that we should establish surveillance throughout the colony?"

Masar fights back a snarl of frustration. He disdains Gaeda and Tomesk for their words. Resents Fonu for not defending Effegen. He knows what Effegen wants, and he wants to give it to her. But Nikkelo told him once, *No one needs a sycophant.*

"I believe that...increased surveillance, on a temporary basis, just until we can find who is responsible...may be our best option."

Effegen nods at once, curt, expressionless. "Very well. Fonu, present me a surveillance strategy first thing in the morning. We will vote on the measure together. And I will prepare a statement for our people. Excuse me."

She turns from them, walking out of the apartment. Masar, his muscles tight with frustration and anger, tells Fonu, "I'll report to you on Jun's ideas for surveillance."

Fonu says, "Come find me after. I doubt I'll sleep tonight."

Nodding, Masar leaves the apartment. Immediately he sees the crowd in the hall, and Dom at the front of it, leaning brokenly against someone from his family on Two. Effegen, short but regal, goes to him, taking his hands in hers. Dom collapses, his family and Effegen barely cushioning his fall. Effegen, though smaller than him, pulls him into her arms, and Dom weeps like a baby.

"I'll speak to Jun as well," Effegen says, half an hour later, when the crowds are dispersing and Dom has left, Kereth's body borne away on the float stretcher.

Masar nods, and they walk on, toward the courtyard. For a short woman, Effegen's stride is impressively long. Masar matches it easily, and neither of them says anything. But he feels antsy in the face of this silence. Effegen radiates distress, though her expression betrays nothing. After a while he says awkwardly, "I know you don't want surveillance. I don't want it, either. I wouldn't suggest it if I didn't think—"

"What I don't want is for the Spokes of the Wheel to bicker among themselves like we were no better than politicians," Effegen says. "I'm as guilty as anyone. I care too much about the others thinking I'm weak."

Masar hesitates. He's never seen any hint of this from her, but also—"Nobody thinks you're weak."

"Just naive, then."

"My Star—"

"Oh gods, will you just call me Effegen?" she snaps at him, composure fracturing. "At least when we're alone? I'm just a person, Masar. Do you know how rarely I hear my true name in this colony? Nikkelo always called me Effegen." The mention of their friend makes a tight ball of grief gather in Masar's throat, but he swallows it. He wants to say something comforting, but Effegen makes a furious sound. "We were all of a purpose before we left the Treble. Now there's factionalism, and the colony knows it. Even you, who love the Wheel—your true loyalty was to Nikkelo. If Fonu hasn't earned your trust, why should anyone else trust them?"

Masar wishes she was wrong, but he's well aware that his loyalty to Nikkelo turned out to be a loyalty to the man, rather than the office. He believes he *would* die for any member of the Wheel. But his life— only Effegen is worth his life. And that is a crime against his office.

They walk down in silence, and when they reach the courtyard, there are many people standing around, whispering in groups about the bombing. Their eyes and whispers follow Effegen. She has a soft, comforting smile for all of them, a way of conveying strength and grief at the same time, and many nod their heads in acknowledgment. Many don't.

In the elevator car she asks, "What can I possibly say to our people so that they will forgive me for putting them under surveillance again?"

"Tell them you love them. Tell them you would do anything to protect them."

Effegen half sighs, half laughs. "You think sentiment would move them that much?"

"They're used to people in power saying that they hate them. Everywhere we have ever gone, hate was all we could expect. You might be surprised at what your love can do."

She looks over at him, her brow furrowed in thought. "If only the colony believed in me as you do, Masar."

The car sinks toward Level 1. Masar says, "I'm not alone in believing in you. Nikkelo believed in you so much that he risked the lives of many collectors to stop the Kindom from learning your name. He knew that protecting you was essential for our future."

She makes an impatient sound. "I knew about that mission before it went ahead. I told him not to risk you all. He disobeyed my orders."

"And so would I," Masar says, "if it was the right thing to do."

She gives him a look. "Really?"

Masar stares straight ahead for fear of what she will see in his eyes. "I'll always tell you the truth. I'll always fight for our people. I'll be loyal to you till my last breath."

"But disobedient, if necessary?" she asks dryly.

"If necessary," he agrees.

The elevator arrives, and the courtyard on Level 1 is quiet, no gathered crowds, just a few small crews headed toward storage. Masar and Effegen walk toward the casting labs, and Effegen has gone quiet and pensive again. A surge of protectiveness comes over him, a desire to stand in front of her and block her from harm. She has never asked for that from him, nor asked it of Nikkelo, according to Nikkelo himself. But did Nikkelo fully appreciate her vulnerability? The softness in her, under the strength? Nikkelo spent his years as River wandering the systems with his collectors. The uninterrupted time that Masar has spent with Effegen these eight months—Nikkelo never had that with her. So perhaps Nikkelo didn't see that while she may have the bearing of a queen, she has the shoulders of a young woman. Should any person, young or old, carry so much?

"There should be a funeral dance," Effegen says quietly.

He considers it and nods. "That's a good idea. It'll bring the people together."

She asks with a smirk in her voice, "Will you dance?" His expression must be telling because she laughs, warm and beautiful, and the tension in her fades. "Someday, Masar, I'd like to see you dance."

He is thankfully spared the need to respond by their arrival at the labs. They step into a large, low-lit room, lines of casting desks turning the space into a grid. The casting hub itself, originating on *Drae's Hope* and reworked by Jun into a modern, meticulous instrument, stands at the center of the room, glowing. Masar sees Jun at once, standing before the hub like a god surveying its planet, her attention on the fluctuating colors and her hands weaving casts through the air. Luja is working the desk nearest to her, and keeps sending her little anxious glances, like she wants help but is afraid to interrupt.

Masar and Effegen walk down. When he reaches Luja's desk, he touches her arm gently. She still jumps, looking up at him with startled eyes. Her smile comes at last, timid.

"All right, kid?" Masar asks. "I didn't know you were on shift."

"Couldn't sleep," she admits, glancing awkwardly at Effegen. Effegen smiles, and Luja, as if remembering herself, bows over her hands. "It's an honor to see you, my Star."

"None of that," says Effegen. "It's mortifying when young people treat me like an inaccessible crone."

Luja smiles again, still timidly.

"Stop interrupting my casters," Jun says, coming alongside them with a look of grumpy humor. She winks at Luja, who gets back to work. Jun faces Effegen. "You're filthy, my Star. You should wash."

Masar grumbles in annoyance. Damn woman doesn't have an ounce of tact. Effegen smirks. "Funny you should be so concerned about my hygiene. Bene says you haven't been home in two days and I should be wary of the stench."

Jun smiles wryly. She does look worse for wear, clothes wrinkled, one of Liis's knit caps pulled down over her ears. Masar snags on the realization that Effegen and Bene have been casting each other over the past few minutes. It makes him feel a strange combination of joy that she has Bene's support—and envy to think of them sharing such casual intimacy. He hasn't seen Bene since he and Jun visited the caster pirates over a week ago.

Jun addresses him and Effegen. "Come with me."

They follow her to the small office in the far corner of the lab. Inside, there's an oversized armchair with a blanket on it, rumpled like Jun may have recently napped there. He should make her go home after this. Though of course there's no time. He's in as much need of a shower as she is. Who can shower when Farren Eyce seems to be falling apart?

Now that they're alone, Effegen asks, "Have you learned anything?"

Jun tosses a number of views into the air, pointing things out as she speaks.

"There's a camera in the courtyard on Level 3. I've run a cast to see if I can find anyone going down the hall to Dom's place who doesn't live in the housing block. Now it's a matter of cross-checking why nonresidents would be there—friends, family, service workers. As you know, there are no cameras in the hallways."

"The Wheel is considering expanding surveillance," Effegen says woodenly.

Jun seems to check out, as if reviewing something on her ocular, before she snaps back. "I can understand that...But I think it might be a dead end."

"Why?" Effegen asks.

Masar narrows his eyes. "What have you found?"

Jun hesitates, looking cagey. "Well...first let me remind you that I'm an anarchic con artist who doesn't play by the rules..."

"Jun," Masar warns.

"I hacked Dom's casting array. I didn't want to wait to ask him, given what he's going through, and he's got cameras in his apartment that I wanted to access." Masar and Effegen give her disapproving looks, and she shrugs. "We can debate the ethics another time."

She draws one of the views into prominence—it shows Dom and Kereth's apartment, including the half-collapsed kitchen. Jun homes in on the oven. "The bomb was in there, as you know. Kereth got home late from work and started making herself some food. She triggered the explosion when she opened the oven door."

Her voice goes a little hoarse as she says it, and Masar realizes that she watched the footage—watched Kereth blown apart by the pipe bomb. Memories of Dom's screaming rattle through him like an icy breeze. Dom wasn't home when it happened. He'll never forgive himself for this.

"Does it show who planted the bomb?" Effegen asks.

"Dom opened the oven door two days ago. No explosion. And he would have seen a pipe bomb of this size. That means whoever planted the bomb did it in the past forty-eight hours. Problem is, whoever did that...I can't see."

A pause, and Masar's adrenaline spikes. He looks at her sharply. "A Hood program?"

Chono and Six both have the Hood sequestered in their neural links. If the Kindom has them prisoner, couldn't it hack the program out of their heads?

To his relief, Jun snorts. "That *would* be impressive. But no. It's less subtle than that."

She tosses a graphic into the air, a timeline outlining the hours between when Dom opened the oven door and when Kereth did. Jun explains, "In those forty-eight hours, there were three power fluctuations in Dom's apartment. One lasted two minutes. One lasted fifty seconds, and one lasted a minute and a half. During those fluctuations, the cameras in Dom's apartment go dark. For someone who moved fast and knew what they were doing, any of those gaps would have been long enough to enter the apartment and plant a bomb."

Masar's thoughts race with the implications. It's Effegen who gives voice to his dread. "Are you saying that these power fluctuations in Farren Eyce are actually being used to conceal the movements of the avatar and its agents?"

Jun, staring at the timeline, rubs the back of her neck. "It seems... very possible."

"But most of the power fluctuations last less than ten seconds," Effegen says. "That's no time to accomplish anything. What does it mean?"

"That the avatar is cunning," Jun says. "It smatters the colony with innocuous fluctuations so that it only appears to be a result of the strain on the power grid. The longer fluctuations are localized to places we're not paying attention to. Dom's apartment, for example. And I've found two dozen more of these longer outages, all over the colony, but nowhere that seems to be important. A bar on Level 3. The construction zone in the Market District. The elevators, once. I'm sorry, Effegen. This avatar... It's been attacking us almost since we arrived."

"To do what?" Effegen presses. "Plant more pipe bombs?"

Jun admits, "I don't know."

Even as she says it, her eyes turn distant, either casting or thinking. For a few moments no one speaks, but she doesn't come back, seems only to slip deeper into her thoughts.

"What?" Masar asks.

She shakes her head, far away. "Liis would've seen it." She's not looking at either of them, talking more to herself than to them. "Whenever I can't get a grip on what's happening, whenever I can't see it clearly, I ask Liis. She... she can always see it."

There's such longing in her voice, but also shame—and it recharges the shame in Masar. He can't see it, either. Something is happening, and he can't see it.

Effegen, her voice very gentle, says, "Jun . . . you've seen it now."

Jun blinks and looks at her. Rather than dwell on what she said, Effegen asks, "Can I assume that the reason surveillance may not work is because the avatar can continue to shut off our cameras with these power fluctuations?"

Jun nods, fully returning to the room. "That's my fear, yes."

"Now that we know what's happening, can we fight it?" Masar asks.

Exhaling, Jun says, "I've got my casters combing through the longer power fluctuations. I'm hoping they'll find a pattern that we can use to identify how the avatar is doing this. If we can find the method, we can build a means to stop them."

Masar knows her well enough to detect the doubt in her expression, the frustration and vulnerability. He thinks of her when she came back from the caster pirate den, ear and neck covered in blood, eye red and swollen from the avatar's attack on her tech, and looking so furious he thought she might blow up a nearby casting hub just to exorcise her helplessness.

Effegen says, "Our best hope is to discover the identity of the avatar. To figure out what it wants. Has it made any more direct communication with you?"

Jun scowls. "No. The little shit has been quiet since we went to Level 2."

Effegen looks pensive. "And you still don't think it's Aris the Beauty?"

Jun shakes her head. "No. Aris is loud and cocky in the real world. The avatar is loud and cocky in the casting net—but it's also a guerrilla fighter. It . . . hides in the trees. It wouldn't expose itself the way Aris has. Not publicly."

"But perhaps she works for it?" Effegen presses.

"The moment I have proof of that, you'll know."

Effegen nods, taking this with equanimity. "I've been thinking about your loud and cocky avatar. There's something childish in how it addresses you, isn't there? Can you think of anyone who has this level of contempt for you?"

Jun flinches. "Yeah. Tej. Maybe even Luja, for all I know. But neither of them has the casting skill to do this."

She restlessly crosses her arms. She looks somehow thinner like that, as if holding her own body reveals how little body there is. Masar wishes Liis were here, too.

"This isn't just about Jun," he reminds them. "Jun has no personal connection to the collectors or Kereth. The farm attacks and the fire and even these shrines that keep getting vandalized—none of that targets Jun specifically, or proves it's targeting her alone."

"It's after the colony," Jun says. "It's obviously after the colony."

"But this *pettiness*," Effegen says, clearly grappling with something. "The first time I met Six, I asked them about their relationship with Esek Nightfoot. All the years they spent gathering information against her and harassing her with what they knew. They admitted that half the purpose was just to fuck with her." Jun snorts. Effegen smiles wryly. "The things happening in Farren Eyce, they have that same tenor. It's not just a desire to sabotage us. It's a desire to fuck with you, Jun. To fuck with the colony. Maybe even to fuck with Six."

"Six?" Masar says, surprised. "There's no proof of that."

"But now that we know someone has been communicating with the Treble, we can certainly assume that they know Six's true identity. It's common knowledge in Farren Eyce, and anyone *here* working with someone *there* would have told them the truth. This may only be a hunch, but the way the avatar is acting... It's almost as if it's taking a page out of Six's book."

"Are we overcomplicating this?" Masar asks. "Whoever is trying to sabotage us *must* be the Kindom."

"The avatar was insulted when I suggested it worked for the Kindom," Jun replies.

"Deflection."

"No." She shakes her head. "It's smart but it's also emotional. I'm sure it's lying about some things, but not this."

They fall silent, pondering, and Masar feels useless to offer solutions. Gods, what good is he, if he has no solutions?

Effegen exhales. She looks around at them. "So we are back to the original question. Who, if not the Kindom, would have a vendetta against us?"

By this clause, and by the blessing and authority of Makala, fecund and lovely, I confer all my tangible property, all my financial holdings, and my majority share in the sevite trade, upon my chosen heir, Esek Nightfoot. She shall henceforth take my title and, as matriarch of the Nightfoot family, direct its financial, military, and political maneuverings, until such time as her death, and the transfer of all to her beneficiary. May none who love our goddess stand against her. May all people respect the destiny that Makala has birthed.

If Esek Nightfoot should be dead upon this reading, then my possessions and power fall to my great-granddaughter, Riiniana Nightfoot, to be assumed immediately, regardless of age.

excerpt, the Last Will and Testament of Alisiana Nightfoot, Clause II. Dated 1663, Year of the Trick.

CHAPTER TWELVE

1663

YEAR OF THE TRICK

Verdant
Sevres Continent
The Planet Ma'kess

Watching her through the crack of the bedroom door was a fascinating experience. Alisiana so rarely handled official business in her private rooms. She was a woman of strange boundaries and careful systems, and while she never let her guard down, there was something slightly more human in the way she presented herself in the underground apartment of the Verdant tower. Tonight, for example, she was *almost* smirking, something she never did in formal engagements. She stood in the foyer outside her bedroom. A man and a child stood before her. All their profiles were visible—a case study in Nightfoot architecture. The sharp jawlines and sculpted noses, the warm golden skin. Alisiana was just a few months shy of one hundred, and she carried that age with a striking dignity, her back still straight, her posture imperious.

The man was Torek Nightfoot. His grandfather, Sorek, had been Alisiana's right hand for years. Alisiana had trusted Sorek, though she had not loved him. The only Nightfoot Alisiana had ever loved was her uncle Caskori, long dead, and her lack of love for her relatives was a dose of poison in the family line. Even the trust she had for Sorek had not transferred to another after his death. Certainly not to his grandson, Torek, who managed the sevite contracts that kept the pipeline between Nightfoot factories and jump gates intact.

He was very rich, Torek Nightfoot. Very handsome. But he looked at the moment like he was smelling something foul, his nostrils twitching. This seemed to be the primary source of Alisiana's amusement. But then she ignored him completely and looked at the child.

"Well," she said, brisk. "You've gotten taller."

"Thank you, Riin Matri," said Riiniana Nightfoot, her fine chin tilted up, her expression solemn. She was just thirteen. "Are you feeling well?"

Alisiana snorted. "Why? Do I look very bad?"

The girl's eyes widened. "No, Riin Matri, of course not, I—"

"Hush. To children the old always look like crypt keepers. Can you believe I was younger than you once? Though, never so sickly."

It was true. Riiniana's childhood had been one respiratory disease after another. She was remarkably thin, as small as Alisiana but without the gravitas of age. Her skin, albeit gold, was paler than Torek's or the matriarch's, and rather than the bright electric-blue eye mods of some of her kin, she had adopted light blue mods, which made her seem wraithlike and peculiar.

Before Riiniana could answer the accusation about her sickliness, Alisiana said, "So. Your uncle's brought you all this way. Why?"

Torek was not the girl's uncle. Riiniana's mother was dead—a suicide; Riiniana's grandmother was a mods addict. And her great-grandmother, Alisiana, was not one to raise a child. So Torek had become her guardian when she was only seven, raising her to one day be the Nightfoot matriarch.

Torek said, "You haven't seen your heir in two years, Riin Matri."

Alisiana gave him a reptilian smile. "I rarely have time for family reunions. My work ethic, as you well know, is what keeps us all so comfortable."

He nodded. "Of course. No one can dispute what you've done for our family, nor the power of your leadership. But someday, Riiniana will take your place. It's time for her to learn beside you."

"*My* mother didn't train me," Alisiana said.

"You had nothing to learn from Ti Nightfoot," Torek replied, carelessly stating what most people tended to keep to themselves about Alisiana's mother. "Riiniana has much to learn from you. Lessons none of my tutors can offer her. Your experience and knowledge are invaluable, and will further cement our strength as a family."

Alisiana looked at him drolly and turned back to Riiniana, assessing her. She sighed. "Well, I suppose being tiny doesn't preclude greatness. Tell me, girl—do you really want to leave your seaside home for a life in this damnable estate? Not nearly as pretty, I promise you."

Riiniana said, "I hear that from the top of the tower, you can see all of Sevres."

"That's absurd." Alisiana looked at Torek again. "Have you made her into a romantic? Do your tutors teach her poetry?"

"They teach me everything."

The girl's voice, her challenge, drew Alisiana's and Torek's eyes sharply to her, both of them surprised at her daring. Riiniana held herself with a poise that had not registered at first. Her voice lacked authority, but her posture and her gaze were proud.

"I'm a very good student, Riin Matri. I've already learned from your example."

Alisiana looked intrigued. "Have you?"

"I have. I've learned to see what isn't being said. I've learned to interpret silences."

"More poetry," said Alisiana.

"I know you're thinking of making Esek your heir."

Torek lost some color; it was obvious he hadn't intended them to lay this card on the table. Alisiana narrowed her eyes, lips pursed. Riiniana kept her chin up, and despite her age and sickly demeanor, there was a shadow of the imperiousness in it that defined Alisiana and Esek.

"I've heard the same reports as you," Riiniana continued. "They say that Jeveni union leaders want Esek to take over after you die. They say you'll have to capitulate, to protect the trade. But Esek is selfish. She doesn't care about our family. I know my mother and grandmother disappointed you, Riin Matri, but I'm not them. If you give me a chance, I'll prove it."

Alisiana raised her eyebrows. "You're certainly bolder than I remember," she said. Riiniana swallowed. "Whoever takes over for me will have to face the skepticism of the people and the bad intentions of our enemies. Never mind what the Jeveni union leaders want. Why should I raise up a kitten, when I have a lion at my disposal?"

Torek sneered. "Esek is violent and unpredictable! All she cares about are her own adventures."

"Esek is strong and ruthless," Alisiana retorted coolly, still looking at the girl. "In my experience, those qualities go a lot further in the Treble than politesse and passivity."

"Esek has no vision for our family," Riiniana said.

The figure watching them smirked.

"Oh, no?" Alisiana asked. "Then tell me, child—what is *your* vision?"

Riiniana paused, considering her response, and said, "I want to make our family the most powerful organization in the Treble. I want us to rule all the other Families."

Silence fell for five, six seconds? Torek looked shocked, even horrified. Alisiana was amazed, and then, she laughed—sharp and genuine.

"By the gods. That *is* ambitious! Completely unrealistic and utterly shortsighted, but I commend you for your—"

"It's not shortsighted."

Torek made a soft squawking sound at the girl's interruption.

"Is it not?" Alisiana asked.

"It's simply a matter of getting the right members of the Families to follow us."

"And why, my darling visionary, would any important member of any First Family bow to the Nightfoots, whom they hate?"

"Because if the First Families were united, we could supplant the Kindom."

Interesting . . . very interesting.

Alisiana hesitated. Her expression did not indicate that the words moved her—but nor did it suggest that she was dismissing them out of hand.

"All right," she said at last. "And suppose I turn everything I've built over to you so you can pursue this ridiculous scheme. Esek expects to inherit. What will you do about her?"

Riiniana paused. "I . . . I would appeal to the Clerisy to control her."

"Wrong. You would have her killed. That is the only solution with any chance of success. You have some spirit, girl, I'll grant you that— but if you haven't got the brutality in you to kill Esek, you certainly haven't got the strength to unite the Families against the Hands."

Riiniana said nothing. But it did not seem that she had nothing to say. Alisiana waited her out for some time, got nothing from her, and snorted derisively.

"Fine. If this has been your bid for the matriarchy, I suppose you could have done worse. But I'm hardly about to make a decision here and now. And I'm not interested in hosting people who are so eager for my death to usher them into power. Don't forget, little Sa, that I disfigured my own daughter to punish her presumption." Riiniana said nothing. She must be thinking of her grandmother's face, with its jagged trench of a scar. "Go back to Praediis, child. Read poetry on the cliffs. If I want you, I'll call for you."

Instantly Torek put his hand on Riiniana's elbow. It was clear he thought he'd lost something, some leverage, and he was furious.

Would he punish the girl, who even now stared her great-grandmother in the face and didn't flinch? Yes, she was young, and she had grown up sickly and her mother had been a weakling, but she must have known that in this moment she had to show every bit of strength in her. And she did. But Torek drew her away.

A full minute passed, Alisiana standing in the foyer with a calculating look on her face. Then she breathed out a little sound and strode toward her bedroom, flinging the doors open.

When she saw who was waiting for her, she jerked in shock. Her face flushed red and her eyes turned to slits.

"Esek! Damn you!"

"Good evening, Auntie."

"What in the name of the Godfire are you doing here?! Who let you into my room?"

"I let myself in." A rakish smile. "Aren't you glad to see me?"

"I should call the cloaksaan to drag you out of here!"

"Yes, I saw that they're still following you around. Clearly the Kindom is determined to protect you. They won't bother us tonight."

At that, Alisiana's furious expression shifted. What must she be thinking? What must she be imagining? She made an irritated noise. "Come and sit down."

They went together to a little table in the corner of her room, sitting across from each other. A servant had left tea things for her. Alisiana poured two cups. "I suppose you overheard that conversation with Torek."

"From where I was standing, the real conversation was with Riiniana. What an ambitious little demon she's turning out to be. I guess sometimes greatness skips a few generations."

Alisiana made a dismissive gesture. "Irrational ideas of Treble domination are no sign of greatness. If anything, she's got a little bit of courage in her. And better spies than I thought. She knows about these rumors of your supporters among the Jeveni. I wonder, does she know you planted those rumors yourself?"

A slow smile, pleased and impressed that Alisiana had figured this out. "Well . . . I am notoriously industrious. And so few people actually ask the Jeveni if rumors about them are true. It seemed a shame to not seed the ground. And people seem more than prepared to believe the Jeveni want me for their matriarch."

Alisiana scoffed.

"Not that I need the support of the Jeveni. Riiniana's play for power notwithstanding, we both know the ink is already dry on your will . . . Isn't it?"

Alisiana took her time answering. She sipped the tea and tilted her chin up. "You're not to kill Riiniana. Do you understand me, Esek? Leave her be."

A laugh. "But you told *her* to kill *me*!"

"I mean it. Touch her and I'll have that cleric you love killed."

"What cleric?"

"That wretched mountain of a woman that used to be your novitiate. I know for a fact she's on very unsteady ground, these days. I should have known that you were no good for training clerics. You do it once and what happens? You churn out a murderer of Hands. Well, I could have her assassinated very easily; the Kindom would even thank me for it."

"I assure you, I have no plans to kill Riiniana Nightfoot."

"Good."

"My plan has always been to kill you."

They held Alisiana's eyes, quiet and unblinking, and by degrees they saw emotions cycle across her face. Distaste that became uncertainty. Uncertainty that became disbelief. Disbelief edging toward fear—and with a flick, contempt.

"You can't frighten me, Esek."

"I am not trying to frighten you, Sa Nightfoot."

Alisiana's brow wrinkled. She didn't believe it. She was trying to identify the real game.

"You need more than my signature on the will. You always have. Kill me now and you'll inherit chaos. You may like danger, Esek, but you're not so much a fool that you want to see the Nightfoots crush one another over infighting."

"On the contrary," murmured Six. "That is exactly what I want."

And it was exactly what they would have. For there was another freshly minted will. Dear, reluctant, effective Ilius, aided by a small consortium of peers, had bowed to the pressure of Six's games and finalized all the documents that would eventually turn the sevite trade over to the Jeveni. He had also planted the rumors that the Jeveni wanted Esek for their matriarch. He had done this out of a belief that it was a Nightfoot long game, that these maneuverings would fundamentally solidify Nightfoot popularity and power over their labor force. Which was what the Kindom needed, wasn't it? That Six had managed to deceive him so well was perhaps their greatest accomplishment—so far. Even Yantikye was impressed.

Alisiana was incredulous. Then shocked. Her eyes flicked toward the door. Six smiled.

"Your cloaksaan are guarding the exterior of the building, just as you have ordered them to do. They do not know I am here, and there is a cast loop assuring them that you have gone to bed. Torek and the girl are headed for the airfield. Your servants have retired for the evening. It's just you and me, Riin Matri."

Alisiana's face was caught in concentration—she was obviously sending out a cast of her own. But when she tried to ask for help, she hit a wall. It was not until that wall, that blockage between her neural link and the comm system, that she truly believed what was happening.

"Esek, you cannot be serious about—"

"I am not Esek."

It was the first time they had said it, and the reveal felt decadent. Alisiana seemed baffled. Six reached into their pocket, politely ignoring the matriarch's tiny gasp, and withdrew a palm-sized piece of laminate with an image printed on it. They laid it down on the table between them. Alisiana dropped her eyes, taking it in.

It wasn't a crisp image. Mostly shadow. But it did show more of Six's face than any other cast program had managed to capture in the ten years since Soye's Reach. Six knew that Esek hoarded this image, this indistinct glimpse at their quarry, which she had shared with the matriarch early on in the game. Alisiana's expression gradually shifted. Recognition crept into her eyes, which flew up to Six again.

"By the gods," she said. "Are you that little *flea* Esek has been hunting?" Six smiled. Yes, they were a flea. A nearly invisible, bloodsucking passenger on the underbelly of the Black. "What have you done to yourself?" Alisiana asked. She looked more fascinated than terrified. She dragged her eyes all over Six's face and body, no doubt searching for the flaw. When she looked into their eyes again, she flinched. Six wondered if it was the similarity that made her flinch, or if she saw something in their eyes that was distinctly un-Esek, and terrible.

Suddenly, Alisiana grew calm. It was a remarkable transformation. Her fascination went away. The spark of panic in her eyes went away. Even her body, though it remained as straight as before, seemed to relax a little bit. It was hard to interpret her expression, but if Six hadn't known any better, they would have taken it for relief.

"Is Esek dead?" she asked.

Six crossed one leg over the other, hands clasped on their knee, and said, "Not yet."

Alisiana chuckled. "Then you're a fool. There can't be two of you in these worlds."

"There won't be. Not for much longer."

"So your plan is to become the matriarch of my family? Destroy us from the inside?"

She seemed remarkably unconcerned.

"I gain nothing from telling you my plans, Riin Matri."

"Not even the satisfaction of bragging?" she asked, and must have seen something telling in their face, for she chuckled again. It put Six in mind of Esek. Just as Esek would have done, Alisiana goaded them. "Don't be coy. You're clearly as much a showboat as my niece. What did becoming her require? Five, ten years of your life? Gods, the *pain* you must have endured. And now you come here to play assassin, and you could have just let me think my protégé was murdering me. You could have even killed me while my back was turned, and spared any conversation at all. But no. You tell me you are Esek's little nemesis.

You let me see the wonders that you've done." A tsk. "You wouldn't give away so much if you weren't *dying* to give away all of it. The dead make such good listeners."

Six felt her accusation in their core, a precise arrow. They had expected her to be more afraid. But these Nightfoots were like malicious wolves. Of course they would face death this way.

Alisiana finished the cup of tea, nodding brusquely at the cup in front of Six. "Are you such an uncivilized boor that you won't even take tea with me?"

They uncrossed their legs and placed their hands on the tabletop, framing the cup.

"The tea is poisoned," they explained.

Alisiana's expression faltered. Her hand that was holding the cup trembled once, hard, and she set it down. She sniffed, and the flash of terror in her eyes resolved. Perhaps, up until this moment, she thought she would survive. A lifetime of failed assassinations would give a person that sort of certainty.

"How long will it take?"

"Another half hour at most. I will stay with you."

She blurted a laugh. "How honorable."

"It is also painless. You will fall asleep."

"Fuck that," Alisiana said.

She stood up. Six thought she was going to run for the door, but she didn't. She went to her bedstand and yanked it open. She reached inside, and stopped. She began pushing things around, brow furrowing. She slammed the drawer and whirled on them.

"Damn you."

"I have removed all your weapons from the room. I will replace them before I leave."

"Give me the knife back."

"Why?"

"*Why?* Why do you think?!"

They looked at her, contemplating. There was no way she thought she could defeat them with a knife, so the only explanation—

Their eyebrows rose.

"You want to kill yourself."

"I'd rather do it that way than wait to fall asleep. I'd rather go under my own power than nod off like a doddering old fool."

"I am sorry," Six said. "The poison is undetectable. I need this to look like natural causes. No one would believe that you killed yourself."

Fury flashed in her eyes. And then, true fear.

"I don't want to fall asleep," she hissed. "I want to go out on my feet. I want to go out screaming. I always have." Six said nothing, though this resonated in a deep, burning way. She narrowed her eyes. "What's this really about? You'd do all of this just for revenge on Esek?"

Six pressed their lips together, exhaling through their nose. It was almost a laugh, though they saw no humor in this.

"My motivations are slightly more complicated than that."

"Oh, you're a *complicated* assassin. How original. Indulge me."

"Jeve," they said.

She paused. She was still standing next to her nightstand, her body rigid. Suddenly her shoulders dropped. A grim smile spread across her face.

"Jeve," she muttered, and shook her head. "That damned moon. If you knew how many times I've wished that Caskori never bought that fucking sphere of jevite." She huffed a laugh and looked at them. "Well, what is it? Trying to make up for the crimes of your ancestor? Lucos Alanye was a fool, you know, and a tool of his betters, but he wasn't innocent. I suppose you're trying to make amends for what he did."

This had actually never occurred to Six, who felt nothing toward Lucos Alanye beyond vague contempt. All their sense of familial connection was installed in Drae sen Briit, Alanye's lover, the woman who had helped her people escape to Capamame. *She* was the ancestor to whom Six felt a pull. She was the one who got her children off Jeve, who risked her life and ultimately lost it to protect them. And what had become of those children? Lost to the machinations of empire.

Murdered by Esek. And in Six's case, transformed by bloody purpose. What grief Drae would feel, to know what had become of her line.

Six asked, "Have *you* ever tried to make amends for what you did?"

"What I did was stop a Treble-wide war!" she said waspishly. "We traded two million cave-dwelling vermin to save a hundred million Treblens. Genocide may have not been our aim, but it was a happy consequence. And I scraped the survivors up off the floor and gave them the only work they're good for. They were born on their knees. Where else should they be? I only wish your fucking ancestors had never made it off the moon!"

It was very transparent, these insults. She must be hoping that Six would lose their temper, put her down in the violent way she wanted. Six remained in their seat. Seeing her ploy fail, Alisiana deflated. She put her hand on the bedpost, steadying herself. Six saw it come, a flicker of exhaustion, and a flash of panic as she realized what was happening. As if to fight against it, she only held herself straighter. Her fingernails picked nervously at the bedpost.

"It takes a certain person to enjoy the annihilation of two million people," she mused. "Perhaps I underestimated what that would really mean . . ." She looked at them with fierce, hateful eyes. "It was my idea, you know. I told the Kindom their best recourse was to destroy the moon. I didn't think they would do it. I . . . never *wanted* it to happen." Six only looked at her, intrigued by her sincerity, which did not end there. "I should never have suggested it. Two million people . . . That's a high body count, even for me."

Six murmured, "Perhaps they will have their revenge."

That made Alisiana snort, a slightly drunken sound. "Who'd have thought my first assassin would end up being the one that got me?" Six didn't understand at first, but she explained, "Some pitiful Jeveni acrobat. He tried to kill me, and because he did, Alanye tortured him and he told us about the jevite. I was young. When I became matriarch, I knew I needed to establish myself in some extraordinary way. So I decided to go after the jevite. And now, all these years later, that's what's killing me." She laughed again, bitter, and wiped a hand across her eyes. She swayed a little and gritted her teeth. Her other hand was still twisting at the post of the bed. "I killed Caskori, did you know that?" she demanded—and yes, Six did know. Not even Esek knew it, but Six did. "One of his lovers was a Kindom spy. They stole all the proof I had of their involvement in the genocide, and retained all the proof of *my* involvement. They trapped me, used it to make me more compliant. It wasn't the first time Caskori's actions threatened me, but it was the last. He was the only person I ever loved, and I had him killed. I wept for days. I had to hide from everyone so they wouldn't know. I thought I would weep forever. Do you want to punish your enemies, little look-alike? Make them kill the ones they love."

Six thought of Chono. They said, "Safer not to love at all."

Alisiana's lips ticked upward. Her hand wrenched down against the bedpost. There must have been a gouge in the wood, because she had torn herself off a shard four inches long.

Six sprang at her. She tried to drive the spike of wood toward her throat, but they were too fast. They caught both her wrists. She screamed and struggled and they worried about bruising on her wrists. Only they didn't have to grip her hard at all. They flung the piece of wood away and turned her in their arms, crossing her arms over her chest and pinning them there. They towered over her and bent to her as she struggled.

"Enough, Riin Matri, enough. I will make sure you die on your feet."

"Damn you," she snarled. She fought a little more and then sagged against them, panting. By now it would be difficult to keep her eyes open. Six could no longer see her face, but they knew she would fight it to the last. "Damn you. I hope my niece rips your face from your skull. I hope she breaks every bone in your body."

Six thought how satisfied Esek would be to hear Alisiana say so.

"Enough, Riin Matri," they said again. "Som is coming for Esek, too."

She was having trouble holding herself up now. Her struggling ceased altogether, but she made little whimpering sounds of resistance. For several moments neither of them spoke. Six hated the intimacy of this, had not touched anyone like this in years. But they couldn't just drop her onto the bed.

"You'll be me someday," Alisiana said. She was slurring. Six grew very still, but the words hit like the precise blow of a stave. What did she mean? Her head began to sag. "Taken out by the last person you expect. Forced to ... kill ... the one you love ..."

Six flinched. *I do not love anything*, they thought. But Chono swam before them like a mirage, her gray gaze taking in what they did and reproving them.

"You'll die underground," mumbled Alisiana. Six thought of the bombing of Soye's Reach, of Yantikye recovering their burnt black body from the depths of the avalanche. They thought of the biodomes on Jeve, and the slaughtered millions buried underneath. Alisiana said, "Everything you want ... will fail." Her head fell against their shoulder, body limp. Six could see her face. It was twitching, fighting, but her eyes were closed. Her mouth hung open, a grotesque gape, and yet she whispered her prophecy like an oracle. "You'll die alone ..."

Six wanted to cover her mouth, to crush her larynx, to stop her voice. Her last words were almost impossible to hear, and yet they slid into Six, and rooted themselves.

"You'll ... never escape."

CHAPTER THIRTEEN

1664

YEAR OF THE CRUX

Farren Eyce
The Planet Capamame

Hours later, the funeral is all Jun can think about.

Thousands had gathered to the Market District promenade to watch the services, and tens of thousands more watched on cast from their homes or workplaces. The people in the Market District were haggard, their pain as much anxiety as grief. Whispers and arguments have run wild in the colony since Kereth ben Dane's death. Even if many want to believe it was some terrible accident, the fact that it has affected a collector, after the deaths of three other collectors, is too much for even the most obtuse and resistant colonist to ignore.

Perhaps this is why the Wheel implementing more surveillance didn't get a worse reaction. Oh, there have been plenty of objections, lots of anger to be sure, but it's contained on all sides by the resolve of the other colonists, whose desire to be protected has temporarily outweighed their desire for privacy.

Nevertheless, Jun was restless at the funeral. She kept scanning the crowd, thinking how easily another explosion could decimate them. Jun's best casters were in the labs, surveilling for any hint of trouble. Not a single red flag waved, yet Jun wished the whole time that she was with them, afraid that they would miss something, afraid some power outage would presage a disaster. Somewhere, Jun knows, the avatar is biding its time.

At the funeral, Gaeda assigned Jun a position at the far edge of a large platform ("You have to be present; you're a leader," the old woman had sniped). The massive crowd spread out below, and Kereth ben Dane held pride of place. Her body lay wrapped in silks inside a narrow coffin that they have since burned in the sublevel crematorium. Dom stood next to her, and the Wheel and Masar and a few other high-ranking people formed a half circle around him. Gaeda wielded the authority of the Stone with a power and gravity that had the crowd transfixed. Prayers poured from her in Je, and Jun's translator bot relayed each evocation of a merciful goddess come to gather her child into her arms. There was no talk of the consuming Godfire, no reference to Som and their hungry hands. There was only the promise of Sajeven, ceaseless kind. Even Jun, neither religious nor Jeveni, felt an unexpected comfort listening to the death rites.

Now those rites churn in her mind. Thoughts of her near death on *Drae's Hope* rustle inside her. She wonders what Liis would look like, standing on the platform next to her coffin. Liis would not weep and shudder as Dom had done, his body half broken under grief. Liis would stand calm and stony as a monument. And then, she would burn down the worlds.

Because Liis is real, Jun tells herself. *She's coming home. She's real.*

"Fires," says Bene. "Are you casting right now?"

As if shifting from one reality to the next, Jun turns to look at him. Her eyes are gritty.

"I'm not casting," she mutters.

"You can stand to take one night off," he says.

"No, we can't," grunts Masar.

Bene sighs, and Jun takes in her surroundings. The Market District has transformed. The thousands who came to grieve and pray this morning are now caught up in exultant celebration. Jun doesn't quite know what to make of the concept of a funeral dance grounded in joy and pleasure. The only funerals she's ever been to were somber. But here, musicians with cast projectors are filling the colony with music, and the people are dancing and singing. Children run around with streamers. Lovers hold each other close, unselfconscious. Some hundred feet or so from Jun's position, the Wheel sit as a group, dressed in their finest and looking happier than Jun has ever seen them. Even Fonu has put aside their pinched look for once. There are smiles and laughter and raised cups, stomping feet and clapping hands. It makes Jun tense, to see the Wheel surrounded by so many people, no protector in their orbit. They had insisted on the symbolism of their actions, and lectured Masar that he couldn't stand around them and brood like a cloaksaan.

Masar, of course, is annoyed with them, and his annoyance seems to skyrocket when Effegen leaves her seat and tears off onto the dance floor, looking young and happy.

Bene says, "There are collectors all over. I can see Kinby and Eda from here. You should try to relax for a few minutes. Come and have a dance." He looks at Masar. "Both of you." Jun imagines that the grimace on Masar's face echoes her own. Bene looks fond and exasperated. "Don't you dance, Masar? I thought all Jeveni danced."

Masar says with the reflexiveness of an axiom, "Dance is the heart song of the Jeveni. When we worked underground on Jeve, the slightest wrong move could mean our deaths. It made it all the more important to exercise our bodies when we had the freedom and safety to do it. Dancing is a powerful release—whether of joy or sorrow."

Jun is amused by the recitation, especially since he looks right now like he's never moved his hips in his life. Bene, on the other hand, gazes at him anxiously, besottedly. It would be adorable if it didn't make Jun want to roll her eyes. She looks out over the crowd, thinking about the constraints of the body. Bene, too, was a miner. On Najic he risked his life every day to mine copper. On their farming station, Luja and Tej faced violent punishment if they ever stepped outside the boundaries set for them. As for Jun, she had the Black itself as her playground—but however expansive the world of her mind, casting traps her in her body. And she knows better than ever that it is a trap. That she can be suffocated and made to bleed, and no amount of intelligence seems sufficient to prevent it.

Maybe it *would* be good for her to dance. Exorcise some of this restlessness and frustration. But Liis is too far away. The avatar is too near. There's a roiling in her, and if she danced, it might explode out from her fingers in a cast fit to raze the whole colony.

But she wishes Masar would dance. Fuck's sake, she even wishes he would dance with Bene, let himself have a little joy. Effegen is out there. They could dance together, the three of them, and finally acknowledge their ridiculous and immature attraction to one another (Jun was *never* this silly over Liis). She hardly wants to think of her cousin like that, but at least she knows Masar would be good to him. Doesn't look like he's going to give into that impulse, though. Hands clasped behind his back, he's looking very soldierly tonight, very stern. When she met him almost a year ago, he was an argumentative and surly asshole, but there was also humor in him, a cockiness that she hasn't seen in months. Not since Nikkelo died.

Suddenly Luja is there, eyes bright and actually smiling, looking more alive than Jun thinks she's ever seen her. She wears a pretty blue dress, hair put up in clips. She grabs Bene's wrist, exclaiming, "There's some people over by the elevator bank. They're dancing a station jig! I swear I remember Grandmi dancing it when we were kids, the exact same one! Hurry!"

She drags him off. The joy Jun feels at seeing her relaxed and happy edges up against a deep ache, not only because the sight is rare, but because Luja didn't invite Jun to join them. She feels petty for caring. Jun is Luja's mentor, she runs the casting labs, and the poor girl deserves to have a break from her boss. Besides, Luja's and Tej's memories of their family dancing would certainly not have included Jun, who left when they were so young. So it shouldn't bother her. It *does* bother her. It only makes her think how naive her hopes for reuniting her family always were.

She realizes, embarrassed, that Masar is watching her. She flicks a glance at him. His eyes, even the silver one, show amusement. "What?" she mutters.

"Why don't you go with them?" he asks.

"Why don't you go find Effegen?"

His ears turn scarlet. They're easier to see, now he wears his hair short. His scowl is petulant, nearly amusing enough to pull her out of her foul mood.

"Fuck off," he says, and she chuckles.

The music is thunderous. Pounding feet create a wild percussion. Jun has seen funerals where the bereaved competed with one another to see who could look the most devastated. Not these Jeveni. Their faces are turned up, caught in laughter and passion and sometimes ecstasy. People dance alone or in groups, families dance, parents with children spinning in giddy circles. And lovers dance—close, intimate dances that shout survival.

If Liis was here, perhaps Jun would dance. Perhaps she would pull her lover into a quiet, dark place, and they would move their bodies together, and every touch and every sway would bleed into Jun like a transfusion, and all her doubts would fade...

A bicycle cart driver nearly clips them, startling her. There are dozens of these drivers in the Market District, carrying food and drink for the people on the perimeter and the dancers who emerge from the throng. Masar, watching the careless driver speed on, admits, "I keep thinking what a good hiding spot a bicycle cart is for a pipe bomb."

Jun grimaces. Well, she *hadn't* been thinking that!

"The casters have been scanning for evidence of explosives all day," she reminds him. "That includes here. If there was anything suspicious, they'd find it."

Masar shakes out his shoulders. "Once, I got into a firefight with some guardsaan on Braemin. We were tracking a Hand who was trying to buy secrets about us. I was hit and Uskel dragged me out. I remember hearing an explosion. Later I learned that one of the guards had thrown a grenade at my people. We never even got the bodies back."

Jun says nothing. He's told her very little about his life before they met. She realizes that they are...friends...but they're not the type of friends who talk about their past or their feelings or their—well, anything, really, besides how annoying they find each other. And yet she has a sudden thought of what it must have been like for him, to see Kereth ben Dane blown apart, and know it was the same fate that met his friends.

She should say something. Some comforting thing. Instead, she jabs Masar with her elbow, nodding toward the Wheel. Dom is there, seated between Fonu and Hyre. He looks wrung out, one foot tapping restlessly.

"Have you spoken to him yet?" she asks.

"Yeah, this morning. Before the funeral. He's pretty numb, didn't seem to understand half the questions I asked him. He doesn't remember anything suspicious in the past few days, and Kereth seemed fine."

"What about when he was on Level 2? Did anybody down there—"

"Not to hear him tell it. He's had his eyes open for the slightest sign of trouble. Nothing." Masar's jaw flexes, the tattoos shifting on his face. "He thinks it's his fault. Just kept saying it was his fault. That whoever it was should have come for him instead of her."

"They probably *were* coming for him," Jun says. "Kereth and Dom had the same work schedules. They thought he would be there when it went off. Kereth was...collateral."

"It doesn't make sense," says Masar quietly. She can barely hear him over the music. He's staring out into the dance, eyes vacant. "Whoever killed the other collectors did it up close. They only took out their targets. Made it look like suicide. Why was this different?"

Jun shifts, antsy. The music changes, the drumbeat faster than before, and a huge cheer of recognition goes through the crowd. Jun doesn't know the song, but she wants to plug up her ears just to spare herself a headache. Or maybe the headache is from what Masar said.

She scans for one of the bicycle carts, wondering if she can get something without alcohol in it. The last thing she expects is to see Tej, not ten feet away and apparently oblivious to her. She looks him over, slowly and with some annoyance. He left the apartment yesterday morning, ostensibly for his work shift, and she hasn't seen him since. The fucking trouble he gets into. Even now, he looks unkempt, jaw patchy with stubble, clothes askew. He's standing with someone, some tall person in a blue cowl whose face Jun can't see. He looks angry, hands moving restlessly as he spews words Jun can't hear. Suddenly someone on a bicycle cart skids up to them. A young man. He's also wearing a cowl—which pricks Jun's attention even as his face pricks her memory. She nudges Masar's side again and nods toward the small group.

"Are cowls a regular fashion statement at funeral dances?" she asks.

Masar, not answering, watches the unfolding argument. Tej and the bicycle rider are talking heatedly now, voices raised enough that even with music blaring around them, Jun can hear the sound of it if not the words. The third person in the group, back still turned, puts a hand on each of their shoulders, as if to gentle them. Something in the figure's posture is familiar.

The bicycle rider says something, and Tej charges him. They slam together, the bicycle tipping over and bottles spilling out and rolling across the floor. Tej makes a wild, incoherent sound of rage, and they hit the ground, brawling. Masar and Jun sprint toward them as others gather around, and the person in the blue cowl disappears into the crowd, face unseen.

Masar gets there first, grabbing Tej by the shoulders of his jacket and lifting him as easily as if he were a child. Tej keeps kicking and screaming obscenities, his nose bloody and a shiner already spread across his cheekbone. Jun jumps between him and the bicycle rider, who is up on his feet again and shouting at Tej.

His cowl has come off, and bright red hair spills over his shoulders. In shock Jun recognizes him: the boy from the caster pirate den who stood in the back. His mouth is bloody. At first he only has eyes for Tej, but when he notices Jun, his expression freezes. He half steps back from her, like she is far more dangerous than Tej's fists.

Inanely she asks, "How's Level 2?"

"I'm not doing anything!" he cries, half panicked. "It's your fucking cousin—"

"Fuck you!" Tej slurs. He's definitely drunk. "You talk about her again, I'll kill you!"

"Hey!" Masar's bark startles them. "Knock it off, both of you. Som's ass, this is a *funeral* dance! You can't fight here."

"What's this about?" Jun demands.

"Nothing," Tej grunts, defiant as ever—though his eyes cut away. His cheeks are flushed even without the beating. "It's none of your business."

The bicycle driver turns to pick up his bike. A few curious onlookers help gather up the bottles, which he seems not to care about, shoving a few into the cart again and racing off, away from the heart of the dance and toward the elevators.

Jun whirls on her cousin again. "Gods' sake! What are you doing?"

"Fuck off!"

"Hey!" Masar looks furious. "Keep that up and I'll be the one punching you. She's the head of your family. Show some respect."

Jun doesn't have time to be surprised before Tej laughs. He sounds almost hysterical, hocking phlegm onto the ground. "Since fucking when?! She's no family of mine."

It stings worse than Jun expects, but she drives past the hurt. "And what about Luja? Is she still your family? She's having the most fun she's had in years tonight, and if she sees you pulling this shit, it's going to ruin—"

"Luja?" Tej interrupts, anger shocking into confusion. "What do you—is she here?"

"Of course she's here!" Jun exclaims. "She's dancing!"

"What?" And now his confusion is alarm. "No, she—she said she was staying home."

"Tej, what the fuck?"

"Where is she?"

"Near the elevator bank, I—"

He runs off. They watch him go, and after the first stall of confusion, Jun's heart thumps. Dread pools in her stomach like blood. She looks at Masar and sees his trepidation. They both start to move to follow Tej, when—

Are you enjoying the dance?

There's no ping before the avatar's message overlays her vision. It is simply there, dragging her to a startled halt. Masar stops, too.

"What is it?" he asks.

Tell him to go after Tej. Tell him to go protect Luja, if he can.

She meets Masar's eyes, her senses surging with horror.

"The avatar?" he asks.

She masks her tech so it won't hear her. "My cousins. Find my cousins."

"I can't." Masar's eyes cut toward the Wheel. Jun understands. His obligations lie elsewhere from her family. She'll have to go herself.

Stay where you are.

Gods and fire, can it fucking read her mind? She hisses at Masar. "Find Effegen, then. Tell the collectors to get the Wheel out of here. And evacuate the Market District."

He sprints off. Jun, forgoing the drama of the visual messages, says dryly, "I'm not one to obey orders. Let me guess. I do exactly what you say or you kill my cousins? Is that the game?"

The answer comes in a string of messages:

Would that be the best way to control you?

I understand you spent many years trying to reunite your family.

You must love them very much.

Will you protect them above everything else? What about Liis?

Would you protect them above Liis?

Jun grits out, "Liis is going to find you and pull your tongue out through your throat."

Liis is far away. Liis is useless to you now.

"Okay, then *I'll* pull your tongue out through your throat."
She can feel laughter in the response.

Not if I get you first, Sunstep.

Jun refuses to satisfy it by dropping into the net. She holds her firewalls, accepting its messages but leaving no other corner of her exposed to attack. Next, holding that line of communication, she gathers her Hood from its closet, deep inside her, and slips it on.

She keeps comms open, but the avatar won't be able to see her, what she does or where she goes. It won't be able to track her movements. Its message is immediate.

Daring.

Jun, already jogging in the direction of the elevators, answers via message this time.

I'm done playing games with you. Tell me what you want or fuck off.

I want to know how dangerous you are. Everything I've seen you do has been defensive. Do you know how to strike first? Do you know how to be brutal?

What, like a cloaksaan? I thought you didn't work for the Kindom. Maybe you're not sure on that point?

Like a flash of irritation, viruses barrage her casting network, but Jun dispels them as easily as tearing fingers through cobwebs. It's sticky, yes—clings to her protection programs, but it's incapable of penetrating the firewalls. She lets the avatar burn itself up with attacks as she reaches the elevator bank. There's a small group of dancers, but no Luja and no Tej. She wishes she had trackers on them. She sends out casts to them both, and gets nothing.

She tries another cousin. "Bene? Where are you?"

He answers, speaking loudly over the music. "Hey! I'm dancing with Effegen. We're near that tea shop you like."

She exhales. "Look, stay there. See if you can reach Tej or Luja. I'm coming to you."

She ends the comm, jogging back into the heart of the dance. She looks over toward the Wheel and finds them on their feet, standing close together. They look like people who are trying to be casual but can't quite hide their concern. Masar must have spoken to them already, but he isn't with them. He'll be looking for Effegen amid the dancers. Jun pings him her and Bene's location, and the avatar bursts back into her awareness—

I'd rather be a Hand than a Wheel spinner.

Congratulations. You're abhorrent.

I'd rather win on strength than die on principle.

Jun is some hundred feet away from the tea shop. She gets a glimpse of Bene's green jacket through the throng. But a moment later, something else snags her attention—

A figure in a blue cowl.

Jun comes to a halt, watching. This is the same tall figure who held Tej and the red-haired boy apart. They slip past little knots of chattering friends, headed not into the dance but toward the market stalls and shops—and into a section of the Market District that's still under construction. With a thump, Jun remembers: The Level 5 casting hub is back there.

She jogs after the figure in blue. The avatar says:

What about you, Sunstep? You want to die on principle? You want your family to die for the Wheel?

I didn't realize those were my only options.

Maybe. What if I told you there's a pipe bomb in the tea shop next to Bene?

Jun fights down the wave of panic that wants to consume her. She can't see Bene's green jacket anymore. She casts Masar a warning but gets nothing back from him.

What if I told you there's a bicycle cart full of explosives headed right toward the Wheel?

Ahead of Jun, the blue cowl disappears between some shops.

They're too chatty, whispers Liis in Jun's thoughts. *They're trying to goad you into taking a specific action. Stop listening to them before you get yourself killed.*

Thank you for that, love, Jun thinks dryly. And, *Please come home.*

She comes upon the construction site and slows to a quick walk, more careful now as she pursues the figure into a network of drywall.

Intermittent floodlights mark the way, leaving plenty of shadows behind. The music from the dance is muffled now, but she listens for the slightest tread of sound, casting out like a fishersaan tosses a broad net. They're definitely moving toward the casting hub, but her fishing confirms that the hub only runs power and comms on Level 5; it's disconnected from the larger casting net until construction is finished. She watches the hub, sees it thrumming like a heartbeat. It's about fifty feet away.

Are you listening, Sunstep? I'm not inclined to hand out chances. Give me something I want and maybe I won't kill your entire family.

And what is it you want again?

Come back to the dance and maybe I'll tell you.

Jun's just around the corner from the casting hub now. Gods, she wishes she had the Som's Edge pistol Ricari gave her. There's a sound of machinery being opened, the whir of a drill. Jun looks around for a tool, a pipe, any kind of weapon. There's nothing. She messages the avatar:

We can dance later. Gotta go.

She cuts and masks the connection, turning into a doorway. The casting hub stands in the center of a small room, pieces of its paneling swinging open. Standing over it, just five feet away, is the cowled figure, bending to some task. They're taller than Jun. She makes her voice as hard and intimidating as possible:

"What the fuck are you doing in here?"

The figure straightens. There's surprise in the movement, but no shock or fear. Slowly, they drop the cowl and turn to face her.

"Hello, sweetheart," Aris the Beauty says.

Jun returns her smile, but thinly. "Funny meeting you here."

A bright laugh. Jun looks at Aris's hand, sees that she's holding something. Poised, almost, over the open controls of the casting hub. She shifts her hand enough that the light catches just so. It's a coin.

"And what is that?" Jun asks, though she can recognize a portable program coin.

"Some jobs call for hardware," says Aris.

"This hub doesn't connect to anything more exciting than a comms array and utilities."

Aris's eyes gleam. "Nothing to worry about, then."

Jun steps aggressively toward her, and suddenly there's a gun pointing at her face.

"Ah-ah-ah," warns Aris. Jun holds very still, watching her. It's not even the twentieth time she's faced a gun head-on. And yet the knowledge that all the guns should be in the Farren Eyce armory—the knowledge that none of her friends have guns to save her with—makes this particular showdown a little more... tense. Still smiling, Aris tells her breezily, "I have someone chatting in my ear who wants me to kill you."

Jun snags on that. In her chest has been growing the conviction that Aris must be the avatar after all, but—

"And yet, you haven't killed me."

"It seems... premature. A big risk."

"A risk you've gotten Tej involved in?"

"That silly boy. He doesn't even know what he wants."

"What do *you* want, Beauty? What does that coin do?" Aris doesn't answer. "Why was Tej afraid when he found out Luja was at the dance?"

"Is she? Poor little thing."

"What are you—"

"Hush."

She cocks the gun. It's an old model, with a hammer. Maybe it was Aris's before all of this happened—confiscated, like the Som's Edge. Maybe Aris and an entire crew have snuck their way into the armory and are even now about to descend on the dance.

Jun casts to Masar.

You better be evacuating the Market District.

Aris's head tilts, eyes going momentarily distant, as if she's receiving a message. Jun uses her distraction to shift her body weight forward. Aris's attention returns, her look pitying.

"Gods and fire, you do evoke intense emotions, don't you, honey?"

Jun casts a virus at the hub, and in a sudden panic that it is being attacked, it starts shrieking with alarms. Aris jumps, jerking toward the hub, then back toward Jun, who is already running at her. The gun goes off, but in her surprise Aris has aimed wide. Jun slams into Aris, both of them spilling backward onto the surface of the casting hub. They slide right across it, toppling onto the other side. Jun thinks of the brawl between Tej and the red-haired boy, and she realizes that she is brawling just the same, punching and kicking in uncoordinated desperation. There are hands in her clothes, grasping, tearing hands and nails like the sharpened points of little daggers, gouging into her skin. She's hit the ground hard, a jarring impact between her shoulder blades, and Aris is on top of her. She still has the gun and she's trying to get her bearings, to aim, to fire. Jun hasn't got long nails, but she rakes at Aris's face with every bit she's got, frantic and animal.

Aris cries out. Jun brings her knee up as hard as she can, socking her right between the legs. There's a gagging sound of pain, and Jun rolls Aris under her, grabbing for the hand with the gun. She gets Aris's wrist, shoving up as another bullet goes off. Dust and plaster rain from the ceiling. Jun is practically screaming with the effort of holding Aris down, pinning the gun, but this woman is taller and bigger and stronger than her. Pain explodes in the side of Jun's head, either a fist or something harder knocking her onto her back again. Aris is cursing and spitting like a cat. There's blood in Jun's mouth and she gets a groggy, almost comical image of Aris fighting with her own cowl, staggering to her feet, and dragging the garment off. Suddenly she looms over Jun, a fanatical violence in her eyes. There's a cut near her eye, bleeding. If she thought killing Jun was premature before, she doesn't now.

Liis, Jun thinks. *Liis...*

With a shriek Aris wheels away from her, firing at something else. Jun sees a figure, big and unstoppable, barreling into the woman. They hit the wall together, like a battering ram. Aris's head strikes hard. Her face goes dazed, her body collapsing. In a revelation of joy and relief Jun sees Masar stumbling upright again, looking down at the woman with his back to Jun.

"Masar," she gasps, choking on dust.

He looks unsteady. She can't see his face. He braces himself on the casting hub.

"Masar?!"

Disoriented, head throbbing, Jun struggles to sit up. He turns toward her, ashen in the yellow light, a hand clutched to his side. Dark blood flows between his fingers, spreads across the fabric of his shirt. He drops to one knee with a choked gurgle and falls forward like a building coming down.

CHAPTER FOURTEEN

1665

YEAR OF THE HARVEST

Praetima
Nikata Leen, an Island
The Planet Kator

"Seti Moonback is still missing," Ilius says.

He's watching her, looking for a reaction, but Chono doesn't rise to it. They're in the back room of Praetima's largest temple, Chono refilling her tin of sevite grease. Icy rain beats against the roof, with intermittent punctuations of thunder. Today is New Sun, the first day of the religious calendar year, and the temple nave is overflowing with waterlogged parishioners come to receive blessings. When Ilius first arrived at the temple, it was to inform her that hundreds of people are at the gates of Praetima, hoping to receive her benediction. But the Secretaries have shut the city down. Because Seti Moonback is still missing.

"Anyone could be her agent," Ilius says. "Closing the gates is a reasonable precaution. A blow against Nikapraev would galvanize her followers and undermine our authority."

Chono scrapes the sevite grease smooth. Her fingertips are blackened from anointing the hands of the parishioners. This is the seventh day since the meeting in the Centrum. Seven days performing rites at the Godfire temple. Seven days since that person Yantikye sent a message to Six, and the fourth time in as many days that Ilius has come to her with some new entreaty. His desire to reclaim her trust, to justify himself to her, is exhausting, all the more because his message never changes: *Appeal to the people for peace*, he begs her. *Publicly address the Jeveni.*

Chono says, "Every day, I recite the prayers for peace and war's end. This is the most I can do in my current office, and I should think it makes my position clear. I'm not a politician to give fiery speeches, Ilius."

"You certainly gave a speech when you returned to the Treble with that data flood!" he jabs. "Your actions have been distinctly tepid since."

Chono turns to him at last, eyes hard. "Shall I anoint your hands?"

He grinds his jaw. "You have to speak against Moonback."

Chono raises an eyebrow, and he exhales noisily, thrusting out his hands. She dips a finger in the tin and draws a circle on each of Ilius's palms.

"You can't possibly want her to go unchecked," he says. "Who knows what she would do if she snuck into the city?"

"Nothing good, I'm sure."

"Then why won't you help me?"

Help me, he says. Not *Help the Kindom*. Not *Help the Clever Hand. Help* me, *your old friend, the one on shaky ground, the one who needs your patronage.* Chono gives him a flat look. "This is the third time you've told me about Moonback's efforts to raise an army. Reports I can't confirm for myself. You've cut me off from the larger casting nets of the Treble."

"For your protection! So no one can hack into your comms and—"

"I only know what's going on in the worlds because you can't prevent Esek from speaking to her family, and you can't prevent her family from reporting to her."

Indeed, Six's nightly haranguing of Esek's relatives has been a rare spot of amusement in the past week, and in this matter at least, Six has not kept her in the dark. She knows what Six knows, about the Treble's ever-worsening unrest, about the people's rumors and excitement surrounding Chono's return from the dead, about the hateful response to the Rule of Unification. But Six has *not* told her what the message from Yantikye said—nor if they have responded to it.

Ilius snaps her attention back. "You trust the *Nightfoots* more than you trust me?"

"It's absurd that you expect me to trust you when there's a collar around my throat."

"Chono, we have given you your freedom! We have—"

"You have stuck me in a room at the top of a very pretty prison and made promises you haven't kept. You've set the Secretaries up as inviolable dictators of the Treble. You've claimed you'll free up the jump gates, but travel is still sluggish. You've punished Moonback's overeager cloaksaan, while simultaneously flooding the planets with your own guards, with a mandate to stomp out uprisings. And you've closed your gates to worshippers, cutting yourselves off from the people you purport to serve." She pauses, taking in the slow deflation of his expression. "Ilius," she murmurs. "There are some things that are more dangerous than Seti Moonback."

She turns from him. She goes back into the nave, where the line of penitents stretches beyond the temple doors, out of sight. She's been here since before dawn, and it's past noon. Her legs and feet are killing her. A middle-aged man approaches the Godfire's altar.

"Burning One," he rasps, overwhelmed and reverent.

Chono smiles, gently anointing his palms. "May the New Sun burn justice and mercy into your heart. And gods keep you well."

The man's eyes are wide and damp. Chono fights not to show her discomfort. She's had hundreds of these experiences already. She's drowning in the awe and admiration of the Praetima citizenry, with no end in sight. As the man withdraws, she looks out on the crowd. There are guardsaan stationed throughout the temple. It doesn't escape her notice that she hasn't seen any cloaks since her release.

Ilius appears at her elbow, clearly intent on saying something else in the pause between parishioners. Chono forestalls him—

"Those guardsaan are a crass touch."

"We have to protect you. There could be assassins."

"The Godfire will protect me."

"The Godfire *is* protecting you. With these guardsaan."

A teenager approaches, presenting her hands, expression hopeful.

"May the New Sun burn justice and mercy into your heart. And gods keep you well."

"Gods keep you well, Cleric Chono," the girl says earnestly. "And gods bless the Clerisy, now Aver Paiye is gone."

Ilius's attention points at the girl, as if he were sighting her down a rifle. The teenager doesn't appear to notice him, too focused on smiling at Chono before she leaves.

"Stop glaring at my parishioners," Chono warns.

"They love you so much," he muses. "They love you like you're the salvation of the Clerisy. Do you know what some of them have started calling you? The People's Kin."

She casts him a barbed glance, the sort of glance she has directed at thoughtless novitiates, or kinschool students who threatened her and Six, or rich businessaan who wanted her to condone their abusive labor practices.

"You are crowding my altar," she says.

Ilius balks, his brow pinching with sorrow.

"You have to forgive me," he whispers. "Please, Chono, for the sake of all the trust you always held in me, you have to forgive me. I am *trying*. I swear to the Godfire. I am trying to steer us toward justice."

She looks at him without answering. She believes that he believes what he's saying. She even wants to believe what he's saying. And yet . . .

"Well, now. Where's my blessing?"

Ilius's and Chono's eyes snap forward again, startled to be taken so unawares by Six's arrival. Six wears an excellently tailored black suit, the shirt underneath a vivid green, collar open to reveal their sharp collarbones. The spattering of rain on their shoulders and in their hair is attractive rather than disheveled. They've recovered from the prison, gained back some weight. Their umber skin is warm as sunshine and their eyes are magnetically bright, and they radiate all the self-satisfaction of a grand entrance.

Chono, reorienting herself, takes note of the guardsaan in the nave, who have slipped closer. Ilius is as stiff as a block of ice. The other parishioners watch them.

"Hello, Esek," she says. "Shall I bless you?"

Something glitters in their eyes, a touch of amusement, like this is some inside joke.

They ask, "What do you do, when your penitents have turned their backs on the Godfire? Gods forbid the apostate should have the benefit of your holy acknowledgment, Cleric Chono."

"No one is beneath my acknowledgment."

"You hear that, Ilius? There's hope for you yet."

Chono doesn't know what they're doing, what this public performance amounts to. The guardsaan watch suspiciously, and Ilius looks repulsed. He says, "I thought you were working in Blue Spire today, Sa Nightfoot. Didn't you have meetings with your family?"

Six wags a finger. "Now, now, Secretary Redquill. The Kindom may have had rights to my schedule very recently, but we all know I am not a cleric anymore. My business is my own."

"Then what is your business?" Ilius asks coldly.

Six ignores him, facing Chono again. "How many hours have you been at it?"

"About seven."

"You're past due a break. Deserter though I am, I know my God-texts. You have responsibilities outside this temple, don't you, Burning One?"

Chono hesitates. Technically, they're right. On holy holidays, clerics are beholden to a tradition of solitude and contemplation. She owes the Godfire at least three hours of prayer—which she had intended to offer tonight. She says as much, and Six grins.

"Nonsense. This line stretches a mile and it keeps growing. You'll be here right up to midnight if I allow it. Do you really want to start New Sun in defiance of your gods?"

"What's your point?" asks Ilius hotly.

Again, Six ignores him. "I'm going outside the city, to visit the praevi distilleries on the coast. I know how you miss the sea, since leaving Pippashap. You should come along with me and do your prayers on the beach, while I get drunk."

"That is out of the question," Ilius declares.

Finally, Six turns to him. They raise their eyebrows, imperious and amused. "How so?"

"You can't leave the city."

A sharp laugh. "*You* can't stop me. You have pardoned Chono and me of all crimes, and unless we are criminals, you have no right to control our movements."

"We are not letting anyone into the city. If you leave, you can't come back. And as for Chono—she remains beholden to the Kindom. She will complete her duties in Praetima."

Chono knows the look on Six's face. Oh gods, Ilius has walked right into a trap.

"You amaze me, Prudent One!" Six raises their voice to well within earshot of the crowd. "Why would you deny Chono the right to leave Praetima? Is she your prisoner, that she can't even perform her prayers on the beach if she wants? That seems very cruel. And very counter to all the messages you've been sending about the faith and trust you place in her."

The nave becomes unnaturally quiet. Chono has no doubt that these people will spread what they've heard from one end of the city to the other—and beyond that, to the Treble entire.

Ilius looks . . . apoplectic.

He controls himself, though composure was never his strength, and half turns into Chono's space. "I've told you. We're not letting people into the city."

Six replies in their slightly too loud voice, "It's our choice whether to leave Praetima. And of course it's your choice whether to let us back in."

"It's not safe," Ilius whispers to her. "We can't allow it."

"You'll have to say so to all these people," Six replies.

"Sa Nightfoot—"

"Don't," they interrupt, voice dropping. They look at him the way a spider must look at its silk-bound captive. "Don't test me, dear Ilius. I'll make *such* a scene."

Chono watches their exchange without comment. She's rather intrigued to see what will happen, almost amused with Six, as she would have been at their antics at kinschool. Gears turn in Ilius's eyes. Maybe he's secretly casting the rest of the Secretarial Court. Maybe Ravening and Songrider have been here this whole time, passengers in Ilius's ocular implant. A full ten seconds pass before Ilius's pinched look pinches tighter. A clear sign he's lost.

"I'm sending a warcat of guardsaan with you. For your protection."

"Of course." Six nods.

"When you're back, Chono, you'll continue the blessings. Otherwise these people will be very disappointed, and I know you don't like to disappoint. Also, there are formal celebrations in the Nikapraev ballroom tonight. You will both demonstrate your friendship with the Clever Hand by appearing."

And no doubt a hundred newscasters will broadcast it to the Treble.

All Chono can think is that Ilius is a very different man from the one who kept his own company and counsel, and sent her little gifts of information, and never seemed to give a damn what his kin were up to—beyond how he could use the facts to pad his collection of secrets.

Six, for their part, smiles a cool, feline, troublemaker's smile.

"I never miss a party."

Six has requisitioned them a driverless taxi-pod, and as soon as they are inside it, they raise Jun's scrambling tech, enclosing them in a bubble of protection. In the street, the rain has unexpectedly receded, and pale sunshine bathes the city. Holiday crowds venture out. Decorations have gone up, streamers and flower garlands and flags. This year, the bakeries are making cookies and candies that look like sheaves of wheat, for the Year of the Harvest has begun. Children wear yellow. Chono thinks about last New Sun, which she celebrated on Pippashap. There, the children who had picked their genders in the previous year got special acknowledgment, hair woven with silver tinsel. One of them, a child who Cleric Paan had hurt, danced all day with tinsel in her hair, carefree for the first time in months. And Paan was dead.

The taxi-pod trundles down brick roads, heading for the city gates.

"Is this about Yantikye?"

Six, their Esek performance vanishing, stares forward. It's not the first time Chono has tried to make them talk about this. But the most she's gotten out of Six is that Yantikye is a long-standing associate of theirs, a Quietan revolutionary, a pain in the ass. When Chono and Esek were hunting Six, she concluded that Six had no associates—only employees of circumstance: the fighters who killed Esek's novitiates on K-5 station. The decoys who all got killed at Soye's Reach. Here and gone, tools in Six's long game with Esek. The idea that Six worked with someone consistently over all of those years fascinates and discomfits Chono. That she has not met this person yet feels like a barb in her side.

Chono glances back through the rear window. A warcat follows close.

"Not sure how you expect to meet with him with no one noticing," she remarks. "Am I meant to distract them while you hare off?"

A faint smile on Six's mouth. "And deny you the opportunity to meet my old friend?"

Chono narrows her eyes. "I thought you didn't want me to meet him. You wouldn't even show me his message."

A memory coin, slotted into Six's neural port. Crushed under their boot, afterward.

Six says in an unexpectedly peevish tone, "I did not...want to involve you in this."

Chono's nostrils flare. "Involve me in what?"

"Yantikye the Honor wants to speak with us. In person. He is... insistent."

"I didn't think you could be moved by someone else's insistence."

"*You* insisted we come back to these damned systems. Was I not moved by that?"

She ignores this. "I still can't believe you have an *associate*."

Six chuckles mirthlessly. They look out the window as they pass through the gates of Praetima, guns and cast surveillance trained on the taxi-pod until it slides onto the road, transitioning to high speeds. Six says, "I am capable of working with others."

"All evidence to the contrary."

Their lip curls. "Yes, well...I suppose it has always come more naturally for you."

They mean Esek, of course, and Chono can hear the indictment, the subtle scorn. It makes something white flash through her. "You think working with Esek came *naturally* to me?"

Six shrugs. "It seemed to."

Chono swallows down the very vile things she could say right now. "Then you weren't paying attention."

They study her, as if searching her face for proof of something. A lie, perhaps? Finally, they clear their throat. "We are to stop at the praevi granary for a drink on our way to the coast. That is the only instruction I have received. Yantikye says that if I do not bring you, he will just find another way to make contact. So here you are."

Chono takes this in, surprised. It had not occurred to her that

Yantikye would want anything to do with her. She asks, "Is he dangerous?"

"Yes, of course. But I do not know what he wants. Whatever it is, I doubt I will like it."

Chono processes for several moments, and says, "A praevi granary? I've never seen you drink praevi. Even when I thought you were Esek, I never saw you drink it. That should have tipped me off, now that I think about it. She drank praevi like water."

Rocky outcrops outside the city walls give way to rolling plains. A pale grayish sky spreads for miles. The sunshine has retreated. Six says, "I do not care for praevi."

Chono huffs a baffled sound. "You transformed your entire body into a clone of Esek, but you draw the line at drinking praevi?"

Their nostrils flare. "I drew many more lines than that."

"Such as?" Chono challenges.

"For one, I did not fuck every pretty thing I came across."

Heat crawls up her neck, cheeks flushing. Six looks amused.

"I suppose that is one kind of line," she grumbles.

"And I did not kill you."

She narrows her eyes. It's only when she says, "I know," that they seem satisfied, as if her concession somehow lends them the upper hand. They look out the window again.

An hour passes.

In time, the taxi-pod crests a hill, and she gets her first view of the Avos Sea, stretched out in a glittering sheet. The dozen or so miles between them and the coast are all praevi fields, rich red grains like dried blood, and many farms and distilleries dotting the landscape. Across the sea is the continent of North Avo, and far east on that continent's northern tip, there is a crater in a mountain that used to be called Soye's Reach.

The road leads down to a few buildings—the granary itself, a small house, and an open-air bar where a few other patrons are milling about. When the taxi-pod slides to a halt, Six and Chono look back at the Kindom warcat, which has also parked in the graveled lot. Six smirks.

"Shall we drink?"

At the bar, the other patrons give them startled looks of recognition, and the barkeep widens his eyes just shy of alarm.

"Sa Nightfoot. And...Cleric Chono. Welcome. This is...You honor my farm."

Six sidles up to the bar. "Don't I just? What have you got here?"

He nervously and lovingly describes for them the half dozen praevi types available, and Six orders two glasses of a kind called Blood Moth, aged thirty years. Chono notices that the guardsaan have not gotten out of their warcat. She accepts the glass that Six hands her, and Six, all theater, holds their own glass up in a salute.

"To the prudence and viciousness of the Secretaries," they say, and toss the drink back.

At those words, something shifts in the barkeep's expression. It's subtle—Chono almost misses it. With a tense smile, he pours Six another glass and says, "If you like Blood Moth, perhaps you'd like to taste an older vintage?"

"Something from 1638, maybe?" Six asks.

"Year of the Quill," agrees the barkeep. "Of course."

A code, Chono realizes.

"I keep it in the cellar of my home. Why don't you join me for a tasting?"

Six's smile is viperous, just as Esek's would be at the prospect of a rare vintage. But Chono thinks the smile is also a threat. If this barkeep double-crosses them, he'll die for it.

He leads them past the granary, behind the house, where a staircase drops into darkness. Chono throws a cautious glance back at the graveled lot. The warcat idles, engine purring, and it's some surprise to her that the guardsaan have not exited to demand where they're going. The barkeep descends first, then Six, then Chono, and the staircase is steep. They end up in a cellar. Lights come on, revealing wall-to-wall racks full of glittering bottles. There's a tasting counter, and a door in the back that Chono notes suspiciously. The barkeep takes a bottle off the rack and fishes tumblers from the shelves under the counter, setting up not three drinks but four. He pours out a healthy measure, sets the bottle down, and wipes his hands on his apron.

"I'm just going up to the kitchen to gets some things. The praevi goes well with cheese."

He doesn't wait for Six's leave, hurrying instead toward the door in the back. Chono and Six watch him disappear, watch him leave the door open. They're both as still and tense as jungle cats preparing to spring. If there will be an ambush—

"Hey there, little killer."

Chono spins around. One of the walls racked with liquor bottles has pushed outward, revealing a secret door. An older man and a young woman stand in the frame. How they appeared so silently is inconceivable to Chono. She throws a look at Six. While Esek would respond to this moment with showboating, Six is silent, humorless, glaring.

The man is Quietan, his face dark and lined and his hair a short mop of locs. Two thick leather belts cross his chest in an X, sheathed with dozens of small knives. He's shorter than both of them but broad-shouldered and muscular as a bull. The very image of the weathered sailor. He smiles widely, seeming pleased with himself. The woman next to him has his same build and coloring, the same shape to the eyes, though hers are a darker, deeper brown. Her face is a lesson in surliness.

"Well, now," says Yantikye the Honor. "Shall I get you a bag to throw up in?" He looks at Chono. "When this one started their grand experiment, they tried to make themself like praevi. They always got sick. Not sick this time, Sa Nightfoot?"

"Yantikye," drawls Six, "do not embarrass me in front of Chono. You know how vain I am. And you know how little I like your surprises."

A throaty laugh. "What's this coldness, old friend?"

"You summoned me here like you were my feudal lord. I told you not to contact me."

"Maybe you don't get to call the shots anymore."

This comes from the young woman. Her accent is thick around the

Katish they are all speaking, clearly unused to the language. Six takes her in, smiling faintly.

"My, my, Graisa," they say. "You are grown up."

"And you're just the same."

Six cocks their head. "Really? No change that you can discern?"

"I don't care what your face looks like. You're the same. Hunting your own purposes and never with a thought for the ones that helped you."

When Esek furrowed her brow, it was always sarcastic, a pantomime. This look on Six's face is openly surprised. They ask Yantikye, "What lies have you been telling her?"

Yantikye waves a hand. "Oh, never mind. She's grown up strong and smart, but not the warmest of my children. Graisa, gods' sake. Steady on, nah?"

She answers him in Qi, "I'm very steady, Da."

Despite his chastisement, Yantikye looks pleased by his gruff daughter, jerking a thumb at her and telling Six, "Was her that got that newscaster into the room with you, to give you our message. This whole rendezvous, Graisa planned it."

"And I'd like it to count," says Graisa.

"We are here, are we not? Make your case."

But instead of answering them, or instead of Yantikye speaking up again, Graisa turns her dark gaze on Chono. To Chono's surprise, she bows over her hands.

"Cleric Chono. I have many friends and allies in Pippashap. It's an honor to meet someone who has so much of their respect. I didn't think a cleric could be worthy of my loyalty, but I trust these friends. I trust that what they say about you is true."

Chono has watched and listened to many newscasts of Pippashap Quietans extolling her virtues, but curiosity still gets the better of her. Switching from Katish to Qi, she asks, "What do they say?"

The young woman seems surprised and pleased by her grasp of the language and answers her in kind. "They say you did far more than stop Cleric Paan. They say you ate their food and spoke their language.

If they came to you seeking advice, you didn't clobber them with God-texts. You helped them rebuild after storms. You never treated yourself as more important than them. You gave services to Capamame as well as the Godfire." She pauses, expression sharpening. "They say you protected them from secretarial corruption and cloaksaan raids."

Chono pauses, unsure how to respond. It's true that when she came to Pippashap, the Secretaries had been overtaxing the Quietans, and she petitioned for corrections that they had to reluctantly adopt. And there was one terrible month of no wind and bad fishing, when a clutch of cloaksaan arrived on Pippashap searching for a fugitive and would have torn the water city apart if Chono hadn't stopped them. Chono recognizes that these actions mattered to the Quietans, but they were the bare minimum obligation of her office, and probably far less than she could have done for the impoverished city.

Quietly, Chono admits, "My time in Pippashap was . . . very happy."

She sees sidelong the way that Six looks at her, as if they didn't know that.

Yantikye breaks in, "Happy, nah? Even though you had to murder a cleric?"

That he would mention this strikes her as a test. She looks at him coolly. Killing Paan, exerting the Godfire's justice, plucking out one evil in the starry sky of evils hanging over these worlds—it did not make her . . . *unhappy*.

"Cleric Paan was a rapist," says Chono.

They seem to wait for her to say more. When she doesn't, Yantikye gives an appreciative nod, and if anything, the respect in Graisa's expression deepens.

"What is it that you want from her?" asks Six abruptly, voice clipped. They look primed for a fight, static-charged and tense as a tuning fork. Chono doesn't understand.

Graisa the Honor says, "We want her to do what she did on Pippashap, but for everyone."

Chono's gut clenches. Six chuckles humorlessly. "Oh, only that?"

Graisa scowls at them. "I suppose you think that is not too much to ask of *one woman*."

"Well, she wouldn't be alone," says Yantikye cheerfully.

"Would she not? Perhaps you intend to be her ally? Or her handler?"

A chuckle. "So distrusting."

"I told you from the beginning, Yantikye. I am not interested in your causes."

Graisa snaps, "We're not asking you to be." She looks at Chono again. "Burning One, please. You don't know me, but my motives are righteous, like yours. The ones I work with—we've fought to protect vulnerable saan, just as you have. We've defied the Kindom's authority, just as you have. But until you came back from Capamame, so few of us believed that true, lasting change was possible. We've had to content ourselves with small victories and constant setbacks. But you." She exhales, as if in the presence of some unfathomable revelation. "*You* are proof that the Kindom has limits on its power. If you allied with us, the combination of your influence and our resources might finally be enough to force a reckoning. We could put down not just one Cleric Paan but every corrupt Hand in the Kindom." Her expression is proud; even the pleading in her eyes is proud. "Surely that is what you want?"

Chono looks at Graisa closely, thinking, *This girl could have been a resident of Pippashap, dodging Cleric Paan. She could have been a kinschool student, raised up for purpose. She could have been an Ironway, dispossessed and forgotten. I've met this girl, so many times.*

Chono says, "You do sound righteous, Graisa the Honor. But I came back to the Treble to see five thousand wrongfully imprisoned Jeveni freed. I came back to defend the rights of the Jeveni who never left. From Capamame, I've watched reports on the rising number of resistance cells. Have any of those cells put their energy toward protecting the endangered Jeveni? No. Have they used their fight with the Kindom to remind people that the Jeveni are mere scapegoats for Kindom atrocity? No. This Treble you imagine, freed from Kindom oppression: What room have you made in it for the Jeveni?"

Graisa looks taken aback. She casts a searching look at her father, who appears simultaneously impressed and amused. If Graisa is the visionary, he is the tactician. He looks at Six, nods his head at Chono, and says, "By the gods, I see why you always hated her working for Esek. Must have been torture, to see such a woman groveling like that."

Chono's face flushes. She bites out, "I never groveled for anyone."

"Everyone has to grovel sometimes. You think I didn't grovel for your friend here? You think they never groveled, to get what they want? I could tell you stories."

Six's nostrils flare. Chono is... unaccountably queasy at the thought of them groveling.

Yantikye carries on, "Anyway, it's beside the point. You want to know if our vision includes the Jeveni. Yes. Have we failed them so far? Yes." He doesn't sound particularly cut up about it, but he looks her in the eye. "Things are different now. We need everyone united in this fight. The Rule of Unification has been just the next step in a crackdown on the Treble. Guardsaan and marshals everywhere. New taxes, huge inflation, hardly anyone allowed to travel. We can't have it. Something's got to change. And the people would rather see you at the helm than an ugly fucker like me. After all, you convinced *Esek fucking Nightfoot* to put the Jeveni in her will. Just—*give her fortune away*! You're a miracle worker!"

Chono narrows her eyes. "You know that's not true. You know that changing Esek's will had nothing to do with me."

"But there has always been a significant difference between reality and perception," says Graisa, without irony. "To the people, you're the cleric who tamed a Nightfoot. Who stood up for the Jeveni. Now they see the Jeveni as a symbol of their own oppression."

Six makes a low growly sound, and Chono flares with irritation. "The Jeveni aren't mascots. They're human beings."

Yantikye chuckles, but Graisa nods. "Yes, we know. We know that now."

The naivety of youth. No civilization could overcome such a

deep-seated prejudice that quickly. If these resistance cells that the Honors refer to had to choose between an uptick in their own freedoms and saving Jeveni lives, Chono is certain what they would choose.

Six says, "I assume you have done everything possible to spread Sa Chono's reputation as a woman of the people."

"We've hardly had to." Yantikye smiles. "Her name is everywhere."

"I'm not a mascot, either," Chono says.

"If we wanted a mascot, we wouldn't be speaking to you. We'd just spread rumors and put words in your mouth. But that's not enough. We need action from you. Partnership."

She recalls Ilius beseeching her to make a statement against Moonback. So many people invested in her taking action.

"Do you know what will happen if I help you raise more resistance?" she asks quietly. "Hundreds of thousands of people will die. Innocents will be caught in the crossfire. They will pay the price of the war, as they always do. Why should I be eager for that?"

"If people don't fight for their own freedom, no one will," Graisa replies, earnest. "But you're right, Cleric Chono. We can't simply throw thousands of guerrilla fighters at the Kindom. We must be smarter than that."

"Smarter how?" Six asks, cold as ever.

"There are significant reasons why no one has taken a real go at the Kindom. You ask the average Treblen if they could do without the secretaries and cloaks, and they're all for it. Who wouldn't like to get rid of taxes and power-hungry murderers? But it's not just the Brutal and Clever Hands, is it? It's the Clerisy. And if you ask people to turn on the Clerisy, you're asking them to turn on their gods. Hardly anyone is willing to do it."

Six looks at Yantikye. "You told me once that the Secretaries were the most powerful Hand of all. You said it was economics and law that would shape the Kindom."

"And it will. It has. Which is why we have to bring the Secretaries low. Only the gods can do that. That's where you come in, Cleric Chono."

Chono glares. "By using religion to foment war? I won't turn on my gods."

"But the average cleric *would*," says Graisa. "The average cleric already has. To most clerics, the *Clerisy* is god. Power is god. That's why you're different. You prove that the Righteous Hand can live up to its name, that it can actually serve the Treble."

"You are speaking in abstractions," Six says tensely.

"Action is not abstract," says Graisa.

"So you want Chono to act. Act *how*?"

Graisa is eager to explain, "We want you to speak against the Rule of Unification. We want you to persuade other clerics to do the same."

Chono nearly laughs. "I'm sorry, Sa Honor, but you must not realize— I've never been popular among my kin clerics."

"But there is one cleric who respected you very much."

If she means Esek, then—

"Aver Paiye," says Six, expression shifting with revelation.

Chono blanches. "He's imprisoned somewhere. Stripped of his rank. He was instrumental in all the crimes of the past year—"

"Reality and perception," says Yantikye, holding out his hands as if weighing two different items. "He may have accepted culpability and resigned, but we have insiders who say he never believed in the Rule of Unification. And even disgraced, he retains more allies than any First Cleric in centuries. I've got intelligence his own family head, Oyun Paiye, stands by him and resents the Kindom for ousting him."

This catches Chono's attention, not only because Paiye always loved his older sister, but because Oyun supporting her brother over the Kindom's judgment is...significant. What other First Families might toy with rebellion?

Yantikye goes on. "If you and Paiye spoke out against the Kindom, it would light a fuse. Other clerics would follow. And with the Cloaksaan fighting among themselves over whether to serve Moonback, the Secretaries lack a reliable military arm. If the Clerisy rebelled against the rule, the Kindom itself would have to change."

Six makes a low sound, full of distrust. Chono shifts on her feet.

She feels the appeal of it—of forcing the Hands to fight among one another, to change or die. But while the Secretaries have their ranks of hired guardsaan, the Clerisy has no standing army. Its army would be the people, risen up on behalf of their gods, flocking to the Kindom's religious wing in droves and laying themselves open to slaughter.

"You're flirting with a holy war," Chono says gravely.

Graisa shakes her head. "With you and Aver Paiye working together, we think you can persuade the rest of the Kindom to stand down. We can avoid war altogether."

"You expect me to believe that you do not hunger for a war?" says Six, looking at Yantikye. "It is the only thing you have ever hungered for."

Yantikye smiles wolfishly. "What can I say? I've grown."

Six sneers. "There is no way the Secretaries will let Chono talk to Aver Paiye."

"We can manage it," says Graisa with a touch of arrogance. She looks at Chono. "We have insiders, like that newscaster. We've bought certain guardsaan. We can get you to Paiye, and if he agrees, we can broadcast his message alongside yours. We've got people who handle this sort of public relations operation. They can make it work; they can make it good. The Kindom won't be able to retaliate without martyring you."

"And suppose they are happy to martyr her?" asks Six icily.

"We can protect you," Yantikye says. "We can get you out of Praetima."

"It is too dangerous."

Six speaks with finality, as if the decision is up to them and they've already made it. Chono cuts them an irritated look.

"So protective," Yantikye observes.

"You only want to use her."

"Oh, don't get moral with me, little killer. We both know you want to use her, too."

The words slip between Chono's ribs, clean as the thrust of a blood-letter. She gives Six a quick look, then forces herself to focus on the

Honors. She doesn't want them to see how Yantikye's statement affects her. She doesn't want them to know how *aware* she is of Six in this moment, of their furious eyes that seem to be trying to burn the Quietan man alive.

"Where is Aver Paiye?" Chono asks.

"Chono," Six growls.

Graisa says, "He's here on Nikata Leen, though not in Praetima. He's under heavy guard. I'm sorry, I won't tell you more until you agree to help us."

Chono nods, ignoring Six's tensed body. Graisa looks at her with such hope, while Yantikye's expression is more . . . appraising. Suddenly he reaches over, takes up both his and Six's glasses of praevi, and swallows them both with the ease of a performative drinker.

"I suppose we've given you enough to think about," he says. "And we've been down here long enough. You ought to go out before your escort gets suspicious, nah?"

He's right. Six grunts, already turning to go, no words of goodbye for their old associate. Chono, too, starts to turn, but Graisa surprises her by touching her arm. Chono stops, looking at her. The young woman's stare is urgent, penetrating.

"You will consider it, won't you, Cleric Chono?"

She hesitates, conscious of Six's blistering glare. But Six is not her keeper, so she nods, cautiously. "I'll consider it. I don't promise anything, but I'll consider it."

Graisa is too gruff to show relief, but her short nod is satisfied. Yantikye claps. "Excellent! Now don't you scowl like that." He points at Six. "I followed your lead and kept you alive for years. It's about time you returned the favor."

"Everything you did was to your own benefit," Six replies.

"That's why we've always liked each other. We're both so transparently selfish."

They lock eyes for several seconds. Chono watches. On the one hand, she's unnerved by Six's hostility, put off by Yantikye's indifference, worried about what hangs between them. On the other hand, to her sickly surprise, she's jealous. Yantikye was a part of Six's life for years. He has known Six in a way that she never did, and perhaps never will.

His words to Six beat in Chono's breast: *We both know you want to use her, too...*

He puts a hand on Graisa's elbow, drawing her away. Chono watches them disappear into the secret door, pulling the liquor rack shut after them. The barkeep has not come back. Six clears their throat.

"We should go," they say, and head for the stairs.

Chono follows them. "Who knew you had such interesting friends."

She's utterly unprepared for the vitriol in their voice when they snap back, "I could befriend every criminal in the Treble and never be as guilty as you for *your* associates."

Stunned, Chono halts on the stairs. She knows that they don't like this plan, she knows that they are afraid of something, but why is she the object of their anger? Six, noticing that she has stopped, looks back at her. Light and shadow bifurcates their face, hides their ruined ear in darkness. In this moment, at this angle, they look nothing like Esek. And yet, they look *exactly* like Esek. They are a creature of the Black Ocean, ledger soaked in blood, a serpentine operative of the most deplorable undergrounds and criminal dens—and to them, she will always be worse than the worst thing they ever did. Because she belonged to Esek.

She waits for them to say it. She's certain they're finally going to just say it. The hatred they feel. The contempt they will never let go. But instead, they twist away without a word. Chono can do nothing but follow them up the last steps, ready to burn alive with her own anger.

But when they reach the ground level, walking around the house and past the granary, they both stop. The bar is empty. The barkeep is missing. The patrons have vanished, unfinished drinks still sitting on the counter. Chono and Six stand perplexed. Chono looks toward the Kindom warcat some thirty feet away, idling just as before in the graveled lot. She walks slowly forward, angle changing to give her a view behind the bar. There she finds the barkeep, lying in a pool of blood. Gunshot wound to the head. She rounds on Six again. They look ready to ask some question, but their gaze slips past her. Their eyes narrow—widen—

"Get down!"

And they hurl themself at her, just as gunfire zings past her ear.

CHAPTER FIFTEEN

1664

YEAR OF THE CRUX

Farren Eyce
The Planet Capamame

He wakes to a tight and aching pressure in his abdomen, mouth dry, throat sore. There's something wrapped around his middle, and as his eyes blink hazily open, he's met with an overhead light, a pale gray ceiling that he recognizes at once as a hospital room. He takes slow inventory of his body. This was something Nikkelo taught him and the other collectors. How to assess themselves for injury, and how to assess the seriousness of the injury. He drags his awareness up from his feet, through his calves and thighs, his pelvis; follows the path up his belly, where an ache thumps like a heartbeat—then through his chest and throat and head. It's only his abdomen that's been injured, he concludes, but it has the feel of a mortal injury, recently curtailed. The last time Masar almost died was after the firefight in Ycutta. The last time he was seriously injured, he lost an eye on *The Risen Wave*. It's a skill, learning to live with Som's pursuit. He wonders if he's gotten rusty at it.

"Masar."

He blinks twice, the cybernetic eye glitching. There's a chair at his bedside, and Effegen is sitting in it. She looks ashy with exhaustion, dark smudges under her eyes, but she smiles.

It takes him several tries to get words out, his sandpaper throat protesting.

"My Star," he rasps.

To his embarrassment her smile widens, her eyes filling with tears. He furrows his brow in distress, and she swallows, leaning closer to him. "Listen to me. You're all right. The bullet went through your side, through and through. It broke a couple of ribs and caused a lot of blood loss, but the surgeons were able to stabilize you, and it didn't hit any organs. You've got a shipload of regeneratives working on you right now."

"Jun," he whispers, memories coming back in fits and starts. "The gun—"

"Jun is alive," Effegen says. "The woman who attacked her was Aris the Beauty. We have her in custody now."

Masar frowns. Custody? How? Farren Eyce has no jail.

He tries to remember what happened. He was warning Effegen, warning Bene, and Jun went dark on his cast. He realized she must have raised her Hood. The little asshole was about to get herself killed. It was pure luck, seeing her on the other side of the market, headed into the construction zone. It still took far too long to reach her. A little later, and she would have been dead.

"Aris," he whispers. "What did she do?"

Effegen rises from her chair, picking something up off the end table.

When the little spoon touches his lips, he swallows down ice shavings, glorying at the relief of the moisture and cold. Effegen gives him a second spoonful, then puts the cup down. Instead of backing up, she stands leaning over his bed, and he has the sensation she wants to touch him, but refrains.

"She had a program coin that she was preparing to insert into the Level 5 casting hub. Our casters examined the coin. It contained the same virus that attacked Jun's aural and ocular tech. We think the plan was to release the virus into every neural link that was drawing on the hub for power or comms. That would have been several thousand people. We assume the plan was to at least destroy the crowd's tech. At worst, they meant to seriously injure anyone affected by the virus. Aris does not admit that she's the avatar. And she doesn't seem to know who is."

Suddenly Masar remembers Tej arguing with the redheaded boy. The person in the blue cowl, standing between them—that was Aris. And when Tej realized Luja was at the dance, panic filled his eyes. He knew there was going to be an attack, and that his sister was in danger. But he didn't try to warn anyone else. Why wouldn't he have warned anyone else, unless he was working with Aris?

Tears burn in Masar's eyes, a blur of anger and grief. He knew that Tej was unhappy, but this? It'll kill Jun; it'll devastate Bene and Luja. Why didn't Masar see it?

Effegen touches his shoulder. Then, to his surprise, she cups his face, her thumb brushing beneath one of his eyes. He feels the cool impression of her jevite rings. She's never touched him like this before. He sees the entreaty in her eyes, as if she is commanding him to come back, to stay in his body, to be with her. But he wants to leap out of the bed. He wants to rip the colony apart, find the monsters under the floorboards, and crush them.

He forces the tears down. "Aris wasn't working alone. There was a man on a bicycle cart. And there was"—he swallows, feeling like a traitor for saying it—"there was Tej. He was—"

"We know," someone says.

It's not Effegen this time. Something crosses her face, a flash he can't interpret, before she looks toward the door. Masar looks, too. Fonu sen Fhaan stands in the frame, looking even surlier than usual. It seems they only just appeared. "Praise Sajeven, you survived," they say.

Masar recalls Nikkelo, stepping onto the deck of *The Happy Jaunt*, greeting him, grinning at him. *You survive again*, he'd said.

Within hours, Nikkelo was dead.

"My River," Masar rasps.

He tries to sit up, but the dull pain turns sharp. Effegen makes a chastising sound. Fonu steps closer and warns, "Moon arise, lay still. You don't have to stand up to give me your report."

"Let him rest," says Effegen.

"We need his version of events."

There's seething tension between them. Uncomfortable, Masar recounts everything he can think of, starting with the moment when Jun first drew his attention to Tej's argument with Aris and the red-head, and the fight that broke out, and the avatar contacting Jun. He describes Jun and him splitting up to warn different people, and a glance passes between Fonu and Effegen. He keeps telling his story, trying to think if there's anything he didn't really notice at the time. Some small thing that, now remembered, will slot a key into a lock, but there's nothing. He describes finding Jun, tackling Aris, realizing he'd been shot...

Effegen speaks aside to Fonu. "It's just as Jun said."

Fonu's lips compress, and Masar asks, "Where is Jun? She must know more about what happened before I arrived."

"Stay calm, Masar," Fonu answers.

Masar's brow furrows; he's no less calm than at any point in the past few minutes. In fact, it's Fonu who seems agitated now, and Effegen radiates some emotion he can't interpret. The two Spokes stare at each other, a silent, noisy conversation.

"What does Jun say?" he asks again.

Fonu slowly turns their gaze away from Effegen and back to Masar.

"Let me explain to you what we know. But please understand, this is all privileged information. It's important that no one rush to conclusions."

Masar holds his tongue, knowing better than to show the irritation that this unnecessary warning causes him. Apparently satisfied, Fonu nods.

"First of all, the redhead you spoke of is called Jasef sen Clime. Both he and Tej Redcore have been missing since the events at the dance. Multiple witnesses, including you, saw Jasef leave before the attempted attack. Others, including Luja Ironway, say that Tej was near the elevators when it happened, but afterward, no one appears to have noticed him leave. The cast cameras have coverage of both of them on Level 2, but then, we lose them."

They say the words with an ominous scowl, like they're pronouncing judgment.

"There were power surges," Effegen starts. "We lost camera access on Level 5."

"They were clearly wearing Hoods," Fonu retorts.

Masar hesitates. "Jun already investigated that. There's no sign that—"

"And who would know if she was lying?" they interrupt.

In a flash, Masar realizes what Fonu means. He shakes his head. "No. She—"

Fonu holds up a hand. "We searched the Ironway apartment. There were explosives and other bomb-building materials in Tej's room. There was a gun. Furthermore, our casters examined Luja's and Jun's private casting hubs. We found the virus that was nearly released at the funeral dance. They built it."

Masar has no voice, too shocked. Fonu takes advantage of his silence. "There was also encrypted correspondence between Jun and Aris the Beauty. We can't crack its code, but that she was hiding it is, of course, damning."

Staggered by the accusation, Masar opens and closes his mouth. He finally says, "That's absurd. Jun has been trying to help us fight the avatar since—"

"Has she?" interrupts Fonu, sharp as a razor. "None of us were there on *Drae's Hope* when the avatar supposedly attacked her. None of us saw what happened in the caster pirate den, besides Jun and Bene. No one saw what happened between Jun and Aris at the dance."

"Aris was pointing *a gun* at her!" Masar cries.

"You could have misinterpreted what you saw—"

"Jun *saved* the Jeveni," Masar exclaims. "She saved all of us on *The Risen Wave*."

"And perhaps that action has stopped us from seeing her true intent. I'm sorry, Masar, but you can't be objective. Jun is your friend. Bene is your lover. Probably by Ironway design."

Masar flushes, too shocked to speak, but it is nothing to the fury that suddenly glints in Effegen's eyes, more dangerous than anything he has ever seen from her. "If you believe Masar is that naive, then you are a fool."

Fonu sniffs. "We are all fallible people."

Masar recovers with a jolt. "Then think about the fallibility of this evidence! This correspondence that you found, this virus on Jun's casting hub. You say she and Luja used their personal network access?" Fonu pauses, as if detecting a trap, but nods. "Don't you find that a little *odd*? Don't you think a terrorist mastermind might carry out their work with more sophisticated tools than a standard home casting hub?"

"Tej is a butcher's apprentice," says Fonu. "Luja is new to casting. We don't think they knew any better."

Masar's temper boils over. His voice rises to a boom. "*Jun* would know better!"

He throws the blanket off. Pure adrenaline holds back the pain, and he's on his feet. There's dizziness—a surge of cold and heat through his body—but his vision clears. He stands a foot taller than Fonu, and he lets that height make a giant of him, looming over his River. Fonu looks stunned.

"Jun would *never* have left herself exposed like that! She would have buried her family under protections. Whoever did this is *framing* her! How can you not see that?!"

Fonu warns him, "Control yourself."

"Where is Jun now?"

"We have all the Ironways in a secure location."

"You *jailed* them?" He turns toward Effegen. "You have to stop this. This won't be the last attack the avatar tries. We need Jun. And Luja— what if she's the only one who can help us find Tej?"

Effegen looks sick with guilt, but her voice is steady. "I'm not a dictator, Masar. My leadership still beholds me to the entire Wheel, and all our votes are equal. Right now I'm outnumbered. Gaeda, Fonu, and Tomesk want the Ironways held until—"

"Then Hyre is with you?"

"Stop this at once," cries Fonu. "How dare you try to foment unrest in the Wheel? Are you a servant of Sajeven or not?"

"I am a servant of my people, Sa. The longer you hold Jun, the more danger we're all in."

"I am perfectly sensitive to danger—"

Masar ignores Fonu, looking at Effegen. "Let me talk to Jun."

"Out of the question!" Fonu cries.

Effegen says, "You're injured."

"I'm fine," he lies. "I want to talk to her, now."

Fonu grits out, "*You* do not give orders to the Wheel—"

"All right," Effegen interrupts. The River makes an apoplectic sound, which she ignores. "You can speak to Jun. But if you so much as sway on your feet, I'm making you come back here. I'll have you sedated if I have to. We need you healthy, Masar."

Perhaps they do. But they need Jun more. Masar is more sure of it than ever. If it could hack Jun's hub well enough to plant this evidence, the avatar is even more dangerous than he thought. And if the avatar meant to orchestrate an attack on the funeral dance, who knows what else Tej and Jasef sen Clime are preparing to do?

"You know," says Jun Ironway, "there is something to be said for a matriarchy."

Masar sits across from her at a small table in a requisitioned private office. They're in the newsnest, which the newscasters of Farren

Eyce have vacated under Hyre's orders, relocating to a different part of the colony. The newsnest has private offices, contained in a larger office space in the government quarter of Level 8. These offices share a hallway, have no windows. They're easy to guard. And now some of the rookie collectors (Eda and Layez and Iyrini and Siel) have requisitioned the retired uniforms of the Jeveni sentries and stand guard throughout the office space.

As for the particular "cell" where Masar finds himself, Hyre had the desk and the sofa replaced with a trio of makeshift cots. Bene and Luja are sitting on one of the cots, Bene with his arm over her shoulder. He looks calm but tired. Luja wears a blank expression, as if she always knew this would happen, and has dropped down into the blankness she learned on the farming station. Masar, body sore, chest tight, holds Bene's gaze. He's shocked by the compassion in Bene's face, the obvious concern for Masar's health. Even now, stuck in a cell by Masar's superiors, Bene is worried about him.

Masar snaps out of his distraction, looking at Jun. "You really think a matriarchy would solve our problems?"

"Absolutely," she drawls, fingers tapping the table in the restless gesture of a caster who can't cast. "If the Jeveni had a matriarch, this farce would never have happened to my family. How *is* Effegen? Her Wheel has lost its basic sense of reason and there doesn't appear to be anything she can do about it."

Bene says, "It's not Effegen's fault. She wants us freed."

Masar nods agreement, entreating Jun, "This wasn't her idea."

"In my whole life I've only had my access to my neural link cut off twice, and both times it was by your Wheel. Remind me, Masar, who saved all your godsdamned lives again?"

"Look, don't get sassy with me, I—"

"They *arrested* my cousins." Jun seems to bite the words. She gestures at Bene and Luja. "I brought my family here to be safe and you've *locked them up*. Do you know what I could—"

She breaks off, chokes the words down. Maybe she knows that Fonu is watching via the surveillance camera in the ceiling, and this tack won't convince anyone of her innocence. She looks away. He watches her. He's never been on opposite sides with Jun, never worked counter to her or experienced the brunt of her genius as a weapon raised against him. Most of the time, he treats Jun like an obnoxious sister, poking at her grumpiness, treating her skill set like a coworker's aptitude for math. Now, for the first time, he contemplates the idea of being Jun's enemy. Of seeing her turn her brilliance against Farren Eyce. He'd be a fool not to quail at that.

"I'm going to get you out, Jun. All of you. Once we find Tej and Jasef, we'll be able to get to the bottom of how you were framed—"

"I know how I was framed," she interrupts with a sound of disgust. "Whatever fucking virus the avatar threw at me last week, it must have penetrated some of my firewalls and hacked a line into my private casting hub. From there it could have taken over Luja's as well. If I had access to the casting net now, I could find it before it causes any more trouble."

Masar feels cold from the top of his head to his toes. Jun has access to *everything*. The casting lab. The life support systems. The *gate key*.

She seems to understand what he's thinking, because she smiles a little. "Don't panic yet. Access to my private hub isn't the same as access to the colony. But we can't afford to be complacent." She taps the side of her head. "It's got a drill in my head. And it'll just keep drilling deeper until we stop it."

Masar nods slowly. "I guess you told Fonu all this?"

"I told them they'd better stay away from me once I get out of here."

"Jun."

"You think I can't get out of here, Masar? You think I need a neural link to get out of this little jail? The longer I'm locked up here, the longer we're all distracted by this story of my complicity, the more time the avatar has to roam. And act. And hurt people. So I am getting out of here. I'm going to find Tej myself, that little fucking shit, and—"

She cuts herself off, throwing a glance at Luja. But Luja is still wearing that blank, numb expression. Bene gives her arm a little squeeze. He says quietly, "We didn't know it was this bad, with Tej. I should have kept a better eye on him."

To Masar's surprise, Luja says, "Tej is an adult. He made his own decisions."

There's a hardness in her voice that Masar isn't used to hearing. She blinks a little, looking at Jun. "You're so determined to protect me and Bene. But what about Tej? What's the Wheel going to do if they get him?" She looks at Masar. "Lock him up? Send him back to the Treble? Are you gonna send us *all* back to the Treble, if you decide we did this?"

Masar's side throbs. He can feel the regenerative medicine, stitching him together like a thousand needles. He wants to spare Luja's feelings, but he won't lie to her. "I don't think they'd send you back to the Treble. Jun has too much information. There'd be a concern about the Kindom... torturing her. Torturing all of you."

"Let's not get ahead of ourselves," Bene says. "Masar will prove that we're innocent."

"I will," Masar swears. "I'm gonna get you out."

"Not Tej, though," Luja says. No one answers, and her voice goes cold. "You know, Emos used to say that Tej was born looking for trouble. If he were here now, he'd say he saw it coming." She looks at Jun. "You're no better. You always expected the worst."

Jun blanches, startled and hurt. Bene says, "Luja, that's not true—"

But Luja pulls away from him. She goes to another cot and curls up facing the wall, pulling the meager blanket over herself. Masar sees the same bleak helplessness on Jun's and Bene's faces. Masar feels helpless, too.

He leans closer, whispering to Jun, "Let me get you out the *right* way. If I exonerate you, then you get the pleasure of the moral high ground. Break out and they'll always distrust you."

"They'll distrust me regardless. Fonu hates *strangers*, remember?" She uses the Je word with disgust. "Gaeda is suspicious of anyone who doesn't worship Sajeven. And Tomesk is a wannabe despot."

Masar swallows a thickness in his throat. He doesn't want to believe this. He doesn't want to believe the Draeviin abhor the non-Jeveni, or that his Wheel could so fail their legacy of uncompromising justice. But there's no point in defending them to Jun right now. He knows a better tactic, anyway.

"Since when do you care whether the people in charge trust you?" he demands. She narrows her eyes. "You've worked outside the cover of the establishment your entire life. You don't do what you do to make leaders happy—you do it for your own reasons. Eight months ago, you wanted to save the Jeveni and your own life, so that's what you did. Now, maybe you don't give a shit about the Jeveni right now, and I wouldn't blame you. But you give a shit about your family, and you give a shit about stopping this avatar. So stop sulking about what the Wheel has done to you or thinks of you. Use your *head*, Jun, not your ego."

Eyes still narrowed, she considers him. It's very quiet in the room, no outside voices penetrating the locked door. Dryly, Jun asks, "You been practicing that speech?"

"No, I had godly inspiration."

Over on the cot, Bene chuckles. Even Jun allows herself a half smile.

"Fine," she says. "Get me out, if you can. But I won't wait indefinitely."

Masar exhales. "Your casters will want to help you. What should I tell them to do?"

"Track every power outage that lasts more than ten seconds. Look for patterns. Tej and Jasef may be working for someone smart, but they're just a couple of boys following orders. They'll make a mistake, probably as soon as they get hungry."

"All right," he says.

"And another thing—"

But suddenly the door opens. Fonu appears, their face pinched, studiously ignoring Jun. She looks at them with a lazy, malevolent patience, like a vulture biding its time.

Fonu says to Masar, "I need you to come with me. There's...a disturbance, outside."

Confused, worried, Masar makes to stand. Halfway up, the movement sends a flash of pain through him, and he braces himself on the table, wincing. Bene is off the cot in an instant, and despite his embarrassment, Masar allows the younger man to help him stand up the rest of the way. In irritation he notices Fonu has gone tense, as if they expect Bene to attack.

"You've got to rest," Bene says.

"He's not wrong," Jun agrees.

Masar smiles faintly, straightening to his full height and moving toward the door. As he walks past, his fingers reach out on instinct, brushing against Bene's. He doesn't say goodbye.

In the hallway, Masar glances up and down the row of doors. Aris the Beauty is in her own repurposed cell toward the end. What happens when they catch Tej and Jasef and whoever else is involved in this? Will the newsnest become a permanent prison?

Recovering his strength, he looks at Fonu warily. "What's going on?"

"I don't know," Fonu admits. "A crowd has come down from Levels 9 and 10."

This makes no sense. Levels 9 and 10 are the farms, and above them are the surface and the dome. Is it a protest from the farm workers?

Fonu apparently has no time for his confusion. They stride off, and Masar follows, lucky that his superior height can make up for his careful gait. The hallway leads into a larger office space. There's a receptionist at the main desk looking anxious, and Masar is nauseated again by the sight of Eda and Layez in uniform, guns at their hips. They nod at Masar, respectful, and he nods back, but wonders if they have any conception of the gravity of their presence. The risk it poses to everything Farren Eyce is meant to represent.

Outside, there are more armed and uniformed collectors, a line of five standing between a crowd and the newsnest suite. The saan in the courtyard do indeed appear to have come down from the above levels, many of them still standing on the staircase. Masar clocks their expressions, searching for hostility and threat. To his surprise, they look mostly curious, even excited. Like spectators at a Som's Catch tournament.

Fonu and Masar step through the line of collectors. Only then does Masar realize that some of the saan at the front of the crowd stand out from the rest. They're not wearing farming clothes, or even the casual attire of colonists going about their day. They are cloaked in heavy coats, dusted white. Snow melts onto the ground around their big boots. Masar recognizes the faces of expeditioners who he hasn't seen in weeks.

A figure steps out in front of the crowd, shorter than most of the rest but projecting an intensity that puts Masar in mind of bombs about to go off. They cast back the hood of their coat, revealing a head of tight black twists and a face beaten with frost.

"Sa Fhaan," Liis Konye murmurs, her feet apart, her hands loose at her sides. "I think you have something of mine."

These are my oaths, until I die.

To obey the Godfire first, and above any other god or saan.

To echo in my life the character of my god—mercy, justice, and incorruptibility.

To serve my god by serving my people, whose lives I place above my own, whose care and protection shall inspire my actions, whose crimes I will curtail and forgive, and whose innocence I will defend, even to my death.

I will not buckle. I will not relent. I will be steady in purpose. I will shine like a burning star, bright and righteous as my god.

Else may it burn me up, and forget my name forever.

The Formal Oaths of the Righteous Hand.
Dated 138, Year of the Cliff.

CHAPTER SIXTEEN

1665

YEAR OF THE HARVEST

The Coast
Nikata Leen, an Island
The Planet Kator

A second shot pierces the air as Chono drops behind the bar, Six practically on top of her in a tangle of limbs. Adrenaline kicks her senses into gear, the smell of the hard-packed dirt, the bite of the wind, the whistle of a third bullet and the crack of it impacting wood—

"Single shooter," Six tells her. "They're in the granary. Second floor."

Chono shoves out from underneath them, both of them taking up a crouch.

The sniper fires another shot.

Six asks, "Do you have a gun?"

Chono scowls. "Where would I have got a gun?"

Six reaches inside their coat with one hand and down toward their pant leg with the other. They pull a pistol out of an ankle holster and hand it to her, brandishing their own larger handgun. Chono examines the chamber. Ten rounds. Six presses a second clip into her hand.

"This is what you must do. Move to the end of the bar, then fire on the top-left window. Cover me and I will rush the granary."

"You'll be completely out in the open."

"That is why you are going to cover me."

Chono doesn't like it. She doesn't like the stillness of the Kindom warcat. She doesn't like the sound of another shot, skipping across the top of the bar and exploding a row of glass bottles. She and Six cover themselves against the spray of glass shards, then look at each other again. Chono nods. She keeps low and moves toward the far end of the bar, while Six moves in the opposite direction. Another three shots, goading them.

"Ready?" Six asks.

Chono says, "Do it."

And springs to her feet, already firing. She finds the top-left window unerringly, firing one round after another as Six sprints for the granary. She counts the bullets as she tracks their progress. Three left. Two left. One—

Six hurls themself into the door, which smashes open against their shoulder. Chono drops to a squat, expelling the empty clip and loading the new one as fresh gunfire sprays the bar top, the sniper clearly back in the game. Chono takes a new position, pops up long enough to fire, and drops again. If she can keep them distracted while Six gets to the second floor—

But this time the answering gunfire doesn't come from the granary— it clips the side of the bar not three inches from her face. She jerks away, spilling onto her back. There's sharp glass under her, and from this position she sees the edge of the lot and the warcat. A guardsaan has appeared beside it.

But this guardsaan is not here to help her.

They stalk toward the bar, full body armor and lowered faceplate, a rifle aiming for her.

Chono fires. Shots pepper the dirt by her feet. The guardsaan advances, and Chono lays down half a dozen rounds as she gambles on her life, leaping up and springing around to the other side of the bar, out of the guard's range but fully in view of the granary. Yet no sniper fire takes her out. Six must be up there already. She squats, peeks around the edge of the bar, and sees not just one advancing guardsaan, but a second. This one runs for the granary. Chono stands, fires—and the first guardsaan closes in, but a bullet drops them in the dirt.

Six has the sniper's rifle.

The second guardsaan closes in on the granary. She sprints after them.

More gunfire rains from the second-story window, but the angle is bad and the guardsaan slips past it, getting closer as Chono gets closer, both of them running full tilt at the doorway. They reach it at the same moment, slamming into each other, falling into the close and dusty darkness. Chono, mercifully on top, strikes at them, and a fist comes out of nowhere to connect with her jaw. Pain explodes in the side of her face, ear ringing. She twists, grappling for control. They grab her by the shoulders, wrenching and rolling her under them. She brings her knee up hard into their groin, and the leather padding isn't quite enough to stop their grunt of pain—just before they headbutt her.

For a split second she goes weak, stunned and spinning. The headbutt has knocked the guard's helmet loose. A shaggy-haired, grimacing man appears, and gloved hands wrap around her throat as he straddles her waist, a boulder of weight pinning her helplessly beneath him.

Remember your forms, drawls Esek.

She grabs his wrist and bicep, breaks the strength in one of his arms, and hooks a leg over his. She flips him almost over her head, rolling sideways with him and striking his temple as hard as she can. He rakes at her face, nails sharp, opening up the skin like razors. As if from a thousand miles away, she glimpses another guard in the barn. A bullet takes them out.

Shame on this guardsaan, for growing his hair long. She gets a fist-ful of it, cracks his head down on the hard floorboards, but not hard enough. There are teeth over the back of her wrist, biting so hard she screams. Her gun is missing. The guard's, too. They are like wild ani-mals, snarling and frantic. Chono punches his face hard enough that his teeth let go, and blood runs down her wrist and fingers. She hits him again, breaking his nose with a wet crunch—and sees a flash of steel.

She jerks back, barely avoiding the slash of the knife toward her throat. He drives at her side, and she grabs his wrist, slamming it down on the floor with her injured hand. The guard has ripped open the side of her palm, the pain excruciating as she tries to hold the knife immo-bile. A flailing arm—the guard swinging at the side of her head. She blocks to avoid the worst of it.

"Chono!" someone yells.

There's no time to answer. The guardsaan is snarling, and she is thrashing and spitting and then wrenching the knife off him, fling-ing his arm wide, exposing the gap between his chest and backplates. She drives in, right there in the sweet spot under his ribs, and feels the separation of muscle and bone. She yanks the hilt down, and his body loses strength beneath hers, throat spasming.

Chono hears pounding footsteps. She pulls upright, taking the knife with her, and prepares to leap up into the next fight—

But it's Six. They're racing down a ladder from the second story of the granary, sniper rifle in hand and looking at her in a way Esek never looked at her—the borderline of panic.

Beneath Chono's body, the guardsaan is limp, his eyes staring. She staggers off him, half stumbling until her back hits the nearest wall. Her legs turn to jelly, and she sinks into a sitting position. Six is there in moments, snapping at her, "Hold still!"

She trembles with adrenaline, the pain in her hand pulsing. She can see the guard's face from this position, blood pooling under him. She blinks, and his face turns old, cracked open, and his body is skinny and broken inside its red cleric's cloak, and Caskhen Paan is dead—he deserves to be dead—monster and rapist—he—

She blinks, and it's the guardsaan again. Chono breathes in raggedly and tries to stand up. Six's hands on her shoulders push her back down.

"The warcat," she gasps. "There might be more—"

"It drove off," Six interrupts.

They're checking her body for injuries, hands skating over her limbs and sides, her chest and belly and the back of her head. When Moonback's cloaks did this, it filled her with terror, but suddenly all she can think of is when she was shot on *The Risen Wave*, and the person she thought was Esek drained their own blood to keep her alive. Now, Six's face is an iron mask, but when they try to touch her hand, she yelps, and their eyes widen.

"I'm okay," she says, pushing aside the past. "I'm... I'm okay. Are you okay?"

Six nods, but there's a ripening bruise on the side of their face, blood on their mouth. The sniper on the second story must have got in a few jabs before Six took them out, but they show no sign of serious injury. Chono, bruised and still winded, grabs their arm with her good hand.

"Help me up."

They do. For a moment the both of them stand still, Chono getting her bearings, Six looking her over. She touches the side of her face, tracing out three gouge marks that at least aren't bleeding very much. She takes in the scene of the granary. There are two dead guardsaan, her own victim and the one Six shot, halfway out the door. Six squats beside the latter, examining them. They pull the helmet off to reveal a woman's blank-eyed face.

Six says, "I do not think these are Kindom guardsaan."

Chono looks down at the familiar uniforms. "Why?"

"If the Kindom was trying to assassinate us, it would not send its guardsaan to do it. It would hide its actions better."

Chono agrees. Does this mean that whoever is responsible wanted to frame the Kindom? She can think of several parties who would do that. Seti Moonback. The Khen family, wanting revenge for her murder of Cleric Paan. The Nightfoots. Last year, someone put a hit out on Esek. Does this latest attempt come from the same source? Is Esek even the target, this time?

"What do we do?" she asks.

Six stands up again, dusting off their hands. "What do you want to do?"

The question surprises her, but Six meets her gaze, expectant. She swallows. "From where I'm standing, we have two options. We can return to Praetima, or we can strike out on our own. Both are dangerous, but—"

"We cannot run, Chono."

She expected them to be thrilled at the prospect of getting out from under the Kindom's thumb. "Why not?"

They pause, measuring. "You cannot burn your goodwill with the Kindom."

"The Kindom obviously can't protect us. Maybe it doesn't want to."

"If we run, we declare ourselves as dissidents."

Chono steps away from them, temper flaring. They're right, of course. What will happen to the five thousand, if Chono and Six disappear? But she is sick of holding services in the Praetima temple, sick of Ilius's mournful looks, sick of being watched.

"You must hold on to the power that you have, Chono," Six says. "You must remain the venerated cleric. It is our only leverage."

"Yantikye would have me lead an uprising," she retorts, as if parading a counteroffer.

Six smiles thinly. "Yantikye wants to use you."

"Yantikye says *you* want to use me."

Six doesn't reply, and she feels oddly guilty. Their Esek eyes, those gorgeous, forge-bright eyes, that face with its exquisite structure, that full mouth pressed into a line—all of it captures her like a net. Does she trust them or not? She must decide.

Six says, "Yes. I do want to use you. Everybody wants to use everybody. But unlike Yantikye, I do not want you to be hurt."

Chono isn't quite sure how to respond to that mercenary logic. Reluctantly, she looks over at the graveled lot, noticing for the first time their taxi-pod smoking from its engine, pockmarked with gun-fire. Clearly the guardsaan meant to cut off their escape route.

Wearily she says, "I'll have to ask Ilius to send us help."

Six's lip curls a little. "Yes, I suppose you must."

"It seems risky, summoning the Kindom."

"Yes. Which is why you should send the cast to Ilius alone. His politics are as despicable as any secretary's... but I am reasonably certain he does not want you dead."

So it is that they find themselves back in Praetima. And, less than two hours later, standing in the Centrum of Nikapraev. But tonight it is almost empty, just a half dozen guardsaan, and Ravening, Songrider, and Ilius holding court upon the dais. Every door into the Centrum is shut, and the vastness of the gleaming space makes Chono imagine standing on the surface of Capamame, the opaque sky endless above, and the stretch of barren miles reminding her how very, very small she is.

Songrider wears a contemplative expression. Ravening looks surly and gruff. Ilius stares at Chono, his concern for her embarrassingly bald. The doctors have treated the wounds on her face, and wrapped her hand in thick regenerative bandaging. The ripped meat of her palm throbs.

After a silence of nearly thirty seconds, Six huffs.

"Kata's tit, what a warm welcome we're receiving. Don't you people know the niceties of conversation? 'Why, Sa Nightfoot, I'm so glad you're alive. I hope your injuries aren't too serious. Please, please forgive us for letting assassins overpower and replace your escort'—"

"You should not have needed an escort," Ravening says. "Your determination to leave Praetima shows your reckless intransigence. If you had listened to Secretary Redquill when he tried to dissuade you—"

"You think assassins got to us because we were outside Praetima?" Six interrupts. "That's not how assassins work. Remember, I've trained cloaksaan. They'll find a way to their quarry, no matter what."

"Your attackers weren't cloaksaan or guardsaan," Songrider reminds them mildly. "We've traced them to Teros."

That was fast, Chono thinks.

"They're insurgents," Songrider continues, "trying to strike a blow against the Kindom by taking out high-profile targets. You made their job easier by leaving Praetima."

"What makes you so sure they were insurgents?" Chono asks.

"We've seen a groundswell of violence in the past day. Protests have transformed into uprisings overnight."

Chono wonders, are these the same resistance cells that Yantikye and Graisa claimed were simply waiting for an excuse to light the fuse? Or are they spontaneous and disorganized?

"That doesn't tell me why you think the assassins were Teron," she says.

"We've linked them to a terrorist cell in the city of Trin-Ma. It has been under siege for twelve hours—the governor has fled and the insurgents are nearly in control."

A twist in Chono's stomach. The familiar name of that city, which she has tried to forget for twenty-five years. Six slaps her shoulder, gripping tight as they laugh. "By the gods, Chono! Your own birthplace! You'd think they'd want their famous daughter protected."

"Whatever the insurgents originally wanted, they are bought actors now," Ilius says. "In the past week, they've received an influx of money and weapons. My informants have traced the origin of those resources to Seti Moonback. She's also funding uprisings on Ma'kess, Kator, and Quietus. Pippashap itself has become one of her strongholds. And Principes, as well."

Nausea pushes toward the back of Chono's throat, but Six makes an intrigued sound. "Huh. All precious places to our hearts. Home cities. The location of our kinschool and of our most significant assignments."

"Those are just examples," Songrider interjects. "The uprisings are everywhere, and many secretaries have been targeted."

"Where is Moonback getting her funds?" Chono asks. "Her family?"

"Not that we can prove," muses Songrider.

"Amazing, isn't it?" says Six. "Who'd have thought ousting Moonback would come back to haunt you, Prudent Ones?"

"We're in no need of your sarcasm." Ravening's voice drips acid. "Nor your levity. We believe that Seti Moonback intends a wide-scale assault on Kindom strongholds."

Chono says, "However many Brutal Hands Moonback can rally, the guardsaan of the Treble will outnumber them a thousand to one."

Songrider leans forward. "The mathematical chances of Moonback's success are not the problem here. Her rebellion is a rot that will spread sickness through the Treble. If the people believe we are fighting each other, it will erode their confidence in us. It will encourage more uprisings. It will bring chaos. The entire point of Kindom law is to *reduce* chaos. It is the purpose of the Secretaries. It is our calling from the Godfire."

Six laughs. "You are utterly delusional if you think Treblens still believe in the unity of the Hands. You have eaten your siblings in the womb to make yourself bigger and stronger. Moonback is the underdog now. Oppressed people love an underdog."

"The Cloaksaan have terrorized Treblens under Moonback's leadership," Ilius points out.

"Something you didn't seem to mind until recently," says Six.

"Oh, and I suppose you minded it?" Ilius asks scornfully.

Six spreads their hands apart. "I'm simply offering some free advice. As soon as you removed Moonback from power, she set her sights on destroying you. If she pursues that aim, she'll make herself a cult figure. People will forget her evils because they'll see her as standing up to tyrants. It's no use you saying she was a tyrant first. You simply do not understand the difference between reality and perception."

Yantikye's words, thinks Chono grimly.

"I suppose you would have us ignore her movements altogether," accuses Ilius.

"I would have you give me back the sevite trade before you destroy it with your petty infighting."

"We are *fighting* for the Treble!" Ilius shouts. Chono has never heard him raise his voice like this, has never seen such open hatred on his face. His whole body trembles with it. "And we all know that's not something you care about! It doesn't matter to you how many die in a civil war among the Hands, or how many innocents suffer for the shortsightedness of insurgents. All *you* care about is your profits, and gods know war needs sevite. You are a misanthropic, self-interested barbarian. If children died at your feet, you would step over their corpses and tell your novitiates to burn them as fuel!"

Six's eyebrows shoot up. "That's very colorful."

"For all we know you're in league with Moonback yourself!"

"Ilius," Chono says, baffled.

But he looks quite wild now, shoving a finger at Six. "All of this is down to your crimes and disloyalty! You allied with Jun Ironway, a known criminal caster from a terrorist family. You allied with Liis Konye, a cloaksaan defector and traitor! You allied with a secret, *illegal* Jeveni government and no doubt promised them the trade so that they would be loyal to you after Alisiana died. You helped them leave the Treble and sabotage the sevite trade so that you can hoard their knowledge and use them as a weapon against us!"

He breaks off, shuddering from the intensity of his outburst. Dead air follows after him. Chono wonders if this has been the theory about Esek and her work with the Jeveni all along. The Kindom's hunger to reopen contact with the Capamame Jeveni only seems more dangerous now.

Chono flicks her eyes at Ravening and Songrider, who are tense. Ilius has obviously given something away that they wanted to hold close. As for Six, they make a purring, pleased sound. But she thinks their pleasure is not an Esek act, but their own mean-spirited delight to see how much trouble they have caused.

Chono says, "You're mistaken about Sa Nightfoot's intentions with the Jeveni."

"Prove it," Ravening booms. "Both of you. Tell the Jeveni to negotiate with us."

Chono tamps down her frustration. "We cannot ask them to do something that is against their interests. And as long as you keep the five thousand imprisoned—"

"I will not negotiate with you," Ravening interrupts. "You're both lucky we didn't hang you as soon as you arrived. You may think yourself highly valued in the Treble, Cleric Chono—and you may see yourself as the untouchable scion of a First Family, Sa Nightfoot, but you are neither of you above the reach of our authority. If we have to, we will destroy your reputations past repair and throw you out of this city and onto the mercy of people who will *hate* you once we're done! See how safe you are then!"

Spittle flies from his mouth, sweat lathering his brow, and the sheer satisfaction he takes in making the threat is...remarkable. There's something refreshing about having any pretense of goodwill between them abandoned. Chono wonders how Ilius feels about this threat, but he seems not to have even heard it. He's staring at Six like a fighting pit dog on a shredding leash. Six, to Chono's annoyance, is staring back at him with a smirk that demeans his very existence.

Then Songrider's crisp voice fills the Centrum. "Day after tomorrow, the Secretaries will vote on two crucial matters intended to strike at Moonback. First, we will formally appoint a new First Cloak. Second, we will approve attacks on Moonback's main strongholds. That includes Trin-Ma, Pippashap, and Principes, and some of the other cities where she is funding terrorism. The purpose will be to annihilate the insurgents before their cancer can spread. Once we complete our vote, you, Cleric Chono, will speak to the newscasters and condemn Moonback as the orchestrator of your assassination attempt. You will publicly and enthusiastically support us in any and all efforts to stop her. And you will call on the Jeveni to equip us with the information we need to strengthen the sevite trade infrastructure, so that we can fight Moonback more effectively. None of these actions are negotiable. Will you honor your vows or not?"

Chono doesn't react right away. She's still processing phrases like *annihilate the insurgents* and *any and all efforts to stop her.*

"I..." She pauses long enough to demonstrate her consideration. "I will not."

The three secretaries stare down at her. Ilius has finally stopped glaring at Six, his attention shifting toward Chono, his eyes panicked. She focuses on Songrider and Ravening, the former icy, the latter looking on the verge of violence.

Ravening says, "You will defy us, then?"

"I will not betray my gods for you. I will never support the wholesale destruction of cities that are full of innocent civilians. By the gods, Principes houses a kinschool."

"We have evacuated that kinschool," says Songrider.

"Have you evacuated the other children living in those cities?"

"These early strikes will prevent wide-scale war. It will save millions in the long run."

"That is the logic the Secretaries used seventy-five years ago," Chono says, "when they murdered the Jeveni to prevent a resurgence of the jevite trade. You should know better than to think I'd share that philosophy now."

"And what about the Jeveni?" Songrider tosses back. "You have been very protective of them, very determined to see the five thousand released. How can we do this, or refrain from arresting the other Jeveni in the systems, if we discover that they are themselves insurgents?"

Chono wears her composure like armor, but she is full of the thought of what happened to the Ironways on K-5, and the surviving Alanyes on Braemin, after Esek attacked them. How she spread the lie that they were terrorists in order to defend slaughtering them. It was a lie that went down easy, in the Treble. Lies always seem to.

"I will not condone this kind of violence."

Songrider's hands grip the armrests of her chair. Ravening leans forward, malicious. "You underestimate our resolve."

"I don't think so. I've seen the cruelty of the Kindom firsthand. What's the worst you can do? Kill me? Then kill me." And gods, what a blessing that would be! Delivered from all these evils and every choking memory, and perhaps reborn on another world, on cool, crisp Capamame, or somewhere even farther away. Somewhere unreachable. "Kill the five thousand. Kill everyone who stands against you. But you won't have my blessing when—"

"Oh, shut up, Chono."

Six cuts her off like a scythe. She looks at them, bewildered, but they ignore her with all of Esek's disdain, eyes on the secretaries. "We all know how obnoxiously principled you are. Be quiet while I speak to these people in concrete rather than flowery terms. Maybe it'll get through their thick skulls."

Songrider lifts her eyebrows. "I beg your pardon, Sa Nightfoot?"

"You talk so casually of bombing Principes. Have you forgotten that it's Nightfoot territory?"

Ravening sniffs. "All territory in the Treble belongs to the Kindom."

"That is quite debatable. But certainly if nothing else, you can concede that the First Families have the right to defend their interests. Why, for example, Trin-Ma is rather important to the Khens. And the Paiyes rely on cities like Pippashap for their seafood imports. As for my own house, we can't support indiscriminate carpet-bombing of—"

"It is not indiscriminate," Ravening interrupts. "And no First Family will want to protect a city that has fallen to criminals and rebels."

"I am Riin Matri of the Nightfoots," Six reminds him. "I *am* a First Family. I'll tell you straight, we handle our own affairs. Your...interference isn't welcome, and we won't stand for it."

Songrider leans forward again, looking amazed. "Are you *threatening* the Kindom, Sa?"

A laugh. "Well, you did threaten us. So now we have threatened you back. It *is* New Sun, after all. We should begin the year as we mean to go on."

Chono barely stops herself from kicking them.

"We could arrest you right here," Ilius bites out.

"Now that *would* make for a fun evening. Try it and let's see what happens."

Chono quickly interjects. "Sa Nightfoot is tired and frustrated by the attempts on our lives. Don't make the mistake of escalating hostilities by arresting her—"

"If Sa Nightfoot resists our efforts to stop Seti Moonback, then she is as good as declaring for Moonback herself."

"Yuck," Six says. "I'd rather fuck a sea elk. I'd rather fuck *you*, Ilius."

Chono shoots them a message.

Shut up.

They ignore her.

"Besides, the question here is whether you can get away with all these threats you're making. I think you're all very insipid, but maybe intelligent enough to realize that when walking on a razor's edge, you have to be careful you don't overstep."

"We won't be intimidated by a recalcitrant blowhard," Ilius says.

"All your prior actions to the contrary, dear Ilius. Beloved writer of wills."

Ravening slams the round stone gavel onto the table, maybe because it's the loudest and most startling sound he can make. Six still grins at it, amused. Chono cuts a look at the guardsaan by the door. Their hands are on their guns, just waiting for a signal.

Ilius's finger bracelets make a short, discordant music—but his dismissive gesture causes the guards to stand down. Ravening, for his part, chuckles in a slow, murderous way.

"Take Cleric Chono and Sa Nightfoot back to Blue Spire," he orders. "They will not leave its grounds, and if they try . . . shoot them."

Chono looks at Ilius again. He says nothing. One of the guardsaan has her by the elbow. She shakes him off, turning and walking under her own power. Six comes, too, at a lazy stroll, calling back, "Do be wary, before you dip those pure white tippets in fresh blood. For our ghosts will come after you."

CHAPTER SEVENTEEN

1664

YEAR OF THE CRUX

Farren Eyce
The Planet Capamame

The Level 2 casting den is abandoned. Masar stands in the empty apartment, all its equipment stripped out, nothing but a flattened pillow left behind. This was the first place Fonu's collectors checked, after the events of the funeral dance and the capture of Aris the Beauty. But the scene has changed since they were here. There is now a body in the room.

Jasef sen Clime sits against the wall, one leg bent under him, a bullet wound in the center of his chest and a thick smear of blood on the wall from where he slid down. His head tips at a strange angle, his eyes half closed. The shock of his red hair puts Masar in mind of Uskel, broken open on the staircase steps.

Masar knew already that Tej and his compatriots had got ahold of guns somehow, but to have it proved again makes him feel sick. The only people with access to the armory are a couple of high-level collectors (himself included), the Wheel, and Jun. When Masar reports this death to Fonu, will they find a way to use it against the Ironways? Or to argue that Liis killed the boy?

It's Liis who sent him here, just nine hours after her return. Masar has spent the intervening hours shut up in his apartment, Effegen's stern command forcing him to lie uselessly in bed. But he couldn't relax, body lit with the desire to act. When Liis's ocular message reached him, it was brief.

I found one of them. Dead already.

Now, standing before the scene Liis discovered, he thinks about the moment when he first saw her outside the newsnest. Her utter calm. Her razor edge. He was both incredibly relieved to see her and surprised at his own fear. What would Liis Konye do in the face of Jun's arrest? She was capable of terrible violence, but she was also admirably controlled. Could the endangerment of her lover crack that control?

Fonu, damn them, had stepped forward with an ill-advised bravado. "Sa Konye. We didn't realize you were coming back to Farren Eyce so early in the expedition."

Liis's answering smile was chilling.

"Should I believe that if I'd come sooner, you would not have shown the terrible, bad judgment of arresting the Ironways?"

"There are things about the situation you don't yet know, namely—"

She interrupted, "Tej Redcore is affiliated with whoever murdered Kereth ben Dane and the collectors. He has fled, and his apartment is full of evidence that implicates his family in the actions of the avatar. You have taken this evidence at face value and, shortsightedly, arrested the Ironways while you consider your next move. What exactly don't I know about the situation?"

Fonu had blinked in surprise, then shot back, "I wonder how you know so much about it if you're not involved yourself."

"Godsdamnit," Masar had muttered.

"Your casting corps isn't particularly good on security without Jun to guide them," Liis replied. "And I was trained by the Brutal Hand. Imagine what the avatar is able to do in these lax circumstances."

The crowd behind Liis (swelling, since her arrival) began to murmur, fretful, and unnerved, and angry. Masar remembers the feeling of it, the pressure in the air, the rampant discontent in Farren Eyce reaching a fever pitch.

Into this harrowing atmosphere, Liis had said, "I'll find them."

Fonu narrowed their eyes. "What?"

"Your search for Tej and his coconspirators has been fruitless. Don't interfere, and I'll find them for you."

"They've got nowhere to run. *Your* interference is not necessary."

"I could hide from you for a lifetime in this colony," Liis replied. "At the very least, Tej has the help of an expert caster. It could be weeks before you find him, and I won't tolerate the Ironways staying in your jail for that long."

"You have no say in the matter," declared Fonu.

Masar had begged the goddess for Liis to be temperate. She looked at Fonu, steady and silent, and after a moment Fonu seemed uncertain. Perhaps they were thinking what Masar was thinking: that Liis had chosen, out of respect, not to vocally threaten them. But the threat was perfectly obvious on her face. Who could stop her, if she took action? The line of uniformed collectors between her and Jun was not nearly enough to hold her back, and when Masar sent little glances at them, he saw that the collectors knew it. They were sweating with nerves.

"Sa Konye is a free citizen," Masar said, hoping to de-escalate before Fonu well and truly fucked themself. "What she chooses to do is her business, granted she breaks no laws."

The crowd chattered with agreement, clearly on Liis's side. Her past as a cloaksaan is well known to Farren Eyce, and most people fear her a healthy amount—but her legend as a defector has bred respect and even reverence. Few would side with Fonu over her.

No doubt feeling the crowd turn on them, Fonu had scowled. But finally, Liis's stare quelled their bluster. "Fine," they groused. "If you think you're superior to all the collectors in Farren Eyce, conduct your search."

Masar could have laughed at that, if things weren't so strained. Liis nodded deferentially, and though she isn't a sarcastic person, Masar couldn't shake the feeling that there was mockery in it. Fonu said, "I suppose you'd like to see Sa Ironway?"

"No need," Liis replied, already turning on her heel, her heavy coat swishing around her ankles as the crowd parted for her. "I'd know if you had hurt her."

Now, standing in the abandoned casting den, Masar wonders where Liis is. Why she called him here and then left. When the door to the apartment opens, he whirls around expecting to see her—but it's Effegen who steps into the room.

The Star of the Wheel is just as pale and weary as when he saw her in the hospital. For all her demands that he get some rest, it's clear she hasn't slept in far too long. They look at each other without speaking, and she closes the door after her, stepping farther into the room. She doesn't quail at the sight of the body. She regards Jasef with a cool, thoughtful expression, and murmurs a Je blessing, and asks at last, "How long?"

Masar grunts. "A few hours? Recent, anyway."

"Someone cleaning up shop, perhaps?"

"It could be."

Effegen nods, staring at the boy for so long that Masar begins to wonder if she is even seeing him—if her mind has gone somewhere else. If she is thinking of other bodies. Other deaths. Nikkelo, perhaps? Or members of her own family?

"Did Liis send you here?" he asks.

Effegen hums. "Though not Fonu, it appears."

"Can you blame her?"

"I don't blame her for anything. I'd hardly blame her if she attacked us. After everything Jun has done for this colony..."

"It's not your fault."

"Isn't it?"

"No."

"We have broken Jun's trust forever. I am the Star of the Wheel, the figurehead of our government. It's my responsibility. And my failure."

"Jun is a spiteful little shit, but she's not irrational. She'll understand that she can't blame the whole colony, or even the whole Wheel. Liis and Bene will knock some sense into her."

"Yes, Bene," Effegen says, with a pained smile. "Do you know I sometimes tease him by calling him Capamame? The dear friend."

Masar can't decide which emotion is stronger: amusement at the appropriateness of this, or jealousy that the two are close enough to have nicknames.

"What does he call you?" Masar asks, unable to help himself.

She looks at him, her eyes soft. "He calls me Effegen."

Masar thinks of the times she's asked him to call her Effegen. Suddenly he realizes why. It was not some attempt at informality. She and Bene are friends because Bene does not treat her like an unapproachable Spoke of the Wheel. He calls her Effegen, and in calling her Effegen he lifts the burden of her responsibilities—not completely, not all the time, but just enough to help her breathe. And all this time it could have been Masar lifting the burden with him, and he's been too proud to do it.

"Effegen," Masar whispers.

She looks startled, and then almost shy. She moves forward till she is right in front of him.

"I keep thinking about Drae sen Briit," she says, her hand drifting to the pocket where he knows she keeps the little book of Drae's speeches. "She had...so much hope in Capamame. In *us*—that we would make her dream come true." Her eyes rise to his again, and the grief in them is terrible. "Will you forgive us?" she whispers. "You dedicated your life to making this world possible. You sacrificed so much, and this is the best we've been able to do. Will you forgive the Wheel for its failures? Will you forgive me?"

His heart aches. "There's nothing to forgive...Effegen...There's nothing to forgive."

Her eyes finally lift to his. He wants to comfort her. He wants to touch her. He'll call her Effegen as many times as she needs, if only it will soothe her.

But a message pings in his ocular. He sees the shift in her expression, sees that she has received it as well. They reach for it in the same moment.

Come to Caspir's Bar on Level 3. Now.

The bar is a small establishment, about half the size of the Ironway apartment and tucked into one of the residential quarters. The owner, Caspir, is not there when they arrive. The door is shut and the window dark, which is strange given it's only early evening. Masar might fear some interference by the avatar, but he sees a light far in the back of the shop. He steps inside, Effegen behind him. The bar itself is empty, the little tables as well, except for one high-top in a corner, with a lamp overhead. Liis is sitting there. Dom ben Dane sits with her.

He's bent over his cup, shoulders sunken, his profile a snapshot of defeat and grief. When Masar approaches, and Dom lifts his head to look at him, his eyes slide right past Masar and land on Effegen with blooming horror.

"No." He turns a panicked look at Liis. "No, you said it was Masar coming, you said—"

"You'll have to tell both of them regardless," Liis interrupts in a quiet, unreadable voice.

Masar glances at Effegen, sees her confusion, and when they are standing next to the high-top, Dom's panic only intensifies. He clutches his cup and desperately shakes his head at it.

"No," he says again. "No. No."

"Dom," Masar tries.

"No, I can't," he says. "Not to her, I can't. I won't. I—"

Liis's fist comes down so hard on the tabletop that it cuts him off like a knife.

"That's enough," she says, voice wintry. "The only reason you've still got all your fingers is because you were wise enough not to test what I can do to you."

"Liis," Effegen reproves.

"Forgive me, my Star." Liis shows no remorse. "I simply don't want us to waste any more time."

Dom turns the cup again and again between his hands, trembling. Liis stares at him in a way that Masar has never seen her stare at anyone, even as intense and powerful as she is. It's the stare of a cloaksaan. It's the stare of someone who is prepared to beat someone to death.

"Dom," he says, stunned by what he sees, terrified of what it might mean. "Dom, what is it? Tell me. You can tell me."

Dom raises his head, looking at Masar with wet, red eyes.

"They were going to kill Kereth," he rasps. "You have to understand . . . They were going to kill Kereth."

Liis takes something from under the table and places it down for all to see. It's a handgun. Dom flinches as if she's struck him.

"Tell them," she says.

He swallows. "It was never supposed to go this far. In the first couple of months they just wanted help getting more rations, more resources. It was never supposed to go this far."

"Who?" Masar asks.

"Aris was in charge. Or at least, I thought so at the beginning. I don't know how many there are, but Aris usually sent Tej and Jasef to talk to me."

"Tej and Jasef sen Clime threatened to kill Kereth?" Effegen says. "Why didn't you come to us? Why didn't you tell us?"

"The two of them are half your weight," Masar put in. "What threat were they to you?"

"Tell them," Liis repeats.

"I—it was—we were so young, you know, Masar?" Tears are streaming down his face now. "We didn't have anything. The work—we risked ourselves every day and we never got anything. I never got to see Kereth and there was no money to send back to her. I thought I was going to die! I wanted her to have something. She barely had enough to live on, working the factories. I thought she might starve."

His voice chokes off, like this outburst is the most he can manage. There's something thick in the back of Masar's throat, the terror closing in, making his side throb and his eye glitch and his lungs compress.

"There was a secretary," Dom whispers. "And he...had people all over the Treble. One of them was Aris. She told me he had a buyer who would pay me a lot of money if I...if I told them what I knew...about the Wheel."

Silence falls, soft as snow on the plains of Capamame. Masar doesn't speak because he doesn't understand what he just heard. He has the strangest experience of dissonance, as if Dom had just spoken in one of the few languages that Masar doesn't know. He's bizarrely inclined to call up his translator bot, to check the words back.

But very slowly, the meaning penetrates Masar's confused thoughts. Nonsense syllables restructure, becoming words so terrible that he thinks he may have been shot again. His insides go icy, then hot, his limbs suddenly weak. There is no one in the Treble whom the Wheel placed more faith in than the collectors. Their sword and shield, their sworn protectors. Masar has known Dom since they were both seventeen-year-old recruits, flush with the pride of their enterprise and the future they imagined. Never, in even the darkest moments, would Masar have suspected—

Effegen whispers, "Oh, Dom..."

"We had nothing!" he cries, unable to look at her. "You made us live with *nothing*!"

Masar can't move. Liis says, "Tell them."

Dom looks like he'd rather choke on glass. He looks like the only thing that scares him more is Liis.

"It all went wrong," he moans. "It went so wrong, it...I was working on a fishing crew on the coast. I was meant to sneak over to Ycutta and make the deal without anyone knowing. Then Nikkelo contacted me and told me about the mission. I thought at first he knew, but he—he didn't know, he was just warning me, in case things got hot for all the collectors. So I stayed put in Ycutta and thought it would all blow over when I didn't show, but..."

He trails off. Masar has a sudden, acute memory of the battle in Ycutta, the guardsaan charging in, the attack on their positions. He remembers something knocking him over onto his back and not being able to breathe, and blood choking him and streaming between his fingers where he was clutching at his own neck, at the bullet wound there. He remembers passing out and waking up slung over Uskel's shoulder, and passing out again—and when he came to on Nikkelo's ship, half the team was dead.

"I didn't think the collectors would get hurt," Dom whispers.

Liis answers with a coldness that makes Masar's already chilled body drop another few degrees. "I said, *tell* them."

Tears stream down Dom's face. He won't look at anyone now. He opens and closes his mouth like he can't speak, and then all of a sudden he *is* speaking, a torrent of words.

"I never heard from Aris or that secretary again. Then I got to Farren Eyce and...she was here. She said if I didn't help her that she would tell the Wheel what I had tried to do, so I helped. But what she wanted kept getting worse. So when I said I wouldn't do it anymore, not even to save myself, she threatened Kereth. She showed me this... this cast program connected to Kereth's neural link that could...that could blow it up, and she said that if I didn't do exactly what she said, she would kill her. So I had to do it, see? I *had* to!"

"Do what?" Masar's voice is raw.

Dom weeps harder. He confesses brokenly, "She wanted the senior collectors gone."

Effegen draws in a sharp breath, whispering, "By the gods."

Masar, on the other hand, can't breathe at all. He looks at Dom for five seconds, ten seconds, head swimming with the image of Uskel's body on the staircase, and Leios dangling from a noose, and Roq with the puncture wounds of five thick carpenter's nails in the side of their head . . . Murdered, all of them, and not by a stranger. By a friend.

Masar moves like a whip crack. He has the gun, and with the force of a hurricane behind him, he pushes the muzzle against Dom's temple, pushes Dom's whole body back so his head is pressed into the wall and held there with the weight of the gun, and Masar is towering over him and snarling into his face, "You fucking coward. You fucking traitor."

"Masar!" Effegen shouts.

"We would have done anything for you! If you needed money, we would have shared ours. If you needed blood, we would have given you our blood. We would have torn our own hearts out to make yours keep beating! You fucking traitor!"

"I'm sorry!" Dom sobs. "I'm sorry, I'm so sorry! They were going to kill Kereth."

"We would have protected her!" Masar screams at him, spraying spittle.

"Masar, don't!" cries Effegen, in tears.

"Why not me?" he shouts, frantic to know. "Why didn't you kill me?"

"I—I—I—"

"Why are they dead and I'm not?!"

"I couldn't—you're too—I didn't think I could make it look like a suicide!"

Somehow, this is worse. This is so much worse.

"You don't deserve to *breathe*," Masar hisses at him, pushing the muzzle even harder into his head. The trigger feels *so good* against his finger. "I should beat you to death with this gun. I should drag your body out of Farren Eyce and throw you into a snowdrift to rot like a fucking—"

A sharp pain explodes in Masar's wrist and another in his thigh. He stumbles sideways, the muscle going numb, and when he barely keeps his feet and whirls around, Liis has the gun, her expression fierce and warning.

"Calm down," she says, voice very soft.

Masar rises to his full height, the pain in his wrist and abdomen and the numbness in his thigh too distant to matter. There's a monster inside him, a monster woven together from the death sounds of his murdered friends, explosives and gunfire, nooses and nails, and the impact of a hundred-foot fall. A growl rises in his throat, a threat. Liis points the gun at him.

"Sa Konye, stop!" Effegen orders.

Liis ignores her, eyes on Masar. "We need him to exonerate the Ironways."

"I'm going to *fucking* kill him!"

"I don't give a shit if you do—so long as it's *after* we have what we need."

Masar's chest heaves; that monstrous creature pushes at the boundaries of his body, snarling to get out. His vision blurs. Grief has lit him on fire from the marrow of his bones to the hairs on his skin. He and Liis lock eyes. Dom hugs himself against the wall, sobbing.

Effegen says like a general corralling her troops, "No one is killing anyone today. Both of you stand down *right* now!"

Liis continues to hold the gun, but then she gradually tips it down. Masar feels the first inklings of his reason come back, as if Effegen's voice is a lure hooking in his belly, dragging him to shore. It's not until his breathing slows down that he realizes he was on the verge of hyperventilation. Slowly, very slowly, some of the tightness in his body unlocks, the fighter's instinct dropping back. Leftover adrenaline floods him till he's shaking, and he can't stand the sound of Dom's tears. He moves away, crossing half the distance of the bar to stand with his back to them, trying with all his might to get himself under control. His face is wet. Why is his face wet?

After some time, he hears Effegen's voice. "Did you kill Jasef sen Clime?" Dom must nod, because she asks, "What about Tej? Is he dead, too?"

"I couldn't find him," Dom says, tear-clogged and pathetic.

Masar scrubs at the water on his face. Effegen says quietly, "I value the life of every person in Farren Eyce. I revere the collectors for all they did for our people. Even now, that includes you. But what you have done..."

Dom makes choked, miserable sounds. *Som devour you*, Masar thinks. *Som devour you...*

"There can be only one redemption," Effegen says. "You have to tell us what you know. Everything that you know. Why this is happening. What the avatar wants. You have to tell us, Dom...or Kereth won't know you when you die."

Seconds pass, full of Dom's heaving gasps. All at once his breathing goes quiet. When he speaks, his voice is empty, monotone. "This person you keep calling the avatar...I've never spoken to it. The avatar worked through Aris, and Tej and Jasef worked for her. Maybe there are others. I don't know. Tej—he likes to talk. Jasef was always trying to get him to shut up. Tej said the avatar works for the same secretary who wanted to buy your names."

Masar slowly turns around. Dom is folded in on himself, arms crossed over his belly.

"The secretary sponsored them. He gave them work, paid for their education. Once, someone broke Tej's hand, and the secretary covered his surgery. That's how he got people to work for him. He gave them what they needed, and in exchange they were his informants."

"Even now that they've ended up in Farren Eyce?" Effegen asks.

"That's..." Dom's brow furrows. "That part doesn't really make sense...Apparently the secretary disappeared after the mission in Ycutta. Then in the first month on Farren Eyce, the avatar showed up, saying the secretary was back and he wanted to sow chaos in Farren Eyce. And Aris and the others—they were all for it, because they hate this place. I think they hate everything."

Effegen looks hawkeyed. "Is the avatar here or in the Treble?"

"Tej thinks it's in the Treble. Aris says it's here. I don't think either of them is sure."

Effegen presses him. "What else?"

But he shakes his head hopelessly. "I don't know. I don't know."

She pins him down with her stare, cold as a glacier, utterly implacable as moments and seconds pass. Abruptly, she addresses Liis. "Go outside."

Liis looks at her. Thinks. Asks, "Why?"

"Because I said so."

"What are you going to—"

Effegen snaps, "I am the Star of the Wheel. This is my colony and this is my colonist. I am responsible for both. I am responsible for you. Now go outside."

At first Liis just stands there, gaze flat. Effegen raises her head, steady with resolve, unafraid of this former cloaksaan. Masar is convinced that Liis will refuse, but after a few seconds, she turns away. She takes the gun with her, stalking out of the bar.

Several seconds pass with no sound but Dom's congested breathing. At last, Effegen looks wearily at Masar. "I should send you out, too," she muses.

"I'm not leaving you alone with him."

"No, I suppose I wouldn't expect you to." She takes in a deep breath, looking at Dom again. Her weariness vanishes into determination. "You've testified against Tej, and we already have evidence of his crimes. What about the other Ironways?" Masar goes tense with fear. "There's evidence against them, too."

Dom sighs and swallows, his gaze fixed on the far wall. "It's nonsense," he says.

"How do you know? You said yourself there could be others working for the avatar. Why shouldn't we assume all the Ironways are involved?"

Masar feels sick.

Dom says spitefully, "Because Tej freaked out after the avatar almost killed Luja on *Drae's Hope*. He didn't give a shit about Jun, but he loves Luja. He tried to talk to me alone, to see if I would protect him if he went to the Wheel. But Aris found out about it and told him the avatar was only trying to kill Jun. I'm not sure he believed it. He was frantic. Just kept saying how they needed to leave Luja out of it. Look, why would the avatar attack Jun and Luja if it was working with them?"

Effegen is dispassionate. "Maybe the attack was fake."

Dom's wet cackle is incongruous after so much sobbing. "That sure would be a twist."

Masar wishes he had the gun; he wants to kill him for that laugh. Then, her voice perfectly composed, Effegen asks, "What about Bene?"

Several moments pass, heavy as if there were steel weights holding Masar down. When Dom looks up at them both, Masar is shocked to see a grimacing smile.

"That would kill you, wouldn't it?" he says roughly. "Both of you... so in love with that boy. And what if all this time he was a traitor?"

"Is he?" Effegen asks, stern, unemotional.

Dom's expression twists, gone cold and hateful as he says, "You judge me for wanting to take care of my wife. For wanting to save her. You're no better than me. See what you'd do, to save the ones you love."

Masar doesn't answer. *You killed the ones I love*, he thinks.

As if he had heard him, Dom's face crumples in anger and pain. "Go on! Judge me. But what if Bene *is* a traitor? What will you do then?"

Masar feels the monster curling into shape inside him again, feels all the aches in his body retreating with a fresh surge of adrenaline. He doesn't need a gun to kill Dom.

Effegen breaks in, like the snap of a branch. "Is Bene involved or not?"

Dom drops his eyes. All his bluster evaporates. "I don't believe the avatar for a second that it wasn't attacking Luja and Jun. You know Bene better than me. Would he work for someone who hurt his family?"

No, thinks Masar. *He would do anything to keep his family safe.*

If Effegen is relieved, she doesn't show it. "Who is the avatar?" she demands.

"I don't know. I don't even think Aris knows."

"What about the secretary? You did direct business with him. What's his name?"

"Nobody knows that, either," Dom says. "Insulated as a snake, that one..."

Effegen's nostrils flare.

"What else do you know?" Masar asks, the first words he's managed to speak in minutes. His voice sounds alien, his vocal cords raked with sandpaper.

Dom smiles, faint and defeated. "I know the newsnest won't do for a long-term prison. What'll you do when you find Tej? What will you do with me? You'll have to execute us."

Effegen says, "I'm not executing anyone."

Fresh tears drip onto Dom's crossed arms, his whole body sunk with despair. "You'll have to...Nothing for it. This place..." He looks at Masar. "We fought so hard for this place. But it was just a dream. It was never real."

Masar growls, "It'd be a lot fucking realer if people like you weren't here."

A hacking laugh. Manic revelation brightens Dom's eyes. "Exactly! Exactly. That's the problem, isn't it? It's the people who came here. We never stood a chance. We brought too much poison with us, on that jump..."

Masar doesn't answer. Effegen doesn't answer. How can they? For Dom may well be right.

CHAPTER EIGHTEEN

1665

YEAR OF THE HARVEST

Praetima
Nikata Leen, an Island
The Planet Kator

When they were very young, Six's da told them that they would grow up to be an excellent drover. They had an affinity for animals; the kai sheep ate from their hand, and they were good at echoing Da's herding calls, even at five. In the northern lands of Teros's Aal continent, there were limited options for work. Droving brought in decent money and a fair amount of security, since Teros depended on its meatpacking industry. Six, who even that young knew that the purpose of droving was to prepare animals for slaughter, often wished that they could do something else. Leave Teros, even. Maybe live in a big city, like Riin Kala. But Da was adamant that they must keep a low profile, live a humble life, cherish their survival. So Six resolved themself to a future of leading kai sheep to slaughter.

Now, having become a different fashion of murderer, Six stands on the balcony overlooking Praetima. It is a dark, icy night, with intermittent sheets of rain and groaning winds whipping against Blue Spire. Shielded under the canopy, Six wears a film of mist, clothes damp and chilled through. Down in the city proper, fires have broken out, seemingly impervious to the rain. From time to time Six hears the *tat-tat-tatting* of gunfire. Guardsaan scour Praetima for anyone who might have been involved in the assassination attempt. The two other port cities of Nikata Leen are getting similar treatment, as are many more cities in the Treble, Six suspects.

It is all performance. They won't find the assassins. They probably aren't even really looking for the assassins. The Kindom has shut down gate access again, ostensibly to curtail Seti Moonback's movements, and riots have broken out all over the Treble. With so many wild animals in the street, the guardsaan have become drovers, herding the crowds toward violence and death.

Six has little admiration for protesters. They've never placed much store in group action. They prefer the precise efficiency of a sniper's bullet to the battering ram of a mob. Really, they didn't know Praetima's populace had this level of energy in them, all chaotic and far-reaching. What must things be like in Trin-Ma or Riin Kala?

Something lights up about a half mile away, a burst of flame and a cracking like the rupture of the sound barrier. The explosion looks to have occurred in the commercial district. Six wishes that Jun Ironway were here. They are themself a capable caster, but she would have no trouble sneaking through the blocks the Kindom has placed on cast communication. Ah, the typical, shortsighted methods of the tyrant. Cutting the people of Praetima off from their casts will only foment this uprising. It will do the same in other cities. And the day after tomorrow, the Clever Hand will vote to blow those places up.

The doors to the balcony open, and Chono comes alongside them. They haven't spoken to her since the events in Nikapraev, when they shouted down her rebellious threats and drew the attention of the Hands away from her with threats of their own. Something she clearly did not like. The tension between them is like a spring stretched to its breaking point.

"What did Ilius say?" Six asks.

Chono has spent the past half hour in her private room, conducting a heated argument with Ilius via cast. Six could hear very little through the door and came outside to resist the temptation to throw a spy cast into the room.

Chono engages the scrambler tech. "What do you think he said? 'Esek will be the death of you. You need to publicly disavow her and fall in line with the Kindom.' Et cetera."

Six chuckles. "Poor Ilius. I wonder if he would feel better knowing that he was never serving the Nightfoots in the first place." They cut a glance at her. "And that you are not serving them now."

Chono wears her flat, unreadable expression. Not for the first time Six wonders if Chono ever loved Ilius. They themself find him queasily undesirable, but Chono was friends with him for years, and their sexual relationship lasted longer than any of her other affairs. Her anger at Ilius for working for "Esek" seems deep and personal. Six wonders at this, feels irrationally jealous that she shared such intimacy with someone else.

Six looks out over the city. More gunshots in the distance. That building that exploded is burning and smoking. The rain has stopped, and in its absence, it's easier to hear the sounds of people shouting and chanting through loudspeakers, voices carrying across the city. Six remembers when they and Chono were in Lo-Meek, tracking Jun Ironway, and people flooded the streets because of jump gate closures. The same old story, never resolved, and Praetima's prison will be stuffed full come morning. Its morgue, too.

"I need you to get a message to Yantikye."

Six knew it was coming, but it still chills them.

Chono says, "I want to meet with Paiye. As soon as possible."

In a neighborhood due west, something lights up like a solar flare, booming across the city. Gods, what is happening out there? Six wants to sneak out of Blue Spire. To go into the fray. They are very good at controlling their impulses but very bad at resisting a fight. And if they answer Chono's request now, it will be a fight such as the two of them have never had.

There was a time they fantasized about fighting with her—an explosion of accusation and recrimination and, ultimately, revenge. She had become Esek's creature. She was the tool of Six's enemy, a perpetrator of Esek's crimes. It was unforgivable, and they thought that they would have to kill her. Instead, they nearly drained themself of blood to keep her alive. There is too much history with Chono. Too much *feeling.*

She is clearly waiting for them to speak, but instead they turn from her, heading back into the warmth of the suite. She follows.

"I'm going to go down to the gymnasium," they announce.

She makes a growling sound. "Six..."

"We will talk when I return."

Chono mutters something, but she doesn't try to stop them. In the elevator they send a message to the concierge at the front desk, ordering that a guardsaan be sent to them for sparring practice. Beating a Kindom tool to pieces sounds very satisfying, at the moment.

The elevator trundles down to the second story of the hotel, delivering them to a large, well-kept gymnasium that they have used nearly every day since their release from the prison. There is beautifully maintained, state-of-the-art equipment, as well as a sparring circle and various nonlethal weapons racked on the walls. The room is empty. Six isn't sure how many people are staying in Blue Spire. Is it possible the Kindom emptied the hotel out to make it Six's and Chono's exclusive holding cell? Not a bad idea. Perhaps Six can figure out a way to lock Chono in her room. How else are they going to keep her alive, the righteous fool?

Itchy with anger, they unbutton their jacket, which is wet and stubborn coming off. Their movements are slightly erratic. They toss the jacket onto the ground with a splat and yank off their fine silk shirt. This leaves them in just the spotless undershirt and the fitted trousers and the boots that probably cost more than two months of Da's droving income. Gods, the relentless luxury of the Nightfoots, and of all these preening, greedy, repulsive people.

Behind them, the gymnasium door opens. They turn, expecting to find a guardsaan.

It's Chono.

Of course it's fucking Chono. Six has seen footage of Chono standing like an immovable boulder in the face of Esek's tirades. Enduring threats and screaming fits and, once or twice, violent blows, and never backing down while somehow, simultaneously, never seeming to challenge. Of course Chono won't be intimidated by Six's retreat from their rooms. Of course she will follow them down here and make herself a wall impossible to shoulder past.

Six still tries.

"Go back to our suite."

Chono raises her eyebrows, not answering, not acquiescing. Six's body vibrates, like all the self-control they've fostered over the years is reaching a limit. Who else but Chono could do this to them? They recall that day in the planetarium of *The Risen Wave*, when the Wheel first showed them that they had jumped to Capamame, and Chono said in a tone that brooked no argument that she was going back to the Treble. And that Six was going with her. How angry Six had been at her. How helpless in the face of her command.

Another door opens. Six glares at the guardsaan coming in, who asks uneasily, "You need a sparring partner, Sa?"

Chono speaks first. "You may go. I'll spar with Sa Nightfoot."

Six grits their teeth. "No, you won't."

Chono ignores them, already shedding her coat. She lays it over one of the benches framing the room. Her bandaged hand sends a pulse of fury through them. The nail marks on her face make them want to kill something.

"You're injured. You can't spar."

"It's my nondominant hand. I'll be fine. Anyway, I'm not going to let you beat a guard unconscious just to exorcise your frustration." She looks at the guardsaan again. "You can go."

With a last nervous glance at Six, he does, quickly and with obvious relief. Furious, Six reengages the scrambler tech, taking an aggressive step toward her. "I do not want to spar with you, Chono. Go back to our suite."

Chono strips down to her undershirt. She was badly injured on *The Risen Wave*, and for a month afterward her doctors wouldn't allow her any strenuous activity. But once she got her bill of health, she started going on jogs with Liis Konye and practicing the calisthenic exercises that she first learned in kinschool. Now, with her muscular arms and square shoulders displayed, she looks in the prime of health. But whereas Six found their own outlet by sparring with Liis and a couple other collectors, Chono never joined such exercises.

Six says, "You have not done any combat training in over nine months. I will hurt you."

"I haven't forgotten the forms," Chono says, voice clipped. "Or don't you remember what happened at the distillery today?"

Six rakes their eyes over every inch of her—just as they would assess any opponent. Chono notices, glares, and her ears go slightly pink, as if humiliated by the perusal. She rotates her arms, flexes her shoulders, rises and falls on the balls of her feet, perhaps to draw attention to her height advantage and broader build. Something fiery and competitive purrs to life in Six.

"Three hits to the torso and the loser concedes," they say at last.

"Let's make it six . . . for old times' sake."

Their lip curls. "Let's make it *four*, for old times' sake."

Chono chuckles, grimly, tightly. "Four." She nods, her old kinschool name ringing a bell between them. "All right."

"Open hand," Six adds. "We don't need you breaking something."

Her nostrils flare. "Fine," she says.

Six nods once—and runs at her.

She barely gets her arms up in time, thrown into the defensive as they breach her personal space, a barrage of strikes beating her back. Six swings low, and she dodges left, smacking clumsily at their arm to deflect them. They don't relent, teeth set as they press her back. Off the mat. Toward the wall. Chono sets her stance and pivots right, jabbing at them. Six's knee comes up into her thigh, and her guard drops just long enough for them to chop the side of their hand into her rib cage.

Gasping, she staggers back from them. Six lets her, standing a few feet away now and vibrating as they watch. The satisfaction is exquisite. The anger feels cleansing. She touches her tender side and gives them a scathing glance.

"Open hand, huh?"

Yes, they suppose using the side of their hand like that is not strictly in line with the rules, but Chono's annoyance brings a venomous smile to their lips. She won't be able to use the one hand to hit them like that—not with the wound in the meat of her palm. But Six has never been above playing to the disadvantages of their quarry.

Chono snorts. "You see? You *do* want to spar with me."

The thought that she knows this, knows them, can see into them, sends a lance through their chest. They go at her again, a hurricane. This time, she is ready. She doesn't have their raw talent. She never had their skill. She's outmatched and underprepared, but she doesn't seem to care, and she doesn't back off. Six rains blows on her, battering her arms as she defends herself.

"There is no need to take another hit," they mock. "Yield."

She drives her heel down toward their foot. They barely avoid it, forced to drop back half a step. Chono takes her first offensive strides, striking out three, four times. But on the last blow she overextends. Six slips under her guard again. Instead of striking her, they grab her. She chokes in surprise as they move behind her, arms under her armpits and holding her arms locked behind her own head. Her back is hard against their chest. Pinned.

"Yield," they pant against her ear.

She tries to kick one of their legs. Six tightens their grip and she makes a sound of pain.

"Yield."

"No," she snarls.

Six lets go and stabs their fingertips into her kidney.

Chono gags, doubling sideways. Six knows what it feels like: an electrical current of pain, all ice and heat, immobilizing. She drops to one knee and shudders through it. Six circles around to stand in front of her, looking down at her with satisfaction...and a niggling sensation of guilt. There's sweat on her forehead and beaded on her shoulders and collarbones. A flush spreads across her chest and throat, like watercolor. She's panting raggedly.

"That is enough," they say. "I told you, I do not want you hurt."

To their surprise, Chono hacks a laugh, levering herself onto her feet again. "Too bad."

Their brows hike up. *Too bad?*

"I'm not your fucking sidekick," she snaps. "You can't stop me being hurt."

"I—"

"Is that what that scene in Nikapraev was about? You wanted their attention off of me so you threatened and insulted them with a Nightfoot uprising? I don't need you to protect me."

"You fucking well do."

She charges them, fists up, any pretense of open hands forgotten. They feel a flash of surprise, and answer her attack. She's aggressive this time, using her height and superior muscle to hound them backward. Every time they meet her blows, it sends a jolt shooting up their arms. They relish it. They see her relishing it, too, her eyes burning, her teeth clenched, and when she catches one of their blows and flings their arm wide, exposing their torso, Six sees the light of victory on her face—

And then they punch her shoulder and take her legs out from under her.

Flat on her back, she gasps at the ceiling. Six stands over her, breathing hard through their teeth and consumed with rage and satisfaction.

"That is three–zero, Chono. Maybe you should consider that you *do* need my protection."

Chono lays her head back on the mat, staring up into the lights. She says nothing, and Six paces around her, their anger like a tide, their self-control wavering. They snap at her, "You were reckless in the Centrum."

Chono scoffs. "*I* was reckless? You were—"

"I behaved exactly as Esek Nightfoot should behave. I was in every particular what they expected of me. But *you*."

Chono rolls to her knees and stands up again, glaring at them.

"What should I have done? Said I would support them in razing cities?"

"You could have used your lauded wisdom to argue for a more temperate reaction."

"They wouldn't listen!"

"You did not try. You were like a bomb about to go off. You were not the calm and measured Chono. You were a person on the verge of open rebellion. What, by the gods, were you thinking?" She looks taken aback, which only annoys them into mockery. "Perhaps you are sick of being the well-mannered Chono?"

"What the fuck good did it ever do me?"

Six's lip curls. "Your patience and generosity of spirit have made you what you are to the Treble. People trust you because they believe you will be the cooler head when injustice rears up. They believe you will protect them."

"I *am* trying to protect them!" she cries, stepping forward like a bull with set horns. Six holds their position. "I'm trying to stop the Kindom from attacking them! If Paiye can help me do that somehow—"

"Yantikye did not dangle him in front of you because he believes it will stop the violence. All these uprisings across the Treble—you think he is not fomenting them where he can? Yantikye wants to *escalate* the violence. He wants to use you to do it."

"You think I'm so naive I can't see that? I can still use him to get to Paiye."

"And then what?"

She pauses, glowering. Six huffs. "You are smarter than this. How else could you have survived Esek than by being smarter than this? And yet you antagonize them."

"*You* antagonized them!"

"Because I *can*. Because my life is forfeit anyway."

Chono flinches back, stunned. Her voice comes out disbelieving. *"What?"*

Six makes their face into the cold mask they trained it to be after they left their kinschool. A mask modeled after Chono. But suddenly Chono runs at them, shoving them in the chest, her first body blow in this pointless game of theirs. They don't stop her.

"What do you mean it's forfeit?"

"Chono—"

She shoves them again. This time they're not prepared for the strength of it; they stumble. Chono cocks her fists again, and she batters them across the gym. Six deflects her, dodges her, looks at her in a mix of exasperation and entreaty. She is being absurd. Like some hyperactive puppy. Why should this make her so angry? Surely she already understood this was coming?

"We agreed to do this together! If this is some fucking suicide mission for you—"

"You are still being naive," Six shoots back, spinning free of a hard jab, catching her arm and flinging her back from them. "We both knew the danger we were in, coming back here. The difference is that there is no place for Esek Nightfoot in the Treble. You think they will give me back the sevite trade? No, they will kill me to stop that happening. At best I can cause useful mischief for a while. *You*, on the other hand—you can survive. If only you would play it right! If you would be more careful and not provoke them!" They block her next strike. "Gods' sake, Chono—you could be the First Cleric!"

Chono's hands drop. The perplexed furrow of her brow doesn't last. Her eyes widen, first with disbelief, then horror. Six wills her to understand what they have always known.

"That's ridiculous," she chokes out.

"What is ridiculous is that you do not see how many players have this in mind for you. Have had it in mind from the beginning. Why do you think Aver Paiye made you his attaché on that tour in '61? Why do you think he made you accompany me on the mission to find Jun Ironway? And why do you think these secretaries want so badly for you to work with them? They want to lift you up, Chono. They want to legitimize themselves through you."

Chono pales. Can she really not have seen it? She was never a foolish person. Perhaps she survived through a certain degree of denial, but—

"I don't want that," she whispers.

Six looks at her incredulously. "Do you want the Jeveni protected? Do you want the five thousand released and the First Families held to account? Do you want to challenge the corruption of the Hands and operate as a check against their unrighteousness? How better could you do that than as the First Cleric?"

"No," she says, stubborn as a kai sheep, fierce-eyed as the wolves that stalked the drovers. "The First Cleric is just another powermonger. The First Cleric will have to be a ruthless political mastermind. I won't turn myself into someone else, Six. You may have been willing to do that, but I'm not."

They raise their eyebrows, surprised at the hit. "You hold me in contempt, I see."

"What else should I hold you in?!" she snaps.

Six is so startled they can't conceal it, their face gone slack as an unprecedented emotion swells in them. She reminds them, "You mutilated your body so you could take the place of a woman you despise! You did it as some irrational bid to supplant the Nightfoots with the Wheel. And the Wheel didn't even want it! It was a waste. That *scheme* was a *waste*!"

"My schemes are not over," Six whispers.

"No, clearly not!"

"Everything I have done has been to achieve a goal I believe in. And I have achieved my goals. I *did* replace Esek Nightfoot. I *did* supplant the Nightfoots, and I did give the trade to the Jeveni. And yes, I failed. But do you think that was the end of it for me? I *will* rip apart the

Nightfoots and the Kindom. I *will* have revenge for the Jeveni. And for myself."

Chono laughs, stunned, incredulous. "You haven't learned anything, have you?"

Six's body burns. "Perhaps you thought I would be content to follow you back to the Treble like a dog, and be some symbol of how the great Chono can redeem even Esek Nightfoot herself?"

"*What?!* What are you *talking* about—"

"I had a choice. I could retire to Capamame and cover all the mirrors and finally have some peace. Or I could come back here and pursue my goals a different way. A new way."

Her arms flex with the current of her anger. There is something quite... beautiful about Chono.

"And what way is that?" she rasps.

Six stands firm and unrepentant. "Everything I have done since I came here has been to protect you. Everything has been in the hope that they will raise you to First Cleric. Where I failed, you can succeed. If only you will be wise enough to see it."

Of everything they have said, she lands on, "Protect me?" Her voice is as soft as the child Four whom they knew in kinschool. The child who never raised its voice and yet could look at other students in a way that had them slinking off from her, confused and wary.

She says, "This has been your scheme? To protect me. And die doing it?"

They grimace. "I am *prepared* to die. I thought it was obvious to you by now that I regard your life as more valuable than mine." She gapes at them. In exasperation they cry, "You say I have not learned anything. But none of this was a secret I kept from you! To succeed in a mission, you must be willing to use the right person for the right job, at all times, without ego. Surely you have known that you are the right person? The one who can make true change."

"You... fucking—" She breaks off. "You've done *nothing* but keep secrets. You hid the truth about Ilius from me. You hid your aims in coming here. You made plans for me as if I were your student, with no consideration for what *I* want. You may as well be a teacher from Principes, selling my body for your own ends!"

They balk, shocked. "That is *not*—"

"If you trusted me at all—" she began.

"What do you need my trust for? I am inconsequential—to all of this!"

She runs at them, unleashed. A lifted arm, an easily deflected strike, and Chono drops under their guard, fist cracking against their abdomen. Six chokes, wheezes. They bring their elbows down to catch her, but she is already darting back. In petty fury she cuffs them hard against their ruined ear, snaps their head sideways, and when they stagger upright again, her foot comes up, kicking them square in the chest.

Six flies back, catching air for a split second before they hit the ground with a grunt. Chono, panting hard and radiating fury, stands over them.

"That's four–three," she sneers. "I win."

Six lies on the mat for several moments, stunned. She boxed their ear! It's ringing, throbbing. The place where she kicked them—did she crack their ribs? Perhaps not quite, but still. Even at school, in their most heated sparring matches, she never hit them like that. It surprised them sometimes, because when she fought other students, she could be frighteningly violent, ruthlessly inventive in her attacks. But not with them. Now they wonder if all that time, she was pulling her punches.

She prowls away from them. They watch her, her hands on her hips, her back turned and the muscles of her shoulders locked. For a long time neither of them says anything. Six finally sits up again, head a little fuzzy. *You may as well be a teacher from Principes, selling my body for your own ends!* Her words sit heavy in their chest.

The silence goes on and on. *If you trusted me at all*—she said. But what does it mean to trust? They never trusted Yantikye, or anyone they worked with. They trusted the Wheel to accept the sevite trade, and it didn't. They trusted Esek to be what Esek is—and she was. But

Chono...She is too deep in them, too consuming. She has haunted their thoughts and she has paced them across the systems and she has known them as no one else could. A threat to them, in her very person. Quiet and terrible.

"You would not be like other First Clerics," they say. "You would be like a seed planted in the Riin Cosas garden. A poison to our enemies and a redemption to those who can be redeemed."

"Fuck you, Six."

"I have never intended to force it on you. I thought you would pursue it yourself."

"Why would I *pursue* being First Cleric? Why would you expect me to want that?"

"Esek taught us both the importance of power. You came back here to change the Treble. I thought you would use a chance at power to do that."

"If Esek taught us anything, it's that power is a disease. By the gods, Six, if you had tried to talk to me about this even *once*!"

They glower in confusion, sitting with arms clasped around their knees as they study the floor. They feel inexplicably sulky.

"I did not think we needed to talk."

"Why?"

"I do not...I have not done much talking, these years."

She makes an exasperated sound. They swallow, throat dry.

"I have not...put much store in trust." Shocking themself as much as her, they add, "But if I trust anyone, it is you."

The gesture brings her up short. They stare at their arms, but they can feel her watching them. It is quiet again, and she has stopped pacing. They can hear her breathe. There was a time, in their kinschool, when they would share a bed with her, just to stay warm. And when nightmares shot Six awake, they listened to her breathe and fell asleep again.

She sits down next to them, not looking at them, arms around her knees in a mimic of their posture. They feel a flicker of hope, which embarrasses them.

"Why would you want me to be First Cleric? Half the time I think you hate me."

They scowl. "Why?"

"Because of Esek. Because I...followed Esek. Because I loved Esek."

Even hearing it makes them rabidly angry, furiously jealous. They look away again. "You have certainly been foolish in your loyalties. That does not mean I hate you."

She answers, "'How I despair of you, Chono.'" Six looks at her in surprise. She speaks in a voice of clear, calm recitation. Her beautiful orator's voice. "'How I wonder at the disappearance of my old friend. Where is the righteousness we promised each other? You have fit yourself inside the mold of a monster, and in the end you will be no different from her.'"

Six recognizes their own letter, written to her nearly a decade ago. They sniff.

"That letter was not about hate. I have *wanted* to hate you. I planned to kill you, once. I was going to do it after I killed Esek. But you are very irritating, Chono. You did all these good things, and you made it impossible to hate you. You did not fit inside her mold, after all."

They can see, sidelong, her surprise, and perhaps—is that pleasure? Why does that embarrass them more than anything? They mutter, "This plan to meet with Aver Paiye. It is a bad idea."

"Yantikye was right. The people need their gods. They need to see that the representatives of their gods want an end to violence in the Treble. Yantikye may be hoping I'll use this to spread wider violence, but that doesn't mean I have to play it his way."

"I do not even know how Yantikye means to bring you to Paiye. We are prisoners in this place. The moment you try to leave, you will be declaring yourself for the insurgents."

"Then we will have to plan very carefully," she says. Six doesn't respond. After a while she tells them wearily, "I'm not a leader, Six."

Six shrugs. "Sometimes we do not have a choice about what we become. My da wanted me to be a drover. *I* wanted to be a cloaksaan, to go unnoticed. Now I am the matriarch of the Nightfoots."

Chono climbs to her feet again, wincing. She holds out her hand to Six, and after a pause they accept it. She pulls them up, and they take her hand, turning it over to look at the regenerative bandages. She holds still, letting them touch her. Shockingly, she seems not to have torn her hand open again. Her hand feels strange. The last time they touched like this, her hand was much smaller.

She says, "Whatever I become, I'm not content for you to let yourself be killed like some melodramatic martyr."

They shift restlessly. "I am a survivor. They will have to pry my life from under my fingernails. But I am also practical. If I am killed, that is an acceptable outcome. For you to die—that is not acceptable. Not when you can do so much in these systems. Especially now."

"And you could transform the Nightfoots," she retorts. They grimace in distaste. They realize they're still touching her hand, and drop it. She says, "Why don't we proceed from the agreement that neither of our deaths is an acceptable outcome?"

Six thinks this is very naive, but they decide not to argue. Finally, reluctantly, they say, "I can get a message to Yantikye. He will want to move quickly."

She's Chono, so of course there's no smugness at winning the argument—but there is a touch of satisfaction, her gray eyes heavy as a stone upon Six, who turns away, picking up their shirt. "I am going to hate this very much," they tell her.

The smile in her voice is unmistakable. "Thank the gods you have a gift for endurance."

By Sajeven's own mercy, every citizen shall have the measure of resources necessary for their survival and comfort. Every occupation shall be available to any person who can work toward and demonstrate the necessary skills. Every crime and injury shall receive fair deliberation and avenues of restitution. Every person shall be equal, and valued, and protected. For Sajeven loves the forgotten, and the rejected, and most of all the one who reaches for truth, though they risk their life to do it.

excerpt, the Charter of Farren Eyce, in Sajeven's Name.
Section A, Part 2. Dated 1651, Year of the Level.

CHAPTER NINETEEN

1664

YEAR OF THE CRUX

Farren Eyce
The Planet Capamame

I suppose I'm curious," Jun says. "What was your endgame?"

Released from her own prison, vindicated before the colony and no happier for it, she now stands in a different cell. This one boasts its own sink and mirror. Aris the Beauty regards herself in the reflection, her manner less vain than contemplative. Did she ever imagine that it would come to this? Locked up in a repurposed office on the other side of the universe, coconspirators either shot or fled, and no help from the avatar who seems to have been her leash?

Aris hums. "Not sure what's in it for me, telling you that."

"Nothing," Jun admits with a shrug, a flat smile. "It just seems strange, wreaking havoc like this. All right, some secretary paid your bills a few years ago. Fine. But this is an impressive level of loyalty. You're fucking with the only barrier between you and a frozen planet. Seems a lot to risk just for loyalty. Unless it's ideological or some shit, but even if you believe in the Kindom—the Kindom is forty light-years away."

"It's got nothing to do with the Kindom," Aris says. "You can work for a Hand without working for *the Hands*. You think the people who worked for Esek Nightfoot when she was alive were serving the Kindom?" A snort of laughter. "Isn't that what torments Cleric Chono?"

Jun considers this. The avatar insisted it did not work for the Kindom—it even showed contempt for the Kindom. But does that mean it could never be loyal to a specific person *within* the Kindom? After all, there must be hundreds of Hands who value their own agendas far above the agenda of the Kindom, who even hate the Kindom as much as the avatar seems to.

"Dom says the secretary stopped speaking to you after a bad job in Ycutta. Is that true?"

Aris meets her eyes in the mirror's reflection, but she doesn't answer. It feels like a confirmation. Jun murmurs, "Very loyal indeed, to hop back into his service after years of abandonment. Seems pretty desperate."

"As desperate as giving up your years of independence to ass-lick the Wheel?" Aris retorts. "You were Sunstep once. Now you're just an errand girl."

"Oh, *I'm* the errand girl?" Jun asks. "Som's ass, you're the one setting fires and tearing up shrines like some rebellious teenager. And from where I'm sitting, it doesn't seem like your boss cares much what happens to you now."

Aris chuckles, turning around, eyes alight. She really is a striking woman, as beautiful as Esek in her way. But there was an effortlessness to Esek's beauty, curated by wealth. Good clothes, good skin, good nail beds. She was beautiful just by existing under the cover of her privilege. Aris... She has the air of humble beginnings. Someone who *was* an errand girl, perhaps, for a tradesaan or a pirate ship or a First Family boss. Someone from nothing, who made herself into this new person with the secretary's help. How loyal would Jun have been, if she had such a benefactor? If Six had stayed in her life, perhaps, and helped her and guided her and given a shit about her? Would Jun sabotage her own house, for a debt like that?

"The secretary must have a name," Jun says. "What is it?"

Aris laughs. "Sweetheart, you're adorable."

Jun smiles a little, a smile like a mask, concealing something deep and ravenous. This—this is the clue that matters. This secretary. Because if the avatar is the link to the secretary, the secretary is the link to the avatar. She can use the secretary like a trail of breadcrumbs, leading her to her prey. And she will have her prey now. Nothing will protect it from her.

"I've already got my casters scouring every inch of your history. I'll find the secretary, one way or another."

Aris grins at her. "So find him."

Jun's nostrils flare.

"Where's my cousin?"

Aris shrugs. "Hiding in the sewers, probably, and pissing himself. Silly little kid, Tej Redcore. Still wonder what the secretary wanted him for."

"I assumed it was because his stepfather knew about the Wheel," Jun says.

"You really think Tej got info on the Wheel just because he had a Jeveni stepfather?" she scoffs. "He wasn't smart enough for that. Just a useless kid, trying to look useful. You know the type—wants to be a big saan because the world makes him feel small."

"Yeah, I think I'm looking at one of those right now," Jun replies.

Aris's lip curls. She takes a step toward Jun, head tilted to one side with malicious curiosity.

"What would you give me to get your cousin back?"

Jun says, "I would give you the opportunity to go back to the Treble."

Aris studies her for a long, hungry moment. Suddenly Jun knows that this is what Aris really wants—to go home. To leave Capamame behind, to be folded into the arms of her beloved benefactors. Could this be why she and the others are working for the secretary? Do they have some idea that in doing so, they'll earn a route back home? But no one in the Treble, and only a few people in Farren Eyce, can control the jump gate. Without the gate key, it's an unbreakable vault.

Recovering, Aris declares, "I'm not a traitor," but she says it like someone who could most certainly be persuaded to betray.

"No," Jun says. "You're a survivor. A pragmatist. And what are you going to do, if you stay here? Wait for the Jeveni to build you a proper prison, and rot for the rest of your life among people you hate? Or you could help me. And I'll find a way to put you on a shuttle and slingshot you to whatever system you want."

Aris's face twists. "I don't know where your cousin is."

"The secretary? The avatar?"

"I don't know their names."

Jun snorts. It was worth a try. "Just as well for you. If you go back to the Kindom, they'll torture you for information. Throw you away when they realize you don't know anything. Probably kill you out-right, just to keep things clean."

Aris's eyes narrow to slits. She prowls forward another step. "And you think you're any safer with your masters?" she mocks.

A voice in the corner of the room says, "That's far enough."

Liis. Standing in an imitation of ease, she is ready to spring at any moment. Jun flicks her a glance, feels a pull in her stomach. It's been two months since they've seen each other, and yet they've barely spoken. Jun is caught between an ache of need and a depth of shame. In a single day, Liis uncovered more about the threats against Farren Eyce than Jun and Masar have in weeks. *I couldn't see it*, Jun thinks. *But Liis could. Liis saw through Dom. What does Liis even need me for, in this life? What use am I to anyone?*

"What's the matter, lovely?" Aris asks Liis. "Don't trust me to behave?"

Liis doesn't respond. Liis is stalwart, her stare like a rifle sight. For weeks Jun has had nightmares that Liis was never real. Just a fantasy born of her isolation and helplessness. But now, here she is. And Jun is afraid to touch her.

Aris gives Liis a slow, lascivious look, then turns to smirk at Jun. "Your girl really is so beautiful, isn't she? To think what fun we could have had."

Jun snaps, "I'd rather fuck a snake than a lackey."

Aris sneers. "You're a Wheel spinner. You work for people who were ready to toss you overboard." She snaps her fingers. "Quick as that. And not just you but your family. You gave everything to this colony. Risked your life and saved all of ours, and for what? You may be free now, but how long will that last? We'll be cellmates, mark my words. And they'll put you in the ground if they can. But first they'll find Tej. You know what they'll do to Tej."

Does Jun know? Maybe they'll just send him back to the Treble, useless as he is. And if the Kindom don't kill him, he'll be out on his own, as unable to defend himself as a newborn. Jun recalls the days before she left K-5 station for the Riin Kala Academy of Archivists, when all her family would gather in the workroom of the family shop, to share food and time and laughter, and there were so many of them: Great Gra and Jun's grandmothers, and her uncles and aunts. The twins were barely five. Now she fears she will not see Tej alive again.

"Think about your options, Aris," Jun says. "If you have anything to trade, now is the time."

Aris spits on the ground. "You've still got an enemy in the walls and no way to fight it. I'll take my chances."

Jun nods slowly, thinking how little she blames Aris for this. Jun has her cast access back. She has the whole breadth of the Farren Eyce casting net and her channels to the Treble besides, and yet she feels naked from the outmaneuvering of the avatar. Maybe Aris is right, betting on a different tile.

"Fair enough," Jun agrees, and leaves. Liis follows.

They don't speak. They walk out of the hallway and out of the newsnest and into the courtyard of Level 8. Bene and Masar are waiting for them. But no sign of Luja.

"She went to the lab," Bene explains. "She wanted to work her shift."

Jun looks at him in bewilderment. "Her shift? Her shift is covered."

"That's what we told her," Bene says. "I think she needs the distraction."

Guilt slips icy fingers between Jun's ribs. Of course. Why go back to the apartment and lie in bed and relive the atrocities of her farm station bosses, when she can bury herself in a cast and pretend that Farren Eyce hasn't just subjected her to similar violations?

"I should go find her," Jun says.

"You should give her space," Masar replies. "She looked...very angry."

Jun snaps, "She should be angry."

Masar doesn't rise to her temper, nodding. "Yes. She should."

She glowers silently. They're all silent. There are two collectors-turned-sentries standing outside the newsnest, and two more inside, but otherwise the level is abandoned. The Wheel, whose Spokes convened to see her and her family released, are gone now. Hyre and Effegen were clearly sorry about what had happened. Gaeda seemed reluctantly humbled, Tomesk uncomfortable. Fonu sen Fhaan, though—their expression was stolid.

Jun's afraid that if she keeps thinking about it, she'll start screaming. She looks at Bene. "You need sleep."

"We all need sleep," Liis remarks.

Jun shakes her head. "I have to piece through everything I missed while my neural link was off, not to mention see whatever mess they made of the apartment. I assume all the evidence the avatar planted is available for my review?"

This is for Masar, who says, "I made sure that Fonu cleared it."

She nods. She takes him in, processing for the first time how pale he is, the circles under his eyes, the blankness of his expression. Dom ben Dane is also in the newsnest—no, the *prison*. Locked away for murder, for betraying the family that loved him. Masar is the only one left, of that original crew. Grief hangs on him like a shroud. A grief you never recover from.

"I'll rest if you do," she says.

He snorts, humorless. Bene says, "I'm going to walk Masar back to his apartment." He looks at Liis. "You make sure she sleeps; I'll make sure he does."

"Deal," Liis says.

"Fuck's sake," mutters Masar.

"Fuck's sake," Jun agrees, and shakes her head.

Masar tells her, "We have a meeting in the morning. With the Wheel. They want to talk about next steps."

Jun stalls in disbelief. She feels briefly detached from her body, and then thrust into it again with a crack like thunder.

"Next steps?" she repeats, icy. "The Wheel wants to talk to me about next steps? The Wheel arrests my family, takes my cast access, puts me in a cell, and now it wants to summon me to a meeting to discuss next steps?"

"Jun—" Bene tries.

"How fucking *dare* they—"

"What else should they do?" Masar asks. "Leave you out of it and be ripped apart by the avatar for their pride?"

"Godsdamn you, Masar, if there wasn't so much between us, I would *hate* you for this. For this place, for bringing me here! You told me your Wheel was incorruptible. You said the Spokes resigned at the faintest hint of corruption. Well, where are my resignations?"

"Arresting you was foolish," Masar says. "Not corrupt."

"It was *suicidal*! The Wheel is lucky I don't steal us a ship and leave for good!"

Masar's expression hardens, color rising in his face, and Jun is ready and eager for a screaming match—but it's Bene who speaks next.

"You can't blame all of Farren Eyce for the actions of a few members of the Wheel," he says quietly. "By that logic we're all responsible for every action the Kindom ever took."

"We *are* responsible!" Jun snarls. "I should have built a bomb and dropped it on Riin Cosas! We should have torn the Treble apart, all of us; we should have killed every Hand in the Kindom for what they've done and then maybe we would never have had to come here. Gods, I hope Six razes them all to the ground!"

Bene startles her by losing his temper. "We're not in the Treble! And the Wheel are not the Kindom and the Jeveni aren't responsible for Fonu being an ass. This is our home now. You want to drop bombs? Drop one on the avatar."

"Aris and Dom are our only leads, and neither of them know who the avatar is."

"Find the secretary," he says.

"I don't know how!" Her voice cracks. "I'm in the dark. I don't know *how*!"

Bene looks at her with fierce belief. "Yes, you do. I know you do, Jun. Don't give up. Not yet. We have to be somewhere in this damned universe. I'd rather be here than anywhere else. Wouldn't you?"

She doesn't answer. Her eyes burn. She thinks, *If we weren't here, Tej would be protected. Luja would be protected.*

But it's not true. Tej got caught up by this secretary long before Farren Eyce. And if they hadn't come to Capamame, where would they really be? Still on that farm station? Or maybe, best-case scenario, Jun would have booked them all passage to a frontier station. Would that be better? Would that be safer?

Liis says in a low voice, "I'm taking you home now."

Jun looks away from her, suddenly ashamed, as if she were a recalcitrant child being herded off by her minder. She grunts, "I'll be at the meeting," and turns to leave.

No one says goodbye.

Liis's footsteps shadow hers, and Jun isn't a tall person, but she feels like she's flying across the courtyard toward the staircase, all her emotion in her gait, like she can stomp it out onto the stones. As they get closer, Liis says, "Let's take the elevator down."

Jun is incredulous. "It's only one floor."

"You're on the verge of hyperventilating. You need to relax."

Jun wasn't aware. Now she feels the tightness in her chest. But no, she doesn't need to relax. She can't relax; she's not tired at all. She's surging with adrenaline, lit up like a casting hub, and her hands are shaking. She takes the stairs, practically jogging in her haste. She has some absurd idea that she can outrun Liis on the stairs, outrun the logic and care of this woman who she's missed with her whole soul and now can't even bear to look at. *I was useless without you*, she thinks. *I'm helpless without you. Please be real.*

On Level 7, she strides toward their quarter of the housing block. It's midnight, and the hallways are almost empty. Every once in a while they pass someone who recognizes her. Jun watches for suspicion, for distrust, for threat. But gets only curiosity and surprise.

Who among them believes that she was behind the bombing? Who among them would happily see her and her family thrown out of the colony to freeze and die aboveground?

She bumps a cast off her wrist, wanting to get a lead on the damage to her apartment. She can instantly identify the fingerprints of Fonu's collectors, all over her casting hub, all over her files. She finds the planted evidence, the fake messages between her and Aris, the program that attacks casting tech. She's surprised at how convincing it all is. She thought it would be so obvious that someone had planted it. She hated Fonu for being taken in. Now, for the first time, she remembers that this is the avatar, its work clever enough to have fooled her if she were on the other side of this. It's made a delicate, effective job of it. It's used her family like a multitool. When she finds it, she's going to light its tech on fire.

"Jun," Liis warns. "Please. Breathe."

Jun ignores her, though she does try to obey, conscious of a burn in her lungs, a slight fuzziness to her vision. At the same time, she walks faster. The apartment door comes into view, like a vault containing the secrets she needs. She casts the lock open, stepping inside.

Her threshold is a trip wire, and the trap springs fast: a net thrown over her head, a cage snapping down around her. She whirls toward Liis, blocking her entry. She snaps at her, "Turn off your tech."

"What?"

"Turn it off, now!"

Jun can feel it already, slithering through her neural link, aiming for her ocular.

"Now!" she says again, and drops down into the net.

It's there. Of course it's there. It was always going to be there, lying in wait, this damn slithery sea creature of a thing. It hurls a new virus at her, something it hasn't tried before. Immobilizing as a paralytic. Sparking yellow cables wrap around her ankles and her wrists, winding up her arms like tentacles. The avatar is a genderless, featureless human shape, full of the Black, and with a jerk it flings her onto her back, reeling her in and tunneling inside her.

In the real world, Jun senses Liis in the apartment—she feels for her in the cast and finds a dark space. Her tech is turned off; she's safe. Jun grabs hold of the cables, digs in her heels, and uses the momentum to lever herself up onto her feet again. She hurls a pulse of malware up the length of the cables, and the coils release, shrieking and slinking away from her.

It's too late, though. She can feel an array of viruses attacking her from every angle, like thousands of tiny spiders racing across her skin. She makes her skin into iron, and the attack stutters. The spiders, unable to dig deeper, slide uselessly over her shell, and she sweeps them up in handfuls. She digs through their bodies. She peels them apart, using pins and needles to hold them open as she finds what makes them tick.

The avatar hurls another attack at her. She raises a firewall, bright as the sun, and repels it. For once, the avatar isn't talking. For once, there's no smugness or mockery. It exudes a hatred she never knew anyone but her could feel, the hatred she felt when Six came to her and told her Great Gra was dead, the hatred she felt when she first learned Esek's name.

She's not afraid of the avatar's hate. She'll use it. She'll use the sloppiness of hate, the imprecision of its efforts. She finds the venom glands, the origin points of the poison, putting it under a microscope and learning its structure. The better to replicate. She gives herself hundreds of hands, thousands of fingers, and casts out toward the hub in her bedroom. The avatar's planted evidence. The blueprint.

Her jaw seems on the verge of cracking. Heat hits her in waves, and the pain starts.

"Fuck," she growls through it. "*Fuck.*"

Too many spiders got under her skin before she could stop them. They've surged into her tech. Her eye and her ear are stinging, burning. The virus feels like it's in her brain, burrowing through her layers of protection to get at her neural link. If it distracts her with enough pain, it may succeed. Her armor has chinks in it already, and the shield she's raised has started to fade around the edges, the relentless assault chipping away at her.

"Jun!" Liis's voice barely reaches her—a sharp edge of panic. "Jun, you're bleeding."

Yes, she's bleeding. Her ear, her eye, both are bleeding. She thinks of Masar's cybernetic eye, the pain he tries to hide. She can live with a cybernetic eye. She can live with one deaf ear.

"Jun!" Liis snaps. "What do I do?"

What does she do? There's nothing she can do. She is the sword in the waking world. Jun is fighting on a different plane.

"Wait," Jun gasps. "Just wait."

Something leaks down her neck. Her vision swims. She recalls her early days at the archivist's academy. She recalls the lessons of her teachers, how to turn casts into a story, how to turn code into a narrative, and manipulate it, and control it, and that was the magic of casting, that was the true power that lay open to her. Her teachers taught her—use your ocular to envision the stories. They taught her—use your aural link to hear the code, to hear the whispering messages. But her aural link and her ocular are about to explode.

Jun closes her eyes. She turns them off.

The apartment is shockingly quiet. She hears Liis's anxious breathing, feels her nearness and helplessness. There is lightning in the air. Lightning at her fingertips.

"Almost there," she whispers. It is the only reassurance she can give.

She no longer sees the shape of the avatar, or the virus spiders, or the venom flooding through her. The attack is on the very cusp of her neural link now, disintegrating her shields. It'll slit her open and strip her for parts, take everything it can. She draws on instinct, on the hours, days, months, years of her craft. She feels messages pinging in her neural link, and she knows the avatar is trying to speak to her. But she can't hear those messages, can't see them, can't communicate with anything but the casts between her fingers, the raw code, stripped down. She cannot visualize the virus spiders in her tech, so she imagines them, their opaque bodies, their filament limbs. She winds their code together. She pulls from the virus blueprint in her hub. She forms a blade, curved like a sickle. A threshing blade.

And she weaves a program of her own. A magnet like a sucking black hole, a thing of inestimable power drawing out the poison of the spider bites. And it's *beautiful*. It's so beautiful, this program, as beautiful as the Hood when she first breathed it to life. She feels such tenderness now, despite everything. Such deep love for the thing inside her, the thing that has kept her alive, that has made her what she is.

Easy now, love, she remembers Great Gra saying, the first time she ever grappled with a securities code. Eight years old and squinting so hard she could barely see, and Ricari's big hand on her shoulder. *You're on to it now. Nice and easy.*

"Nice and easy," she whispers.

And slices the avatar's virus out of her own body.

Her aural link and ocular spring back online, rescued at the final hour. She opens her eyes inside the net and sees a sea of spiders crumbling to dust. She sees the avatar, too—writhing backward, riddled with lightning. Jun storms forward, scythe aloft, and swings.

Her blade cleaves the avatar from shoulder to hip. It yawns open, like a piece of fruit split in half and all its flesh exposed. She sees it then. Straight down to the core. Its exquisite construction. Its beautiful architecture. Dozens of firewalls. Perfect camouflage. She sees a half dozen connections it's woven between itself and the Treble, for it's not in the Treble at all. Liar, liar, little liar, it's pure Capamame, built from the networks and the hubs of the colony. She cuts it again. She plunges her hands inside it, going for the roots.

She finds it then, right in the thick of its coils.

"There," she cries, her fingers like tubes, sucking up the data she's unveiled, greedily swallowing the secrets it can't keep anymore. Its name, its name—it's right there, it's so close.

A pulse knocks her back, breaks her hold. She tries to drive in again, but a glass wall has sprung up, thick as the rock of Farren Eyce, clear as water. She watches the avatar stitch itself back together. But the pure anonymity of its shape has suffered. It looks more human than before. It almost has a face.

"I'll find you," Jun snarls. "I'll fucking find you."

But she's flayed it apart. It's too weak to respond. There's a stuttering sound, a glitch in her vision, and the avatar winks out.

Jun bursts free, stumbles, and Liis's hand is there, grabbing her elbow. Liis's arms catch her, hold her up.

"Okay," Liis says. "Easy."

"I almost got it," Jun gasps.

Liis swims into view. Jun feels like she's seeing her for the first time since she got back. Her brows furrowed with worry, scars creasing, mouth a hard line. Her knit cap is incongruously beautiful for its familiarity, and her eyes, those oil-slick eyes—

"What happened?" Liis asks.

Jun pulls away from her, staggering farther into the room. Her shoulders and chest are heaving; her body is soaked in sweat. She feels . . . feral. Monstrous. She faces Liis again and thinks of all the times her lover has emerged from a fight, blazing with life and ferocious as Som.

"I almost got it," Jun says again. "I almost got its name."

Liis eyes her. "What does that mean?"

"It means the avatar is in the colony," she says, "and I've got it on the run.

"Jun—"

"I'm *so* close to it."

"Jun, you're injured. You're bleeding—"

Jun barks a laugh, delirious with victory and exhaustion and the nearness of her own death, which couldn't have her in the end. Som went hungry.

"Jun," Liis says, urgent and commanding. "Look at me."

Only then does Jun realize that her eyes have been skittering across the apartment. She wipes the back of her wrist across her face and her ear and it leaves a rusty streak behind, but the bleeding has stopped. Her fingers feel numb and her limbs are shaking. Distantly it occurs to her that she might be in shock. She feels as if she is on a shoreline, and a tsunami is rolling in, ready to drag her under. But she looks at Liis, and Liis is the single point of stillness in all the universe, a dam that holds the tsunami back.

"Breathe, Jun," Liis tells her.

Jun breathes, stares at Liis and breathes. Then, with a growl, she throws herself at her.

They collide in the center of the apartment. Jun thinks that Liis will hold her off, try to make her sit down or drink water or some other thing she doesn't need. Instead, Liis catches her around the waist, shoves her against the wall. The first kiss is relieved, but the second is desperate.

"You're real," Jun groans. "Gods, you're real."

Liis grabs her hair, pulling her head back and nipping her throat; Liis's mouth, Liis's growl. Her fingers, scraping at Jun's skull. Jun drags her back into a kiss, tongue and teeth and the boiling point of weeks apart.

Liis pants against her, "Are you okay? Tell me you're okay."

"I'm okay. Just—just kiss me, I'm okay."

Liis's hands slip under her ass, hefting her up. Jun locks her legs around her, and Liis pins her to the wall. They roll into each other, burning alive and dying of thirst, and it feels so good Jun could weep. Maybe she is weeping. She pushes Liis's knit cap off her head, the black twists of her hair longer now, riotous. She cups Liis's face, touching the burn scar on her jaw and the gouge on her cheekbone, all monuments to her survival. She feels Liis's abdomen against hers, and Liis's arms around her body, sheets of muscle holding Jun together. She licks into her mouth and Liis yanks them away from the wall, toward their bedroom.

"I missed you," Jun whispers, voice broken with the weight of her aching, care-battered, love-devoured heart. "I missed you."

Liis growls, "Same," and spills her onto the bed.

It takes too long to get their clothes off. Something definitely rips. When Jun loses patience, she reaches a hand between them, finds where Liis is already hot and wet and needing her. Liis gasps into her mouth and Jun swallows the sound, pushing inside with a groan.

"I thought you weren't real," she says shakily. "I thought—"

"I'm real," Liis says, in her fierce, consuming voice, pushing her own hand between them. "Feel me, Jun. I'm real."

In relief, Jun does. It lacks all finesse. It's clumsy and perfect. Jun must look a wreck, disheveled and exhausted and blood on her face. She can't possibly be beautiful right now. But Liis is always beautiful. Liis smells like sweat and the green salve she uses on her arm, and somehow, still, like the wild winds on the surface of Capamame.

Then Liis flinches above her. Jun draws back, worried, and notices how Liis is bracing herself on her left arm so she can use her right hand between Jun's legs. Jun rolls her onto her back, sitting astride her hips. She reaches for the seam of the prosthetic arm.

"It's fine," Liis says.

"It's not fine," Jun answers.

When it's off, just the sleeve cap cupping the most vulnerable skin, Liis breathes a sigh of relief. Jun kisses just above the cap, nuzzles her breasts. Starts crawling down her body.

"Come here," Liis breathes. "Jun, come here."

Jun ignores her, putting Liis's legs over her shoulders, gripping the dense muscle with a sigh of joy. "You're real," she whispers, and bends to her.

CHAPTER TWENTY

1665

YEAR OF THE HARVEST

Easwa
Nikata Leen, an Island
The Planet Kator

The cottage sits on the shoreline of the coastal village of Easwa, dunes behind it and a road that disappears over the rise. There are five guardsaan outside the cottage, and all of them, Yantikye explains, have been paid off. Same as the concierge of Blue Spire, the one who got Chono into the servant quarters of the hotel and, from there, smuggled out in a refuse cart.

On the shore, the bought guardsaan watch as Chono and Yantikye approach in a skiff. Two of them come down to help secure the skiff to a rickety dock, and another holds out their hand to Chono, helping the cleric come ashore. Chono, embarrassed at the loss of her Quietan sea legs, accepts the help, whereas Yantikye leaps onto the dock, fleet-footed and perfectly balanced. He smiles broadly at the guardsaan, all sharp incisors.

"All right?" asks Yantikye.

One of the guardsaan, thick and heavy-browed, grunts. "Your credits came through. But the guard changes in an hour. If you're not out by then, I'll arrest you myself. Probably be a reward in it."

"Very clever," says Yantikye. "If you betray us, my people will release the proof that we paid you. Also I have a friend who will find you and kill you. Nobody wins."

A gruff snort. "Just be gone by the hour."

"Not a problem. I'm sure Cleric Chono won't need much time. Will you, Cleric Chono?"

They look at each other. Chono feels a low twist of dislike for this man, and wishes that Six was here. She knows why they had to stay behind—someone needs to be in Blue Spire to hold off any Kindom that might ask after her. Six had barely been able to contain their anger, their refusal, but Yantikye was insistent, and Yantikye was right. *I'll protect her with my life*, he said, and because Chono wanted this to work, she made Six yield. But their absence makes her restless.

Ignoring Yantikye, she addresses the guardsaan.

"Where is Cleric Paiye?"

"*Cleric* Paiye?" he jeers, and a couple of the others laugh. "He's no better than a civilian. But you call him cleric if you like. He's inside."

Chono is about to ask if Paiye knows that she's coming, but then she looks to the cottage and sees a large window, and a figure passing by it, as if he had only just been looking out. She starts to walk up the path toward the cottage and realizes that no one is following her. She looks back at Yantikye.

"I doubt he'll talk to you in front of me," he says. "I'll watch the skiff, and keep these saan entertained. One hour, Burning One. Our friend won't like it if I don't bring you back safe and sound."

Chono doesn't respond, and walks up the path to the cottage. The door is ajar. She knocks anyway and is somehow unprepared for that familiar, sonorous voice calling out to her.

"Come along, Chono. There's no need to be shy."

With those words, he erases the ten years between this moment and the one when they met. He makes her a freshly coated cleric again, young and eager to leave the days of Esek behind. Determined to impress him with her righteousness and hard work, to be worthy of her mantle. Now, the coat hangs familiar on her shoulders, and the last vestiges of her naivety are gone, but Aver Paiye still has the power to make her feel like an untried child.

She pushes the door open and goes inside.

It's a small room, not unlike her cabin on Pippashap. A kitchenette on one side, a bed in the corner, and a stone fireplace built into one wall, with a little table and two chairs in front of it. Paiye is sitting in one of the chairs, a teapot and tea things laid on the table for them. He pours, not looking at her. She looks at him.

It's been less than a year, but the gray in his hair has completely eclipsed the darker strands that were there before. He's lost weight. The flesh around his throat sags like a caruncle, and his body is swallowed up inside a fishersaan's sweater and loose trousers. Instead of the fat Godfire ring she remembers, he now wears the three-chained finger bracelet of a Kata devotee, its myriad beads all white. His face has a weather-beaten look, as if he's spent too many hours walking the beach, against the wind.

"Come and sit," he says, dropping hard disks of cinnamon sugar into the teacups and using a little spoon to stir the sweetness in. He still hasn't looked at her.

Chono goes to the empty chair and sits down, watching him prepare the tea. It's a traditional Katish tea service, she realizes—something given for honored guests. Ilius used to make her tea like this, back when they were lovers and always met in his Riin Kala apartment. Each element of the service symbolizes generosity, a giving of one's most valuable resources. The cinnamon sugar dates from a time when sweets were a luxury. The tea leaves themselves, grown in the Katish lowlands of the Kray East, are expensive. Paiye scoops a thick spoonful of clotted cream from a jar, dropping it into the teacups. Traditionally, one does not stir the cream in. The guest is meant to taste its thick buttery texture before it dissolves. To recognize the preparation and care that went into the service.

He pushes the cup across the table to her and raises his eyes. They look at each other. They don't speak.

Chono lifts the cup and drinks, letting the dollop of cream touch her lips and sucking the tea through it. A rude slurp is, in this Katish tradition, a sign of enjoyment and gratitude. Truth is, she can barely taste it. The bitter leaves and the sweetened cinnamon and the cream all come and go from her awareness. She sets the cup down and bows over her hands.

"Gods keep you well, Burning One."

Paiye, holding his own cup, smiles drolly over the rim and drinks. His eyes move across her, assessing, and she tries to bear his scrutiny without reaction.

"The Jeveni who came back nine months ago told us that you were badly injured on *The Risen Wave*. Was it a cloaksaan who shot you?"

Chono hesitates. "It was a Jeveni," she says at last. "Friendly fire."

He takes another sip, eyebrows quirking. "Friendly fire...A telling choice of words."

The way he says it—he means that she is a traitor. She chose the Jeveni over her own kin. She has to hold very still, to remind herself of the stoic and practical person she used to be, the emotionless operative of her Hand, who could suffer interactions with spiteful people and never lose her purpose.

"Do you know why I've come?" she asks.

"I have some idea. I do wonder how your handlers found me. I may retain my devotees in the Treble, but there are people who would kill me if they knew where I was." He puts down the cup of tea and gives her a level look. "Are you here to kill me, Cleric Chono?"

The question irritates her. "No." He tips his head to one side, perhaps thinking of Cleric Paan, whom she did kill. Were his crimes worse than Paiye's? No, but they certainly evoked more violence from her. She has no desire to kill Paiye. Though he does deserve it.

"Very well," Paiye says. "You never struck me as the type to demand apologies. Are you here for a New Sun blessing?"

"I'm here to discuss the Rule of Unification."

Paiye raises his eyebrows. "What about it?"

A muscle feathers in her jaw. She answers calmly, "The Kindom has insisted that the rule will restore peace. Are you aware that it's done the opposite? The Secretaries made promises to increase jump travel and reduce violence. Instead, they've escalated those problems. And now they have an enemy in Seti Moonback. There is no First Cloak, no First Cleric. The Secretaries hold absolute power, and they're abusing it at every turn."

Paiye sips his tea. "That *is* concerning."

Chono tries to parse his tone, to gauge whether the indifference is an act, or a mockery.

"I've met people who want to intercede. They think you can help them."

"Yes, I've met those people, too," he says. "Their ideas are quite interesting. Trade upon my followers in the Treble. Leverage me as a symbol, to force the Secretaries to step back." He chuckles. "Of course, *you* are the symbol they care about. Your name and face are everywhere: the martyr who came back to life with the Godfire's own justice in her hands. The People's Kin. They speak of you with reverence. Those who trust you, that is. There are debates all over the newscasts on whether you have become a political radical. I didn't expect it to be true."

Chono doesn't react. Paiye smiles a little. He picks up his teaspoon, beginning to stir the half-melted cream into the rest of the tea, turning the dark amber color thick and pale. He speaks in a toneless voice. "I was integral to passing the Rule of Unification. I threw the Righteous Hand's power behind the Secretaries. Why would I speak against them now?"

"You supported it as a survival strategy. The Secretaries gave you a choice: public execution or honorable exile. You acted in your own best interests...again."

The last word is a dart she can't help throwing. His placid expression wavers. "How cynical you've become. You think I would support the Rule of Unification simply to save my own life? You think I saved my life at all? I am on borrowed time, Chono. I did what I did because I believed it was the only way to protect unity in the Treble."

"And do you still believe that?" she asks. He looks as if he wants to answer but stops himself. "In the past twenty-four hours alone, the guardsaan have killed thirteen hundred protesters across Ma'kess, Kator, and Teros. I doubt Braemin and Quietus have gone unscathed, but of course we've never been good at reporting all the little atrocities committed against those planets, have we?"

He is silent.

"They're planning to carpet-bomb a dozen cities across the Treble," she tells him.

A flicker of reaction, and then nothing.

"I know you, Sa. I see through your mistakes to the motivations that drove you. You want peace. But the Secretaries aren't peacekeepers. They're lawmakers; they consider their edicts inviolable and they're prepared to do anything to defend them. They're wielding power like a sword they don't know how to use, all while the Cloaksaan are cracking under a schism. Do you want to see Seti Moonback raise an army of Brutal Hands? Is *any* of this what you wanted?"

"And what do you want, Chono?"

"I want peace, too. I want justice."

He snorts. "And this is how you mean to achieve it? You must realize the Secretaries won't bend to the Clerisy. Indeed, I doubt that's even what your people want. This will simply lead to a wider-scale uprising. Tens of thousands of people would die. It would dwarf the Jeveni Genocide. Gods and fire, Esek herself couldn't make you spoil for a fight, and now you want an interplanetary war. I should have known better than to reunite you with her. Clearly those months on Capamame have given her all the time she needs to corrupt you."

Chono nearly laughs. Yes, of course, this must be how it seems to him. When he told her not to board *The Risen Wave*, and she went anyway, he read it for a statement of alliance—to Esek. She wants to tell him it wasn't Esek that drove her onto that ship. It was Six. The only thing she wanted was to protect Six. Protect them from Esek, who was already dead.

But once the irony of Paiye's misunderstanding passes, his hypocrisy takes center stage. Chono sips her tea. "Strange of you, to mention corruption."

His nostrils flare. "Order is a check against corruption; it's a check against chaos. Have we failed? Perhaps, at times. But the Treble has thrived for centuries, and the Kindom is the reason why. You think the people on their own can hold these systems together? We keep resources circulating. We make jump travel possible. We hold the Families in check. Without us, the Treble would descend into anarchy. Yet you want to lead an uprising!" He scoffs. "Gods, did I ever think you were wise?"

Chono almost smiles. "What would you have me do instead? Become the First Cleric?"

He looks at her sharply, like someone whose closely hoarded secret has come to light. Chono feels vaguely satisfied. Six was right. Paiye's expression mellows into acceptance.

"I see you abhor the idea. Are you really so imperceptive? Do you know how many lives I've saved? How many family feuds I've quelled? How many wars I've stopped? That is the power of the First Cleric. That is the power you could have."

"Yet you were happy enough to see me killed on *The Risen Wave*."

He gives her a mocking look. "There it is. Perhaps you *do* want an apology, after all."

"I assure you, I don't."

"Come now, Chono. I was once your confessor. Unburden yourself to me, child."

Her lip curls back. "I will not *unburden* myself to you."

"Shall I unburden myself to you, then? *You're* the cleric, after all, and I am the penitent."

"I don't want your confession."

"Of course you do. And not just my confession, but my contrition. My remorse. You want me to bow before you and beg for forgiveness. But you are the one who betrayed *me*."

Chono stares at him, unblinking.

"Betrayed *you*?" she repeats, very softly.

"You were my choice, Chono. I would have raised you above any First Cleric in history. After you finished tracking down that wretched caster, Sunstep, I meant to bring you back to Riin Cosas and begin training you to replace me. I saw your time with Esek as a boon. You would understand the Cloaksaan better than most clerics. You would understand the threat of the Nightfoots as many of our kin don't. I thought your natural righteousness would rise above the temptation of Esek. But I was wrong. You could have trusted me, trusted that what I did was in the best interest of the Treble. Instead, you disappeared with the Jeveni and their criminal government, and then you came back and tore the Hands apart. What is that if not betrayal?"

He is all disdain, and Chono feels a poisonous thing gathering momentum inside of her, with boulders for hands, hands strong enough to smash a man into the ground and keep smashing until—

"Betray you," she repeats, in the same icy whisper. The thing inside her finds a flaw in its own restraining chains and starts to lever the links apart. "Did you receive the report I sent you on Cleric Paan?"

His face shutters. No matter. Chono, utterly motionless in her chair, feels the violent righteousness of the Godfire swelling within her.

"I sent it specifically to you. I gave you the names of the children, and their families who he threatened into silence. I told you he'd set his sights on another child. I waited for your response. I waited two weeks, thinking maybe it hadn't reached you. I sent my report again, and that time I got a response. It was an order from a lower tier than you, directing me to take my concerns through the proper channels. So I did. No one answered. Did you receive the report?"

His skin has lost some of its color, the gray making him look old and decrepit, and for the first time there's a flicker of shame in him.

"Chono, you must understand—"

"Did you know what the kinschool masters did to the children in their charge? You knew about the recruitment tours. Did you know how they sold us into the beds of saan whose patronage they needed? I was sold five times before Esek fished me out."

"Chono—"

"Did you know what *Esek* did? Your own cleric? How she murdered innocent families to get what she wanted? How she terrorized people for crimes as minor as *existing* in her orbit?"

He leaps at that. "You yourself served Esek. What right do you have to—"

"Close your mouth or I will kill you."

She speaks as softly as a breeze, and his eyes widen, doubt and fear clouding his expression. She hears Six's voice, naming her: *Student Four. Quiet and terrible.*

"I don't need you to answer these questions," Chono murmurs. "I know the answers. And I know my own guilt. If the Godfire burned me up for following Esek, it would be justice. But you..." She draws the word out with a growl. "You say 'betrayal' with the same mouth that damned a ship carrying over five hundred civilians. You say 'betrayal' with the same mouth that never spoke against Cleric Paan. You broke the laws of Remembrance Day to send cloaksaan onto *The Risen Wave*, and you hid behind stories of Jeveni rebellion that held no truth. 'Betrayal' is too tame a word for the pattern of evil that winds its way through your career. You wanted to train me up to replace you? Bless the gods for sparing me that fate."

Paiye flinches but doesn't say a word. Apparently he believes her threat.

"As I said, my associates want you to partner with them in standing against the Secretaries. And as you said, that would lead to open war. You assume they are my handlers and that I want what they want. You're wrong."

His eyes cut at her, startled.

"My associates would drive the Treble to violence and uprising. They would turn the people into martyrs. I came here to hold the Kindom accountable. Not to spur them to slaughter more innocent people."

Paiye looks wary. "So what *do* you want?"

Chono tilts her chin up. "I want to speak to Oyun Paiye."

He blinks at her. If she has startled him already, she has mystified him now. "What?"

"Your sister," Chono says, as if she could mean anyone but the leader of the Paiye family, a woman of ponderous resources but notorious privatism, utterly indifferent to the outside world until it threatens her profits. A woman who did always love her little brother. Chono continues, "Oyun is on good terms with Khen Ookhen Obair. She can persuade him to speak to me as well. And as you know, I already have the Nightfoot matriarch's ear."

"Chono, what are you—"

"I'll allow that Khen is a problem, given I murdered his uncle. And there is of course the matter of the Moonbacks. But Revel Moonback sent Seti away to kinschool because he despised her, so I doubt he'll support her now. Also, I have some leverage over him. That's the four Families, all of whom are beholden to you for protecting their interests when you were First Cleric. So I need your help to bring them together."

Paiye is silent for a long while. Chono lifts the teacup, sipping. The cream has entirely dissolved. There's a silt of cinnamon sugar at the bottom of the cup.

"You never intended me to help you start a war," he says.

"No," she says. "That was your presumption."

"You want the First Families to rally behind you and take the brunt of the conflict."

"Why ask mortal saan to fight a giant when you can send another giant to fight for them?"

"Do you have any idea the price they'll exact?" he asks. "Everything they'll want from you, in exchange for their help? You think it was bad bowing to the Kindom? Wait till the First Families have you on your knees."

Chono regards him pensively and says in a quiet, firm voice, "No. I will not bow again. Not to you or any Hand. Certainly not to the Families."

Paiye curls his lip. "When did you become so arrogant, Chono? When did your oaths to the Kindom fall so low in your estimation? You'd betray all your kin for some wild gamble with the First Families? You say you won't bow, but what about the Godfire? Your oaths to the Kindom are caught up in your oaths to our god. Are you so prideful now that you will refuse to bow to the Godfire that you claim to serve?"

She watches him for a beat of three, four seconds. Musingly she says, "Do you know... it's very strange that we purport to be the servants of the Godfire. We are so much more like the Six Gods." She turns her spoon in the cup of tea, watches the swirl of liquid, watches the light glint off the spoon. "The Six Gods are vain and jealous. They want worshippers to love them just for existing. They tell their people to bow, no matter what. Just like the Kindom." She raises her eyes again. "But the Godfire has never asked me to bow. The Godfire has no ego. The Godfire burns through ego. It burns through all corruption, all injustice, all pride. In time, no doubt it will burn through me as well." She leans closer. "But until that day... I will *not*... bow."

Paiye swallows. "You will fail."

"I certainly may."

"Esek will betray you."

"I understand why you think so."

"The Families won't work together."

"But they will work toward their own best interests. The Clever Hand is throwing trade and law into upheaval. Esek isn't the only one annoyed by the threat to her family's interests."

"What makes you think a war between the Kindom armies and the armies of the Families will result in any less death?"

"Perhaps I won't ask the Families to use their armies. Perhaps I'll tell them to leverage their assassins and take out one Hand after another, until they get what they want."

Paiye looks stunned, and then despairing. "You've become brutal, Chono."

Has she? What else was she supposed to become?

"Will your sister speak to me?"

He studies her for several moments. She can see him, weighing her scheme against the prospect of a war. Weighing the good of his family against the supremacy of the Kindom that ousted him. She has lost her faith in him, and yet her faith in him is her only hope: her belief, under layers of resentment, that he *does* want what's best for the Treble. Will he agree with her about what is best?

At last, he speaks. "I can make an introduction."

Chono nods. "Good. I'll await your word on the matter."

With that, she wants no more of him. She stands. "Thank you, Sa. Gods keep you well."

"If I may, Cleric Chono..." He stops her. She looks at him coldly, and his worried expression shifts with a vague smile of affection, almost paternal. It makes her stomach flop. "I do have one question. This...scheme. Is it your idea, or Esek's?"

Chono adjusts the collar of her red cleric's coat, replying, "It's mine."

A long pause.

"Are you sure?" When Chono doesn't respond, he asks, "Are you sure that she is not simply manipulating you toward some goal of her own? One of your greatest gifts, I think, was that you knew Esek better than any of us. You may not have had the courage to stand up to her, but you certainly understood her. Are you sure you understand her now, and are not just a tile on the game board?"

Chono ponders. It's natural, of course, to transfer this question to Six, to ask herself if she truly understands her old schoolkin. Haven't they admitted that they want to use her, just like everyone?

But her thoughts return to Esek, long dead. What did Esek want, really, from Chono? What did Esek want to use her for? To Esek, she was absolutely a tile on the game board. But there were times when she also seemed to be a gambling partner, both of them laying the same bets, both of them risking the same stakes. What would Esek tell her now, as she stands on the brink of this new mission, with everything to lose?

Bet high, Esek would say. *Bet everything. Never yield. Die on your feet.*

Chono is just debating how to answer Paiye's question, when her gaze flicks toward the window, wondering if the hour Yantikye gave her is up—

She stops. Standing here, she has a clear view of the dock. But the skiff, and Yantikye, are gone. And there are dead guardsaan on the beach.

She barely has time to process what she's seeing, when the crack of an explosion drops her onto her face. She expects to feel a rain of debris as the cottage comes down around her, and she hears Paiye cry out, and she covers her head with her arms—before realizing in confusion that it was a concussive bomb. Ears ringing, pulse gone wild, she rolls to her knees, reaching for the gun Six made her strap to her thigh. Something kicks her hand away and stomps her other hand down onto the ground. Her barely healed hand. Bones shatter. Flesh splits apart. The gun skitters away, and Chono pivots on her other knee, kicking out. Through her muffled hearing she recognizes a dull shout and someone hitting the ground.

She launches to her feet—bodies collide with hers. She's wrenched sideways, driven back, slamming into the window behind her. Glass cracks behind her skull, her vision haloes and goes black, and someone punches her so hard in the gut that she gags, doubling over. Only the arms holding her keep her from collapsing. Only sheer furious will stops her from passing out. One of the hands on her wrist twists, wrenching the already broken fingers. She chokes and screams, and tries to focus. She's snarling and spitting like an animal, and four guardsaan are holding her against the cracked window.

A voice says, "That's enough. Don't hurt her."

Chono's knees turn watery. There in the middle of the cottage stands Ilius.

In his small round spectacles with that piece of hair curling over his forehead, he looks as boyish and out of place as ever. But in the tippet of his Hand, all appliquéd with the high honors he has won, he looks suddenly...vicious.

Chono stops fighting the guards, but they hold her no less firm, one with a hand to her throat like a collar. She clocks Paiye on the ground near the fireplace, the table and the tea things all in pieces around him. No one holds him down. They don't have to. On his knees, he's trembling, and there's a bleeding gash on his cheekbone; he squints, looking uncertainly at Chono, then at Ilius. Ilius, seeing the direction her gaze has gone, turns to regard the former First Cleric. Paiye snorts a shaky laugh of recognition.

"Secretary Redquill. I see the Clever Hand is finding more and more interesting uses for you. Since when do you lead raids?"

Her hearing comes back sluggishly. Ilius's voice goes from distant to close. "This called for someone relatively important. It's not every day such high-level clerics turn mutineers."

Paiye laughs again, but it's furious. "You are a *child* playing in those robes, Redquill. They wouldn't have even wanted you if you didn't know so much about Nightfoot and Chono."

Ilius ignores this. "You broke the terms of your release, Sa Paiye. You were strictly forbidden to engage in any private conversation with unapproved visitors."

Taking in the broken cups and teapot, Paiye says, "My good manners got the better of me. I was never one to turn away a guest."

"I understand," says Ilius. "But we've had an aural link to your cottage since you came here. Your treason is on record. Again."

Only then does Chono realize she never raised Jun's scrambling tech. Too distracted by speaking to Paiye again. Self-loathing unspools in her body, and then, anger. "He hasn't done anything. He refused to rise against the Kindom or speak against the rule."

Ilius looks at her slowly, and she knows how empty her words are. His eyes are very bright—but not with tears.

"I warned you," he says quietly. "I told you over and over to be rational. But you just...wouldn't listen."

She has been so cold to him, so indifferent to his pain. She's indifferent now, as well—and yet she thinks perhaps she feels it more than she did before. How hurt he is, not by her betrayal of the Kindom, but her betrayal of him. Just as Paiye was hurt. Chono looks at Ilius urgently, trying to reason with him even as their years of friendship assail her. The early conversations via messenger and cast. Their first shy meetings in Riin Kala. The sleepy, philosophical debates they carried out in the aftermath of sex, each trying to come up with a better solution to a moral quandary. They were such . . . intellectuals. They were such hypocrites.

"I listened, Ilius," she tells him. "I just think you're wrong."

His glare is icy. "So it would seem."

"I have to follow my conscience. We're both sworn to the Godfire. I—"

"The Kindom is the *instrument* of the Godfire," he snaps. "We are the *Hands* of the Godfire. We protect the Body, the people, and we do it with the full confidence of our gods. *You*, of anyone, ought to know that."

"The Kindom serves the Godfire," she retorts. "It is not the final word."

"If you would only put aside your juvenile rebelliousness and think clearly, you would remember that the final word of the Godfire is peace, under the Kindom. Unity, in the Treble."

She hurls back, "That is a self-serving argument, and always has been."

He seems amazed at her. But there's resignation in his eyes, as if he always knew it would come to this. Shame quickens her pulse. Not for what she's done, but for her own naive and myopic choice to befriend him in the first place. To misunderstand the true foundation of his morality, which was never the maintenance of good but the maintenance of order.

He takes a gun from a holster behind his back, and Chono jerks as if someone has hit her again. She's never seen him hold a weapon, not in all the years she's known him. *Why* did they send him to do this, when any guardsaan captain would do? Is it to punish her? To punish ·*him*, for loving her?

"You said you have associates who want to use the Clerisy to raise a rebellion." His voice is flat. "Who are they? Esek? Or maybe those Quietan spies who met you at the distillery?"

Chono nearly flinches to realize how much he knows. She should have anticipated it. She doesn't answer him, and he narrows his eyes.

"The Jeveni, perhaps? Why else have you refused to parlay with them?"

"The Jeveni have nothing to do with this. All they want is to be left alone."

"I don't believe you."

"Ilius, this is absurd, I—"

He turns with mechanical efficiency, aims at Paiye, and shoots him in the leg.

The old man screams, toppling sideways and clutching at his calf as blood spurts out of him. He screams the way people who have never suffered scream. Pure shock and disbelief blended with the immolating pain. Chono shares his horror.

"Ilius, don't—!"

"Tell me the truth, then. Tell me who you're working with. Are there other Jeveni spies in the Treble? Are you in league with Seti Moonback?"

Chono can't think how to respond.

Ilius directs the guardsaan. "Bring her here."

They yank her away from the window. They wrestle her over to Ilius and shove her down onto her knees. He looms over her, gun held loosely, comfortably, at his side. How much has she never known about him?

"Chono. I don't want to hurt you. Even now, I want you to live." He sounds both sincere and distant. It chills her. "But you have to tell me who my real enemies are. I've watched you for years. You're not a rebel. You've served your entire life. So who are you serving? Is it whoever wrote you those letters in that box?"

Goose bumps race across her skin. Six's letters that she left on *The Makala Aet*. She comforted herself at the time that the chest's self-destruct lock would prevent anyone from getting inside. Now, it occurs to her that Ilius, the information broker, the wielder of operatives from every trade, could obviously have found someone to open it.

And realizing that, her strongest, most overwhelming sensation is the same one she had when her kinschool master sold her for sex. A sickening flush of exposure and humiliation.

Ilius's lips compress in what might be a smile, if his vindication didn't look so unhappy.

"They're rather obscure, the letters. I gather that you and Esek have been hunting this person for some time, but that your loyalties were somewhat divided. Perhaps you've allied with them now? Does Esek know?"

Chono exhales slowly. "Whatever you read, I am absolutely certain you don't understand it. And whoever you think I'm collaborating with—you couldn't be more wrong. I came here to save the five thousand. It's you who've collaborated to make that impossible."

He ignores her, looking at Paiye. "And what do you know about it? You had spies on Esek for years. You must know something about this mission she was on. Why she was working with the Jeveni. What they want."

Paiye, blanched white and clutching his leg, wet all over with blood, sets his teeth. He looks at Ilius balefully. "You are a *waste* of that uniform," he says. "We made so many mistakes, and you Secretaries have learned *nothing*. You'll never conquer Chono this way. She—"

Ilius shoots him again.

But not the leg, this time. Blood sprays hot across Chono's face, and she hears the heavy, deadweight thunk of Paiye dropping back. It takes her a moment of staring to realize that the shape now collapsed at rude angles is not the former First Cleric—but his corpse. Her ears are still faintly ringing. Her mouth is open.

"Tell me the truth," Ilius orders her, a slight tremor in his voice now, as if cold-blooded murder has pushed him further than he realized. When she looks up at him, his eyes are white-rimmed. And her contempt for him melds with pity. He has blood on his clothes. He is a brilliant man, and the most foolish kind there is.

She pushes aside the horror of Paiye's execution. Pushes down the fear that her own is next. "You want to believe that everything I've done was to serve someone else. That I'm just a tool. That's easier for you to accept than the reality...I don't work for anyone else. And I will *never* serve the Kindom again. I'm your enemy. Forever."

A blaze of rage and denial fills his eyes. Then, something clicks off inside him. All his emotion falls behind a screen. He sniffs.

"Very well, Cleric Chono." He looks at the guardsaan and gestures the gun at her, almost casually. "Take her now."

Hands grab her up again. Chono stares at Paiye's body, at the brain matter dripping and clumping around his head, and the bizarre twistedness of a shape that was once so regal, so beloved. Through the whooshing whine in her ears, and the bluster of the guardsaan moving her out, she hears someone speak to Ilius: "Should we raid the suite at Blue Spire?"

Sweating with fear, Chono hears his answer: "Not yet. I have plans for that one."

CHAPTER TWENTY-ONE

1664

YEAR OF THE CRUX

Farren Eyce
The Planet Capamame

Masar is one of the only people in Farren Eyce who has his own apartment, and he sometimes feels guilty for that. Such a wealth of riches for one person: the oversized armchair and a kitchen with an island, the tall wardrobe that came from *Drae's Hope*, and a bed with a thick woven comforter that belonged to his grandmi. Everything is packed too close together, but big as he is, Masar still likes the smallness, somehow. He could have opted to share an apartment with some of the other collectors, but in those early days after jumping to Capamame, he felt split open with grief over Nikkelo, and the new eye was challenging him. He wanted privacy, and the Wheel allowed it.

But now, with Bene puttering around the kitchen, a soft presence, it occurs to him that it's not so bad, sharing space. Usually Bene is chatty, but he's quiet tonight, standing at the stovetop on the island, cutting up vegetables and setting a pot of water to boil.

"I hope you like noodles," he says with an embarrassed smile. "It's all I can make."

The apartment doesn't have room for a table, so Masar is sitting on a stool on the other side of the island. He makes a gesture that says noodles are fine and tries not to watch Bene too obviously. It's hard, because he feels so clouded with worry and regret. There are dark circles under Bene's eyes, and he looks older than his years, mouth turned down at the corners while he throws spices and herbs into a pan. A rich, aromatic smell fills the apartment, and there's the hiss of the vegetables tossed in. Steam rises off the pan. The pot of water starts to boil.

"You don't have to cook for me," Masar says, just for something to say.

Bene gives him a dry smile. "Liis and Jun haven't seen each other in weeks. Believe me, it behooves me to steer clear of the apartment for a few hours."

Masar scowls. He had to listen to Jun have sex once—and though he didn't know her very well, it was probably just as uncomfortable as if she'd been his cousin. But Bene only looks amused. He stirs the vegetables. He dollops curry paste into the pan.

Masar says, "You can spend the night, if you want."

It's the least he can do, isn't it? Give Bene a soft place to rest? Of course, then it occurs to him that they would have to share the bed, which is certainly big enough, but—

Bene cuts him a look, shrugs casually. "All right."

"You look tired," Masar says.

A snort. "I didn't exactly sleep well last night. I don't know if I'll sleep tonight, either."

"Because of Tej?"

"Because of everything."

Yes, everything. Masar doubts he'll sleep much, either. Not with Dom in his head—the sounds of his weeping and the abject misery on his face. It makes Masar's nerves light up, as if someone were shocking him with electricity. There is no pity in him, no inkling of compassion. Thinking of Dom makes his shoulders lock. He wants to hit something, to punch a hand through the wall, to rip the apartment into pieces.

He controls himself. He doesn't want to scare Bene.

"Thank you for..." He hesitates, trying to think how to say it. "You defended Farren Eyce to Jun. That couldn't have been easy, after what we did to your family. So...thank you."

Bene gives him a funny look. "What you did to my family was give us a home."

"Yes, but—"

"The twins would have died on that farm station eventually. And I'm lucky I lived so long in the mines. You don't know what it was like there, Masar." Something crosses his face, a haunting. "Grandmi was always sick. We barely had enough to eat. I had to change my gendermark because the men kept threatening to kill me."

Masar's stomach drops. He knew about the gendermark, but not why Bene changed it. Cautiously he asks, "Do you...want to be a woman?"

Bene shrugs. "No, not now. Maybe someday, again. The point is I barely survived. Call this colony flawed, but no one's come into my home and slaughtered half my family here."

Sometimes Masar forgets that Bene was in the Ironway shop when Esek Nightfoot killed his father and uncle and Great Gra. It must have felt very much like watching Medisogo shoot Nikkelo in the head, or like realizing that Uskel had carried him to safety while the guardsaan mowed down the rest of their team. A collapse in the foundation of the world. A black hole opening up inside, never to be filled.

Bene cooks. Masar watches.

"Do you resent Six?" Masar asks.

Bene hesitates, not looking at him. "Why should I resent Six? They did the only thing they knew how to do."

"It's their fault Esek Nightfoot went after your family in the first place. And then they put you and your cousins... Well, the homes they found you weren't safe."

Bene gives the noodles a stir. "I haven't got space in my heart for resentment, Masar. I'm too tired. This life... It's made me too tired. All I want now is to be with the people I love."

Masar flushes a little, knowing that he falls under the cover of Bene's love. But he doesn't deserve it. He doesn't have Bene's forgiveness and grace. Resentment burns through every vein in his body. Every muscle is a contraction of anger and grief. He never thought of Bene as tired, as worn out by the cares of the past, but now it almost feels comforting. Masar is tired, too.

A few minutes later the noodles and the stir-fry are ready. Bene stirs it all together and adds big hunks of crumbled cheese and ladles it into two bowls. Masar, restless, comes around to the other side of the island so they can stand together and eat. It feels different from sharing meals and space with other people. On his missions, he made it a point to befriend everyone he met. But he didn't really want friends—he wanted people to give him the information he was looking for, and that want superseded all other wants. Every once in a while he went into a city somewhere and picked up a lover, but those encounters merely scratched an itch. They didn't have the intimacy of eating noodles in a tiny kitchen with Bene.

Sidelong, he watches Bene finish his meal and wipe sauce off his chin with the back of his wrist, which is oddly endearing. Masar clears his throat and takes both the empty bowls. He washes them hurriedly, focused, determined. He thinks if he gets this part over with, he can turn to the more serious task of convincing Bene to take the bed while he sleeps in the armchair.

When arms slip around him from behind, he nearly jumps out of his skin, assuming an attack—realizing embarrassingly late what's really happening. To his surprise, Bene doesn't pull back at his reaction.

Instead, he presses his face between his shoulder blades. Masar looks down to see Bene's hands laid very lightly over his belly and sternum. He swallows against a wave of desire and gathers his strength to pull away. What good could he possibly be to Bene tonight? All he can see is Uskel's body on the steps. Roq shot and Leios hanged. And Nikkelo, whom he loved, whom he served and adored—

"Bene," he says, voice rough with apology, putting his own hands over Bene's hands, telling himself to lift them away.

"Masar," Bene whispers back.

When a soft knock pulls their attention to the front door, Masar's heart pounds like he's heard a gunshot. Bene untangles from him, and Masar exhales in relief. But it doesn't last. Because the person at the door is Effegen.

"I know it's late," she says. "I hope this is all right."

"Of course," Bene says, as if it's his apartment and not Masar's.

He steps aside for her, and she comes inside looking careful and uncertain. An unusual expression on her face. Masar hasn't seen her since they brought Dom to the newsnest, since she presented the new evidence to the Wheel and shamed them into acknowledging what it proved. Since then, she's put aside her official robes. She wears a wrap dress, with a shawl draped over her body. She's put her hair in a braid. Her smile, when she sees Masar, is weary and a little droll, as if she's embarrassed to be here.

"I thought you might both be awake still," she explains.

Masar realizes that she must have known that Bene was here. Maybe she gleaned it from surveillance? No, Bene would have told her.

"I was just making sure he ate something," Bene says. "Have you eaten? We could make more noodles."

He takes her hand, leading her deeper into the apartment. How can he just...touch her like that? So familiar? And she accepts the touch easily, like it's nothing new. It makes Masar antsy. Just a few hours ago she was interrogating Dom ben Dane about the Ironways—ready to confront the reality that Bene might be a traitor.

Effegen demurs. "I ate a few hours ago." She's surreptitiously inspecting the apartment, obviously curious. Her eyes drift over the armchair, the bed, the kitchen island. She's never been here before. She looks at Masar, takes stock of his frozen posture, and flushes like someone caught. "I'm sorry for intruding."

"Oh," Masar blusters. "I—no. Not at all. Please—would you like to sit?"

"No, no." She gestures placatingly. "I'll only stay a moment. I'm sorry, I just wanted to check on you." She smiles at Bene. "Both of you, I mean."

Bene is still holding her hand. Does he know that she was ready to condemn him on Dom's word? Bene says, "I'm all right. We could all probably use some sleep."

Effegen chuckles grimly. Her eyes flit toward the bed, almost with longing. How long has it been since she slept? There are dark circles under her eyes, same as Bene's. Yet they seem to take comfort from each other, from their fingers tangled together, from the ease of being in each other's presence. Something sick and twisted fills Masar's belly.

"Any leads on Tej?" Bene asks.

She shakes her head. "Not yet."

"I don't think he has the skill or the temperament to hide indefinitely," Bene says. "He'll make a mistake and..."

Bene trails off, glances away, like he doesn't know what comes next. Prison, for Tej? Something worse? Suddenly he gathers himself into a sterner posture, saying, "I'm sorry. I know how inadequate that is, but... I'm sorry. We should have watched him better."

With a flash of annoyance, Masar says, "It's not your fault."

"Maybe not, but he's our cousin. We should have known this was—" He breaks off, looking frustrated and helpless. "Well... no wonder people like Fonu distrust the non-Jeveni."

Strangers, Masar thinks, and his hackles rise.

Effegen says, "No one who truly knows you could distrust you, Bene."

Annoyance tips over into anger, like a jaw clamping on the back of Masar's neck. He looks at her, incredulous. "How is he supposed to believe that?" he demands. "Our own River imprisoned him. And *you* were ready to believe he worked for the secretary!"

He expects Effegen to balk at his tone. He's never spoken to her like that, so accusing, so furious. But she watches him with a preternatural calm. It's Bene who looks alarmed. "Masar. Don't."

"Don't what?" Masar snaps. "Don't admit that we would have turned on you? Just stand here and pretend to be friends when we both betrayed your trust?" He looks at Effegen in disbelief. "How can you let him believe you trust him when just a few hours ago—"

"Masar, she told me!" Bene exclaims. Masar looks at him in confusion. "She told me what happened with Dom. She told me she questioned him about all of us. Gods, what else was she supposed to do?"

Masar doesn't know what to say, his anger hitting a brick wall—but then it spills over the top.

"She was supposed to protect you! *I* was supposed to protect you! I was supposed to protect all of you. Everyone in this fucking colony— it was *my* job to protect them." His voice is raw. He can barely breathe. "It was *my* job! Fonu can't do it. Nikkelo isn't here. My collectors are dead! How the fuck can you stand there and apologize when we've failed you like this?"

"Masar," Effegen says quietly. "This isn't your fault, either."

"Of course it is!" he shouts. "Dom was *my* responsibility! He was blackmailed and trapped and he was murdering our friends and I didn't see it. I couldn't see it! Whose fault is that but mine?"

Bene's eyes are wide, distressed. Effegen says, "Nikkelo's, for one."

She may as well have put a knife through him. He steps back from her, shocked, incensed. How dare she— How could she—

"Nikkelo is *dead*!" he snarls.

"And that makes him faultless?" she asks, with that same disorienting calm, her eyes steady, her posture exact. "You say you're responsible for Dom. Nikkelo was responsible for all of you. He should have seen what was happening to Dom—how strained he was. The impact of his poverty. He should have discovered who it was trying to sell the names of the Wheel."

"He tried!" Masar exclaims. "He did everything he could!"

"And I was responsible for Nikkelo," she continues, as if he hadn't said it. "I am responsible for all the Wheel. I'm responsible for all the collectors. I'm responsible for the Ironways and every person in this colony, from the Draeviin who revere me to the black marketers who hate me. By Sajeven's own mercy, Masar, *I* am responsible. It's at my feet, not yours. I absolve you."

He makes a choking sound. "You can't."

"Can't I?"

"You told me to find the threat. You said, 'Whatever it takes.' And what have I done? Who have I saved?"

For the first time, her composure cracks. Her nostrils flare, and the green of her eyes goes sharp as a fire burning through a gemstone. "Did you forget that bullet wound in your side?"

He blinks rapidly. His response is completely inane. "I'm fine."

Bene makes an exasperated sound. He exclaims, "You were shot! You were shot protecting all of us!"

"It's nothing."

Effegen says angrily, "Why is it nothing that you were shot?"

"I—I—" He stumbles over his words, reaching out uselessly for a handhold, finally returning to: "You can't blame Nikkelo!"

"Why?" she asks. "Because you loved him? So instead I should blame you? Would that satisfy you, Masar? Would you finally forgive yourself for Nikkelo's death, if you could take all the blame on yourself?"

He stares at her. Bene's eyes widen, looking back and forth between them as if he's afraid of what's going to happen. Masar fights against the impulse to scream at her. But what would he be screaming at? He would be screaming at himself for not protecting Uskel. For losing Ademi in the firefight on Braemin. For leaving Nikkelo behind.

"I have to go," he says.

Bene catches him by the wrist. "Stop," he says, quiet but urgent. "Please, just... stop."

Masar goes rigid at his touch. He glares at the offending hand, and glares at Effegen, feeling cold and cruel. "Kata's *tit*, what do you want from me?"

"I want you to stop blaming yourself," Effegen says.

"I can't!"

"I want you to let us comfort you."

He takes another step back, breaking Bene's grip on him. He blinks rapidly, nerves exploding through his body at the soft entreaty in her eyes.

"I—I don't need that," he says. "I don't need that from either of you."

A beat of silence. Bene says, "Maybe *we* need it."

Masar feels on the verge of panicking. Damn his small apartment, there's nowhere to run. Effegen is between him and the door.

"You have each other," he says. "Take comfort from each other. You don't need me."

"I don't *need* either of you," Effegen says, sounding impatient.

Bene moves toward him again, and Masar is too stunned to react. He feels the younger man's hands, just the tips of his fingers, against his hips. Light. Cautious. Bene looks up at him with beseeching eyes.

"We love you. Don't you know we love you?"

Now Masar is definitely panicking. His eyes widen in alarm. He looks at Effegen, almost accusingly, and she looks a little panicked, too. As if she didn't expect Bene to state it so boldly. But with a helpless gesture, she nods. Her eyes are wet. "We do. We love you."

He looks down at Bene—Bene, who is still touching him with such gentleness, gazing up at him, soft and hopeful. "Do you love us?" he asks.

Masar swallows. "Even if I do, it—"

"It's enough," says Effegen, slipping forward.

"It's not, it—"

"It's enough," says Bene, pleadingly, and his grip tightens, and he's rising up to him—

The warm comfort of his mouth. The feeling of their chests pressed together. The low, wanting sound in Bene's throat as he deepens the kiss. Masar, helpless, kisses him back. Raw desire floods him, and he feels himself pulling Bene in, pulling him closer, gorging himself on the nearness and taste of him. When Bene pulls back, Masar sees in exhilarated confusion that Effegen has come close. Bene reaches out a hand to her, pulls her in. Her lush curves, brushing Masar's arm. Her nervous, hungry eyes.

"Masar," she whispers.

His heartbeat is a wild drum. He glances once, uncertainly, at Bene, and Bene nods, but he can't do it, it's not right, she's his Star and he is just—

She puts a hand behind his neck, lifting up onto her toes to kiss him. It snaps his control. He cups her face, bends to her, moaning. His thumb brushes the jevite studs in her ear. Her kiss is more aggressive than Bene's, needier, and with the feeling of Bene still against his chest and the feeling of her pressing into his good side, he's surrounded by them.

She jerks away with a gasp, stumbling—the Star has *never* stumbled. "You're hurt." She looks fretfully at Bene—pauses—seems distracted. She kisses Bene, a quick, hungry exchange that washes Masar in heat, and jerks back again. Her eyes, all green and gold, are desperate. "We can't. He's hurt."

Bene looks unconcerned, even relaxed. He lifts up into Masar again, kissing him on the throat, reaching for his belt. "It's all right. We'll be gentle with him."

Masar almost squeaks. He can't move. Effegen, however, seems to have just needed permission, and then she and Bene are both touching him, leading him, conspiring against him together. They crowd him toward his bed. In minutes they've laid him down, his pants stripped off, his shirt pulled open.

Masar feels a strange combination of bafflement and fear and desperate arousal. He is swept up in the current of them, unable to resist. Bene crawls over him to kiss him more. He straddles his upper thighs and pulls off his own shirt, revealing his chest and shoulders and arms—muscular, but softer than Masar's own body. There are scars from his life of mining. There are calluses on his warm hands. Blinking, dazed, Masar sees Effegen rise from the bed, unwinding her shawl. As she sheds her clothes, she watches them, watches how Bene lowers to kiss his chest, and Masar shifts restlessly, head tipping back. Bene bites his nipple, and Masar hisses through his teeth, looking at Effegen again. She's taking off her rings, setting them on the bedside table. Her eyes are hot and greedy and reverent.

"You're both...so beautiful," she whispers.

Naked, she is all curves and skin like burnished copper. Her full thighs. Her belly. Her breasts. Bene sits back and reaches for her. She comes to him. They kiss, her hands gripping his shoulders, their mouths familiar to each other. Her hips flare out in unbearable temptation, and Bene grips them, smiling against her lips. Masar feels ravenously jealous, one of his hands lifting tentatively to touch her naked thigh. Goose bumps race over her skin, and her eyes snap toward him. She lays her body alongside his. She cups his jaw, kissing him, tongue stealing into his mouth in a way that makes his scalp tingle.

"All right?" she asks, earnest and worried, her eyes sliding down to his injured side.

He's breathing rapidly. He looks down to find Bene watching him with predatory eyes, thumbs stroking the hinges of his hip bones in a way that is...distracting.

"I—" Masar swallows, looking back and forth between them. "Are you sure?"

In answer, Bene groans. He scoots back, pulling Masar's underwear down just enough to reach his sex. He bends over him, uses his mouth, and Masar's whole body locks.

"Oh—gods—"

Effegen stops the sound with her kisses, or else—she swallows them, moaning back. Pleasure like ocean waves rocks him forward and up, seeking more. His side aches, but he barely feels it. He winds his fingers in the silky mop of Bene's dark hair, and Bene's throaty groan vibrates through him. Effegen leans over him, kisses his chest, his throat, his lips. She licks into his mouth, her breathing ragged with want. In a sudden burst of long-restrained need, Masar slips his hand between her warm thighs, tasting her whimper, feeling the silk of her as she shudders. Bene's hand slides up her thigh; his free hand grazes Masar's belly. Masar touches her firmer, deeper, wanting her so much. With a sharp, breathless laugh, Effegen tugs Masar's hand away.

"Not yet," she teases him. "Don't distract me. Lay still."

He can't. It's too much to ask, now that he has them. He wants to touch them. He wants to tie them down and explore them without interference, make their sounds into a chorus, devour them whole—

But they, it seems, mean to devour him first.

Much later, they lie together in a sated quiet, bodies cooling. Effegen is half asleep between them, her curves dewy with sweat, her face pressed into Bene's neck. Masar, on his good side against her back, runs a slow, soothing hand up and down her thigh, and Bene, catching his eye, winks.

Masar nearly blushes.

The mischievousness fades from Bene's expression, turning to tenderness as he urges, "You should sleep."

Masar gives a wry smile. "So should you."

Bene chuckles, eyes rolling closed, his face a picture of blissful relaxation. "I'm nearly there," he admits.

Watching him, Masar feels a slow, delicious lassitude stealing over his own body. Effegen is warm against him, and watching the soft rise and fall of Bene's chest is hypnotic. He pauses to simply look at them, taking in the lines and curves of them, the muscle and the softness, their skin flushed from exertion. He marvels at himself, that he is holding the Star in his arms, and Bene wanted it. They all did. This unfamiliar sensation—comfort, joy—it almost frightens him. So much to want. So much to lose…

"You're thinking very loudly," mumbles Effegen.

Bene snorts, nuzzling his face into her hair, eyes still closed.

Masar, embarrassed and pleased at their teasing, says, "There's a lot to think about."

Effegen puts her hand over his on her thigh, squeezing. "Rest now. Tomorrow I'm taking you to the doctor to make sure we didn't break you."

Masar grins. In fact, his body feels fantastic. A little soreness in his side, but they were gentle with him. They forced him to be careful, which was both frustrating and arousing, with their bodies crawling all over him, touching him, touching each other. He thinks of watching how she stroked Bene into release; how Bene and Masar both used their hands to make her come. The strain in her body, her ecstatic cry. He doesn't remember ever experiencing sex like this, rich and intense and healing.

Effegen's breaths even out, her body relaxing into sleep. Masar looks at Bene across her body. Bene opens his eyes long enough to give him a lazy smile, then closes them again. In moments, he's sleeping, too. They seem to drag him with them, their relaxation a curative, until he drifts away.

And sleeping, he dreams.

In the dream, he and Jun are walking through the service tunnels of *The Risen Wave*. But it is a dream, so she is also Effegen, and also Liis. Overhead lights flicker, and somewhere gunfire is going off. Jun-Effegen-Liis weaves a cast between her fingers, like a seamsaan knitting a cloth, and her brows are drawn together in focus.

"That better work," Masar says.

"Fuck off," she answers, and pulls her hands apart so that the cast stretches into a tightly woven net, which is somehow also a star. The links are razor sharp, glinting and terrible. She regards the net thoughtfully and says, "We're missing something."

Masar's skin crawls, and then he looks up and there's a figure at the end of the tunnel. He stops short, staring at it, but Jun-Effegen-Liis doesn't stop.

He calls to her, "Wait."

She ignores him, focused on the cast, walking toward the figure. It is deep in the shadows, cloaked by the darkness, and radiating malevolence. Masar realizes that his shotgun is on his shoulder, and he unholsters it, pointing at the figure as Jun-Effegen-Liis keeps walking forward.

"Wait!" he shouts. "We're missing something!"

The shadow creature spreads arms made of night, and she slips inside them, disappearing into a sudden flash.

Masar's eyes open. The light is a yellow diagonal, cutting across the bed. He blinks rapidly, confused. Effegen is still in his arms, sleeping peacefully. He looks across her body for Bene, but Bene isn't there. Masar looks around, looks for the origin of the light. It's the door, he realizes. Staring blurrily, he watches it crack a little wider, and a figure slips through it, out into the hall. It takes him a few seconds to understand that the figure is Bene. The door shuts after him, drenching the room in darkness again.

At first Masar lies in silence, still climbing out of sleep. He considers waking Effegen, thinks Bene must have told her where he was going, but she is breathing deep and even. He draws carefully away from her, makes sure the blanket replaces his arm over her body. He finds his clothes by touch, flinching a little as he bends to pull up his pants. He puts on his shoes by the door, glances toward the bed again, and slips out into the hall.

Bene is already out of sight. There are three routes from Masar's bedroom to the courtyard center of Level 6. Wincing at the lights, Masar considers the time. It's predawn. Far too early for Bene to have gone for a shift at the construction site. Is he returning to his own apartment? Why would he have gone without saying goodbye?

Masar thinks climbing out of the cozy haven of the bed must explain why there's a chill racing across his skin. He has a strange, confused combination of impulses. To hurry down the hall and see if he can catch up to Bene. To comm Bene. To comm Jun—why would he comm Jun? Why is he hesitating to comm Bene?

Why is he pulling up a cast, linking into the surveillance program, pulling up the cameras in his neighborhood—

He finds Bene immediately, halfway to the courtyard and walking with his hands shoved in his pockets. He moves fast, hunching forward. Masar follows him.

It would be easy to catch up to him, but Masar keeps back. When Bene reaches the courtyard and gets into the elevator, Masar waits in the shadows of the housing block, duplicating the casting views so that he has an image of every level. Bene rises through Farren Eyce, the government district, the farm levels, and as Masar watches in confusion and dread, he goes all the way to the surface.

Power fluctuates in the colony. The elevator goes dark, and when the lights come back, Bene is gone. Masar taps into the surveillance on the surface and finds it has gone dark, too.

Comm Jun, he thinks again. *Comm Bene.*

Instead, he gets on the elevator. All the way up to the surface, his insides twist with the leftover ache of his gunshot, with the glitching of his eye, with the memory of Bene's kiss—

The elevator whooshes open. He enters the closed-air atrium that leads onto the airfield.

"No one saw me," Bene is saying.

"You can't know that," Tej's shrill voice retorts.

"I told you I would—"

But Bene's voice cuts off. He swivels toward Masar, and their eyes lock. Bene's expression shutters like a steel curtain. No one speaks, no one breathes, until—

"Shoot him!" Tej cries, shoving a rifle at Bene. "Shoot him!"

Masar stares, disbelieving. There's a squeezing in his chest, like a vise tightening his rib cage, bone and muscle compressing against his lungs, against his heart. Ventricles constrict, arteries go slow and sluggish, as the utter horror of it devours him.

But before Bene can take the rifle, before Bene can shoot him, Masar's cybernetic eye goes out. And then explodes with pain.

The measure of a true Hand thus remains their obedience to the Kindom entire, for all traitors show the first sign in their kinschool days, through acts of intransigence.

excerpt, the Ethics and Principles of Kindom Rule,
by Secretary Millok Dustrow. Dated 917, Year of the Soil.

CHAPTER TWENTY-TWO

1665

YEAR OF THE HARVEST

Praetima
Nikata Leen, an Island
The Planet Kator

They're in the gymnasium, engaged in their fifth round of press-ups, when the door opens. Six listens to the tread of several different sets of boots, perhaps four or five. Continuing with their set, eyes focused on the mat between their hands, they sense the movement at their periphery, figures shifting into a loose circle around them.

Six reaches a count of fifty and relaxes onto their knees, sitting up to observe the grim faces of the guardsaan. They're armored, but without helmets. They have guns, but they don't draw, hands resting instead on the pommels of their batons. One of them, the captain, takes a small step forward.

"Forgive us for interrupting, Sa Nightfoot."

Six rises smoothly to their feet and strolls toward the biggest gap between the guardsaan. Batons come out. A flash of panic in those faces. But Six ignores them, walking to the pull-up bar in the corner of the training court. They hear restless grumbling. The guardsaan cautiously come up behind. Six leaps and catches the bar, beginning a rapid series of pull-ups. They send out a cast, reaching for Chono's signal. What comes back is a silent void. They reach for Yantikye next. More of nothing. That quiet animal violence in the center of them begins to hum, rage like a solar flare, and underneath it, hammered down and rejected—terror.

Behind them, the captain says, "Riin Matri, we need you to come with us."

Six works to a count of twenty, then drops down onto their heels. They rotate toward the guardsaan, who have them cornered now and look foolishly self-assured for having accomplished it. Six, arms hanging loosely at their sides, feet apart and head tilting to one side, smiles with all of Esek's grotesque and threatening humor.

"Why is that?"

The captain tips his chin up. "Where is Cleric Chono, Sa?"

"Napping as far as I know."

"That's not true. She was apprehended in Easwa half an hour ago."

"Was she really?"

"Cleric Chono is accused of treason."

"Treason?" Six tsks. "That doesn't sound like Chono. Are you sure you haven't arrested her doppelgänger?"

"Sa Nightfoot, if you would come with us—"

"Where are the cloaksaan?"

The captain looks taken aback. After a cautious moment he says, "Sa?"

"I just think it's interesting that the Clever Hand thinks they can take me with *guards*."

A new current of unease moves through the group of five, two of them glancing at each other; two others, their batons still drawn, flex their grips. Six assesses each of them in turn, quickly ascertaining the weaknesses: one man favors his left leg, a sure sign of injury; a younger man sneers, all cocksure and eager. But there are strengths, too: The sole woman is rangy, with clever eyes; the biggest man has muscle mass to rival Chono's. Six sends another cast, this time to Graisa the Honor.

The captain says, "Riin Matri, any resistance will be an admission of guilt. We have authorization to take you by force, if necessary."

"But you've already made a mistake," says Six pleasantly. At his blank expression, they explain, "You're standing too close. If you were a few feet back, you could draw on me. At this distance, if you try, I'll have you shooting at each other in less than two seconds."

"We have no desire to shoot you, Sa. We only want—"

"Which means you don't have permission to shoot me," Six interrupts. "Which means you're meant to take me alive. *I*, on the other hand, am constrained by no such orders."

Suddenly, a message comes from Graisa:

Chono taken. Yantikye escaped. We're going to ground.

Even though they knew it already, the words go through them like a blade. *Chono taken… Chono taken…* But Six pushes down their emotion, casting back:

Can you get me out of Blue Spire?

> *No. If you can get to the Braemish quarter in the southeast, we have people who can bring you to safety.*

All the guardsaan have drawn their batons, fanning out to better corner Six, with the big man to their right. The rangy woman to their left. Captain in the middle. Strong fighters, bracketing the two weaker links. A bright electric flame sparks to life at the tip of each baton, crackling, and Six wonders what happened to Chono when she was captured. If they injured her. If she fought back.

The captain warns, "We can have more guardsaan here within minutes, Sa."

Six grins, a feral outlet for all their anger. "By then it will be too late."

The guardsaan charge, a single force, a wave—and Six, like an immovable cliff, breaks the wave apart. They slip sideways into one guard's thrust, the cocky guard. Spinning him in front of them, they kick him hard in the sacrum, propelling him like a doll. He hurtles into the big guard, just long enough to waylay him. The bad-leg guard swings wide, but Six ducks low. His arm comes in too high, baton useless. Six catches him under the elbow, twists, and wrenches, lifting their leg and driving a boot hard into the back of his weak knee. Something pops. A scream. A fist—swinging at Six's face—they lift their arm to block, forearm juddering against hard armor, and the rangy guard swipes at them. They tilt out of reach and into the captain's orbit, but slip under his driving thrust to punch him in the throat. He gags, and Six snatches the gun from his holster. Six shoots him, a deafening report. They spin on one heel and shoot the big guard just as one of the batons grazes their ribs.

Pain like an ice pick drives through them. If it had been a direct hit, they would probably have dropped. As it is, their nerveless fingers lose their grip on the gun, their knees buckling. Something cracks against their jaw, a solar burst, but they roll with the blow, kicking out once to clear their path, coming up on their knees five feet away. They lurch to their feet with room to breathe, limbs vibrating, fine motor skills gone. There are three bodies on the ground. No—two. The baton made Six's shot go wide, and the big guard is getting up, blood streaming from his ruined shoulder, face a contortion of agony and rage. Six shakes the dizziness from their eyes. The three guardsaan come at them, more cautious than before, but determined. They don't draw their guns, surprisingly. The Secretaries really must want Esek alive.

By the time the guardsaan have the courage to attack, Six can almost see straight. They nearly bend over backward, avoiding another heavy swing from the cocky guard. They weave inward, catching his wrist, headbutting him, and slipping the baton from his grip into their own. They spin. They're dizzy. One wobble gives someone the chance to jab with the point of a baton, which Six barely deflects with the flat of their own, but this is the rangy guard, the quick guard, who comes at Six with a barrage of strikes, tirelessly harassing them. Six uses the baton like a rapier, lunging and slicing up a counterthrust, with a clean precision that opens her wide. They sweep their baton clear, duck low, and drive the point up into the vulnerable slit between the torso of her armor and her pelvis. Electricity surges through her body, and she drops into a twitching heap. Six barely ducks the blow coming up behind them, spins, lunges, and has the big guard's baton out of his hand a second later. Wielding two batons now, spinning them once and crouching low, they watch the final two guardsaan lumber at them. One disarmed and with his shoulder blown apart. One—the cocky guard, not so cocky now. Full of wild panic, he hurls himself at Six, who crosses their weapons in an X and breaks the meaty poles against his skull, not even watching him collapse.

The big guard snarls, arm hanging uselessly, sweat sheeting off his face like rain. When he lunges forward, Six drops low. They roll, coming up almost underneath him, levering his whole big body over their own back and spinning to jab each baton point into the vulnerable chinks behind his knee guards. The man's legs go out like broken sticks, and Six, leaping up, drives one more electrical jolt down into the back of his neck. Either dead or unconscious, he twitches limply.

There are four bodies now. The fifth, the one whose knee they dislocated, lies in a heap, cradling the limb through sobs. Six goes to him, smacks a hand against the side of his head hard enough to make his ears ring, and grabs him by his hair.

"How many more guardsaan in the building?"

"I—I—"

Six smacks him again and presses their palm down into the knee. The man shrieks, and Six holds the pressure, relentless.

"How many?"

"None, none, they sent us alone!"

"That's absurd. Who else is out there?"

They press down harder. The guard screams and babbles, "They're circling the hotel! I don't know how many!"

Six releases the pressure a little bit. "Any cloaksaan?"

"I don't know! They didn't tell us—I don't know!"

"Where is Cleric Chono?"

"No one told us—I swear, no one told us!"

Annoyed, Six drives a fist into his temple, knocking him unconscious, and rises. They've shaken off the remnants of the baton graze, aware of an electric burn on their rib cage. They send a cast out to intercept the camera signals in the building, shouldering their way into the connection with a brute force that would make Jun Ironway proud. No sooner do they have eyes on the exterior of the hotel than four ground shuttles pull into the drive, two dozen guardsaan emerging in full armor.

Well, a voice purrs in their thoughts. *How will you get out of this one?*

The Blue Spire concierge in Yantikye's pocket got Chono out through the servant quarters in the south wing, which is divided from the lobby by little more than two hallways. But the hotel staff will need to escape that way, and Six thinks that Chono would prefer them not to put the staff in the middle of a firefight. So that leaves the main entrance as their route to escape. Very bad odds, very bad. Even Liis Konye might balk at such odds.

But, *Chono was taken* beats in their breast, and they are no good to her captured.

You're no good to her dead, either, says the purring voice, almost a singsong now.

The guardsaan have blocked all the exits, but they haven't entered the building yet. Six strips the dead captain, shrugging on his vest armor, as well as his holster belt. Six takes two batons and two handguns, a third gun tucked into their boot holster. The captain has a belt of magazines as well, which they strap to the opposite side of their chest, thinking of Yantikye and his X of knives. Yantikye got out, Graisa said. But Yantikye didn't save Chono.

They grab a fourth gun from a felled body, zap a recovering guard with the baton, and walk calmly out of the gymnasium. They take the staircase down to the lobby, where a handful of hotel staff are standing around looking anxious and confused. When they see Six, they run for it, all but the frozen concierge.

"Are the doors locked?" they inquire. The concierge's eyes move up and down Six's body, taking in the guns. He looks quite pale. "Lock the main doors," Six orders. "And please lock the gymnasium doors, as well. I'd like to keep certain guests where they are."

The concierge does some quick thing at the station in front of him. Locking the main door will only waylay the guardsaan for as long as it takes them to put a battering ram through it. But it's better than nothing. They look at the fireplace in the center of the lobby, a column of white stone with real coals merrily blazing inside.

"Do you have an accelerant?" Six asks. "Something to help get the fire started?"

The concierge blinks confusedly. "I'm sorry?"

"It would probably be in the supplies closet. Cleaning solutions are fine, as well."

He brings Six a jug of something from the room behind his desk, and Six accepts it with a nod of approval. "Now," they say. "Time to go. Take the servant exit. Walk out with your hands up and they probably won't shoot you."

The concierge looks from the jug to their face. "What...what are you going to do?"

They give him Esek's rakish grin. "I'm going to shoot a lot of people."

His eyes widen, and he hurries to the far end of the foyer before sprinting off.

Six assesses the layout of the foyer, a round room that opens into the larger lobby. They pour the accelerant onto the floor and the nearest furniture, deciding to take cover behind the concierge's desk, which is outside the reach of a potential fire. They'll have a better shot at picking the guardsaan off from this vantage, anyway, and if it becomes necessary to set the place ablaze, there's a decent escape route through the lobby. They're just hopping over the desk when a comm request pings in their aural link, and the signature opens up a gleeful hatred in them. They accept the comm.

"Prudent One," they say, in Esek's casually threatening manner.

Ilius's voice in their aural link is calm.

"Whatever it is you're planning, don't. Your circumstances are dire enough as it is."

"You sent *five* guardsaan to apprehend me, Ilius. I'm *offended*."

"I gave you just enough rope to hang yourself with. If I had sent a force that could actually stop you, you might have surrendered. Now I have proof that you attacked the Kindom."

"Ah. So they were bait. Happily sacrificed."

"Did you kill all of them?"

"I don't *think* so."

"One is sufficient. Cause enough to execute you."

"What I'm hearing is that I have no incentive to behave. There are two dozen guardsaan outside Blue Spire, not a cloak among them. Shall I infer that you're willing to sacrifice quite a few more to take me down?"

"There are two dozen guardsaan now. I have another two dozen en route."

Six considers that for a moment, replies, "And yet . . . no cloaks."

Ilius rolls right past the observation. "If you lay down your weapons and come out of the hotel under your own recognizance, you will not be harmed. You have my word."

"Except for the execution bit. What about Chono?" Six watches on cast as the first dozen guardsaan approach, four of them with short battering rams designed to take out doors much more threatening than the hotel's.

"Chono surrendered without incident," Ilius says. "You should, too. You can still avoid a death sentence, but you have to cooperate."

"I'll take my chances."

"You've murdered guardsaan. You've conspired against the Kindom. You—"

He rattles off a litany of charges, apparently quite satisfied with the act of recitation, but even as he's droning, Six gets another ping in their ocular. They think it'll be Graisa, maybe Yantikye. But when they accept the message, there's no signature at all.

I can get you out of Blue Spire.

Finally, monotonously, Ilius says, "And collaboration with a Quietan terror cell. You can kill a hundred guardsaan, Esek, and we'll still catch you, and all those charges will catch you, too."

Six pauses. They send a message back to the anonymous messenger.

Perhaps introductions, first.

The response comes immediately.

Now, now, Sa. Let's not pretend either of us would give our true names at this juncture.

Six allows themself an entire two seconds to process this statement. They tell Ilius, "I'll make you a deal. You release Chono and forget whatever irrational ideas you have about prosecuting her, and I'll turn myself over."

Ilius huffs a laugh of incredulity. "I'm not sure what's more amazing. The fact you think you're a more important captive than Chono, or the fact that Esek Nightfoot would sacrifice herself for someone else. Why don't I disabuse you of any illusions about your value?"

The comm disconnects, and the four guardsaan throw the weight of the battering rams into the double doors of Blue Spire. The narrow glass windows in the doors shatter, and the battering rams come in for another round, shaking the foyer.

Six, feeling petty, steps from behind the concierge's desk, grasps two handguns, and with pristine economy, shoots two guardsaan through the broken windows.

They're back behind the desk the minute rifle fire sprays the foyer. The next message has a sterner tone than the previous.

The more of them that get inside, the harder it will be to extract you. You need to move now.

Six responds:

Perfect. Just tell me my exit and I'll decide whether or not you're full of shit.

Let's not be hasty. I'm selling a service, not rescuing kittens.

The battering rams start up again, crunching through the nearly decimated doors. Another rain of rifle fire sweeps through the room. Ilius comes back into their aural link, saying, "They have permission to kill you."

Six chuckles. "My family won't like that."

"Your family will be fucking *delighted*."

"And lose the trade to the Jeveni Wheel? I doubt it."

Still, why Esek didn't have the foresight to gain at least a few Nightfoot allies is just one of several incongruities Six has pondered about their old nemesis, who even now leans close in their thoughts and tells them dryly, *You want to talk about incongruity? You're being uncharacteristically thoughtless. The cameras, Six. They can see you on the cameras.*

Six responds by shooting the nearest cameras out of the ceiling, though that's hardly a long-term solution. By some strange turn of coincidence or fate, the messenger reaches out again, just as they are thinking—

You could use your Hood program. It would work better than shooting the cameras.

Six chuckles. So they know Six has a Hood. Or suspect it at least. Rising from behind the desk again, they watch the doors buckle inward and empty two magazines into the gap before bolting across the lobby under return fire, slipping around armchairs and sofas and end tables that all but explode behind them. They reach the bar, clean, unused glasses waiting on the countertop, a row of bottles on the shelves behind, and bar rags under the sink. Six stuffs rags into the mouths of five bottles.

There's a door to the left of the bar. Take it through the kitchen and you'll see a flight of stairs. Go down the stairs.

Six uses the sparking end of the baton to light all five rags. They ask:

What makes you think I have a Hood program?

Jun Ironway gave it to you.

And what's your interest in that?

I said already, I'm selling a service. The Hood is my fee.

The first row of guardsaan breach the doors, and Six hurls the bottles with their flaming rags across the lobby, smashing them into the sea of accelerant. There's a whooshing sound of fire catching, and one of the bottles strikes at a guardsaan's feet. Flames surge up their body, and Six hears the cries of panic, the disorientation. Six spins away from the bar, barreling through the door on the left.

Rifle fire peppers the door a half second later. Impact against their shoulder. Six stumbles forward. Happily, the vest armor protects them, but the hit still sends a shock of pain through their body, like being punched with the narrowest end of a stave. They stagger into a trolley stacked with supplies and, teeth gritted, shove the trolley in front of the door. They look across the kitchen, toward another door, and notice cameras flicking in several corners. They throw Jun's Hood over their body and jog across the kitchen. Sure enough, there's a short flight of stairs leading down into darkness. They message their anonymous benefactor:

Where exactly am I going next?

No more free rides. I want the Hood.

It's not exactly mine to give.

I'm completely indifferent to whether or not you die in that hotel. Either you give me the Hood or I leave you to the guardsaan.

Six reaches the bottom of the steps, entering a small room. There are a half dozen shelves stacked with linens and other supplies. A crashing sound reaches them from above—the guardsaan, breaching the kitchen. Six closes the door behind them, intrigued to find a lock pad on the inside, which is easy enough to engage. The door is thick metal, and the walls are stone. A bomb shelter, probably dated all the way back to the resource wars of the fourteenth century, when the collapse of the jevite trade threw the Treble into chaos. Hardly a good escape route. Six wonders if they've just delivered themself to the Kindom on a silver platter.

Nevertheless, they shoot the lock pad to prevent the guardsaan from breaking in, and turn to consider their prison. The messenger has gone silent, obviously waiting them out.

An underground tomb, muses Esek. *Like Soye's Reach, perhaps? How did you survive that hunting lodge collapsing on top of you?*

These are memories Six would rather not relive. They process their options. They can't give Jun's Hood to a stranger. They cast out to Ilius.

"What are you going to do to Chono?"

It takes him a few moments to respond; perhaps he's disoriented that Six isn't appearing on any cameras. When he speaks, his voice is flat, cold. A performance of indifference. "Chono conspired with a known traitor to instigate a rebellion. Her life is just as forfeit as yours."

Six chuckles, though with a little less control, they'd be screaming.

"You'll make a martyr out of her. Or shall I say, you won't. You and I both know you won't hurt her. She's your weak point, Ilius."

Ilius says mockingly, "Apparently she's your weak point, too. Or is it that little letter writer the two of you have been chasing?" Six's stomach drops. *The letters...* "They seemed quite obsessed with you. And you with them. And both of you with Chono." His voice is hateful. "Whatever the root, you've clearly changed in the past year. But I've also changed, Esek. You can't manipulate me anymore. If we have to execute Chono as a warning to those who defy us, we will."

Six exhales slowly, remembering the words in the letter: *You have fit yourself inside the mold of a monster.*

"Swear to protect her," Six says, "and I'll surrender."

"I don't need you to surrender! You are surrounded. Your family won't help you. The Jeveni *can't* help you. Your terrorist associates are on the run. You have no friends, no allies. You made a lapdog out of me, Esek. But I'll see you skinned and spitted for it."

The sheer hatred in his voice—perhaps he *is* prepared to kill Chono. If he would only say that he won't kill her. If he would only say that she will be safe, Six could turn themself over. They could let themself be killed, even—and fuck the anonymous messenger in their head, fuck Esek's whispering voice, fuck Ilius for thinking he could defeat them. Because if Chono lives, nothing can defeat them. She will be like the Godfire and burn through the worlds.

If only Ilius would say it.

There is a sudden, massive *crack.* Six steps back from the shuddering door. The guardsaan have come with their battering rams.

"Listen to me, Ilius," Six says. "This is your last chance. Protect her."

Ilius erupts with fury, "It's your fault she's in this position in the first place! It's your fault any of this has happened! You—you corrupted her! You poisoned her against her oaths. Anything that happens to her is on your head, not mine! And I won't bend for you ever again. I'm not your tero bird anymore!"

Six says calmly, "Before this is over, I'm going to chomp you into pieces."

"I tried to protect her. I tried to save her from you! All of this, all the danger she's in—it's your fucking fault!"

He sounds grief-stricken, panicked. It gives Six pause. So much bitterness, in Ilius. Trapped by the manipulations of Sa Penrider. Bound to the Nightfoots and their cause (or so he thought). Cursed to a frustrated and futile love for Chono, who chose Esek over him, and chooses Six over him, and Six wants to confess their true identity, just to torment Ilius with another layer of humiliation.

Instead, they tell him, "You'd better pray on your finger bracelets, Prudent One. Pray to Kata, who sees us. I will carve a smile through your throat before this is over. If you so much as bruise her, I will rip your limbs apart. See if I don't."

Before Ilius can respond, Six cuts the cast. But the line, between themself and Ilius—themself and *Chono*, vibrates.

She's as good as dead, says Esek.

No. No, not while they live. They cast out again:

Fine. I'll give you the Hood. But I want something more than my life. I want Chono, alive.

There are a few terrible seconds, when the hammer of the battering ram only punctuates a deathly silence, and then:

Fortunately, our interests dovetail in that department.

Six feels a seizure of hope in their chest, and the battering ram crashes into the door a seventh time.

Transfer me the Hood.

I'll transfer it once I'm out.

You're in no position to negotiate. Transfer me the Hood program, or I'll let the guardsaan have you.

Get to her, Six thinks furiously. *Save her.*

Then there are a thousand voices in their head. The messenger. Ilius.

Jun Ironway practically snarling at them not to bargain with something that isn't theirs. And Esek, of course, sneering, smirking, haunting Esek.

But Chono. *Chono Chono Chono...*

Six extracts the Hood program, bumping it through the cast signal and into the grip of the stranger, who for nearly a minute doesn't respond. Six is just ready to conclude that they've been had, when the next message comes.

There's a sewer entrance under the shelving unit in the right-hand corner of the room.

Six bolts to the shelves, wrenching the unit away from the wall, letting it crash away from them. And there, true as true, they see a round porthole with a handle loop. They lift the heavy plate away, staring down into darkness. Nothing for it. They climb down through the hole, landing in an inch of water and to a sudden flood of flashlights in their eyes.

It's only after a few moments of disorientation that they recognize the shapes looming before them.

Cloaksaan.

CHAPTER TWENTY-THREE

1664

YEAR OF THE CRUX

Farren Eyce
The Planet Capamame

Jun wakes with Liis's back pressed to her front, an arm tucked over her middle. The signal in her neural link goes off a second time, and she blearily recognizes it as a newscast alert she set almost a month ago. She disentangles from Liis, standing beside the bed and pulling clothes on as she bumps the newscast hologram into the air. She's looking at the interior of the Clever Hand's headquarters in Praetima, the Centrum of Nikapraev. Hundreds of secretaries fill the background, and sat in the center of them are Six and Chono.

A voice in her aural link announces, "This is the first sighting of Clerics Chono and Nightfoot since their return to the Treble over three weeks ago, when their release of a data flood indicted several high-ranking Hands for deception, conspiracy, and murder. There has been much speculation in the interim as to what became of the two clerics, with some theorizing a secret trial and summary execution. We're now hearing that they have been pardoned, a report that certainly casts new light on the resignation of Aver Paiye last night, and the rumored disappearance of First Cloak Seti Moonback."

Jun feels movement behind her, Liis pulling on a shirt and coming to stand beside her. Jun casts the audio to Liis's aural link, and they both watch as the First Secretary and his Minor and Major Advocates confer on a dais above Chono and Six. Chono has shaved her head; she looks tired and thin, and Six, for all their gorgeous Esek-ness, is strained around the eyes.

The newscaster says, "We're hoping to hear Cleric Chono speak for herself this morning, with many analysts particularly interested in how she will respond to the announcement of the Rule of Unification, which is a source of upheaval in the Treble. The Secretarial Court will no doubt speak in defense of the rule this morning."

Quietly, Liis says, "That's Ilius Redquill."

Jun shoots her a confused look. "What?"

"The Minor Advocate. They've been replaced by Ilius Redquill."

Jun looks at the hologram again. Redquill is a wan, milky-looking person who, despite the polish of his uniform, seems unkempt. What she knows about him she gleaned from running a rather exhaustive background check on Chono right after the jump to Capamame. He's an information broker, but a low-rung secretary. Certainly not one in line for the Secretarial Court.

For some reason Jun thinks of Six, gaming their way into control of the Nightfoot family, despite how far from the matriarchal line Esek was. Such leaps in position don't happen by accident. They are born of curious twists in fate, or careful maneuvering. When Jun looked into Chono's past, her research on Ilius was cursory. Now, instinct drives her back to him.

She pauses the newscast on Chono and Six. She weaves her casts, conscious of the absence of the avatar, a blankness at her periphery that she can't trust. She cross-checks Redquill's history against known credit-sharing applications, looking for signs of funding dumps. Unexpectedly, she finds a company called Scholar Solutions, and a mission statement:

> **WITH OVER 200,000 LEARNERS IMPACTED AND MORE THAN 1,000 DONORS, SCHOLAR SOLUTIONS IS ERADICATING EDUCATION DESERTS ACROSS THE TREBLE. WOULDN'T YOU LIKE TO BE PART OF MAKING THE FUTURE BRIGHT?**

She says, "He paid for tutoring programs. In-person and gaming modules."

At her periphery, she sees Liis reattaching her prosthetic arm.

She combs through the data, picking up Redquill's signature in backwater villages on Teros, and the sevite factory towns of Ma'kess, and on stations both more and less impoverished than K-5. Dom told them that a secretary patron compensated some of his informants with education. Six had a secretary benefactor who sent them to a kin-school. Perhaps this is just something secretaries do?

Liis asks, "Any students we'd recognize?"

Jun follows the threads of Redquill's influence, and in just a few minutes she finds a tutor who trains students in basic medical care. The tutor had a six-month assignment to an isolationist Jeveni community on Braemin, and among his students—Jasef sen Clime.

Jun's heart thumps. She shows Liis, and Liis makes a low, thoughtful sound. Almost trembling now, Jun scours the records. Jasef even showed up in a Scholar Solutions marketing image. He looks...maybe fourteen? Skinny and underfed. That shock of red hair. There are lines of connection between half a dozen members of his village and the Wheel itself. This would have been Redquill's interest in Jasef. The boy could inform on the Wheel.

She's just begun to look for more when a fresh alert jerks her out of her search. She steps back from the cast, pulling up the new notification. What she sees kicks her in the ribs.

"Liis. Look at this."

Jun snatches out for camera access to the landing field on the surface of Capamame. She's met with a harrowing darkness. The cameras are out. But the alert is clear: One of the midsize shuttles, like the one Jun flew to *Drae's Hope*, has lit up. She reaches for Masar, who should have received the same alert of someone breaking into a ship. But her message gets no response. Could he have turned off his tech? No, he wouldn't have done that. He never does that, not even to give himself a break from the cybernetic eye—

"What about Fonu?" Liis asks.

She reaches for the River and finds a blank space where their comm signature should be. Why would Masar *and* Fonu have turned off their tech?

With a punch of dread she remembers that Bene was with Masar. She reaches out for him, too, growls his name like he'll know better than to ignore her. And gets nothing.

She's already to the door when Liis cautions her, "Boots. Coat."

Shaking, Jun obeys, Liis doing the same, and moments later she has thrown her Hood program over both of them. They bolt from the apartment. There's a voice in her ear. *Run!* Great Gra told her, when the cloaksaan came to the academy and would have captured her for Esek.

> *sunstep*
> *sunstep*
> *sunstep*
> *RUN!*

They reach the Level 7 courtyard in less than ten minutes. Gasping for breath, Jun paces the elevator car as it lifts them toward the surface. She casts for the other members of the Wheel.

"Jun?" It's Effegen, her voice tight, as if she already knows what's happening.

"Someone is trying to take a shuttle," Jun says. "I can't reach Masar or Fonu. I can't reach Bene."

"Neither can I. I'm sending collectors up. They'll be armed."

"I have Liis," Jun says, and the elevator arrives. "I have to go."

They jog through the atrium and through the doors into bitter cold. The clear dome over Farren Eyce stands at quarter power, repelling the worst snowstorms, but far below its capacity to shield them against an attack. Or prevent a ship from breaking out. As Jun and Liis step onto the flat concrete of the landing field, the cold seeps through their clothes. Far off beyond a sea of shuttles, and a seemingly limitless stretch of ice, Jun sees the ember of the rising sun, the horizon smudged in gold. Four high moons crest a pale cloud cover, and the distant shape of *Drae's Hope* is like another moon against the darkness and stars, and Jun feels how microscopic, how insignificant, she is.

But she sees the shuttle, not thirty feet away, engines humming and steaming, and she remembers that in the network of humanity, she can be huge.

They run for the shuttle, Jun hacking toward its control system. A wall blocks her path, the avatar's work familiar to her now. She's just about to try something else when a figure jogs down the gangplank from the open hatch.

Tej.

He's holding a rifle, and it looks far too big in his hands, which are shaking as he points it at them. He looks startled, as if someone told him they were there, and he hoped it wasn't true. Jun stares at him. His few days underground have left him sunken-eyed, grimy, and unwashed. She has a memory of him at the party her family threw right before she left for Riin Kala. A shaggy-haired little boy running around with a smile for everyone.

"Stay right there," he says.

They're less than ten feet away from him. Liis could get him at a run and he might not even have the wits to fire. But Liis doesn't run at him. She watches him.

"Tej," Jun says, bewildered. "What are you—"

"Get in the shuttle," he orders.

"Where are you going? There's nowhere—"

"Get in the fucking shuttle!" he screams at her.

Jun looks at Liis, who gives her a tiny nod. They move forward carefully, hyperconscious of the rifle and his dubious control of it. When they reach the gangplank, he grabs something from his pocket, tossing it down.

"Put those on," he orders. "Do it right now."

They're zip ties. The kind you can find in the construction quarter.

"I'm not putting those on, Tej," she says.

"Put them on or I'll kill Masar!"

Jun hesitates. If Masar is in the shuttle, does that mean Bene is with him? At last she crouches down, picking up the two pair of zip ties. She hands one to Liis, who first binds Jun and then binds herself, pulling them taut with her teeth. Tej lets out a shuddering breath. The circles under his eyes are a dark purple.

"You weren't supposed to come here," he says. Jun doesn't know how to respond to that, so she doesn't. He waves the gun toward the gangplank. "Go!"

Their boots clang on metal, and when Jun stands at the threshold of the shuttle's cabin, she stutters to a halt. She sees Masar first, directly across from her. He's in one of the half dozen flight seats circling the perimeter of the cabin. His feet are bound to the legs of the seat, his wrists zip-tied just like Jun's. His left eye is a clot of blood, tears of it running down his face. He meets her gaze, but when she expects to see fury, she finds instead a horrified grief.

Slumped a few seats down from him is Fonu sen Fhaan. They're unconscious, stripped down to their underwear and zip-tied. Cuts and burns cover their arms. Their hands and feet are bloody, a few fingers at wrong angles. Their head lolls back, mouth open and full of broken teeth. Jun's stomach heaves as she realizes—their right ear is missing.

The third person, standing untied to her left, is Bene.

"Sit down!" Tej barks, coming up and nudging both her and Liis with the rifle.

Jun searches Bene's face for some explanation. His expression is cloistered, impossible to read. Jun sits down beside Masar, and Liis between her and Fonu. The River breathes raggedly, wetly. Their injuries are deep. How did Tej get to them?

The hatch slams shut. Tej approaches, laughing in a strangled way. "Pretty gross, huh? How do you like the ear?" He gags a little, then says in a stab at bravado, "Six would be proud, huh?"

When he kicks Fonu's bare feet, Fonu moans, dripping more blood onto an already bloody chest. Jun looks from Tej to Bene.

"Bene," she whispers. "What's happening? Are you okay?"

"'Course he's okay!" Tej says shrilly. "Aren't you, Bene?"

Bene gives Tej a slow look. "I'm fine."

Tej comes over and punches his shoulder. He's trying to grin again, but he only looks ashen and terrified. Jun doesn't understand. In confusion she starts, "Bene, what—"

"Jun," he interrupts, looking at her with an intensity she's never seen. "Shut your mouth, okay?"

Baffled and afraid, she tries to understand his careful, masked face. But suddenly a third voice says, "I'd listen to him, Jun. You're not in charge anymore."

From within the cockpit, Luja emerges.

Somehow it's not even a surprise. *Of course Luja will be here*, Jun thinks. *My cousins are here, so this is where Luja will be.*

But what she's not prepared for is the blood. Luja's clothes are... *covered* in blood. Red handprints stamp her shirt, her face and neck streaked with it. She holds a wooden carpenter's mallet in one hand and a handgun in the other. There's a knife tucked in her belt. And her eyes—her eyes are like pitch, and completely, repulsively alien.

Jun looks from one cousin to the next. They hardly look like themselves, in this moment. Bene's masked expression. Tej's white-rimmed eyes. Luja with a cold smirk along her mouth, transforming her from the shy girl Jun knew into a malevolent stranger. There's blood on her teeth. Like she's been sucking it out of Fonu's wounds.

"Luja," Jun whispers. "Tell me what's going on."

Luja narrows her eyes in a pantomime of shrewdness. "I told you, you know? Right at the beginning I said you weren't the challenge I thought you'd be. And now look at you. The great Sunstep. The deliverer of the Jeveni. And you couldn't even see it."

Jun swallows, trying to breathe. Her mind bows under a wave of such intense emotion she can barely name it. Then, she takes hold of those emotions the way she would take hold of a cast gone rogue. She gathers them between her hands, so many tangled ropes, and shoves them down so far she doesn't know if she'll ever be able to have feelings again.

She looks from Tej to Bene. "Did you know she was the avatar?"

Tej shifts restlessly, mute. She remembers what Dom said, how upset Tej was after the attack on *Drae's Hope.* How Tej said they had to leave Luja out of it. No, he didn't know. Maybe he'd be less panicked if he'd known. Jun looks at Bene next, raising her eyebrows.

He says in a monotone, "It hardly matters now."

But what else could matter? Nothing matters, will ever matter again, except the specter of Bene's betrayal. She swallows, trying to put it from her mind. She looks at Luja.

"That's some misdirection. The first thing the avatar said to me was that it wasn't Luja."

"I'm *not* Luja," she says, baring her teeth like she's playing at being an animal. She laughs, a short, dead sound. "Luja Ironway was a fragile, helpless kid. She was a station brat at the mercy of Esek Nightfoot. Just like Jun Ironway was at the mercy of Esek Nightfoot. You became Sunstep, right? Well, *I* became Ujan Redcore." She steps farther into the cabin, eyes never leaving Jun. "Let me guess—it doesn't compute, right? I mean, as far as you knew, I could barely cast in a straight line. Why would you think any different? I never went to the archivist's academy. I didn't travel the systems stealing whatever tech I needed. Well, I didn't have to, Jun. I did it all by myself, on a fucking decrepit farming station. I became *twice* the caster you are, and you had no idea. You're only alive 'cause I took pity on you on *Drae's Hope.*"

Jun flits her eyes over Luja—no, Ujan—like there'll be some

physical mark that she should have seen. But of course there's none. *You're talking to the avatar*, Jun tells herself. *Not Luja*. And so she answers, slightly mocking, "Well... not *exactly* all by yourself, was it? You had help, too." Ujan goes still, and Jun raises her eyebrows. "Ilius Redquill, wasn't it? He funded your education. Probably gave you a state-of-the-art neural link." She looks at Tej. "And he paid for the surgery on your hand, right?" She looks at Ujan again. "*I* never had a benefactor, out in the Black. If I had, it wouldn't have been someone *Kindom*."

Ujan's nostrils flare. Her eyes glitter. "You think you know everything? You don't know *anything*. He would never have reached out to me if he couldn't see my potential."

Jun needles her. "So you care what the Kindom thinks of you after all?"

"You think you can be smug about Redquill? Guess who else worked with him." Jun, sensing a trap, doesn't answer. Ujan flashes her teeth. "Six," she says, like it's the winning tile. "They hired Redquill, years ago, and he hired me. Needed my help finding someone who could sell the names of the Wheel. Six got *a lot* of Je bastards killed, Jun. You should have seen it."

Across the cabin, Masar makes an uncomprehending sound. Jun remembers him telling her about a mission that went bad on Braemin. A mission that got collectors killed. Is that what Ujan means? How the *fuck* did Six get involved with—

"Your beloved rescuer," Ujan taunts. "Your trusted ally. About as trustworthy as me in the end, huh?"

Jun struggles to process what all this means. When Liis's knee suddenly presses against her own, it's like a bucket of water to the face. Like Liis is snapping her fingers and telling her, *Focus! All that can wait*.

With a sharp inhale, Jun recovers. Ujan, however, still wants the stage.

"It's no wonder Six worked with Redquill. They knew he could get the best. I tested higher than you on the aptitude exams. I was better than you. I *am* better than you."

Jun nods a few times, swallowing down any trace of emotion. "Maybe," she allows. "They say Great Gra could run circles around any caster in the Kindom. I suppose you got it from him." She looks at Masar, the blood half dried around his eye. She looks at Fonu, wheezing and gurgling through their broken mouth. "You didn't get this from him, though."

"I know!" Ujan cries. She sounds almost...frenzied. "I didn't know if I had it in me anymore! But when you hear that first crunch"—she knocks the mallet against her own head, not quite hard enough to hurt herself but too hard to be rational—"it takes you right back."

She saunters closer. Her body is different than it used to be, more liquid. No, her body is different from the body she showed Jun. The scared kid with her breathing exercises. Those hunched shoulders and distant eyes. Always a mask. She drops into a squat in front of Jun, looking up at her. "Remember that boss I told you about? Who used to break people's fingers for bruising the squash fruit? There's a part I left out. After she broke Tej's hand, I cornered her in a dead zone." Ujan lifts the mallet, and Jun hears Liis suck in a breath right before she feels the sticky wood tap her forehead. "I bashed. Her. Face. In."

Nearby, Tej's shoulders and head flex forward, like he's trying not to be sick. Jun looks at him directly, sees his hollowed-out eyes flicking toward Fonu and snapping away. He nearly vomits again. Jun looks back at Ujan.

"I would have done the same."

Ujan springs to her feet, furious. "No, you wouldn't. Don't act like you would have! You never did shit to protect any of us."

"I thought you were safe—"

"Shut up!" Ujan screams, fury breaking through a weakened dam. "Shut up! You wanted to *think* we were safe! You wanted to be free of us while you were off making your name! If you had given a fuck about any of us, you would have figured out that Six stuck us in two of the worst places the Treble had to offer. Just *stuffed* us there and forgot us after getting our family killed! And *you* weren't *there*!"

"Is that the point, Ujan?" Jun asks, her voice soft and empty. "All of this? Killing the collectors and Kereth and just...making mayhem across the colony? It was your revenge?" She thinks of the utter contempt the avatar always held her in, its childish taunts.

Ujan scoffs. "Don't be so full of yourself. I've got bigger goals than making your life miserable."

"Like destroying Farren Eyce?" Jun asks.

Ujan leers. "Why should I tell *you*?"

More childishness. More taunts. Jun says, "Or maybe your boss hasn't told you the endgame. Maybe Redquill has you in the dark."

Her nostrils flare. There's something pleased in her eyes. "My *boss* has over a dozen people planted in this colony. But he put *me* in charge 'cause I knew there was more to be done than just kill collectors and sabotage colony systems."

"Like what?" Jun asks. "Like attack Fonu sen Fhaan?"

"I didn't just *attack* them," Ujan says, offended. "I'm not irrational. I tortured them for information. You should have seen the look on their face when I took their ear off. They didn't know what they were looking at!"

Tej jerks forward, vomiting onto the cabin floor. Ujan looks over at him with a grimace of concern and impatience. "'M sorry," Tej says, spitting and wiping his mouth.

"Tej, why don't you give me the gun and sit down?" Bene says.

"No!" Ujan shouts. "Everybody stay just as they are!"

Jun looks at Bene, searches that tense, emotionless look on his face. "What about you?" she asks. "What did Ilius Redquill give you?"

Something flickers in his eyes—a trace of *her* Bene. But his voice is flat. "Nothing. I never heard of him until now."

Ujan laughs, poking Bene with an elbow, hands still overburdened with the mallet and the gun. "No, see, Bene is a *new* recruit. Aren't you, Bene?"

"A new recruit for what?" Masar asks. His voice is hoarse. He looks bowed under with devastation. "What are you even doing? Why is Fonu here? Why—"

"Fonu is insurance," Ujan interrupts. "In case your Wheel tries to stop us."

"Stop you from *what*?!" Masar shouts. "Where the fuck are you going to go in a closed system with a shuttle at half fuel?!"

Ujan seems not to appreciate his tone, her expression flattening out. Suddenly, she ducks back into the cockpit.

"Bene," Jun whispers.

His eyes flick toward her. His chin moves, the tiniest shake of the head. She nearly screams in desperation to know what it means. But Ujan storms back in. The mallet is tucked into her belt, and in her free hand she carries a cup. She marches up to Fonu, throwing whatever is in the cup into their face. They come to, flailing. Ujan tosses the cup and smacks Fonu's cheek. They cry out in pain.

"Hey!" she says. "Hey, wake up. Masar has a question for you. Wake up. Go ahead, Masar, ask them."

Fonu looks around blearily, but Masar doesn't ask his question again. Ujan gets impatient. "Masar wants to know where we're going. Why don't you tell him?"

Fonu starts to weep. Jun thinks she might be sick. She never liked them, and they never liked her. But here is a person broken down to scraps, and it horrifies her. Their shoulders are heaving, their face twisted in agony and—humiliation? Is that what it is?

"Go on, tell them." Ujan taps the stock of the pistol against their head. "Tell them where we're going. Tell them or I'll shoot your leg."

Whimpering, Fonu chokes out, "The Treble. You said...the Treble..."

Ujan beams, but it's a lifeless expression, a failed imitation of joy. "That's right! We're going to the Treble! Right, Bene?"

Bene hesitates, and says, "We don't have to bring these people with us. I told you, leave them on the field and the Jeveni will let us go."

"Can't open the hatch again." Ujan shrugs. "Shuttle's surrounded. And they've got guns this time, the hypocritical fuckers."

Sure enough, Jun's casts show about twenty people on the landing field, pointing rifles at the shuttle. Several pilots are operating nearby ships with weapons systems. Jun's plan to hack control of the shuttle seems like a bad one, with the avatar's gun in her face.

"We should make contact with the Wheel," Bene says. "We'll need to negotiate for—"

"Tej!" Ujan snaps at her brother. "What's wrong with you?! Keep that rifle on Liis."

Tej obeys, but he looks faint. There's a tremor in his whole body, and Jun imagines what a big man he must have told himself he was, threatening Dom. But he could never have planted that pipe bomb himself. He could never have been the one who took revenge on the station boss for breaking his hand. He needed Ujan to do it. Just like he needed Dom to kill the collectors. This is all so far beyond what Tej can bear.

"Ujan," Jun says. "The Wheel are trained to die before they give up the gate key. If you think that Fonu will open the gate for you, you're wrong."

Ujan's immediate look of incredulity chills Jun's heart. Her cousin blurts a laugh, shaking her head as if she can't believe how oblivious Jun is.

"Have you not been paying attention?" she asks, and leans closer. "I don't need Fonu to open the gate. They gave me the key an hour ago."

Masar breathes in, sharp and strangled. Jun holds Ujan's gaze, refusing to panic.

"Fonu gave you the gate key?"

"Yeah. For such an arrogant shit they sure didn't take long to break. Less than three hours, though that's with me putting the virus through all their tech. Fully deaf in one ear now, I figure. Blind in one eye. All that's left to do is overload their neural link and watch their brain leak out of the hole in their head. Maybe I'll do the same to yours."

The threat is like an unguent, turning the air to grease, impossible to breathe.

"Neural link torture," says Liis musingly. "That's a popular Cloaksaan technique."

Ujan sneers, "Yeah? Used it yourself, have you?"

Liis says, "False promises always proved more effective than torture, in my experience. I wonder what false promises your master has given you. A glorious return to the Treble? Wealth and prestige? It won't be like that. Whoever you work for, the Cloaksaan will get their Hands on you. And once they have what they want, they'll drop your carcass in a mass grave."

Hatred fills Ujan's eyes. She storms toward Liis, pointing the gun at her head. Jun's chest seizes, but Liis doesn't flinch.

"When we get to the Treble," Ujan snarls at her, "I'm gonna turn you over. Think how much the Cloaksaan will pay for you. And you—" She points at Jun. "Sunstep has made a damn fool of the Kindom over and over. They'll be pissing themselves to buy you from me. Plus I've got a member of the Wheel for them. My fortunes are set."

"Yes," Liis murmurs. "I think they are."

"Ujan," Bene says. "We're practically home free. We've got the key and everything, so why don't we just let the rest of them out and we can—"

Ujan shouts, "What the fuck is wrong with you?! You think I had to give you this chance? You think I couldn't have just left you behind?! I did it for Hosek, you ungrateful shit." She points the gun at him now. "But I can change my mind, quick as I like!"

Bene's voice drops low. "I just want you to live through it, all right?"

She looks at him for a long, wary moment, eyes narrow with suspicion. "I'm not sure about you," she says. "Tej! I'm not sure about him. I shouldn't have listened to you."

"I dunno if they'll let us go," Tej says, like he hasn't heard her. His voice is shaking. "I don't know if they'll let us go, Ujan."

"Of course they will! We've got four high-value hostages." Her eyes light up. "Hey! Now there's an idea! We tell them to let us go, right? And for every minute they don't let us go, we shoot one of you!" She waves the gun around at them, like someone who gets to decide which player is *it*. "We gotta start with the youngest one," she declares, pointing at Fonu and then Liis and then Jun and then—Masar. "Right, Bene?" she says. "That's what Esek told Great Gra, remember? I'll kill the youngest ones first."

Bene's composure fractures, just the faintest strain in his voice. "I don't want to play that game again, Ujan. Look at Tej. I don't think he wants to play that game, either."

"Tej will do what I fucking say! Who do you think kept him alive all these years? It wasn't *you*, was it?" No one answers, and she clears her throat in an overly dignified way. "All right, then. Well, they've been pinging me for five minutes, so let's get this started."

With an operatic swoop, she flings a comm into the center of the cabin, projecting a hologram of Effegen ten Crost.

"Hello!" Ujan says with absurd cheer. "I was wondering when you'd show up."

Effegen assesses the woman before her.

"Good morning, Sa Redcore," she says.

It clearly takes Ujan off guard, her brow furrowing as she must wonder how Effegen knows what name to use. She tries to move past it. "I have four hostages. Fonu sen Fhaan, Masar Hawks, Liis Konye… and Jun. I intend to take this ship off planet. I want you to tell all your fucking people to stand down and let us go."

Effegen says nothing. She is draped in her official green robes, bright with silver threadwork. Her hair is woven in tight braids and gathered atop her head. Her hands lie folded before her, and her expression is deadly calm.

"Ujan," she says. "It's obvious to me now that I made mistakes when it came to ensuring that you and Tej were happy here. But there'll be another time to regret my choices. For now, you must understand something. I will not let you leave Capamame."

Ujan chuckles. "You say that now." She shifts her cast, spinning the view to encompass the people in the flight seats. Jun watches Effegen take them in. Despite all the blood, she doesn't so much as wince. Ujan says, "How will you feel about it when Masar's brains are on the wall, huh? Or when I finish what I've started with Fonu? You want them to live? Let us go."

"There's no need to parade them," Effegen says. "I'm convinced of your sincerity."

"Must be hard, seeing them like that," Ujan says. "Masar's eye is toast. You don't have a lot of those things sitting around, do you? I *think* I can still save Fonu if I get them to a doctor on the other side, but they're definitely bleeding internally."

"Sa," Effegen says. "This verbal sparring is unnecessary. I gather that you mean to leave Capamame System. Since you have Fonu on board, and they have obviously been tortured, I think you must have the gate key. Which is precisely why I can't let you go."

Ujan says, "I'm not bluffing."

"I don't believe you're bluffing."

"You expect me to think you'd let me kill one of the Spokes of the—"

"The Spokes of the Wheel are replaceable," Effegen says. "Everyone in that shuttle is replaceable."

Ujan looks momentarily shocked. Then she recovers, shouting, "Tej! Come here. Come here right now!"

Looking confused and foggy, he comes to her. There's a wobble in his movements, as if he were drunk. Ujan takes the rifle off him, pushing the handgun into his hands and spinning to shove the muzzle of the rifle into Masar's throat. Maybe she thinks the rifle looks more threatening? Her eyes are wide, too wide.

"What about him? You never gave a shit about Fonu, maybe, but I know what Masar means to you. You're practically feral over him. You think I won't kill him?"

Jun watches Effegen look at Masar, who stares back at her stolidly, teeth set. She refocuses on Ujan, voice steady. "You are trying to appeal to me as the person Effegen, because Effegen cares deeply about your hostages. But you are not speaking to Effegen, Ujan. You are speaking to the Star of the Wheel, and it is in that capacity that I tell you: If you try to leave this planet, I will shoot you down."

Jun watches Ujan's profile, sees her rapid blinking. For a moment Jun hopes that logic will prevail; maybe Ujan will see it's hopeless and give in. But instead, a nasty smile spreads across her face as she steps back from Masar and props the rifle over her shoulder.

"Okay," she says. "Fine. So put me in that pathetic little prison. I won't be there long." The invitation for a question goes unanswered, and Ujan grimaces in annoyance. "What I'm saying is—I'll be rescued. See, it's too late, Effegen. I already sent your gate key to the Treble."

Jun's body cycles hot and cold. Some part of her knew that this was a possibility. Those comm links, between the avatar and the Treble. Only strong enough to send messages via text. Perfectly capable of sending the string of code that is a gate key.

Masar rumbles a low curse. Effegen absorbs the information, the only clue to its impact being that she doesn't blink for several seconds, doesn't speak, and Ujan looks cruelly delighted.

"You sent the gate key to the Kindom?" she asks.

"None of your fucking business who I sent it to. Fact is it won't be long till ships comes through that gate. They'll blow the dome apart and take you all in a ground war. Don't worry. They want you alive for the factories. Most of you, anyway. As for me? All I have to do is wait in that prison until I'm rescued, and I'll go back to the Treble a hero."

Effegen remains quiet and unblinking. Then, she lets out a long, slow breath. "Very well," she says, sounding weary, but calm. "That is easily remedied."

Ujan laughs at her without humor. "Remedied? Did you hear what I said? They're going to come through that gate and—"

"They won't," Effegen says. "Because I will destroy the gate."

CHAPTER TWENTY-FOUR

1664

YEAR OF THE CRUX

Farren Eyce
The Planet Capamame

The moment Effegen says it, the weight of it is so profound that there's no need for the zip ties. Masar's legs feel numb. Could he move, if he tried?

He struggles to focus, though his vision is fucked and the pain is working against him. Ujan's mouth opens and closes. Her eyes dart from Effegen to her hostages to Effegen again.

"I—" Her voice gurgles a little. Like a child she blurts, "You're lying!"

"I am not," says Effegen. How cool she is. How straight her posture, how level her gaze.

"You—" Ujan struggles. "You can't! You *wouldn't*!"

"I wouldn't?" Effegen repeats, and the temperature in the shuttle drops. "I wouldn't destroy the gate? To save my people, who I brought here for peace? To save my culture, which the Kindom has tried to stomp out over and over? You don't think I will blow up the gate, to cut them off for good?"

Ujan glances toward the hatch, like she can see Effegen on the other side of it. A stone wall, impossible to step around. Her grip on the rifle slackens, and Masar zeroes in on this. He has been very carefully stretching the zip ties for the past hour—ever since Ujan flattened him with her virus attack and had Bene and Tej hustle him to the shuttle. Bene...

He looks over at him, sees the tension in his body, feels again the sweeping horror but also the most painful hope.

Ujan blurts a laugh, disbelieving. It is a strange, grotesque thing, to watch someone's plans collapse around them. Is this how it was for Six?

"You—you—" she stammers.

"Sa Redcore," says Effegen. "You cannot begin to grasp the things that I would do to save my people. The question is what you will do to save yours. What will you do to save your family? It's time for you to decide."

Ujan's eyes are wide now, panic creeping across her face. In her stunned silence, Bene inches toward her, urging, "I think we should stand down, and—"

She whips toward him, striking the barrel of the gun against his face. There's a gush of blood, and he crumples. Jun starts cursing incoherently. Masar twists the zip ties harder, heart sprinting, frantic to protect this man whom he loves, whose actions he doesn't understand.

Ujan stands over Bene. "Shut up!" she shrieks. "I should have known better than to give you a chance! You're with *them*!"

Bene half shields himself with his hands, looking up at her. The side of his face is swelling up, from the height of his cheekbone down to his mouth. His eyes implore her. He whispers, "Ujan. I love you. Listen to me. I love you."

She kicks him as hard as her small body can, and Bene doubles over, gagging.

Effegen says, "Ujan, you won't gain anything by killing your family."

Ujan spins toward the hologram, shouting, "*You* killed my family! You fucking Jeveni killed my family! If Six had never come to K-5, my family would be alive. It's you fucking people who started all of this, you mongrel vermin motherfucking bastards!"

Effegen murmurs, "Six did not do that because of the Jeveni, Ujan. Six did it because they were alone and afraid—like you."

"I'm not *afraid*!"

Ujan screams it, an earsplitting, hysterical scream. Jun makes a choked sound. She seems to fight it, but her self-control dissolves. Her chest heaves, and she's sobbing, openly, helplessly sobbing, as Masar has never seen. As if all the grief of losing her Great Gra, her home station, her childhood dreams, is just a pinprick compared to this. As if nothing will ever hurt worse than this hurts her.

Ujan looks at her hatefully. "What is wrong with you?!" she screams again, and her voice is hoarse from it. "Stop it! Fucking stop it!" But Jun can't stop. Masar thinks if she could, she would stop. If only to say how sorry she is, if only to beg Ujan to forgive her. Ujan points the rifle at her. "Fucking stop it!"

"Ujan . . ."

Tej's voice is so soft and raw that somehow it defeats all the volume in the room—Jun's sobs and Bene's wheezing gasps and Ujan screaming. She stops screaming. She looks over at him. The handgun has dropped to his side. He looks numb. No, confused. Like someone who wakes up somewhere and doesn't know how they got there.

"I think . . ." His voice is a rasp. "I think we should stop."

"Tej, *shut up*!"

"I think . . . I think Mama would want us to stop."

Ujan freezes. Her rage transmutes into disbelief, and then terror.

"No," she says. "No, no, no, Tej, she told us to survive, remember?" Her voice pitches up. She tries to smile at him, but it's twisted. "Remember? She said everything would be okay if we would just be strong and protect each other. That's what I'm doing, see? I'm protecting you. These people, they don't care about you—"

"I don't think she'd like this," Tej says, and shakes his head, like a frightened little boy, like he hasn't heard a word she's said. "I don't... I don't think Mama would like it, Ujan. I want to stop, okay? I want to stop."

Ujan is facing him directly now, her back to Bene, and Bene inches back from her, levering himself up onto one arm, and then, carefully, one knee. Blood streams from his face. Ujan says, "Tej, it's okay."

He shakes his head. He raises the gun—and points it at her. "You lied to me. You kept all of it from me. You—we—you lied about everything."

Ujan's eyes are wide. "Tej—"

But she doesn't seem to know what else to say. And it's Liis speaking, very calm, "Tej, you're right. You should stop. Why don't you put the gun down? Then it will stop."

Tej blinks rapidly. Behind Ujan, Bene gets to his feet, arm cradled to his side.

Liis says, "Tenje. Listen to me. Put down the gun."

Tej flinches at the sound of his birth name. He turns to look at Liis, still blinking. All at once something hard and horrible consumes his face.

He raises the gun to his head.

Ujan screams.

Liis snaps the ties as if they were threads. She springs forward, slamming Tej into the wall of the cabin. His shot goes wide, lodging above Masar's head. Ujan aims the rifle.

And Bene throws himself against her, arms around her like steel bands. She shrieks, managing to get off a volley of shots that spray the ceiling. Masar is wrenching and fighting now, ripping up his wrists in an attempt to get free. Bene drops his weight forward, hitting the ground with Ujan under him as the rifle skitters away. Jun leaps up, kicking the rifle farther out of range. Ujan shrieks. Tej is screaming, a broken animal screaming, as Liis puts him on his stomach and twists his hands behind his back.

When Ujan nearly slips free of Bene, Jun throws herself forward, hands still bound, and together the two of them hold their little cousin down. Ujan spits like a cat, wriggling and thrashing, and Bene just keeps his arms wrapped around her. He's speaking in her ear, low, desperate sounds—"Luja, stop. It's okay. Tej is alive. You're both alive. Luja, stop now. You can stop now. You can stop."

Suddenly, she flattens out beneath him, sobbing and trembling. Liis has zip-tied Tej, lifting him and putting him in one of the seats, where he stays, body limp. Liis goes to Masar, slitting open his ties with a knife she must have taken from Tej. Freed, Masar kneels down beside Fonu, using the knife to cut them loose. They were making more noise a few minutes ago. Their breathing is faint now, just a whistle.

He hears the hatch on the shuttle open and looks back. A trio of collectors step inside, sighting down their rifles. Liis comes to kneel beside Bene and Jun and Ujan, and she carefully but efficiently zip-ties Ujan's hands behind her back. The collectors sweep for more weapons, and Effegen steps onto the shuttle, and Masar lifts Fonu bodily into his arms to carry them down the gangplank. And he hears Bene, still whispering—

"It's okay now. You can stop. It's okay . . ."

In a reasonable universe, where circumstance is compassionate, and healing supersedes the needs of a crisis, Masar would have the luxury of passing out in his hospital bed. He'd have the relief of a little unconsciousness and some painkillers to white out the agony in his virus-ravaged eye. But he won't let them give him painkillers. Instead, the doctors numb the entire left side of his face, and he's conscious as they carefully extract the eye. He's almost relieved. *I don't like that eye anymore*, he thinks. *I don't want it. Get it out.*

"You're lucky," the surgeon says as she applies the regenerative patch.

"There wasn't much damage to the eye socket or the surrounding tissue. We'll have it healed within a day, but I'm sorry. Your cybernetic eye was the best prosthetic we had. We can give you another, but it won't be as sophisticated, and it'll take longer to acclimate."

Masar says, "I don't want another eye. What are my options?"

The surgeon looks surprised. "I . . . Well, nothing will ever be as good as a prosthetic, but we can run a neural program that'll help with your depth perception and other factors. It usually takes a few days. But it would be much better if—"

"I have to go," Masar says.

"Sa, please—"

"Don't bother," says a voice in the doorway. Masar, disoriented, looks over and sees Liis, standing with her arms crossed. "The Wheel needs him, anyway."

The surgeon mutters about reckless people ignoring advice and hands him an eye patch to cover his bandage. When he has it on, he rises from the bed. He feels a little weak on his feet at first, but slowly, he gets his bearings. He turns his head left and right, trying to get a sense of his field of vision. He's less disoriented than he expected. He nods at Liis, and they start down the hallway.

"Where are we going?"

"The council room," Liis says. "Jun is there. They're making a plan."

"Fonu?"

"Alive. They're in surgery."

Masar swallows. "How did she get to them? How did Ujan—"

"Tej says she lured them to the surface by claiming she had evidence against Jun."

His heart sickens, grief like a whirlpool sucking him down. Of course. The disease of distrust in their midst. Of course this is how it happened.

Masar knows it should be the last thing on his mind, but . . . "Where's Bene?" he asks.

"We put him in the newsnest," Liis says. They walk in silence, Liis considering her words, Masar struggling with his questions. "He says that he didn't know Ujan was the avatar until she and Tej contacted him early this morning. They asked him to come with them to the Treble. He says he was trying to defuse the situation."

Masar doesn't respond. He remembers being driven along toward the surface, wrists bound, and Tej with the gun pressed to his back. Bene wouldn't look at him.

"He stopped Ujan," Masar says, clinging to that moment, to what it seemed to mean.

Liis nods. She looks even more controlled than usual, and that in itself is his clue to the emotion she's trying to master. Softly she says, "I trust him. I think we should trust him."

A sob lodges in Masar's throat, and he chokes it back down.

They walk in silence the rest of the way, out of the medical wing of Level 8 and into the government sector. They pass the doors that lead to the newsnest. Eda and Iyrini stand guard. There are five prisoners now, counting Aris and Dom. He thinks of Ujan, going limp under Bene and Jun, and wonders if she has succumbed to catatonia, or rediscovered her anger. He will never forgive himself for not seeing it. Jun will never forgive herself for not seeing it.

When they reach the door to the council room, Masar misses the doorknob. Liis gets it for him, and he stomps down on the humiliation and vulnerability, stepping inside.

The seats at the round table are full, all the Wheel there but Fonu. Jun, looking gray and empty as a ghost, sits between a couple of her high-ranking casters. There are three engineers in the room, as well. Everyone is grave. Masar looks at Effegen, and though she is a little pale, she is just as composed as she was when she spoke to Ujan.

"Masar." Her eyes skate over him. "We shouldn't have made you come."

"We must act at full strength," Gaeda argues. "We need everyone."

"Come and sit, Masar," Hyre says. "I'll get you water."

They lift their big, elegant body from the chair, and Masar sits down next to Liis. Hyre comes back a few seconds later, offering the water glass.

"Drink," they urge.

Masar, uncomfortably aware of the people at the table watching him, drinks. Then, blessedly, everyone turns to one of the engineers, the gate chief.

"I don't understand why we can't just shut the engines down," Hyre says.

The chief raises a hand, and gate schematics lift from his finger-tips into the air above the round table. He rotates them and pulls in a closer view of the triple engines limning the latticework frame, each engine as large as a warship.

"We can," he says. "But it takes a month. The fail-safes won't let you rush it. It'd be faster to rewrite the gate key."

"So let's do that," Tomesk grits out.

"It's..." The caster to Jun's left glances at her uncertainly. "It's a very...complicated endeavor. The key was written almost a hundred years ago by Drae sen Briit, and someone would have to... that is, with her notes, perhaps, and with time—"

"He's saying only I am smart enough to do it," Jun interrupts, voice a rasp, eyes cold. "And even I would need weeks."

"I have had quite enough of relying on your brilliance," Tomesk declares. "Little good as it's done us in months!"

The saan at the table shift, disquieted. If Masar had a voice, he would scream at him—but his voice is gone. Jun, on the other hand, looks at Tomesk with a kind of deadly calm that reminds Masar how easily she could wreak havoc to put Ujan Redcore to shame.

"By all means," she says. "Solve the problem yourself."

He seems about to launch into another attack, but Gaeda exclaims, "Sajeven spare us your posturing, Tomesk! This is all nonsense. Effegen said she would destroy the gate. All right. How do we destroy it?"

Her snapping voice breaks the frozen silence. The thought of destroying the gate sends a wave of despair through Masar, but he pushes it down. This is what they have to do.

The gate chief says, "We would have to destroy all three engines. Gates can operate even with just one engine online."

"And how do we destroy the engines?" Gaeda presses, impatient.

"Not with firepower," says another engineer. "We don't have Kindom warheads. We don't have anything powerful enough to destroy them, even with their shields down."

No one speaks for several moments. Masar feels raw and fuzzy, useless, his mind drifting toward Bene in his office cell. He berates himself. He can't think of Bene right now. He has to be like Effegen, steady and focused. He looks at her, wanting to find strength in her composure. But all he sees is the strain around her eyes, the tightness of her clasped hands.

Suddenly Jun murmurs, "I saw something written on a mirror... It was attributed to Drae sen Briit: 'Our home shall be our sanctuary. And our weapon.'"

Everyone looks at her. Hyre shifts forward with an air of recognition. "Yes. She gave a speech to the original crew of *Drae's Hope*, before it departed. But what are you implying?"

"*Drae's Hope*," Jun says. "Make it a weapon. Fly it into the gate."

Her suggestion travels like a shock wave across the room, faces clouding with resistance. The Draeviin engineer says softly, "That ship is...deeply important to us."

Jun nods, and though there's sympathy in her eyes, there's also resolve. "I know. I know what it means to love a ship. I know what it means to love a home. But it's the only thing big enough to destroy a jump gate. We could drop the shields around the engines. We could fly *Drae's Hope* remotely. It would be enough."

Masar imagines it. The proud *Drae's Hope*, disappearing into a flash of white. Shards of wreckage scattering across the Black. Everything that ship represents, every possibility it permits, vanishing. He finds his words, raspy though they are. "*Drae's Hope* is a crucial resource. We've always known that we'll need to build another colony someday. We'll need the raw materials of the hull to do it."

"We won't be building any colonies if the Kindom annihilates us," says Gaeda testily.

One of the engineers points out, "The gate is not so far that we won't suffer debris. If a big enough piece hits the planet or, gods forbid, hits us—it could be cataclysmic."

Gaeda throws her hands up. "Moon arise! So what? We're back to square one?"

"The gate is a hundred thousand miles away," Jun says. She sounds like a length of rope being slowly frayed from the bottom up.

"I can show you the calculations," the engineer says.

"I can do the calculations in my head. The chances of something like that—"

Tomesk interrupts, "We don't need *recklessness* right now."

The gate chief shakes his head. "We should focus on rewriting the key."

A caster retorts, "And gamble on the Kindom not invading for weeks?"

"But are we even certain that Ujan Redcore *sent* the key to the Kindom?" asks Hyre. "She could be lying! Maybe Fonu didn't give it to her. Let's wait till they're out of surgery—"

"Of course they gave it to her," snipes Gaeda.

The Draeviin gate engineer leans sharply forward. "What are you saying?"

"You know exactly what I'm saying."

"Sa Fonu is true and loyal."

"It's not a question of loyalty when you're being tortured!"

"So we should ram the gate on the word of a maniac?" Tomesk cries.

"She terrorized this colony for months! Why ignore her threats?"

Into this gathering storm, into the glut of voices talking over one another and getting louder and louder, Effegen says, "Stop."

The arguing breaks down into muttering and mumbling, and as they all see her expression, silence. Effegen waits, then rises from her chair. She looks from one face to another in a way that warns not one of them should dare to speak right now. Walking to the corner of the room where the water pitcher sits on a smaller table, she pours herself a glass and drinks.

Still with her back to them, she says, "Liis Konye. You've been very quiet."

Everyone looks at Liis. Liis looks as calm as if she has spent the past few minutes meditating. "It's my nature to be quiet, my Star."

Effegen turns, smiling faintly. "But not your nature to lack instincts. Or ideas."

A long pause. "No."

Effegen nods. She finishes her glass of water. She walks back to the table, but she does not sit down. Others at the table seem confused by the silence, and Effegen says, "Since this began, I've been thinking about when we jumped to Capamame to escape the Kindom fleet. And I've been thinking of our ancestors, who sent *Drae's Hope* off to build us a new world. There was no shame in retreat, because when your enemy does nothing but hunt, when your enemy is a cruel and tireless stalker, playing by their rules is nonsense."

She pauses, looking down at the table, at her fingertips spread apart and resting upon it, as if she were pinning down and examining the breadth of their history.

"Yet here we are, hunted again. And I find myself asking...what would the hunter do?" She looks at Liis. "You were a hunter. You were the most dangerous hunter the Cloaksaan possessed. What if it's time to stop running? What if what we really need...is a Brutal Hand."

A few quiet murmurs, shifting bodies, eyes glancing at one another and at Effegen, but Effegen has eyes for no one but Liis, who looks steadily back at her.

"So tell me, Liis Konye," she says. "What would *you* do?"

Liis doesn't take long to think about it. Her answer is resolute. "I would find out who in the Treble has the key. Then I would go there and kill them."

The murmuring gets louder. Effegen thinks for a moment, and nods.

"Yes...that does sound like the tactic of a Brutal Hand."

"My Star," Hyre says, "if Sa Redcore sent the key to the Kindom, then the entire Kindom has it. We can't assassinate the entire Kindom."

"She didn't send it to the Kindom," Jun says. She's still looking at

Liis, who looks back at her. Nods at her. She directs herself to Hyre. "My cousin...I don't believe she's a Kindom stooge. I think she threw her lot in with one specific secretary. Ilius Redquill gave her an education, got Tej a surgery he needed. Sent them money. He won Ujan's loyalty and he gave her a mission. I believe she sent the key to him."

"Ilius Redquill is a member of the Secretarial Court," says Tomesk acidly. "Whatever she sent to him, she also gave to them."

"Not necessarily," Liis replies. "Redquill has only just risen to Minor Advocate, and all the reports coming out of the Treble indicate that leadership of the Hands is in upheaval. Redquill is in. Paiye is out. Moonback has disappeared, and I can assure you, that won't be good for anyone. Things are very tricky on the ground."

Gaeda says, "But isn't it obvious that Redquill will have bought his position on the court with his access to a spy in Farren Eyce?"

"Maybe," Jun says. "But he's spent his career hoarding valuable information. I doubt it's his instinct to hand over something like this when his position in the court is so new. But let's just say, for argument's sake, that he *did* share the information with the court. Secretaries are called clever for a reason. They're hardly going to send the key to the Silver Keep, or Riin Cosas, when they don't know if they can trust the other Hands."

Liis speaks again. "We should capture Ilius Redquill and ascertain who else knows about the key. And act accordingly."

Hyre says, "It could take days for you to find him. Longer to capture him. Do we have that much time?"

Gaeda looks at Effegen. "My Star, you yourself said we should blow up the gate. Isn't it simpler and safer to cut the Kindom off entirely?"

Masar's stomach drops, something near to panic gathering in his breast. Hoarsely he says, "I don't think we should do that."

Everyone looks at him. Gaeda raises an eyebrow. "And why is that?"

Masar takes a deep breath. His eye is throbbing. He spreads his hands apart. "For almost a *year* we've promised this colony that we won't force people to stay here. We've promised that someday, we can sue for peace with the Treble and those who want it can return. Destroying the gate, destroying that option—our people aren't ready for it. It'll break us."

He sees their shock. But Effegen, looking at him, holds a light of pride in her eyes.

"We can rise above it," Hyre insists.

Jun shakes her head slowly, thoughtfully. "Not all of us can. My cousins couldn't."

"Your cousins were terrorist plants," Tomesk retorts.

"I won't defend their actions. But Esek Nightfoot ripped their home away from them, killed their family, turned them into refugees. I should think that would strike a chord with you."

"Are you comparing them to the victims of the Jeveni Genocide?!" Tomesk demands.

"She is reminding us," Effegen says, "that there is a unique cruelty to having your home taken from you. What did we do but take so many unwilling people from their homes?"

"It was that or die!" Gaeda says.

"But it had a cost. And that cost will only compound if we take the Treble away from them for good. Masar is right. And I can't break hearts so easily, no matter what I said to Ujan."

"And what if the Kindom invades while we are searching for Redquill?" Tomesk asks.

"If that happens, we will throw *Drae's Hope* at the gate," Effegen allows. "And pray to Sajeven to forgive us."

The table is grim, lost, radiating conflicted opinions. Finally, Jun says, "Send me and Liis. I can help find Redquill—"

"Whoever goes may end up trapped on the other side," Effegen says. "I'm sorry, Jun, but as our head of the casting corps, I can't spare you."

Jun's nostrils flare. "Then Liis isn't going, either."

Liis says, "I'm the best qualified—"

"Unless you want to risk getting stuck over there and have to wait decades while I find my way back to you at standard speed, you will shut up right now," Jun snaps.

Masar snorts a laugh. He wasn't aware he could still laugh.

One of the casters asks, "What about Six and Chono? They're in Praetima. They have access to Redquill, and Six is a known assassin. Why not give them this job?"

"We can't reach them," Jun says grimly. "There's a comm block on them. I don't know if I'll be able to break it, and I don't know how long that would take."

Masar recalls what Ujan said about Six, a betrayal he has not had time to process. If Six worked with Redquill before, if their actions led to the deaths of the collectors, can Masar be sure they're not working with him, still? What do they even know about Six, really, besides their unceasing commitment to their own aims?

Masar looks at Effegen, and Effegen looks at him, and she must be able to see what he is going to say, because her expression darkens.

He addresses the table. "It'll have to be me."

Effegen waits a beat. Her voice is flat. "You have been severely wounded."

"It'll take several days to get anywhere near Redquill. I'll have healed up by then."

"You're our senior collector," Hyre says. "We can't spare you any more than Jun."

"This is what I'm for," Masar replies. "I'm the tip of the spear."

He can feel the unhappiness in the room, but Gaeda says, "We can't afford to be sentimental. If we're going to try this ridiculous scheme, we have to put our best foot forward."

Masar nods. "I won't go alone. I'll bring a team with me." He looks at Effegen, at her frozen, emotionless expression. "Let me do this, my Star."

She goes on staring at him. Then, with a blink, she addresses the Wheel. "We will vote."

Gaeda responds, "I move that we send Masar to the Treble to capture this Ilius Redquill."

Brows knit in concern, Hyre nods. "I second."

Tomesk grimaces. "Agreed."

Everyone looks at Effegen. Regal, poised, powerful Effegen. Her nod is short, her head high. "Very well. We concur. Let's begin preparations. Everyone please vacate the room. I will speak to Masar alone."

There are many looks around the table, Tomesk and Gaeda seeming particularly put out. But nobody argues. The shuffling of people leaving the room becomes a heavy silence. Effegen, standing at the table, and Masar, still seated, watch each other. It's only then that he begins to recognize the emotion behind her mask of calm. It's anger.

"How dare you do this to me," she whispers. Masar stands up, moving carefully toward her. "I nearly saw you killed today. I saw my other lover taken into custody for treason. I'll have to build a real prison for Bene and his cousins. Even if I can prove he's telling the truth, the Wheel may never let him out. And now I could lose you to the Treble. Forty light-years between us. Or death. How much do you expect me to endure, Masar?"

He moves closer, as slow and unthreatening as if she were a panicked animal.

"I would spare you all the grief there is, if I could," he whispers. "But you were right, what you said to Ujan. We are not Effegen and Masar. We are the Star and her collector. Our feelings are immaterial—"

"Damn you, Masar." Her voice chokes off.

He is an arm's length away from her now, and the sight of her like this, every muscle locked against the emotion consuming her, fills him with pain—but also, determination. "Am I not this colony's sword and shield?" he asks. Her jaw tightens. "I have to go."

"Of course you fucking have to go!" she snaps. Masar isn't sure he's ever heard her curse like that before. Her eyes well with furious tears that she somehow keeps from spilling. "I didn't rise to this position by being feeble. Who I love"—she swallows hard—"will always come second to who I serve. But you listen to me, Masar Hawks. You are *my* sword and shield. I am your Star. I *command* you to come back, do you hear me? I command it, by Sajeven and on all the lives of our dead. Swear it."

Masar's throat tightens. He reaches her and lifts a hand to cradle her face, this brave, fierce woman, this inestimable, radiant Star.

"I swear it," he breathes.

She looks at him as if searching for a lie. At last, still controlling herself, she nods once. She raises a hand to hold his hand against her face, and her fingers are cool but trembling.

"All right," she says. "Then what do you need?"

He smiles a little, before real urgency sweeps through him, to do this thing, to go, and return.

"Well," he says. "For starters . . . I'd like my shotgun back."

Being that the three Hands were formed in unity and love, and from the best of all the Kindom's agents and executors, there can be no doubt that the unlikely institution of the rule will be met with equanimity and grace. For what is the purpose of the Kindom but to support itself, in order to support the Treble? And why should three saan, who love one another, be divided rather than rejoice to see one of them lifted just a little higher?

excerpt, the Rule of Unification. Dated 1322, Year of the Long Hunt.

CHAPTER TWENTY-FIVE

1665

YEAR OF THE HARVEST

Praetima
Nikata Leen, an Island
The Planet Kator

They put Chono in a cell in Nikapraev that looks like it might have been an office once. The door is heavy wood and metal. There's a desk and a cold hearth with dregs of blackened wood. She sits down carefully, regarding her hand. They've done better this time than when they gave her a simple regenerative patch for her broken eye socket. Her hand is carefully wrapped, throbbing with the quick healing of strong medicine. Her back is sore from being thrown against the wall, and there's a tender spot on the back of her head.

She keeps oscillating between images: Aver Paiye, awkwardly slumped in the cottage. Ilius, holding the gun and looking at her in accusation. *You made me into this*, his look said. *I never hurt a living soul, until you.*

And then will come Esek. And Chono will think, *I never hurt a living soul, until you.*

It may not be true, but it ushers in Khen Caskhen Paan, a heap of bloodstained robes and brittle brokenness, and standing over him in her memories, Chono wonders if she could do it again. If she *will* do it again, given the chance. What was it she said to Six all those months ago? *I want to be absolved*... And what was it that Six said they wanted? *Recompense.*

Yes, Chono thinks. *I want recompense.*

But for now, she wants rest. It's night in Praetima, and she feels as if she hasn't slept, really slept, since they jumped from the Capamame System. She is exhausted in her marrow, in the links of her DNA. It gives her some comfort to remember how many hours the Kindom interrogators left her to herself, in the Praetima prison. If she lays her head down on the desk now, she knows she'll be asleep in seconds.

Which is why it disappoints her when the locks in the door start clanging, and the door opens to reveal Ilius—two guardsaan behind him.

She hasn't seen him since they took her out of the cottage a few hours ago. He's changed into a clean blue suit, the white tippet pristine. She looks at his finger bracelets, his homage to Kata. Chono always thought, for some reason, that it was Kata's honesty and wisdom that he identified with, that he loved them for their logic and intellect. Why else convert to their temple when he is neither Katish-born nor Katish-raised? But of course it is quite obvious. He has fashioned himself after them, as Six fashioned themself after Esek. A perverse copycat. Ilius must have thought to himself at some point, *Kata is the god of many spies, keen and clever. I will be like a god, with many spies, keen and clever.*

"Kata is a god of honesty," she remarks, as if he has been privy to her internal conversation. "How do you think they'd judge you, Ilius?"

He looks at her without answering, then says something quietly over his shoulder to the guardsaan. Their faceplates are down, but Chono detects a hint of hesitation before they obediently back away. The door shuts after them, leaving the Minor Advocate inside.

With an authoritative air, Ilius folds his hands in front of him, looking disappointed. "You're hardly one to lecture me on godly judgment. You're a terrorist." He says it with the stiffness of someone trying on a speech he'll have to give over and over.

Chono flicks her eyes over his slim and vulnerable body. "Yet you'll stand in here with me, all alone. Don't you know I killed a Hand once?"

His composure falters. Chono isn't sure if she's bluffing, but she certainly knows now that she is capable. She wants to know where Six is, if they're safe, if they're *here*, and wanting that is like a demon inside her. She has let out her demons before, and has the sense memory in her knuckles to prove it.

Ilius grows imperious again.

"You may have been led astray, but I believe you have enough sense left not to try something that irrational."

"Led astray," she murmurs, looking down at her bandaged hand and wondering if he's right. "Led astray... Shall we do this one more time, Ilius?" She raises her eyes to him. "One more philosophical argument, for the sake of all our history? You tell me why your actions are righteous, I tell you why my actions were necessary. We lob Godtexts at each other and argue the finer points of secretarial law. You bluster about moral purity. I evoke the beatitudes." She spreads her hands apart. "Then at the end we can be right here again, nothing gained. But at least we'll say we were very civilized about it."

Ilius looks at her woodenly. He's standing at his full height, which for some reason only reminds her that he's shorter and smaller than she is. His prideful look conceals an abscess of insecurity that will never heal.

He says, "A philosophical argument between like-minded thinkers is always, in its own way, a negotiation. The time for negotiating is over."

Chono is almost amused. "Very well," she says. "I think the opposite of negotiation in this case is judgment. What's your judgment?"

"The Clever Hand doesn't pass judgment in a secret cell. We do it publicly, in keeping with the law. Your trial is set for three days. Time enough for you to prepare a defense. It's tradition for the Minor Advocate to prosecute." She doesn't respond, and he shifts restlessly. "You brought this on yourself."

"Why the wait? Why not try me right away? Even better, why not keep me in the Praetima prison? Closer to the chopping block, isn't it? I assume this will be a capital case."

His jawline tightens; his clasped hands go white at the knuckles. In his pale brown eyes she sees a combination of rage and grief that makes her feel... *nothing*.

She asks wearily, "What are you doing here, Ilius?"

"I've come to give you the details of the case. There's no other reason. I've spent enough effort trying to protect you. And you threw it back in my face. You have no allies left."

Quietly and warningly, she asks, "Are you sure?"

Her meaning turns his eyes to slits. Chono has to put all her strength into not showing her relief. If he had Six in custody, he'd singing it out right now.

"Three days until my trial," she muses. "You think you'll live that long? Esek is coming."

"You have a lot of confidence in that... malcontent, but you're surrounded by guardsaan."

"You wouldn't be the first to underestimate Esek."

His nostrils flare. Color rises vibrantly in his neck and cheeks. "And you wouldn't be the first to underestimate me. We still hold the five thousand."

Chono huffs. "Then you really are no better than Paiye or Moonback. They used the Jeveni as hostages, too. It's as if you took a look at the mistakes of your forebears and decided to repeat them, step for step. Gods and fire, Ilius... How will this make the Treble more secure?"

He swallows. Perhaps he does have some remnant of the integrity he always seemed to value. Perhaps he's convinced himself of the greater good of this pill but is choking on it nonetheless.

"Our predecessors were . . . sloppy," he declares. "They believed false intelligence and overreacted to the Jeveni. We, on the other hand, are responding to indisputable intelligence—that you're an agitator and a threat to order in the Kindom. We'll use whatever measures we must to contain you. Including the five thousand."

"And be dubbed genociders in the aftermath," she says.

"As I said, our predecessors were sloppy. The five thousand are closely contained in the sevite labor camp. Since the Clever Hand took over, we've given them medical aid, food, all the care the Treble would ask of a benevolent government. But if you don't come to heel, a respiratory flu will overrun the camp."

Chono's brows rise to the top of her hairline. She's back in the Treble for just over a month and already things have escalated to biological warfare.

He adds stiffly, "We anticipate forty percent fatality."

Chono stares at him. Her voice is like ice. "I see."

Her eyes must be ice, too, for his gaze momentarily darts away, before he forces it back with false bravado. "This isn't what I want, Chono. I argued against it." Can she possibly believe that? "But the court speaks with one voice, just as the Kindom now speaks with one voice. You've said from the beginning that you came here to protect the five thousand. You can do that now by meeting our demands."

"Which are?"

Hope flickers in his expression. He inches closer to her.

"Reiterate your support for the Rule of Unification. Do it loudly and enthusiastically. Call on the insurgents to stand down. And get the Jeveni to talk to us."

"And here I thought we weren't negotiating," she says.

"We're not negotiating. As I said, these are our *demands*, not our offer."

Chono could smash his head against the heavy wooden door in the space of two seconds and he would be dead before the guards could get inside.

"All of this will certainly fall flat if you execute me in three days," she observes.

"Three days gives you time to prove your obedience. No one knows you've been arrested or that a trial is impending. We can cancel the trial. We can keep your name clean."

Behold the devouring Som, her thoughts whisper, *who eats up the dead...*

"Let me see if I have this right," Chono says. "Seti Moonback is in the wind. Esek Nightfoot is in the wind. Any number of insurgents are in the wind. And you think if I make a speech in the Centrum, that will solve your problems?"

He glowers. "Seti Moonback has fled. Our intelligence shows her hiding in the Kriisturan archipelagoes. Furthermore, we vote tonight to firebomb the cities where the main insurgent forces have holed up. As for Esek Nightfoot." His lip curls. "She is alone, with none of the support of her family. Do you think I'm bluffing right now, Chono? I'm *not* bluffing."

Then round your traitorous head, the Many Blessings of Kata say, *like spirits, living, dead, shall come the spies, oh, tireless, and take you for a trophy, lest you be traitorous again.*

Ilius says, "Esek isn't saving you this time. Will she try? Yes, probably. You've made her sentimental. But when she comes, we'll be ready, and when she's in our custody, she'll be just another piece in our arsenal, and you *will* come to heel, or the Kindom will kill both of you."

Chono murmurs, "If you only knew how many people have tried to trap my friend. If you only knew the disasters that have come of it."

"Do you honestly think Esek can take down all the guardsaan in Nikapraev?"

"I do not."

His eyes sharpen. "Then you agree your only recourse is to cooperate."

In your death, whispers Sajeven, *you will eat the fruits of your life, and whatever ripens them shall ripen your death—either with joy, or regret.*

For once she doesn't try to hide her feelings. She lets the welter of her emotions change her face, all her defiance, her fury at the Kindom's betrayals and her disdain for Hands she once served and her love for Six, her loyalty to them, which is a tree with roots as deep as her soul.

"I do not agree," she whispers.

Ilius's face changes, too, turning shocked, and then angrily desperate. "Chono, as you serve the Godfire—*think*. You've been taken in by radicals. Why do you want to ally yourself with people who only want more violence and death in the Treble?!"

"I would rather ally with them than a self-deceiving tyrant."

He flinches, all woundedness and disbelief.

"I've protected you. I'm the only reason you're alive! The others wanted to kill you!"

"I don't want your protection."

He looks at her beseechingly, his voice a raw plea. "Chono... I love you."

As if that would change anything. As if the words would condemn her own actions and shame her. Chono looks at him stolidly.

"I don't care."

She sees what it does to him, how it opens a hole in him, as if she had shot him the way he shot Aver. The way Medisogo shot Nikkelo. The way Esek shot Coz Ironway.

A blistering silence stretches between them, and Chono pins him to the truth with her eyes—before suddenly, he looks aside. He makes a little gesture with his fingers, face turning as a cast message obviously comes to him. She watches his expression shift from furrowed expectation to slow, dawning amazement. His eyes snap toward her again, full of vindication.

"It turns out your ally isn't the mastermind you take her for. We have her in custody."

Wrists shackled, flanked by jailers, Chono walks into the Centrum to find it packed with secretaries. Over a hundred guardsaan form a menacing perimeter, while on the dais, Ravening and Songrider sit tall. Ravening's scowl looks triumphant, fingers tapping in eagerness to begin. Songrider watches Chono like someone anticipating a fresh assault, but there is excitement in her eyes. When Ilius leaves Chono to join his kin on the dais, he looks grim but satisfied.

He's not alone. The energy in the room is palpable, hundreds of secretaries preening as they gaze down at the figure in the center of the room—their captured quarry. The secretaries may have come for the vote, but they're *here* for this, this kneeling figure, bound at wrists and ankles and with a hood over their head.

The sight of them like that makes Chono's body flare with fear and anger. Without their Esek face to look at, she is consumed by thoughts of what they looked like when they were eight, and the kinschool master made them strip to their underwear and wear a blindfold. They were small but sleek as a fledgling, cool black skin contrasting with the white marble floors. The master made them kneel in the center of the sparring court, surrounded by second years.

"Remember," he had boomed, "that it is easy to be brave and cocky when you feel strong. It's easy when you think you're better than everyone, like Six does. But can you be brave when you're cut down to size? That is the only reasonable test of courage."

He had ordered the students to brandish their hard foam batons (they had not graduated to staves yet) and attack. So the children attacked. They attacked with the wild frenzy of those who think they're about to get their revenge. Chono was the only one who didn't resent Six for their superiority, but when she tried to hang back, the master snarled at her, and she, too, brought the hard foam baton down on Six's body.

Afterward Six was bruised and bloody and had two of the batons in their hands and other students were nursing wounds of their own, including a dislocated knee and a broken collarbone. The master was furious. This wasn't the lesson he wanted to teach. Chono, nursing a swollen cheekbone, had watched the blindfolded Six rise shakily to their feet and stand panting and sweating and defiant as a god—and she burned with pride. When the master locked Six in a cellar as retaliation, still she burned.

But now—now . . . there is no comparing that moment to this, when Six kneels unarmed and alone, surrounded by enough guardsaan to kill them ten times over.

Chono's escorts shove her forward, steering her not to join Six, but to sit in a chair; she makes a triangle of her and Six and the secretaries on the dais. She flicks a glance at Ilius as he joins his kin. He looks at her, and she looks away.

"Welcome, Cleric Chono," says Songrider, all self-satisfaction.

Six's head under the hood cocks a little. Chono's shoulders flex.

"Let's see her, then," grunts Ravening.

One of the guardsaan yanks Six's hood off. Six blinks in the sudden brightness, but there's a gag in their mouth. Even at a distance of ten feet, Chono can see the brilliant light in their eyes—and the four-inch cut slicing down their face, blood a scarlet trail that pools on their collar.

"The gag, too."

As soon as it comes off, Six makes a show of smacking their lips and spitting a thick glob onto the floor, to the grumbles and outrage of the secretaries.

"Well," they say brightly. "This is quite the reception." They look around at the packed Centrum, and at Chono, eyes dragging over her, moving past her—finding Ilius for a hot moment before shifting to Ravening. "I see you haven't gagged everyone. Chono will think you like me more."

The First Secretary says, "This bravado of yours—what good has it done you in the end? We captured you sneaking through the sewers like a rat. You're not as clever as you think, Sa Nightfoot."

Six shrugs one shoulder. "And here I thought my cleverness was keeping you all entertained. What shall we do instead?"

Ravening flares his nostrils. "You're here for trial and sentencing."

"What are the charges?"

"Murder. Treason. Just to start."

Six smiles, unconcerned.

"We know you allied with a Quietan rebel called Yantikye the Honor," Songrider says.

Did they capture Yantikye after all? Chono wonders. Is that why he never sent her any warning when the guardsaan arrived at the cottage?

Six replies, "Never heard of him."

Ravening narrows his eyes. "He was instrumental in helping Cleric Chono conspire with Aver Paiye. You are all connected in a plot to undermine the Kindom. Do you deny it?"

Chono exclaims, "Sa Nightfoot had nothing to do with my conversation with Aver Paiye. I worked alone. That's why I left her behind in Praetima."

But this only garners a cacophony of titters. Songrider mocks, "Even if we had any reason to believe that's true, Sa Nightfoot killed several guardsaan today."

Six shrugs. "They attacked me."

"They tried to arrest you," Ravening says. "You refused to go peaceably."

"What obligation have I got to be peaceable when I'm attacked for crimes I haven't committed?"

Ilius leans forward. "So you're saying you're innocent?"

"That is a philosophical question. I have done many evil things, it's true." A slow smile. "But all our evils give something back. It is a matter of *effects*. What are the effects of my evils? Or yours? Are you *prepared* for the effects?"

"I'm not interested in riddles, Sa Nightfoot," says Ravening. "If you have no legitimate defense to offer on your own behalf, we can proceed with sentencing."

Chono calls out, "You haven't even presented evidence!"

"The Clever Hand has all the evidence it needs."

"She is the matriarch of the Nightfoot family! You can't execute her."

"Perhaps you'd like to offer something in her defense?" Songrider returns.

Chono goes icy, thinking of Ilius's threats. This will be the first volley. If she refuses to cooperate, they'll kill Six. Then they'll start killing the five thousand. Six asked if they were prepared for the effects of their evils. Is she prepared for the effect of her defiance?

Songrider nods sharply toward the guardsaan, and Chono finds herself hauled out of her chair and muscled toward Six, forced to kneel beside them at an angle so that she can see their face and the Court can see hers. They want to witness her agony, to watch the blood spatter her face. Biting, snarling refusal blooms in her chest.

"Here in the Centrum?" she shouts. "Without a single newscaster in sight? You *cowards*! The Godfire will burn you alive for this!"

"We will put sentencing to a vote," announces Ravening.

Chono doesn't bother to watch the secretaries send up their votes by cast. She's panting with fury, with terror. A guardsaan is right behind Six now, the muzzle of a rifle pointed at the back of their skull. Chono tries to lurch toward them and hands grab her, hold her down. *No. No no no no no—*

"Chono."

Six's voice is so soft. She looks at them—and their expression takes her by surprise. It is not Esek's glittery-eyed defiance. They look at her the way that only Six has looked at her. Deep and searching and *seeing*. It is a look meant to comfort, and despite all her panic and despair, she stills at that look, eyes beseeching them.

They say, "You know I never go down without a fight."

Before she can begin to feel what this means, Ilius shouts, "What? What did you say?" Six rolls their eyes toward him, and their smile is slow and pleased. Ilius blanches. He mocks, "You certainly didn't fight when we cornered you in the sewers, did you, Esek?"

Still with that peculiar and unsettling smile, Six answers, "No . . . I didn't."

Chono's pulse jumps, an electric current of realization sizzling through her veins. Ilius furrows his brow—and then his eyes widen. Understanding.

"Shoot her!" he cries, startling the secretaries in the stands, startling Ravening and Songrider. He jumps to his feet, pointing at Six and shouting, "It's a trap! Shoot her!"

There are sounds of confusion, and Ravening seems baffled, but then Songrider is up, jabbing a finger at Six. "Execute the prisoner, now!"

The guard cocks the rifle. It takes many hands to hold Chono back now, for Chono wants to throw herself on Six, to shield them with her body, but Six looks at her, bright-eyed and ferocious, and their look says, *Wait*—

And, expecting them to be shot, she waits.

But nothing happens.

The guard behind Six is frozen. The guardsaan behind the guard are frozen. Chono's eyes snap toward the court, as one, two, three seconds pass, and the room begins to rustle. Songrider thunders, "What are you doing?! I said shoot her!"

But still nothing happens, and this flagrant disobedience jars Ravening into action. "Guardsaan! You are our instruments. How dare you ignore direct orders?"

Nothing.

The secretaries begin to look around, noting the guards that limn the Centrum, dozens upon dozens of them, utterly still. A stillness that does not put Chono in mind of guardsaan. It is the stillness of—

"My cloaks never ignore direct orders," says a voice.

Chono whips her head around in time to see the person that has walked into the Centrum. Not a woman anymore, but a man. A man all in black, cloak swishing around his ankles, his leather pauldron shining, his eyes electric blue. He moves with a predator's silken gait, and stops at last between the dais and Six, facing the Secretarial Court.

Ilius falls back into his chair as if someone had stripped the muscle from his bones. His eyes are wide. Beside him, Ravening looks stunned, and beside *him*, Songrider's mouth is open in disbelief. Ravening says hoarsely, "Sa Moonback…" And, after a beat: "You have not been invited to Nikapraev."

Chono imagines how Esek might respond to this moment—delighted and mocking and full of her own power. Moonback's response is a small, frosty smile that doesn't reach his eyes.

"I am here to supervise my cloaks."

"Your . . . cloaks," whispers Songrider, eyes sweeping the room again, taking in the armored figures at the perimeter. The ones who go unnoticed. So unnoticed, that they can replace whole units of guardsaan without detection.

Moonback says, "You want to use the Brutal Hand as executioners. The First Cloak alone has the right to hold those reins."

There is a beat of stunned silence, and suddenly Ravening cries with irrational defiance, "You are not the First Cloak! You ceded your position through your insubordination, through your funding of insurgents, through your rebellion! Under the Rule of Unification, the First Cloak's power is ours! It is our right to command the Cloaksaan, not yours. You are under arrest by the terms of the warrant we wrote for you! Surrender now!"

There is a pause, and he leaps to his feet, shouting at the ranks of cloaksaan, "You are Hands of the Kindom! You are indebted to the authority of the Clever Hand! Arrest Seti Moonback or you are traitors forever! You will be hunted to the ends of the universe!"

Chono has stopped breathing, his brazenness flushing her with sticky heat. Moonback turns in a slow circuit as he observes the cloaksaan throughout the Centrum. His look seems to invite them to take action, to obey the First Secretary if they wish. Not a one moves. When he faces the dais again, his cold smile turns scornful.

"You secretaries," he muses. "You rely so heavily on laws and words, it's as if you think they have more power than . . . action."

The hundreds of secretaries are buzzy now, anxious. Someone high in the stands tries to leave and finds a gun leveled at their head. This sends them cowering back into their seat and turns the uncertainty in the room to barely contained panic.

Chono looks at Six, amazed but also terrified. "What did you do?" she whispers.

They look at her. Their look is unrepentant.

Ravening's voice strains. "This is treason! You are all *traitors*!"

"You stripped their leader of titles," Moonback replies, cool and steady. "You made the strongest warriors of the Treble into guard dogs and sent them across the systems to bat the noses of your detractors. You treated them like loyal, mindless automatons. Did you really think that they would bend the knee to those who so deeply misunderstand them?"

"We value and respect the Cloaksaan," says Ilius, but it sounds pandering.

Moonback smiles another cold smile. "That was your mistake. You should have exterminated them as soon as you decided to turn on their leader. Even now, they are seizing Riin Cosas in my name."

Chono pictures that beautiful temple gleaming like a diamond. It will be daytime there. The clerics will have no defenses. Horror slithers up her spine.

Ravening's defiant expression wavers for the first time. His voice is forcedly calm. "What is your plan, Moonback? You want to be reinstated as the First Cloak, I take it? And to that end you ally yourself with these"—he waves a hand at Six and Chono—"these agitators? Have you forgotten that *they* brought the data flood that proved your guilt on Remembrance Day? That forced us to depose you?!"

Now for the first time Moonback turns his electric eyes on Six. The two regard each other like territorial cats, gauging the need for a fight.

Moonback remarks, "There's something to be said for unorthodox alliances. Sa Nightfoot gave me the tech I needed to infiltrate Nikapraev. She caused enough disturbance to cover me for the final move. In exchange, I promised to get her and"—a glance at Chono—"this one out alive. What do you think, Esek? Am I a man of my word? Or should I kill you here?"

Chono's heart is sprinting. Moonback hasn't even blinked. Six raises their bound wrists.

"You could at least give me a chance. For honor's sake."

Ilius shouts, "Esek killed Medisogo! She killed your own second-in-command!"

With whispering speed, Moonback's bloodletter darts toward Six, tip coming to rest against their throat. Chono expects a geyser of blood—but Moonback only uses the knife to gently tilt up Six's chin. The two of them study each other, Six hard-eyed and unflinching.

"My revenge is like the moon," says Moonback softly. "It comes in stages."

Now there are hundreds of murmuring voices and soft cries and shuffling bodies in the Centrum. The secretaries look on the verge of a stampede, their terror welling up like the portent of an eruption. Chono looks at Ilius and finds him rising from his chair, maneuvering himself slightly behind it. Songrider and Ravening are too amazed to notice.

Ravening, hoarser than ever and with eyes too wide, rasps, "What do you want, Moonback? Tell us what you want."

In answer, Seti Moonback withdraws the tip of the bloodletter from Six's chin before moving to stand behind them. Six doesn't tremble or cower, but nausea swells at the back of Chono's throat.

Moonback says, "I can appreciate the efficacy of the Rule of Unification. Especially in these... martial times. I simply feel that we gave authority to the wrong Hand. My cloaks, do you agree?"

Every cloaksaan in the room brings one foot down, a stomp of affirmation that makes the secretaries recoil.

Six turns their head, half cocking it toward Moonback, and in a low voice they remind him, "You swore it on your family name."

Moonback answers by bending closer, speaking into their ear. "Tell me something... Esek. If I gave you the choice between your life and Chono's, which would you choose?"

Six whispers, "Chono's."

Moonback smirks. "Does Esek Nightfoot have a heart after all? Seems unlikely."

Six smirks back, but it's grimacing. "Well, we never really knew each other that well, did we, Seti?"

Ravening calls out, "We concede! We resign our majority and will serve the wishes of the Brutal Hand."

Moonback ignores him, still murmuring to Six, "I *am* a man of honor, by the way. I keep my promises. Yet when it comes to you and your Chono, my promises are in conflict. What's an honorable man to do, when I am both bound to release you—and bound to bring you in?"

Ravening shouts, "First Cloak, do you hear us? We concede!"

Moonback's arm comes around Six, almost like a lover, and he slits the bindings connecting their wrists. One of the pair of hands on Chono suddenly unfastens her shackles. She watches tensely as, next, Moonback frees Six's ankles—only to lean close to their ear again.

"What about this?" he croons, and Chono watches the hairs rise on Six's neck. "A head start, hmm? Take your pet... Take her and run."

Before Chono can entirely process what has happened, Six springs up. Six grabs her by her coat, yanking her to her feet. She finds herself sprawling forward, helplessly running for the nearest door, and many secretaries are weeping and screaming, and Ravening cries out again, "We concede!"

Moonback pleasantly answers, "I accept."

And the Centrum fills with gunfire.

CHAPTER TWENTY-SIX

1665

YEAR OF THE HARVEST

Praetima
Nikata Leen, an Island
The Planet Kator

There is no time to feel the horror, or the guilt—no time to con-
centrate on anything except their grip on Chono and the door,
first thirty, then twenty, then ten feet away. But nor is there any chance
of shutting off their eyes, their ears, the sounds. Six sees it in passing—
the shots that take out Ravening and Songrider as Ilius Redquill leaps
off the dais. They hear the percussive riot of rifle fire, and the screaming and the running and bodies spilling down the stadium levels of the

Centrum, but too slow, too late. This is the Brutal Hand in its element, birds of prey coasting over a field full of mice.

The door ahead of them is already swinging—because Ilius has bolted through it. Clever little tero bird, taking flight. Six barrels after him, pushing Chono ahead of themself and ending up in the atrium with three separate doors taking three different routes. A half dozen guardsaan lie dead, their weapons stripped from them. The door on the left swings shut. Ilius's retreat.

"Which way?" Chono gasps.

The cloaks will be right behind them, and Six pauses to orient themself, superimposing Nikapraev's blueprint over their ocular, and sending it to Chono. It's the only way they'll get out alive. Nikapraev's triple spiral is a maze, some hallways opening up into offices and foyers that themselves lead to the outer hallways. Others open into rooms with no exit. Ilius will have made a break for the closest but most inconspicuous escape route, the northeast servant's entrance.

But to the south lie the airfields. And Yantikye is at the airfields.

They tug Chono after them, through the door to the right and into an empty hallway. The sounds of the massacre inside the Centrum are muted but inescapable, and Six has no weapons, and they can't see a single one of the cloaksaan on their ocular—because Seti Moonback has them all Hooded. The price Six paid. But Six still has their eyes and their hearing and their deep instinct for survival. So does Chono. They look at each other, hearing the pounding of boots in the atrium behind them.

Chono signals, and they take up position on either side of the door they just ran through. Four figures surge into the hall.

Six hurls themself at the unsuspecting cloaks. They smash one into another, spilling onto the ground in a reckless tackle of arms and legs and swinging fists. Something hits them hard in the ribs, in the face—their head snaps left and they glimpse Chono catching the arm of the third cloak, twisting it, breaking it, using him as a shield against the firepower of the fourth as Six whips back toward their own challenger and grabs at their hair, striking their head down on the tiles until the helmet cracks.

The flash of a bloodletter, a throbbing pain; the other cloak is on them. The sound of a gun, and Six doesn't have time to wonder who's been shot or who'll be next because they've got their second cloak by the wrist, holding the bloodletter high between them, and driving their knee up to stop the momentum of a downward thrust. They're seized with jealousy and murder, wanting their own bloodletter back, determined to have it again, the prize they won from Esek.

"Six!" Chono shouts.

Somehow they know what to do, rolling sideways, the second cloak rolling with them—and then a gun's report. Two shots more. Six ends up jammed against the wall with the dead cloak's wrist still in their grip, and Chono stands over them, gun held steady in her uninjured hand. Her face is sprayed in blood and her teeth are bared. She's breathing hard but controlled, unafraid but terrifying.

No time no time no time—Six climbs up, snatching the bloodletter and grabbing every gun they see like a greedy child on a treasure hunt. Chono secures two guns in her belt, gripping a third, while Six shoves two into the empty holsters on their calves and brandishes two more. They tuck the bloodletter away for now.

"To the right," Six says. "First conference room on the left. Go!"

Chono starts running, Six right behind her.

The hallway takes them straight past the eastern doors to the Centrum, and the menace of gunfire gets louder again, and the screams fewer. About fifty feet down Chono hurls herself into a door on the left, spilling them inside a dark conference room. She and Six stagger to a halt, for it's not so dark that they can't see the bodies on the far side of the meeting table. Six thought that Moonback would replace the Nikapraev guardsaan with his cloaks in a subtle way. Instead, he appears to have infiltrated the building and taken them out in the moment, even as the Secretaries held court. How did he do it so quickly, with such precision? Esek always took Moonback for a glorified foot soldier. But this is something else.

"Come on."

Chono urges them around the table, toward the door on the far side. They listen. Then they step through into the hallway of the middle spiral.

They're just sprinting toward the corner that will lead them into the south-facing hallway when they hear shouting, a spatter of gunshots, saan running in their direction. Six grabs Chono and together they shoulder into the nearest office—a small one, with a dead guard outside. There's a cold fireplace and a desk that Six thinks they should shove against the door. But Chono drops to a crouch, puts her ear to the door, and listens. When Six joins her, they hear the shooting getting closer. There's a scream. They look at each other, breathing hard, knowing what's out there: secretaries who somehow escaped the Centrum. The scream cuts off outside their door. Boots tromp past.

Chono's voice is rough. "He's going to kill all of them."

A quick swell of nausea forces Six to swallow, but they don't answer, can't answer. If this is on their head, if this is the price they paid for a chance to save Chono, they'll let Som decide if they should be devoured for it. Now, the only hope is to survive the hunting parties long enough to get outside Nikapraev—

Chono's eyes are wide, her teeth set. For the first time Six realizes that some of the blood on her is her own, leaking sluggishly from her hairline.

"Are you all right?" they rasp.

Chono raises an eyebrow, jerking her chin at them. "Are *you*?"

Confused, they follow her gaze and discover that the cloth on their left shoulder is soaked almost black. Chono puts her gun down, reaching for them. She rips aside the collar of their shirt to reveal a deep slice over the ball of their shoulder, pulling open like a macabre grin. Fuck. When did that happen?

"We've got to stop it bleeding," Chono says, before a second later they both flinch at the shattering sound of more gunfire, and voices close by.

They crouch in silence for ten seconds. Twenty. Finally, Chono knee-walks to the desk just a few feet away and starts rifling through a drawer. Six can feel the pain now, a yawning throb. It's bleeding too much. Chono comes back with a bottle of liquor, as well as—Six grimaces. It's a torch, the kind used to light kindling in the fireplace. Chono flicks the switch and a hissing pale blue flame darts out.

"Give me the bloodletter," Chono orders.

Reluctantly, they hand it to her, and she starts heating the blade against the flame, destroying it in the process. *What a waste*, Esek mutters.

"This is going to be really fucking painful," Chono warns them, concentrating. She indicates the bottle.

"Not the right time for a drink, is it?" they ask.

At her chastising look, they grunt, opening the bottle. The grunt turns to a snarl as they pour the liquid over their shoulder, the burn lancing through every nerve. They swallow hard. "We have to get out of Praetima. Yantikye is waiting for us at the airfields."

"Yantikye abandoned me on the Easwa beach," says Chono. Six doesn't answer. There's another stampede of people running past the door. How are any of the secretaries getting this far? Is it a game, to the cloaksaan? Let them flee and then track them down? Chono and Six stay silent, stay low, but after the group passes, Chono says with a hint of tense humor, "This reminds me a little bit of *The Risen Wave*, don't you think?"

Six warns her, "You are not getting shot in the chest this time."

She makes a low sound that might be a laugh, her big eyes fierce as the blade glows and she sets the torch down. With her free arm she shakes off one half of her damaged and dirty coat, switching hands to do the other side. She passes the coat over to a confused Six, leading with the heavy collar.

"Bite that," she orders.

Huffing angrily, they dig their teeth into the thickest part of the fabric as Chono leans closer. They put their guns down even though disarming feels like cutting off their own limbs.

"Try not to pass out," she says.

The pain makes their eyes roll back. They chew and gag through it, trying to think of other pain, worse pain: their entire body, burned alive at Soye's Reach. The reconstruction of their hips. The lengthening of their legs and the series of facial surgeries that turned their skull into a firepit of torture. It feels like Chono holds the blade against them for hours, but it can't be more than seconds, the acrid stench rising, crawling into their nostrils and through their teeth, till they drop their bite and choke a louder sound—but Chono's hand is there, pressed hard against their mouth. The knife is gone. There's smoke and pulsing agony, and Chono's blood-slicked face so close to theirs. Six swallows, afraid they might vomit. They sway forward, pressing their forehead to hers.

"You're all right," she whispers. "You're all right."

Instinctively Six lifts their hands, grabbing Chono's face to stop her leaning back, and Chono's hands are on their wrists—not to pull away but only to grip, tight and possessive, both of them breathing raggedly. Six is slick with cold sweat, but Chono's forehead against theirs feels like an entirely different kind of firebrand, pinning them into their body.

"Our route to the southwest exit is blocked," they whisper. "We must find another way."

"There are over a hundred cloaks in this building. Where can we run?"

Six pauses to think. "I will go first. I will keep the way clear and draw off fire long enough for you to—"

She pulls back enough to glare at them. "We go together or not at all."

"That is irrational."

"Stop being insufferably self-sacrificial."

"I told you. That is what I am here for."

This time she grabs the back of their neck, hard. She squeezes. "Is that why you made a deal with Seti fucking Moonback?"

Six swallows. They haven't touched her like this since they were children, just children, alone together, afraid together, brave together.

"I had to," they whisper back.

"You damned fool." She pushes her forehead into theirs again, like a buck locking antlers, angry and intimate. Her fingertips slip against their jaw. Her breath puffs against their mouth. They would do it again. They gave the first half of their life to killing one person, but the rest of their life will be for keeping this one alive—

Something slams into the office door. They jerk to their feet, snatching up their weapons, and when the door bursts open, it's to three terrified, bloody secretaries with wide-rimmed eyes.

One of them cries out, hysterical, "Help us! Help us!"

Chono slams Six into the wall just as gunfire cuts the secretaries down. The saan's bodies drop like sacks of grain, and a cloak stalks in, faceplate raised to better savor his victims. Two clean shots tumble him on top of the secretaries.

It's silent again, no sound of boots or gunfire. But it won't last. Chono grabs Six's arm. "We have to move."

They step over the bodies and check the hall to find it empty, except for a dead secretary, white tippet flung over their face like a shroud. Six inches up to the next turn of the spiral, Chono at their back, and darts their head around. How they're not seen is a mystery, for there are over a dozen cloaks scattered down the hall. Six shakes their head at Chono and reviews the way they came. Chono projects the blueprint in front of them and shows them a route. If they go north, the hallway narrows and cuts through a wing of offices, with a service entrance into the outermost hallway. From there, they can make their way onto the grounds, cut around Nikapraev's exterior, and head for the southern airfield.

"It's night," Chono whispers. "If we can get outside, our Hoods will protect us."

Six nods. "Go."

They cover her, the both of them jogging down the hall, grateful at least that they're not wearing heavy-duty guardsaan boots. A door on the left opens, a cloak steps out—and doesn't even see Chono before she tackles them, their gun skittering away as she throws her whole weight into their back and wraps an arm across their throat. Six watches her nearly lift them off their feet, hands trying to get at her face the whole time. Six unsheathes the bloodletter, thrusting it up through a vulnerable gap in the armor.

Chono drops the body, and they sprint ahead, reaching the northern wing in minutes. A pair of double doors opens at their shove, delivering them into a wide oval space—a waiting room. Couches and end tables and filing cabinets. There are doors into several offices limning the perimeter, and another pile of dead guardsaan, like discarded garbage amid the office furniture. Directly ahead is the service entrance to the outer hallway.

They're just breaking for it when a boom sets their ears ringing. The room shudders. Chono grabs Six, yanking them down into a crouch and trying to cover them, which they allow only long enough to realize that the ceiling hasn't buckled—the explosion is somewhere else, at least two halls away, but lights are flickering and there's dust coming from somewhere, thick and bitter.

"Fuck," Chono whispers, standing again, stepping toward the hallway entrance—

Which is when its doors fly open, and five cloaks storm the room.

Six throws themself at her, launching both their bodies over a couch in the middle of the waiting room, and they know already it won't be enough. Rifle fire sings above their heads, and in moments the cloaks will come around the couch and pepper them dead, and Six rolls onto their back so they can meet the assault head-on—

"Stay down!" someone shouts.

Six twists their neck around to find that one of the doors to a western-facing office has burst open, figures pouring out of it and firing on the cloaksaan. Six thinks they must be Quietans, or maybe even guardsaan, but—

The firefight is an explosion of sound as different weapons create a horrific symphony—handguns and blast rifles and the boom of a shotgun.

But then it stops. Then it's silent. Six, blinking, sits up again. The waiting room is full of smoke and debris and bodies—all five cloaks, mowed down. Six whirls toward their rescuers. Three lay on the floor, four compatriots kneeling beside them, and Six can't see anyone's face.

Six calls out, "Who are you?"

A big man turns toward them—one eye blue, the other covered by a black eye patch. Chono makes a startled sound, and Six rocks to their feet, half imagining another doppelgänger. As for Masar Hawks, he gives them a slow look and turns back to his people.

"We need to get Siel back to the ship," he says. "She'll bleed out if we stay here."

"Kinby and Iyrini are dead," someone says.

Masar's shoulders tense; his voice is hard. "We have to leave them."

The Jeveni faces turn drawn and agonized, one insisting, "We can't!"

Chono, on her feet, stares at Masar in amazement. "How did you get here?"

He regards her for a moment. "We're here for Ilius Redquill."

Before either of them can react beyond confusion, he trains one cold eye on Six, sharp as the tip of a bloodletter. He kicks aside a bullet-riddled end table, stepping closer.

"Maybe you know why, Sa Six? It was you who hired him to track us down, wasn't it?"

Six's blood ices over. Glaciers amass around their feet, locking them in place, nowhere to run. Chono looks at Six, then at Masar, uncomprehending. Masar is like a bull about to charge.

Six whispers, "I ended that mission."

The bull snorts, his good eye gleaming. "Though not before you got four collectors killed, was it? And no, you didn't end the mission. It went on, without you. Now my people are dying because of Ilius Redquill. If finding him wasn't my main concern, I'd take the time to kill you right now."

Chono steps between them, a hand raised just shy of Masar's chest, as if she would shove him back. He glares at Six, and Six will not insult him by apologizing.

Chono says, "What are you talking about? What has Redquill done?"

Masar's hateful stare holds Six for another beat before he rocks back, shifting his gaze toward Chono. "He has spies in Farren Eyce. Jun's cousin Luja—Ujan—she works for him. She stole the Capamame gate key and sent it to him. Maybe others." Chono and Six stare; horror washes through Six's body. Masar says, "Jun hacked us a way into the city this morning, but we thought we'd have more time to track Redquill's movements and abduct him. Now the whole fucking place is going up like a bonfire. I can't just shoot Redquill in the head. We need to confirm if anyone else has the key. We need the names of the other spies in Farren Eyce. But every time we get near him, the fucking guardsaan get in our way."

"They're not guardsaan," Chono says. "They're cloaks. It's a coup."

Masar pauses, thinking. He casts his own blueprint into the air, though this is a real-time projection. In the northwestern corner of Nikapraev, there's been an explosion.

"Cloaks then. Fine. We can't see the cloaks on cast. We set off a bomb, hoping to draw them away. Ilius Redquill"—he points at a small blue dot within a hallway near the Centrum—"is here. Jun has him tagged, so we can track his movements. He's managed to survive so far. We need to get to him before that changes."

"Let us help," Chono says. "If all he sees is you coming for him, he'll assume you're the same threat as Moonback. If he sees me, I might be able to persuade him to come with us."

Masar narrows his eyes. "Did you know he had spies in Farren Eyce?"

"I swear by the Godfire, I did not."

A stern nod. He looks at Six, lip curling. "And you?"

"I am not his fucking ally," Six says, rage at themself transmuting to rage at Masar.

Masar's mouth twitches with contempt, but he says, "Fine. We have to move now. That office"—he points the way Six and Chono came—"takes us deeper into the building, and from there we can—"

"Wait." One of the other Jeveni runs in from the office in question. "I've got eyes on the hallway. There's at least two clutches heading in from that direction."

Masar curses. Six points at the blueprint. "Head north."

"That goes straight through the main atrium," Masar says.

"But you can cut east here and circle around into the Centrum."

"How far are the clutches?" Chono asks the young Jeveni.

"They're combing the rooms. I give us three minutes, tops."

"We have to hold them off."

Masar barks at his people, "Layez, get Siel on your back and evacuate—"

"She's bleeding out," the tall one called Layez says. "Our ship is two miles away."

"Wait," Six says. They pull up a comm, watching the signal blink. "There is another exit."

Finally, bless the gods, Yantikye's face appears in the air.

"What the fuck is happening in that city?" he cries.

"Are you in the airfields? Under attack?"

"Not yet. The city is going dark. Everything seems to converge on—"

"I need you to bring a ship to Nikapraev," Six says.

Yantikye's brows shoot to his hairline. "The fuck?"

"The loggia on the roof. It is wide enough for your ship. Land there. I am sending some Jeveni to you who need medical help. Chono and I will follow."

"*Jeveni?* What are you—"

"It is our only way out, Yantikye—do it!"

The Quietan scowls and signs off. Six faces Masar. "Take the northern route, all of you. Send Layez and your wounded up the staircase in the atrium. My people will be there."

"Hold on," Chono says. "What are *you* doing?"

"The clutches are two minutes away at most. Do you have any more bombs?"

Masar hesitates, then gestures at one of his people. She pulls off a pack, handing it over to Six. Inside, there are four blocks of plastic explosives, wired and ready.

"All right." Six nods. "The clutches will come through here. I am going to set up the explosives—"

"Damnit, Six," Chono says.

"And rejoin you," they add. "I will be right behind you once the bombs are rigged."

"I'll stay," Chono argues.

"You all need to go," Six retorts. "You need numbers."

Masar says, "All right, let's do it."

He leads his team toward a north-facing office. Chono looks at Six with mutinous eyes, her body almost vibrating as she fights against this plan. Six steps toward her. They put their hand over her heart, over the bullet scar, staring at her fiercely.

"Trust me," they whisper.

She seems ready to scream at them. Instead she wrenches away and races after Masar.

Six wastes no time. They plant two explosive packs against the door that they and Chono originally came through, and two more inside the office itself. They grab one of the dead cloaks, wrenching off his chest and backplates, just as they did to the guardsaan at Blue Spire. Shrugging the armor on, and a helmet as well, they retreat into the northern office—but they don't follow Chono. Crouching, they take stock of their weapons, including a rifle they snatched from a cloak. At this distance, they should have enough cover to hold off anyone who makes it through. Give Masar time. Give *Chono* time.

It is in this moment, as gunfire explodes nearby, and Six hears the encroaching thunder of over a dozen cloaksaan, that Esek shows her face again. Carved with humor, and bloody—especially around the ear. Six resets the charge clips on their guns, determined to wait as long as possible to trigger the explosives.

In their head they hear her, gleeful, *Chono will never forgive you for this.*

No, Six thinks. *But she may live.*

Liar, liar. Always lying.

Six does not believe in ghosts, but they believe in the violent proximity of memories, and that all haunting means is that it *stays*, the thing stays with you, forever. There is no end to the things that have stayed with Six, the things that will appear, when they die, on the long table of their life, but they will gorge themself at that table if it gives Chono even one minute of advantage.

Cloaks charge through the door, and Six hits the trigger.

The sheer concussive power of it knocks Six back, like a rag doll tossed in a tantrum. They hit the ground hard, and black smoke pours over them. It is so much like what happened in the galleria of Ycutta that they lose sense of where they are. Then, twisting around, they peer through the debris. There are bodies in pieces halfway into the waiting room. Ceiling panels are coming down, and the doorway Six rigged is twice as big as it was before. Somewhere in the cavern left behind, electricity flashes, and they see the creeping tentacles of fire.

They are temporarily deaf, half-blinded by the smoke. Yet somehow they can still hear her voice.

Better get up, little fish, she croons. *Better run.*

But just as Six is going to follow her advice, Chono murmurs, *Wait.*

A second later, gunfire peppers the waiting room. Six ducks back into their office. The walls and ceiling and light fixtures explode. Glass shatters, and something zips past their ear, so close it's like the buzz of a fly. *I have survived worse than this*, they tell themself. *Over and over I have survived. I am the kinschool student who escaped. I am the Alanye that lived. I am the Esek that killed Esek Nightfoot.*

They roll onto their stomach, aim their rifle, and start firing.

They hear the aborted cries of two cloaksaan cut down through the smoke. A new assault indiscriminately rakes the air, but no one storms the waiting room. Someone is shouting, voices indistinct with Six's hearing damaged. They fire again, fully aware that this pause won't last. They kip up onto their feet and run from their office sanctuary to take a new position in the next office—just as a grenade flies through the air and into the office they abandoned.

Bad luck, mocks Esek.

The force of the crowd-killer grenade blows through the common wall between offices.

It's only a row of thick bookcases on Six's side of the wall that keeps the worst of it from hitting them. Even so, it takes longer than it should to get up again, struggling through broken wood and scattered, shredded laminate. Glass crunches underfoot. Somewhere in the confusion they've lost their rifle and their helmet. They can hear people in the waiting room now, can see the red sights of rifles tracking through the smoke and debris like a laser show.

It takes all their training, all their anger, all their years, to hold the threads of their bomb-battered thoughts together, and suddenly, they are out of the office—they are in the northern hallway. If they continue north, they can catch up to Chono. And lead Moonback's people to her, in the offing.

They run south.

South, and east, where the outer hallway of Nikapraev is a wall of windows on the city-facing side. They fire on the windows, the sound of the shatter muted in their ringing ears. They leap up onto the sill at the same moment that figures appear ahead of them—and others follow behind. They have little time to calculate the drop beneath them before hurling themself forward. Something hits them in the side, but they keep their form, landing on the balls of their feet and rolling over twice to absorb the momentum. Their cauterized shoulder screams protest, and though the body armor seems to have caught the bullet in their side, they think it may have broken a rib.

They whirl back around, aiming up at the window as two cloaks climb into view. Six shoots them both, watches their bodies twist and fall, and without waiting for another target, they turn. They run. They are on the lawn that spreads out from Nikapraev, rolling steeply down toward the first structures of the city, some fifty feet away. Everything is dark, and Six's ocular seems to have been damaged in the bombing. They can't pull up infrared, completely dependent on what little light their eyes can absorb. But if they can get into the city—

A gunshot in the back sprawls them forward, onto their front and breathing in the smell of mud and grass. Overhead, thunder cracks, and Six's ribs are definitely broken.

Get up get up get up, sings Esek.

It takes everything to do it, and they weave, unsteady, before sprinting for the city. Their lungs scream with the effort; their torso is a wall of pain. Another bullet catches them in the shoulder, and this time the body armor doesn't help. They drop their handgun, arm hanging uselessly from some crucial hinge or tendon, severed.

The cloaksaan are close. The cloaksaan are so close.

How many, do you think? ponders Esek. *Is Seti with them?*

No, Seti will hang back, like a lion pride male letting his females rip the prey apart before swanning in for the best of the meal.

They stumble into a cobblestone alley. The skies open up, sheets of rain turning everything to a haze. A voice in their aural link suddenly pierces the ringing sound.

"Where the fuck are you?"

Chono.

Chono Chono Chono . . .

"Just delayed," they say, bracing themself against a wall and trying to see who has tracked them. No figures in the downpour. They keep moving, blood running hot down their arm and washing away in freezing rain.

"You said you were right behind us. I heard the explosion. Where are you?"

"I am in the city. I will circle around Nikapraev and meet you on the roof. Find Ilius."

"You're hurt," Chono says. "How bad?"

Too late Six realizes their voice is a growl, half-choked and breathless. Their broken ribs drive like spears into their lungs.

"I am fine," they lie. "Stay alive. Meet me."

"Godsdamnit, Six."

Gunfire scythes through the alley. Six staggers down a side street. The cloaks will fan out, surround them. Lionesses, closing in for the kill.

"What's happening?" Chono shouts.

Six pauses, back against another wall, eyes clouded with rainwater. To their right, they can make out a courtyard some fifteen feet away. If they can cross the courtyard into the opposite housing block, they'll have a chance.

"Chono, my dear friend. I cannot talk right now."

"Find cover. I'm coming for you."

"No, no, no," Six pleads. There's blood in their mouth, salty and sour. "Do not do that. Trust me. Please, trust me."

Their voice rasps, their breathing is worse than ever.

"Six—"

She sounds furious, murderous, panicked. *Oh, Chono. You should have known better than to love me.*

"Live," Six whispers. "Please. Live."

They cut the comm, cut her off before she can answer, before she can beg. They force themself to focus on the courtyard, and with their last strength, they run.

They are halfway across when something blows their leg out beneath them. It feels like a brick, caving in their knee, and they drop forward, face smashing against cobblestone, blood flooding their mouth and nose. They snarl and roll, ready to fight again, but the gun in their good hand has flown loose, clattering out of reach, and the other arm is still numb and immovable, a puppet with cut strings.

Esek leans over them in the waterlogged darkness. She is dripping with gore, smiling with glee. Six blinks, and Esek is gone. In her place—two cloaksaan. Four. Standing over them with guns trained. Six glowers in defiance.

But the cloaks fall back, and into their place comes Seti Moonback.

His blond hair hangs drenched around his shoulders. His electric eyes gleam in the dark. He has folded his hands behind his back, water sluicing off the black cloak, beading on the leather pauldron with its three-pointed star. A mockery, now, of the Kindom's unity.

"There you are," says Moonback.

His voice sounds distant. Six is definitely deaf in at least one ear. Collapsed on their back, they worry that they will choke on their own blood. But their leg is destroyed; they can't get on their knees. They use their good arm to push themself up into a seated position, eyes locked on Moonback.

"Where is Chono?" the First Cloak asks.

Six snorts, which clogs their throat with more blood. They spit it out, glaring up at him.

"I may have been rash, giving her a head start," Moonback says. "I was caught up in the theater of the moment and lost my perspective. Should I use you as bait to get her back? Does she love you that much?"

"She has more important things to do," Six replies, though they fear to have Moonback test that statement—fear to know how quickly Chono would risk herself for them. "Anyway, what are you complaining about? You have Esek Nightfoot in your hands."

Moonback smiles, amused. "You must realize you are less valuable than Cleric Chono."

Of course I do, Six thinks, and remembers how Ilius said just the same. No need to dwell on it now. Their extremities are going numb, a strange counterpart to the searing pain.

Moonback shows his teeth. "Chono the Rebel Hand," he says, grandiose. "Chono, the People's Kin...What a surprise she has turned out to be."

Six says nothing. Esek warns them, *This is the part where you banter. Don't you know that I would banter? You can't disappoint him.*

But Six is done with Esek. At the end of their life, they will be themself, quiet and fierce and mean. Their good hand rests on their thigh—within reach of the bloodletter. Slicing Moonback's femoral artery would be a good exit.

"You helped me save her," they say, stalling for time, for strength. "I got you into Nikapraev and you swore to let her live."

Moonback shrugs. "I don't intend to *kill* her. She's far more useful alive. You, on the other hand." He tilts his head. "Your value is...in question."

Six's hand slips under their coat. Their fingers graze the hilt of the bloodletter. Suddenly, Moonback's boot is on top of their hand, grinding down. They nearly scream, vision whiting out as broken ribs compress. When they can see again, Moonback leans over them, eyes flat and merciless. He drops more and more of his weight. Six can barely breathe, the pressure excruciating. Moonback draws a gun and leans closer and taps the barrel against their temple.

"Tell me how to find her," he says.

Six pictures Chono, scaring the eighth-years away when they might have beaten Six to death. Hoarding the letters in the chest. Telling the unrighteous secretaries, though they held her life in their hands, *I will not betray my gods for you.*

"Well?" Seti Moonback asks.

"By all the Six Gods, Seti," they answer, "fuck you."

Moonback's smile is sincere this time. "You know...I was hoping you'd say that."

He pulls back, boot still on their hand, gun level, and fires.

CHAPTER TWENTY-SEVEN

1665

YEAR OF THE HARVEST

Praetima
Nikata Leen, an Island
The Planet Kator

Chono stands frozen, eyes so dry they burn, so dry she can't see, can't hear anything but the empty air of the lost comm—and the echo of Six's staggered breathing, the pain threaded through their voice and the fierce exhortation of their final words. *Live. Please. Live.*

"I have to go back," she chokes out, turning to Masar. "Something's wrong."

They're taking cover in a conference room between the middle and inner spirals of Nikapraev. Masar has just finished wrapping a long gash on his forearm. One of the Jeveni, who Masar called Eda, kicks over the body of a felled cloaksaan, a straggler who stumbled upon them and nearly slipped their bloodletter right between Masar's ribs—before Chono slammed into them and wrestled them to the ground. She somehow got ahold of the knife. Now the cloak's throat is a bowl running with blood, and Eda looks slightly sick, gazing down at them.

Chono's breathing is thready. She tells Masar, "They're in trouble."

Masar looks grim. Jun's cast blueprint hangs in front of him, with its little blue dot. Ilius has not, in the end, made a break for the exits but moved deeper into Nikapraev.

"Where are they?" Masar asks.

She tries to swallow down her panic. "They said they were in the city."

Masar's nod is curt. He glances at the door that will lead them to the Centrum. "I can't stop you from going. But my priority is Redquill."

Chono wants to scream. Her body feels hot and cold at the same time, her injured hand pulsing to the rhythm of her desperate heart. Masar has given her permission. She can go! All she has to do is go!

Except the thought of Ilius assaults her. He could be a risk to Farren Eyce. He could wield the key to obliterating them. He could get away—and she would bear the guilt of not trying to stop it.

But Six—

I've chased you all my life. I've chased you all my life . . .

"You need me," she says. Masar looks at her without responding, without denying it. *Six will live. Six always lives.* She swallows. "Let's go."

He signals Eda and the other one, Qlios, and they take up position at the conference room door, ready for anything—

But unprepared, when they step into the inner hallway, for an unnerving quiet. The route is empty. They head west, and cut left, and the western hallway is empty as well. There are no cloaksaan. No sounds of gunfire. Just a thick, heavy stillness as they come upon a pair of double doors that lead into the Centrum. The Centrum, where she stood less than an hour ago. Where the Secretarial Court made its judgments. Where Seti Moonback made his play. And now, as they step inside, the scene is grotesquely different.

"Gods and fire..." whispers Eda.

Something heaves in Chono's throat, and she barely manages to keep from being sick. The cloaksaan have abandoned the Centrum, leaving their kills behind. The bodies are everywhere. Collapsed back in their chairs, or fallen forward onto the ground, or spilling down the aisles in heaps. The pale blue suits and white tippets are blackened with blood, and there is no movement or moaning to indicate survivors. When Chono looks closer at some of the nearest bodies, she sees headshots, over and over. The efficient Brutal Hand. However many secretaries escaped the Centrum, cloaksaan have spent the past hour hunting them down. Chono has a sudden, queasy thought for the secretaries stationed throughout the Treble. Has Seti Moonback sent his murderous Hands to eliminate them, as well? What are the cloaks who have taken Riin Cosas doing, right now?

Suddenly, Masar booms, "Stay there! Don't move!"

She follows the direction of his shotgun, watches Qlios and Eda follow him. Up on the dais, the corpses of Ravening and Songrider lie motionless—Ravening twisted over the arm of his chair, Songrider flopped forward onto the table in front of her. Blood drips off the table's edge. But this is somehow not the most disturbing sight. Far worse is Ilius Redquill, sitting in his usual chair, as if he is about to hear petitions.

"Are you armed?" Masar shouts, moving swiftly toward the dais.

Ilius doesn't react, face blank, colorless. There's blood on him, which doesn't seem to be his. Chono approaches the steps onto the dais, ignoring Masar hissing at her to stay back. She climbs the steps. She makes sure to leave them a clear shot at Ilius, but she comes within five feet of his frozen body. The view of the Centrum is worse up here. Standing so close to Ravening's and Songrider's bodies chills her, but she keeps her eyes on the only secretary alive.

"Ilius." Her voice is soft. She holsters her gun and holds her hands apart. "Look at me."

Several moments pass before, like a machine coming online, Ilius turns his head toward her. He sees her, but his expression does not change. It is blank, and distant.

"Chono," he mumbles. "I thought you would have escaped. I hoped for it."

She tries not to let that statement affect her. "Just a few loose ends to tie up."

The tiniest smile quirks his lips, but it looks like the rictus of a corpse.

"I didn't take you for the personal vengeance type. I expected Esek."

"Ilius, what are you doing in here?"

His eyes drift away from her, looking out over the carnage. "Those cloaks tracked me all over Nikapraev. I don't even remember...leaving the Centrum."

Chono has seen shock before. Once, in the aftermath of a night with a man who purchased her, she sat in her room with her legs hugged to her chest, skin cold and clammy, and realized in some vague part of herself that she was in shock. She needed to get warm, but she couldn't move, and she could hardly see through her tunneled vision.

Years later, she would see traces of that night on the faces of others: wounded children, brutalized saan, the grief-stricken, and the dispossessed. And now she sees it on Ilius, whose dull eyes pan the Centrum. The sight of so many dead is harrowing enough for Chono. She never particularly loved her kin clerics, but Ilius—he believes in the wisdom of the Clever Hand. He loves the Kindom, with the rabid devotion of those who make devotion their defining characteristic. Now, beholding the fall, he has lost himself.

But whatever compassion Chono may feel, Masar shows none. "Ilius Redquill. I have orders to execute you for crimes against my people. But I'm willing to take you into custody and submit you for a formal trial if you tell us what we need to know."

For the first time Ilius's eyes drift down to the figures pointing guns at him. His brow furrows in surprise. "You're Jeveni," he says, as if spotting a rare bird in an aviary. He looks at Chono. "Where did they come from?"

"Farren Eyce," Chono replies. He looks amazed, and doubtful. "Ilius, your spies in Farren Eyce have been captured. We know they sent you the Capamame gate key. We need to know who else has it."

He blinks down at the Jeveni again, still with that irritating air of a person admiring novelty, before his eyes shift to Chono. "Spies?"

"The people you hired to spy on the Jeveni," Masar says. "Jasef sen Clime. Aris the Beauty. Ujan Redcore. Ringing any bells?"

Ilius smiles in that vague way again. "Ujan Redcore. Yes...I don't remember most of their names, but she was exceptional. She's in Farren Eyce, you say?"

"Don't fucking play with me!" Masar warns. "We know you've been giving them orders ever since we jumped to Capamame. We know Ujan Redcore sent you the gate key." His voice catches, and then he goes on doggedly. "We know you tried to buy the Wheel's names. You killed four collectors."

Ilius frowns, but some of the blank shock in his expression recedes, his eyes gaining focus as he looks at Chono. "That mission was on behalf of the Nightfoots," he says. "If these people want revenge for it, they should talk to Esek."

"And was it Esek who ordered you to kill more collectors in Farren Eyce?" Masar retorts.

"Esek ordered me to cease all involvement with the Jeveni, or the Wheel."

"Clearly you didn't listen."

Ilius looks at him confusedly. "I'm not suicidal. Of course I listened."

Chono's heart skips, then thunders. Premonition and fear. Masar stands like a statue, not reacting, not speaking. Qlios and Eda glance at each other, a flicker of nervousness and confusion between them. Masar leaps up onto the dais. He grabs hold of the table, shoving it sideways, nearly over the edge. Songrider's body falls forward onto the floor. With the table gone, Masar comes at Ilius with the shotgun. He presses it into his chest, pushing him back against the chair. Ilius's eyes widen, but he looks less frightened than surprised.

Masar growls, "Your operatives told us about the secretary that sponsored them, and that secretary was you. They told us how you renewed contact with them after they jumped to Farren Eyce. You told them to sabotage the colony. To kill our collectors. They confessed it!"

Ilius looks at him curiously, not like someone who is facing a gun, but like a scholar leafing through contradictory records.

"That's very strange," he says. "I have not spoken to Ujan Redcore in four years."

Masar pushes harder, snarling, "You're a liar!"

Ilius's brow furrows. The muzzle of the gun must hurt against his chest. It will leave a pair of round impressions on his skin. It will leave a hole in his body, if Masar wants it to.

"She used my name?" Ilius asks.

Masar goes still again, but his eyes track back and forth as if he were reading through a report. His silence seems to go on for ages. Chono, worried that their reprieve in the Centrum won't last much longer, presses him softly, "Did they name Ilius?"

He says angrily, "They admitted he was the secretary that hired them. The one Six worked with to buy the names of the Wheel!"

"Six?" asks Ilius, clearly not knowing who he means.

Masar's eyes snap toward him again. He looks more uncertain than ever. "She never told us who she sent the key to," he admits. "Ujan, she...she never said it was Redquill."

Ilius smiles, ghoulish in his blood-soaked clothes. "There you have it."

From below the dais Qlios demands, "If it wasn't *you*, then who was it? Redcore admitted it was someone Kindom directing her!"

"There are quite a lot of Hands, with quite a lot of motivations," says Ilius thoughtfully, though he doesn't look at Qlios. He looks at Chono. "*You* are a Hand, Chono. Yet I don't understand your motivations at all."

Chono's nostrils flare. She shoulders Masar and the gun aside, which he seems only to allow out of surprise. She puts her hands on each arm of Ilius's chair, leaning over him. His sweaty, bloody smell surrounds her.

"Listen to me. Whoever has the gate key is a threat to everything the Jeveni are doing. We must get that key back. These people"—she nods over her shoulder—"they'll kill you to protect Farren Eyce. You have to give us something, now, before it's too late."

"Like what?" Ilius asks, puzzled.

Chono has to fight not to scream at him. "You have spies all over the Treble. You've made a career out of tracking clandestine operations. If it wasn't you who triggered the spies in Farren Eyce, who was it? Who could it have been?"

"Well, they would have had to know about my operatives in the first place," Ilius says. "And recruited them for themselves."

"Good," she exhales. "Now think. Who could that be?"

Distractedly, Ilius looks past her at Masar. "You say you have some of my people in custody? Which ones did you catch?"

Masar's voice is wooden. "That's not how this works."

"But that must be part of what you want, isn't it?" Ilius returns. "You must wonder who else I worked with, who might be in your colony. How can you ever feel safe, in a world where your neighbor may want to kill you?"

Below the dais, Eda says, "We're Jeveni. We know how to live with bad neighbors."

"Isn't that the point of your colony?" Ilius says. "Isn't the entire facile scheme to create a world where you don't experience the atrocities of the Treble? Lurking spies will make that impossible. So will human nature."

Chono's temper breaks free. She smacks the side of Ilius's head, hard, startling him enough that his eyes snap back to hers.

"This isn't a fucking intellectual debate. Someone Kindom has the Jeveni gate key. Either you help me find out who it is or—"

"Why should I help you?" Ilius asks, with the first hint of temper.

"Why should I betray another Hand? You think I'm disloyal, just because you are?"

"Your kin secretaries are dead. Moonback is hunting down the survivors. There is no peace under the Kindom, no unity in the Treble. Do you want to live? Tell me *who* could have taken over your operatives."

Something mutinous flashes across his face, and in that moment she sees it: He knows.

Chono thinks of Six, out there, alone. And she can't go to them, she can't protect them, because Ilius Redquill is playing games.

She grabs his tippet, yanks him out of his chair, and throws him down. He cries out, falling against Songrider's body. He crawls backward on the dais, away from her. Chono follows him, straddling him and batting away the hands that rise to block her. She draws her gun, putting it under his jaw. His eyes are white-rimmed now. She grabs his collar, lifting him once and letting him drop. His head cracks against the floor. His eyes look fuzzy. She slaps him, hard.

"Look at me," she orders. Ilius makes a blubbering sound. She grabs his chin and shakes it, forcing him to meet her eyes. "Look at me," she says again. "Don't be coy. Don't be clever. Be prudent. Do you believe that I beat Cleric Paan to death? Do you believe that I am Esek's protégé? Now tell me—*who* has the key?"

He stares up at her, stunned. As if after everything she can still hurt his feelings, his meaningless, selfish feelings. His self-interestedness. His ego. Her memories fling her back in time again. They're in bed together, naked and relaxed and smiling at each other. They recover. He asks her to recite the beatitudes, and she does, slightly shy in the face of his admiration. He is so beautiful, so clean and clear-eyed, and he has made her feel clean by association. He has stripped away the filth of her life, the Esek and the Six and the past, and written over it with tenderness.

But what she feels toward that memory isn't nostalgia, or relief. It's pure hatred.

In a strained whisper he stammers, "I—I—I—"

And Eda shouts, "Cloaksaan!"

Chono's head jerks up just as Masar wheels around. A clutch spills in from the far end of the Centrum.

A fist collides with Chono's ear. She lurches sideways, disoriented, as Ilius grabs her hand. Grabs the gun. She thinks he's trying to wrest it off of her. She thinks he means to turn it on her. Instead, his fingers fit over hers on the trigger, and she's too slow to stop what he does.

When seeking virtue, look to the child in the dark. The child in themself contains every future. They may become any great or evil thing. But you, if you are virtuous, will look at this child as the embodiment of all virtues, and deserving to be saved. This is the law, and those who keep it shall be blessed. All you other ones, despair.

The Beatitudes, 1:1. Godtexts, pre-Treble

CHAPTER TWENTY-EIGHT

1665

YEAR OF THE HARVEST

Praetima
Nikata Leen, an Island
The Planet Kator

Their only advantage is the distance between the cloaks and the dais. It puts them just enough out of range for Masar to grab Eda's arm and heft her up. At the same moment Qlios pulls a grenade from his vest and lobs it across the Centrum. It explodes well short of the cloaks, but creates enough cover for Qlios to leap up as well—and in the distraction of all of that, the sound of a gunshot close by has Masar spinning, ready to fire.

Chono is still straddling Redquill. Her body heaves. Masar tries not to look at Redquill's head, tries not to remember how close Tej came to shooting himself. He focuses on Chono, frozen and wide-eyed. There's no time for her to lose it. He grabs her by the shoulders, hauling her up as Qlios and Eda open fire on the approaching cloaks. At first her body feels like dead weight, but with a gasp, she snaps back into awareness. Thank the gods.

They throw themselves behind the high-seated chairs of the fallen court, and the room becomes a cacophony of gunfire. Masar doesn't let himself think about the failure of his mission, of Ilius dead and taking the truth with him. He pushes down the certainty of his own impending death, forty light-years away from the ones he loves.

Suddenly Chono's voice is in his ear. "Rear exit," she says, sounding raw but calm.

Bullets lodge in the chairs in front of them. The cloaks are getting closer. Eda recharges her rifle clip.

"Let's do it," she says. "I'll hold them back."

"Only until we reach the exit," Masar orders. "Then we'll cover you."

"Got it, boss."

She's up, spraying the Centrum with rifle fire, and Masar doesn't know how many cloaks are left, but he and Qlios and Chono leap off the back end of the dais and sprint for the rear exit. He shoves them ahead of him, wields his shotgun, and whips around. His stomach drops.

There are at least fifteen cloaks, now. Swarming forward like snakes in the grass. And Eda—she looks back at him. He sees it on her face, that she's not waiting for him to cover her. He sees Uskel dead on the steps, and Ademi slaughtered in Ycutta, and all of Nikkelo's collectors who died on *The Happy Jaunt*. But most of all he sees Nikkelo. Beautiful, brave Nikkelo, staring down the cloaksaan Medisogo. *May the barren flourish*, Nikkelo said.

Eda rips a grenade out of her vest pocket, sprinting around the chairs. She flings herself at the cloaksaan. A dozen bullets shoot her out of the air, and he sees her fall and break on the ground among them. Half a second later, the grenade explodes.

It's more powerful than the one Qlios threw. The screams are blood-curdling. Masar wants to watch every one of them bleed to death, but someone grabs him and pulls him and—

"We've gotta go. Now. We've gotta go."

They flee, tearing through the rear exit and into a hallway on the right. Masar comms Layez, trying to keep his panic down—

"Are you there? Did you make it?!"

A harrowing silence echoes in his aural link before Layez's voice rings out, "We're on the shuttle. You've got to hurry. The captain says he's gonna take off!"

"Keep him there," Masar shouts. "We're coming. Do you hear me? We're coming!"

But who knows if Six's allies will wait for them. Who knows if Six is alive and whether their allies will be any use otherwise. Masar pushes through the door to the conference room where he wrapped his wounded arm, and they race onward into the outer hallway. A large atrium opens up before them, its spiral staircase winding toward the roof. Gunfire follows, and Qlios yelps, slamming into the railing on the staircase. Masar grabs him, drags him forward.

"Just a graze! 'M fine!"

Chono races up the stairs ahead of them, and Masar shoves Qlios after her. "Run!"

Turning, he rains shotgun fire down the stairs. His body throbs with pain and his heart sings with hate and two cloaksaan fall backward down the steps.

Up ahead, Chono shouts, "Run!"

Somehow, he runs. Somehow, he reaches the roof, standing under the loggia with its columns that rise like ancient trees to wind together overhead. There is a squall whipping across the roof. Rain comes in slanting torrents, wind like a screaming god, and the sky as dark as the Black Ocean. He senses movement behind him, turns to aim and fire—

But the gun jams.

A cloaksaan appears at the top of the stairs, rifle sighting him. He hears Effegen's voice: *I am your Star. I command you to come back, do you hear me? I command it, by Sajeven and on all the lives of our dead. Swear it.*

He's mere heartbeats from breaking his word when something slams into him. He hits the ground just as a shot pierces the air—and Chono stands above him, firing her gun with murder on her face. The cloaksaan drops. Another comes up the stairs. She shoots them, too, and Masar scrambles to his feet, grabbing her arm.

They turn together. They run, run, run and see it through the rain: a shuttle, slightly smaller than the one he and his people brought to Kator. It holds position on the roof, engines rumbling the ground underfoot. Qlios makes it inside. Masar and Chono tear after him, through the hatch. In a daze he takes in the faces around him. Siel and Layez. Two Quietans who he doesn't recognize. One of them leaps into the cockpit. Masar kneels over Siel, checking her newly bandaged wounds—she's still alive. Layez and Qlios are alive. He brought six Jeveni to Kator, and he lost half—

"What the fuck are you doing?"

An older Quietan man stands between Chono and the hatch door. He hits something on the wall, and the hatch starts closing. Chono hurls herself forward as if she will dive through the gap. Masar springs at her, grabbing her around the chest. She twists, breaks his hold. She swings at him. He barely ducks. What would *he* do, if she stood between him and Effegen or Bene?

It doesn't matter. He smashes her into the wall. The hatch door closes and the ship lifts off the roof. Chono screams, incoherent. She shoves him off her, swings at him again. He jerks back, but her fist still grazes his jaw, snaps his teeth together.

"Chono!" he shouts at her. "It's too late!"

To his amazement, she stops. Her body heaves. She is drenched in rain, and yet he can see the tear tracks on her face, a wildness in her eyes that echoes the worst grief he has ever felt, the worst failures he has ever endured. The loss of what he loves most.

Then, mutiny fills her eyes again, and she inhales for a new fight—

But the Quietan man cracks his rifle butt against the back of her skull.

She drops like a felled tree.

The shuttle banks left, shuddering in the harsh winds, and they all barely keep their feet, falling against the walls. Masar grabs a handhold in the ceiling. He grits his teeth. He waits, and waits, and waits for something to shoot them down—but it never comes.

It takes Chono about twenty minutes to come back around. By that time they're in the Black, coasting under the protection of Jun's Hood program, and leaving Kator behind. Siel looks fit to survive her wounds. It's a comfort, but not comfort enough. Eda's last moments are burned in Masar's mind.

Chono groans. They've put her in a flight chair, strapped her in to keep her from flopping over. She isn't bound, but it still reminds him too much of what happened on that Farren Eyce shuttle. He moves to stand in front of her, watching as she slowly raises her head to look at him. Wrath such as he's never seen. But then it disappears. She becomes blank, chillingly calm. This only makes her seem more dangerous.

"Take it easy," he advises her. "We've already administered a concussion patch and treated your other injuries, but you need to try not to move." She stares at him. He exhales. "You'd have died. If we left you there, you'd have died. I can't afford to lose any more people right now. Not now Redquill is dead."

She doesn't answer. He says, "The newscasts are sporadic, but it looks like the Cloaksaan have command of Nikapraev and Riin Cosas. It's unclear what the secretaries and clerics stationed throughout the Treble are doing—or whether Moonback will go after them. They're saying he's going to address the Treble sometime in the next hour. I think it's pretty clear he means to set himself up as the de facto ruler of the Kindom."

Chono grunts, the first real sign that she can think past Six to anything else happening around her. That gives him some hope, and he's short on hope right now. Some unknown Hand has the gate key, and the only clue to who that person is, is dead. There is nothing left now for Masar but sacrifice. He understands that he will break his promise to Effegen. He will never get back to Farren Eyce. He'll either find the one with the key, or die trying, or both.

But he needs Chono's help.

"You knew Ilius better than anyone."

She scoffs. "I don't think I knew him at all."

Her eyes are diamond hard. He says, "I need to contact my people, to tell them what happened. I'm not so proud I can't admit to the Wheel that I failed, but I'd feel better about it if I had something to offer them, some hope that I can find out who has the key."

She looks at him for a long moment. "Ilius knew who it was. He figured it out right before he—" She hesitates, as if trying to decide what happened. Masar wasn't looking when the gun went off. He doesn't know if she shot Ilius, or if he shot himself. Maybe Chono doesn't know, either. She says, "If someone was tracking Ilius's movements, if someone took over his crew and set them against Farren Eyce, there has to be a way to find out who it was."

Masar nods. "Jun's been scouring his history ever since we realized his involvement. Knowing he worked with Six may help us triangulate."

Masar regrets saying the name at once, wonders how she will react, but her face blanks again. He has no love for Six, not after realizing that they were behind the disaster in Ycutta, but he recognizes that Six, too, would be a crucial resource now. And Six is almost certainly dead.

Masar asks, "Do you have *any* theories? Any idea where we could look first?"

Chono doesn't answer. It doesn't seem to be stubbornness. He can see her mind working, but she is not one to speak before she has something to say. Suddenly the older Quietan man—Yantikye, Masar has learned—comes out of the cockpit to stand beside him. He has a good-humored but cocky manner, something hard to read in his too-ready smile. He whistles.

"Damn, but I thought that hit would put you out for longer. No hard feelings?" Chono doesn't respond. He sighs and looks at Masar. "Closest port in the storm is K-3 station. I've got friends there; we can refuel and rest before planning our next move."

"Refueling is fine," Masar answers. "But we're not resting. As soon as I have orders from my Wheel, I'll go where they point me."

Yantikye chuckles. "Look, kid, Seti Moonback is probably shutting down the entire Treble, nah? And we are fugitives. This is a time for lying low."

Chono speaks, her voice quiet, but with an unnerving thread of mockery. "The revolution has started, Yantikye. Don't you want to be involved?"

He raises his eyebrows at her. "I prefer my revolutionaries smart."

"Or at least useful," she replies.

The two of them stare at each other, and Masar can sense some history here, but he doesn't care. "Fine. We go to K-3. We get another ship. For now—"

Suddenly the pilot in the cockpit, Graisa, yells out, "It's him! He's up on casts!"

They all turn toward the center of the cabin as a hologram appears. It's Seti Moonback. He's singed with smoke and splattered with mud. His eyes hold a fierce gleam, victorious and terrifying, and there's a smudge of blood near his mouth, which looks less like a sign of injury than like the mess made by a feeding animal.

Chono unbuckles from her flight seat. She looks briefly unsteady, but she keeps her feet, and all of them stand in a circle around the hologram, listening.

"People of the Treble," Seti Moonback says. "I come to you in the full light of the Godfire, vindicated before the Six Gods. The tyranny of the Secretaries is over. No longer will you see your freedom threatened by weaklings who hide away on a hilltop, divorced from your true needs. I am the First Cloak of the Brutal Hand, and we cloaksaan know what it is to live in the Treble. We know the crime and corruption that plagues you. We know how the naivety of the Secretaries has endangered you. No more. I am formally dissolving the Rule of Unification and instituting martial law under my own Hand."

He pauses. Masar imagines millions of voices across the Black, rising in despair.

"Do not be afraid," the First Cloak says, like a serpent whispering to a mouse. "Consider the beatitudes. I want justice and mercy for every law-abiding citizen of the Treble. I want protection for the child in the dark. I want unity in these systems, and peace under my Hand. My only interest is to empower the First Families to resume trade, to empower the Nightfoots to produce sevite, and to empower all of you to continue your lives in safety."

To hear a Moonback talk of empowering Nightfoots feels... wrong. Indeed, everything about Moonback's words feels wrong, as if he studied at the feet of orators and politicians but lacks the acting skill to carry off such grand speeches. He sounds like someone trying to sound trustworthy. He looks like a monster in a mask.

"This is not to say that we won't face struggles," Moonback continues in that not-quite-right voice. "I must demand complete cooperation and obeisance as we transition to a new power structure. I know that you, who want peace just as I do, will welcome the cloaks and guardsaan in your midst, and submit to the authorities who I send to protect you. Most of all, I know that you will be loyal to the Brutal Hand and aid us in weeding out those traitors and malcontents who even now are trying to erode order across the systems. I will hunt them down, deal with them swiftly and mercilessly. And I will do the same to those who harbor them."

Yantikye mutters something in Qi. The young woman, Graisa, scowls. "He doesn't have enough cloaks to hold martial law in the Treble," she says.

"Which means he has other plans," says Chono.

Moonback continues, "Some of you may have lost confidence in the Kindom and placed your faith in folk heroes and charlatans." Chono goes tight and watchful as a hawk. "Don't be fooled. Those people are not who you think. They are not loyal to you. They are loyal to their own ambitions, and nothing more. To them I say this—" And Moonback's head turns, his gaze taking on a new focus, as if he were looking straight into the shuttle, straight into Chono's eyes. "I know where your loyalties lie. I know what matters to you. Submit to my mercy— and perhaps I will not kill everything you love."

Chono makes a sound so sharp and raspy that for a moment Masar thinks she can't breathe. Her gray eyes are huge, her face caught between horror and hope. Moonback, looking at her, smirks, just at the corner of his mouth. He has her now. He breaks his stare, smiling his fake smile for all the Treble to see.

"Have faith, my people! Liberation is coming! Gods keep you well."

The hologram vanishes. The shuttle is as quiet as the Black. Masar, heart pounding, looks at Chono. She seems to have started breathing again, seems to have tamed her expression—if barely. Suddenly Yantikye blurts a laugh.

"Som's ass!" he says. "They're alive! You heard it, didn't you, Chono? He couldn't have meant anything else. Six is alive."

Chono doesn't respond. Masar watches her. It seems to him that Moonback certainly meant to imply this but that it's as likely a trap as anything.

"What will you do?" Yantikye asks.

It's an odd question; it seems to hold an assumption. As if she will surrender. As if Masar would let her. Chono slowly turns her head toward Yantikye, looking at him with a steady, steely concentration. Thoughts flash in her eyes, plans, plots. Six sometimes wore that look. The look of a mastermind, settling on their scheme.

Her voice is quiet, emotionless.

"We're not going to K-3."

Yantikye, seeming disappointed that she hasn't said anything about Six, makes an exasperated noise. "I told you, I've got friends there. We can plan our next move. Decide how to answer Moonback."

"I don't trust your friends. I don't trust you."

"I've just saved your life!"

She moves so fast that Masar isn't prepared for it. One moment she's standing like a statue in front of him. The next she's on Yantikye like an immovable boulder, crushing him backward into the opposite wall. Shouting echoes through the shuttle. Graisa draws on her. Masar instinctively draws on Graisa, and his collectors do the same.

"Get the fuck off me!" Yantikye warns.

Chono holds him with an arm across his throat and, Masar realizes, a bloodletter just under his ribs. Chono, whether or not she realizes that Graisa has a bullet ready for her, breathes hard into Yantikye's face.

"What happened on the Easwa beach?"

His face twists with incomprehension. "What the fuck are you talking about? I—"

"You were my lookout. I saw the shore right before the guardsaan stormed the cottage. Your boat was gone. You left before they arrived. You never warned me."

"That's not how it happened! Chono—"

"I've asked myself, why would you betray me like that? Why make so much of needing me to spur your revolution, if you intended to hand me over? But it's obvious, isn't it? Six told me you had your own goals. You didn't want me to broker a peace with Aver Paiye, did you? That was Graisa's idea. *You* wanted me to be captured. You wanted a martyr. Even now, you want a martyr."

Yantikye's hands are raised up by his head, as if to prove his innocence, but Masar knows what people look like when they're trying to think of a way out of something. Graisa, gun still up but seeming stunned, looks back and forth between Yantikye and Chono in disbelief. A moment later, Yantikye's eyes go cold, his face twisting with unrepentance. Graisa makes a strangled sound. Chono nods.

"I don't mind so much for myself," she says. "People have used me since I was a child. But you knew Six would risk their life to save me." She leans even closer to him. Her lips come right up to the shell of his ear. Yantikye jerks, maybe in fear, and for a second Masar thinks she's going to rip his ear off with her teeth. Instead: "If they die, I'll kill you. Do you understand? I'll kill you, Yantikye. I am not your symbol or your martyr. You are not my handler. Your best option is to take me where I want to go and run very far away."

She leans back enough to meet his eyes, and there's mutiny in him—but also, very wise restraint.

"Chono," Masar speaks gently. "Chono, let him go."

Five, six seconds pass, before Chono does exactly that. She steps back, sheathing the bloodletter. She looks at Masar with that flat, expressionless face, all business now.

"The entire Treble is going to implode. Moonback will need a decisive, early victory, to symbolize his power. Something to show that he can do what the Secretaries couldn't. It'll be Trin-Ma. My birthplace, yes, but also the epicenter of the uprisings. That's where we'll find him."

Masar shakes his head, despairing. "Chono, I can't help you with this. I'm sorry. I know that Six is your mission, but they can't be mine. I have to find whoever has the gate key. That's all that matters to me now."

To his surprise, Chono looks confused. How can she be confused? How can she not realize that the survival of Capamame and its tens of thousands of civilians is leagues more important to him than one person's life?

"Masar," she says. "Weren't you listening? Moonback's message wasn't just for me."

Masar shakes his head, not understanding what she means. Her expression shifts. Her eyes glint, all fury and resolve.

"Moonback has more than Six," she says. "Moonback has the gate key."

The story continues in . . .

This Brutal Moon

Book Three of the Kindom Trilogy

ACKNOWLEDGMENTS

Writing this novel is the hardest thing I've ever done. I drafted and rewrote and revised *On Vicious Worlds* while simultaneously battling long COVID, struggling through intense anxiety and depression, and watching my extended family suffer losses and upheavals, and to top it off, I lost my job, all while debuting my first novel—an event notorious for throwing writers into paroxysms of terror and self-doubt. And these were just the personal challenges, to say nothing of the toll these years have taken on all of us, as atrocities run rampant and accountability fails and the future looms closer and closer, uncertain.

But as always seems to be the way, there were things that kept me going over the past year. Writing was one of them. Creation is the antithesis of death, which is why so many of us keep turning to art, keep searching for life in stories. But it's not the only thing we turn to, and acknowledgments are a ready space for thinking about the foundations we stand on and the soft places where we land. In that spirit, here's who (and what) gave me strength while writing this novel:

My publishing team. Having people in the industry who love your work and collaborate to make it the best version of itself is an incredible gift. To all the publicists, artists, typesetters, and copyeditors—I'm so grateful for what you've done to get this book on shelves. I especially want to acknowledge the sharp insight and warm encouragement of my editor, Tiana Coven, who read my wretched first draft and gave me the key to fixing it. If you love Jun Ironway, you owe Tiana a fruit basket. And of course, in addition to the Orbit team, I bow over my open palms to my agent, Bridget Smith, who has been my champion from the beginning.

My dog. Finnick, you are the best boy.

My readers. Publishing *These Burning Stars* was stressful, but receiving so much love and praise, from trade reviews to TikTok videos, buoyed me as I rewrote *On Vicious Worlds* at the end of 2023. Watching you hysterically bemoan both loving and hating Esek Nightfoot warmed my diabolical heart.

My friends. Chelsea Bullock, who flew to NYC for my book event and beamed at me the whole time. Margaret Rhee and Cathy Davidson, who made that event possible and have cheered me on through everything. Chelsea Montrois and Katie Grennell, points of light and humor in my life. Lisa Yaszek, an invaluable, passionate supporter. And Ren Hutchings and Rebecca Fraimow, brilliant writers who gave me the feedback and encouragement I needed and whose conversation I have cherished so deeply.

Xena: Warrior Princess. You know what you did.

The authors whose works I read while writing this book, who made me want to be better and better at this. Science fiction is a conversation, and I cherish my seat at the table.

My parents. My brother. My sisters. My nieces and nephews, and all the love that floods me when I think of you.

And Mary. Always Mary.

extras

orbit

orbit-books.co.uk

about the author

Bethany Jacobs is a former college instructor of writing and science fiction. In 2019, she made the leap to the tech industry so that she would have more time to write. When not working on her novels, she is an introvert of predictable habits. She likes reading, cooking, writing fanfiction, and snuggling in bed. She lives in Buffalo, New York, with her wife and her dog. She is the winner of the 2024 Philip K. Dick Award.

Find out more about Bethany Jacobs and other Orbit authors by registering for the free monthly newsletter at orbit-books.co.uk.

if you enjoyed

ON VICIOUS WORLDS

look out for

THE MERCY OF GODS
The Captive's War: Book One

by

James S. A. Corey

The Carryx — part empire, part hive — has waged wars of conquest for centuries, destroying or enslaving species across the galaxy in its conflict with an ancient and deathless enemy.

When they descend on the isolated world of Anjiin, the human population is abased, slaughtered and put in chains. The best and brightest are abducted, taken to the Carryx world-palace to join prisoners from a thousand other species.

Dafyd Alkhor, assistant to a prestigious scientist, is captured along with his team. Even he doesn't suspect that his peculiar insight and skills will be the key to seeing past their captors' terrifying agenda.

Swept up in a conflict beyond his control and vaster than his imagination, Dafyd is poised to become humanity's champion — and its betrayer.

This is where his story begins.

PART ONE

BEFORE

You ask how many ages had the Carryx been fighting the long war? That is a meaningless question. The Carryx ruled the stars for epochs. We conquered the Ejia and Kurkst and outdreamt the Eyeless Ones. We burned the Logothetes until their worlds were windswept glass. You wish to know of our first encounter with the enemy, but it seems more likely to me that there were many first encounters spread across the face of distance and time in ways that simultaneity cannot map. The ending, though. I saw the beginning of that catastrophe. It was the abasement of an insignificant world that called itself Anjiin.

You can't imagine how powerless and weak it seemed. We brought fire, death, and chains to Anjiin. We took from it what we deemed useful to us and culled those who resisted. And in that is our regret. If we had left it alone, nothing that came after would have been as it was. If we had burned it to ash and moved on as we had done to so many other worlds, I would not now be telling you the chronicle of our failure.

We did not see the adversary for what he was, and we brought him into our home.

—From the final statement of Ekur-Tkalal, keeper-librarian of the human moiety of the Carryx

One

ater, at the end of things, Dafyd would be amazed at how
many of the critical choices in his life seemed small at the
time. How many overwhelming problems had, with the distance
of time, proved trivial. Even when he sensed the gravity of a situation, he often attributed it to the wrong things. He dreaded going
to the end-of-year celebration at the Scholar's Common that last
time. But not, as it turned out, for any of the reasons that actually
mattered.

"You biologists are always looking for the starting point, asking
the origin question, sure. But if you want to see origins," the tall,
lanky man at Dafyd's side said, pointing a skewer of grilled pork
and apple at his chest. Then, for a moment, the man drunkenly
lost his place. "If you want to see origins, you have to look away
from your microscopes. You have to look up."

"That's true," Dafyd agreed. He had no idea what the man was
talking about, but it felt like he was being reprimanded.

"Deep sensor arrays. We can make a telescope with a lens as
wide as the planet. Effectively as wide as the planet. Wider, even.
Not that I do that anymore. Near-field. That's where I work now."

Dafyd made a polite sound. The tall man pulled a cube of pork off the skewer, and for a moment it looked like he'd drop it down into the courtyard. Dafyd imagined it landing in someone's drink in the Common below.

After a moment, the tall man regained control of his food and popped it into his mouth. His voice box bobbed as he swallowed.

"I'm studying a fascinating anomalous zone just at the edge of the heliosphere that's barely a light-second wide. Do you have any idea how small that is for conventional telescopy?"

"I don't," Dafyd said. "Isn't a light-second actually kind of big?"

The tall man deflated. "Compared with the heliosphere, it's really, really small." He ate the rest of the food, chewing disconsolately, and put the skewer down on the handrail. He wiped his hand with a napkin before he extended it. "Llaren Morse. Near-field astronomic visualization at Dyan Academy. Good to meet you."

Taking it meant clutching the man's greasy fingers in his own. But more than that, it meant committing to the conversation. Pretending to see someone and making his excuses meant finding another way to pass his time. It seemed like a small choice. It seemed trivial.

"Dafyd," he said, accepting the handshake. When Llaren Morse kept nodding, he added, "Dafyd Alkhor."

Llaren Morse's expression shifted. A small bunching between his eyebrows, his smile uncertain. "I feel like I should know that name. What projects have you run?"

"None. You're probably thinking of my aunt. She's in the funding colloquy."

Llaren Morse's expression went professional and formal so quickly, Dafyd almost heard the click. "Oh. Yes, that's probably it."

"We're not actually involved in any of the same projects," Dafyd said, half a beat too quickly. "I'm just putting in my time as a research assistant. Doing what I'm told. Keeping my head down."

Llaren Morse nodded and made a soft, noncommittal grunt, then stood there, caught between wanting to get out of the conversation and also to keep whatever advantage the nephew of a woman who controlled the funding purse strings might give him. Dafyd hoped that the next question wouldn't be which project he was working for.

"Where are you in from, then?" Llaren Morse asked.

"Right here. Irvian," Dafyd said. "I actually walked from my apartments. I'm not really even here for the—" He gestured at the crowd below them and in the galleries and halls.

"No?"

"There's a local girl I'm hoping to run into."

"And she'll be here?"

"I'm hoping so," Dafyd said. "Her boyfriend will." He smiled like it was a joke. Llaren Morse froze and then laughed. It was a trick Dafyd had, disarming the truth by telling it slant. "What about you? You have someone back at home?"

"Fiancée," the tall man said.

"Fiancée?" Dafyd echoed, keeping his voice playful and curious. They were almost past the part where Dafyd would need to say anything more about himself.

"Three years," Llaren Morse said. "We're looking to make it formal once I get a long-term placement."

"Long-term?"

"The position at Dyan Academy is just a two-year placement. There's no promise it'll fund after that. I'm hoping for at least a five-year before we start putting real roots down."

Dafyd sank his hands in his jacket pockets and leaned against the railing. "Sounds like stability's really important for you."

"Yeah, sure. I don't want to throw myself into a placement and then have it assigned out to someone else, you know? We put a lot of effort into things, and then as soon as you start getting results, some bigger fish comes in and swallows you."

And they were off. Dafyd spent the next half hour echoing back everything Llaren Morse said, either with exact words or near synonyms, or else pulling out what Dafyd thought the man meant and offering it back. The subject moved from the academic intrigue of Dyan Academy to Llaren Morse's parents and how they'd encouraged him into research, to their divorce and how it had affected him and his sisters.

The other man never noticed that Dafyd wasn't offering back any information about himself.

Dafyd listened because he was good at listening. He had a lot of practice. It kept the spotlight off him, people broadly seemed more hungry to be heard than they knew, and usually by the end of it, they found themselves liking him. Which was convenient, even on those occasions when he didn't find himself liking them back.

As Morse finished telling him about how his elder sister had avoided romantic entanglements with partners she actually liked, there was a little commotion in the courtyard below. Applause and laughter, and then there, in the center of the disturbance, Tonner Freis.

A year ago, Tonner had been one of the more promising research leads. Young, brilliant, demanding, with a strong intuition for the patterns that living systems fell into and growing institutional support. When Dafyd's aunt had casually nudged Dafyd toward Tonner Freis by mentioning that he had potential, she'd meant that ten years down the line when he'd paid his dues and worked his way to the top, Freis would be the kind of man who could help the junior researchers from his team start their careers. A person Dafyd could attach himself to.

She hadn't known that Tonner's proteome reconciliation project would be the top of the medrey council report, or that it would be singled out by the research colloquy, high parliament review, and the Bastian Group. It was the first single-term project ever to top all three lists in the same year. Tonner Freis—with his tight smile and his prematurely gray hair that rose like smoke from an overheated brain—was, for the moment, the most celebrated mind in the world.

From where Dafyd stood, the distance and the angle made it impossible to see Tonner's face clearly. Or the woman in the emerald-green dress at his side. Else Annalise Yannin, who had given up her own research team to join Tonner's project. Who had one dimple in her left cheek when she smiled and two on her right. Who tapped out complex rhythms with her feet when she was thinking, like she occupied her body by dancing in place while her mind wandered.

Else Yannin, the research group's second leader and acknowledged lover of Tonner Freis. Else, who Dafyd had come hoping to see even though he knew it was a mistake.

"Enjoy it now," Llaren Morse said, staring down at Tonner and his applause. The small hairs at the back of Dafyd's neck rose. Morse hadn't meant that for him. The comment had been for Tonner, and there had been a sneer in it.

"Enjoy it now?" But he saw in the tall man's expression that the trick wouldn't work again. Llaren Morse's eyes were guarded again, more than they had been when they'd started talking.

"I should let you go. I've kept you here all night," the tall man said. "It was good meeting you, Alkhor."

"Same," Dafyd said, and watched him drift into the galleries and rooms. The abandoned skewer was still on the guardrail. The sky had darkened to starlight. A woman just slightly older than Dafyd ghosted past, cleaning the skewer away and disappearing into the crowd.

Dafyd tried to talk himself out of his little feeling of paranoia.

He was tired because it was the end of the year and everyone on the team had been working extra hours to finish the datasets. He was out of place at a gathering of intellectual grandees and political leaders. He was carrying the emotional weight of an inappropriate infatuation with an unavailable woman. He was embarrassed by the not-entirely-unfounded impression he'd given Llaren Morse that he was only there because someone in his family had influence over money.

Any one was a good argument for treating his emotions with a little skepticism tonight. Taken all together, they were a compelling case.

And on the other side of the balance, the shadow of contempt in Morse's voice: *Enjoy it now.*

Dafyd muttered a little obscenity, scowled, and headed toward the ramp to the higher levels and private salons of the Common where the administrators and politicians held court.

The Common was grown from forest coral and rose five levels above the open sward to the east and the plaza to the west. Curvilinear by nature, nothing in it was square. Subtle lines of support and tension—foundation into bracing into wall into window into finial—gave the whole building a sense of motion and life like some climbing and twisting fusion of ivy and bone.

The interior had sweeping corridors that channeled the breeze, courtyards that opened to the sky, private rooms that could be adapted for small meetings or living quarters, wide chambers used for presentations or dances or banquets. The air smelled of cedar and akkeh trees. Harp swallows nested in the highest reaches and chimed their songs at the people below.

For most of the year, the Common was a building of all uses for the Irvian Research Medrey, and it served all the branches of scholarship that the citywide institution embodied. Apart from one humiliating failure on an assessment in his first year, Dafyd had fond memories of the Common and the times he'd spent there. The end-of-year celebration was different. It was a nested series of lies. A minefield scattered with gold nuggets, opportunity and disaster invisibly mingled.

First, it was presented as a chance for the most exalted scholars and researchers of Anjiin's great medrey and research conservatories to come together to socialize casually. In practice, "casual" included intricate and opaque rules of behavior and a rigidly enforced though ill-defined hierarchy of status. And one of many ironclad rules of etiquette was that people were to pretend there were no rules of etiquette. Who spoke to whom, who could make a joke and who was required to laugh, who could flirt and who must remain unreachably distant, all were unspoken and any mistake was noted by the community.

Second, it was a time to avoid politics and openly jockeying for the funding that came with the beginning of a new term. And so every conversation and comment was instead soaked in implication and nuance about which studies had ranked, which threads of the intellectual tapestry would be supported into the next year and which would be cut, who would lead the research teams and who would yoke their efforts to some more brilliant mind.

And finally, the celebration was open to the whole community. In theory, even the greenest scholar-prentice was welcome. In practice, Dafyd was not only one of the youngest people there, but also the only scholar-associate attending as a guest. The others of his rank on display that night were scraping up extra allowance by serving drinks and tapas to their betters.

Some people wore jackets with formal collars and vests in the colors of their home medrey and research conservatories. Others, the undyed summer linens that the newly appointed high magistrate had made fashionable. Dafyd was in his formal: a long charcoal jacket over an embroidered shirt and slim-fitting pants. A good outfit, but carefully not too good.

Security personnel lurked in the higher-status areas, but Dafyd walked with the lazy confidence of someone accustomed to access and deference. It would have been trivial to query the local system for the location of Dorinda Alkhor, but his aunt might see the request and know he was looking for her. If she had warning... Well, better that she didn't.

The crowd around him grew almost imperceptibly older as the mix of humanity shifted from scholar-researchers to scholar-coordinators, from support faculty to lead administrators, from recorders and popular writers to politicians and military liaisons. The formal jackets became just slightly better tailored, the embroidered shirts more brightly colored. All the plumage of status on display. He moved up the concentration of power like a microbe heading toward sugar, his hands in his pockets and his smile polite and blank. If he'd been nervous it would have shown, so he chose to be preoccupied instead. He went slowly, admiring art and icons in the swooping niches of forest coral, taking drinks from the servers and abandoning them to the servers that followed, being sure he knew what the next room was before he stepped into it.

His aunt was on a balcony that looked down over the plaza, and he saw her before she saw him. Her hair was down in a style that should have softened her face, but the severity of her mouth and jaw overpowered it. Dafyd didn't recognize the man she was speaking with, but he was older, with a trim white beard. He was speaking quickly, making small, emphatic gestures, and she was listening to him intently.

Dafyd made a curve around, getting close to the archway that opened onto the balcony before changing his stride, moving more directly toward her. She glanced up, saw him. There was only a flicker of frown before she smiled and waved him over.

"Mur, this is my nephew Dafyd," she said. "He's working with Tonner Freis."

"Young Freis!" Trim Beard said, shaking Dafyd's hand. "That's a good team to be with. First-rate work."

"I'm mostly preparing samples and keeping the laboratory clean," Dafyd said.

"Still. You'll have it on your record. It'll open doors later on. Count on that."

"Mur is with the research colloquy," his aunt said.

"Oh," Dafyd said, and grinned. "Well, then I'm very pleased to meet you indeed. I came to meet with people who could help my prospects. Now that we've met, I can go home."

His aunt hid a grimace, but Mur laughed and clapped Dafyd on the shoulder. "Dory here says kind things about you. You'll be fine. But I should—" He gestured toward the back and nodded to his aunt knowingly. She nodded back, and the older man stepped away. Below them, the plaza was alive. Food carts and a band playing guitar music that gently reached up to where they were standing. Threads of melody floating in the high, fragrant air. She put her arm in his.

"Dory?" Dafyd asked.

"I hate it when you're self-effacing," she said, ignoring his attempt at gentle mockery. Dafyd noted the tension in her neck and shoulder muscles. Everyone at the party wanted her time and access to the money she controlled. She'd probably been playing defense all night and it had stolen her patience. "It's not as charming as you think."

"I put people at ease," Dafyd said.

"You're at a point in your career that you should make people uneasy. You're too fond of being underestimated. It's a vice. You're going to have to impress someone someday."

"I just wanted to put in an appearance so you'd know I really came."

"I'm glad you did," and her smile forgave him a little.

"You taught me well."

"I told my sister I would look out for you, and I swear on her dear departed soul I will turn you into something worthy of her," his aunt said. Dafyd flinched at the mention of his mother, and his aunt softened a little. "She warned me that raising children would require patience. It's why I never had any of my own."

"I've never been the fastest learner, but that's my burden. Your teaching was always good. I'm going to owe you a lot when it's all said and done."

"No."

"Oh, I'm pretty sure I will."

"I mean no, whatever you're trying to soften out of me, don't ask it. I've been watching you flatter and charm everyone all your life. I don't think less of you for being manipulative. It's a good skill. But I'm better at it than you, so whatever you're about to try to dig out of me, no."

"I met a man from Dyan Academy. I don't think he likes Tonner."

She looked at him, her eyes flat as a shark's. Then, a moment later, the same tiny, mirthless smile she had when she lost a hand of cards.

"Don't be smug. I really am glad you came," she said, then squeezed his arm and let him go.

Dafyd retraced his steps, through the halls and down the wide ramps. His face shot an empty smile at those he passed, his mind elsewhere.

He found Tonner Freis and Else Yannin on the ground floor in a chamber wide enough to be a ballroom. Tonner had taken his jacket off, and he was leaning on a wide wooden table. Half a dozen scholars had formed a semicircle around him like a tiny theater with Tonner Freis as the only man on stage. *The thing we'd been doing wrong was trying to build reconciliation strategies at the informational level instead of the product. DNA and ribosomes on one hand, lattice quasicrystals and QRP on the other. It's like we were trying to speak two different languages and force their grammars to mesh when all we really need are directions on how to build a chair. Stop trying to explain how and just start building the chair, and it's much easier.* His voice carried better than a singer's. His audience chuckled.

Dafyd looked around, and she was easy to find. Else Yannin in her emerald-green dress was two tables over. Long, aquiline nose, wide mouth, and thin lips. She was watching her lover with an expression of amused indulgence. Only for a second, Dafyd hated Tonner Freis.

He didn't need to do this. No one was asking him to. It would take no extra effort to turn to the right and amble out to the plaza. A plate of roasted corn and spiced beef, a glass of beer, and he could go back to his rooms and let the political intrigue play itself out without him. But Else tucked a lock of auburn hair back behind her ear, and he walked toward her table like he had business there.

Small moments, unnoticed at the time, change the fate of empires.

Her smile shifted when she saw him. Just as real, but meaning something different. Something more closed. "Dafyd? I didn't expect to see you here."

"My other plans fell through," he said, reaching out to a servant passing by with what turned out to be mint iced tea. He'd been hoping for something more alcoholic. "I thought I'd see what the best minds of the planet looked like when they let their hair down."

Else gestured to the crowd with her own glass. "This, on into the small hours of the morning."

"No dancing?"

"Maybe when people have had a chance to get a little more drunk." There were threads of premature white in her hair. Against the youth of her face, they made her seem ageless.

"Can I ask you a question?"

She settled into herself. "Of course."

"Have you heard anything about another group taking over our research?"

She laughed once, loud enough that Tonner looked over and nodded to Dafyd before returning to his performance. "You don't need to worry about that," she said. "We've made so much progress and gotten so much acclaim in the last year, there's no chance.

Anyone who did would be setting themselves up as the disappointing second string. No one wants that."

"All right," Dafyd said, and took a drink of the tea he didn't want. One member of Tonner's little audience was saying something that made him scowl. Else shifted her weight. A single crease drew itself between her eyebrows.

"Just out of curiosity, what makes you ask?"

"It's just that, one hundred percent certainty, no error bars? Someone's making a play to take over the research."

Else put down her drink and put her hand on his arm. The crease between her eyebrows deepened. "What have you heard?"

Dafyd let himself feel a little warmth at her attention, at the touch of her hand. It felt like an important moment, and it was. Later, when he stood in the eye of a storm that burned a thousand worlds, he'd remember how it all started with Else Yannin's hand on his arm and his need to give her a reason to keep it there.